THE TE...
LA...
LAS...

DELO...ES FOSSEN

AND

GENUINE COWBOY
BY
JOANNA WAYNE

MILLS & BOON

THE TEXAS LAWMAN'S LAST STAND

BY
DELORES FOSSEN

First published in Great Britain 2012
by Mills & Boon, an imprint of Harlequin (UK) Limited
Eton House, 18-24 Paradise Road, Richmond, Surrey T

© Delores Fossen 2011

ISBN: 978 0 263 89509 4

46-0312

ROM
Pbk

Imagine a family tree that includes Texas cowboys, Choctaw and Cherokee Indians, a Louisiana pirate and a Scottish rebel who battled side by side with William Wallace. With ancestors like that, it's easy to understand why Texas author and former air force captain **Delores Fossen** feels as if she were genetically predisposed to writing romances. Along the way to fulfilling her DNA destiny, Delores married an air force top gun who just happens to be of Viking descent. With all those romantic bases covered, she doesn't have to look too far for inspiration.

Prologue

San Antonio Maternity Hospital

The gunshots stopped.

With her heart in her throat, Mattie Collier waited for more rounds of fire. They didn't come, thank God. And judging from the scene unfolding on the live news report on TV, this was the end of the hostage standoff.

The nightmare was over.

Well, one nightmare anyway.

Blinking back tears, Mattie knew it was time for her to die, *again*.

Another faked death, another run for her life. She'd done it before when she'd gone into the Federal Witness Protection Program six months earlier.

This time, it would be much, much harder.

Harder, because of her newborn baby. Her precious daughter was a mere two hours old. She was too young to be in the path of danger, and Mattie knew it was too big a risk to try to escape with her. If she failed, if they caught her, the unthinkable could happen.

On the muted TV in the nurses' lounge, Mattie could now see the police and firemen outside the four-story hospital. Reporters, too. They had their cameras aimed at the building where Mattie and the others were still hiding and waiting for the official end of the nine-hour hostage standoff.

Their captors, the gunmen who'd terrorized them for those nine hours, had stayed concealed behind ski masks, and Mattie had only gotten a glimpse of them before she and another patient had escaped and hidden in the nurses' lounge at the end of the maternity ward hall. Now, without explanation, their captors had apparently given up and perhaps even managed to get out of the building despite every attempt to stop them.

Any minute, San Antonio PD would storm the hospital to look for injured patients or perhaps even another gunman. The officers would eventually make it to the fourth floor, where she was, and if Mattie allowed them to rescue her, the photographers who were no doubt waiting outside could snap her picture. The wrong people could learn that she wasn't dead after all.

And that was a sure way to get her and her precious daughter hurt, or worse.

With her baby cradled in the crook of her arm, Mattie got to her feet. Not easily. She was still dizzy and weak from the long labor and the stress of not knowing if the gunmen were going to kill them all. The adrenaline had come and gone, leaving her with the bone-weary fatigue and sickening dread that came with an equally sickening reality. She'd barely had enough strength to change into the green scrubs that she had found in a nurse's locker, and she wasn't expecting to regain her strength anytime soon.

A fire alarm sounded and was quickly followed by water falling from the overhead sprinklers.

She glanced up at the ceiling. There were no sprinklers here in the lounge, and that gave her a jolt of panic. She cracked open the door, barely a fraction, and looked out. There were no signs of fire, just the faint smell of smoke. Thankfully, her fellow patient and she were far enough away from that smoke, and the sprinklers would hopefully smother any flames before the firemen could come in and do their thing.

Mattie took some steps, staggering. Neither the pain nor the dizziness would stop her. She knew what had to happen. And it would be the hardest thing she would ever have to do.

Mattie made her way to the leather sofa where Nadine Duggan was asleep. Mattie hadn't known the petite blonde before they'd been taken hostage while in the throes of labor. With no one to help them, Mattie and Nadine had sneaked away from the others and hidden in the nurses' lounge. Nadine and she had cried, hoped and prayed through their labors while trying to stay quiet so their captors wouldn't find them. They'd helped each other and then both had given birth there in the lounge. First, Mattie. Then, a half hour later, Nadine.

Now, Nadine had her own newborn son snuggled against her, where he'd fallen asleep after nursing.

"It's over," Mattie told Nadine, tipping her head toward the TV. "The gunmen seem to be gone, and the police are in the building."

Nadine's eyes were glazed from fatigue. "Is Bo here?"

From their whispered labor conversations, Mattie

knew that Bo was Nadine's husband. Or rather "the best husband in the world," as Nadine had claimed. The love of her life. The answer to her prayers.

Mattie hoped Bo would soon be the answer to her own prayers, as well.

From what Mattie had gathered from the TV coverage, Lieutenant Bo Duggan, a cop in the San Antonio PD, had been on the way to the hospital when the ski-mask-wearing gunmen had stormed the labor and delivery ward. Nadine had been trapped inside, and Bo had been unable to get to her.

Now with the gunmen gone, Bo was no doubt tearing his way through the hostage negotiators, firemen, SWAT and reporters to get to Nadine and their child. Mattie had seen Bo on TV, and though she hadn't been able to hear his exact words, she knew he was pleading for the gunmen to release Nadine and the others. Maybe he'd been successful. After all, something had caused the gunmen to give up the hostages.

"Bo's coming," Mattie promised Nadine.

So were Mattie's tears. She couldn't stop them as she eased her baby daughter into the crook of Nadine's left arm.

Nadine's watery blue eyes widened, and she shook her head, obviously not understanding.

"Protect her," Mattie said. "Tell everyone here at the hospital and the newspapers that you gave birth to twins. Only your husband can know the truth for now."

Another shake of her head. "Wh-why?" Nadine asked.

"Because it's the only way I can keep her safe. *Please.* I have to leave. I have to try to get out before anyone sees me, but I'll be back to get her. When I'm sure it's safe, I'll be back."

Nadine ran her tongue over her chapped bottom lip and took a deep breath. "Are you in some kind of trouble?"

"I will be if anyone figures out who I am."

"Bo can help you," Nadine insisted.

"I don't doubt that he'd try. But all it would take is one picture of me. Or for someone out in that crowd to recognize my face. That might even include the police. The world is watching, Nadine, and I can't risk being seen." And Mattie knew for certain that she couldn't trust her point of contact, a federal marshal, in the Witness Protection Program.

Not after what had happened.

Mattie swallowed hard. "Will you protect my baby?"

Nadine closed her eyes and nodded. Mattie heard the racing footsteps in the corridor. There were frantic shouts. One of them came from a man calling out for Nadine. Bo, no doubt.

Mattie's time was up.

She took one last look at her baby and leaned down and kissed her warm, rosy cheek. And with her heart in shreds, she did the only thing she could do to make sure her child would survive.

Mattie turned and left.

Chapter One

Thirteen Months Later

Lieutenant Bo Duggan didn't like what he saw in the rearview mirror of his SUV. A black van had been several vehicles behind him since he pulled out of the parking lot of San Antonio Police headquarters ten minutes earlier. The van was still there.

Maybe it was a coincidence.

Maybe not.

Bo didn't slow down or speed up. He simply continued his fifty-five-mile-per-hour pace on the drive home. Except he wouldn't go home just yet. Not with the possibility of that van on his tail.

As a veteran SAPD cop and head of the Special Victims Unit, it was always a possibility that someone was dissatisfied with the outcome of a case and wanted to bring that personal grudge to Bo's doorstep. But he wouldn't let it get that far. He already had enough to manage with the other crazy things happening in his life.

What the hell was going on anyway?

The day before, he'd learned someone was running

a cyber-investigation on him. A *deep* one. From an unsecured computer at a coffeehouse, no less. He was still trying to get a list of possible suspects from the partial fingerprints taken from that keyboard. Then someone had tried to break into his SUV while it was in the parking lot at police headquarters.

Now this.

Slipping his phone from his pocket, Bo called one of his sergeants to inform him of the situation and to give him the van's license plate number to run through the database. Bo's second call was to his house, and as he expected, the nanny, Rosalie, answered.

"Rosalie, I don't want to scare you, but are all the doors and windows locked, and is the security system turned on?" Bo asked.

"Yes." But he could tell from her hesitation that she was already alarmed. Probably because he hadn't been able to keep the concern out of his voice. Still, better to be safe than sorry. "Why?"

"Just a precaution." He checked to make sure the black van was still there. It was. "Keep everything locked up tight, and don't let anyone in unless you hear differently from me."

There was more hesitation. "I'm sorry, but someone's already here."

His stomach knotted, and he pushed his foot to the accelerator. "Who?"

"Madeline Cooper, the woman who's interested in buying the house across the street. Remember, she called yesterday to make an appointment with you so she could ask some questions about the neighborhood? I let her in about five minutes ago."

Bo didn't relax. He was expecting Ms. Cooper, just not this soon. And not with that van following him.

"Tell our visitor I'll get there as soon as I can," Bo explained to Rosalie. "And if anyone else calls or comes by, get in touch with me immediately."

"You're scaring me, Bo. What's going on?"

"I'll explain it all when I get there. Right now, I just want to take a few precautions and make sure you and the kids are safe."

He clicked End Call and was about to call for backup before he stopped the van and confronted whomever was inside, but he realized that wouldn't be necessary. The van made a right turn, off the main highway, and disappeared down a side street.

Bo blew out a long breath and wanted to dismiss the incident as mild paranoia on his part, but something in his gut told him he had reason for concern. After twelve years of being a cop, the one thing he'd learned was to trust his gut.

He pressed a little harder on the accelerator while he kept watch around him, to make sure that van didn't resurface. It didn't. Bo made the turn into his neighborhood without any sign of it or any other suspicious vehicle. However, in front of his ranch-style house there was an unfamiliar two-door blue Ford.

Ms. Cooper's probably.

He would quickly answer his prospective neighbor's questions and send her on her way.

Rosalie met him at the door that led from the garage and into the laundry room. Oh, yes. She was concerned. Normally, Rosalie was cool and calm under pressure.

But Bo saw the stress, and the tenseness only accented the wrinkles at the corners of her eyes.

"Everything okay?" Rosalie asked.

"Yeah. How are the kids?"

"Fine. They're playing in the nursery." She glanced down at the monitor she held in her hand. She carried it with her whenever she wasn't with the twins so she would be able to hear them no matter where she was in the house. "So, why did I have to make sure the doors and windows were locked?"

"I thought this black van was following me. I was wrong." Bo kept it at that, but Rosalie's raised eyebrows let him know that she would want to discuss this further. "Where's our guest?"

"Living room."

Bo headed in that direction, and he kept his jacket on so that it would shield his shoulder holster and gun. Best not to alarm Ms. Cooper in case she was squeamish about such things.

He found her just where Rosalie said she would be. Not seated, but standing by the limestone fireplace, where she was looking at a framed photo. He'd forgotten the photo was there, but then he rarely went into this room. Heck, for that matter, he rarely had guests. Between fatherhood and his job, there wasn't much time for anything else.

Madeline Cooper turned. Their eyes met, and Bo made a split-second cop's assessment of her. Tall, about five-nine. Average build. Shoulder-length, straight brown hair. Green eyes. A full mouth. Very little makeup, just a touch of pink color on her lips. She wore matching olive-green pants and a sweater. The outfit was nondescript. Definitely not flashy.

She was not a woman who wanted to draw attention to herself.

But something about her caught Bo's attention.

"Do I know you?" he immediately asked.

"No." Her answer was immediate, as well. Maybe too immediate.

"You look…" Bo didn't know where to go with that. Several things came to mind, including, much to his surprise, that she looked damn attractive. But what also came to mind was that she was "…familiar."

"Oh." It was her only response.

Bo was ready to launch into more questions, but his phone rang. He pulled it from his jacket pocket and looked at the screen. It was Sergeant Garrett O'Malley from headquarters.

"Please excuse me a second. I need to take this call. Duggan," he answered after his guest nodded.

"I ran the license plate on that black van you thought might be following you," O'Malley informed him. "It must be fake. No record of it."

Hell. That was not what Bo wanted to hear. "What about the van itself—was it stolen?"

"That's my guess. I checked, and there were two black vans reported stolen in the last twenty-four hours."

Bo didn't like that, either. "Keep digging. Try to locate that vehicle. And call me if you find out anything else." He kept his instructions vague since he had an audience nearby. Madeline Cooper seemed to be hanging on his every word.

"Is there a problem?" she asked, her forehead bunched up.

"No problem." At best, that was a hopeful remark. At worst, a lie.

He might not know which was the truth for a while.

Bo walked closer, studying her and trying to figure out why bells the size of Texas were going off in his head.

"You have a lovely home," she commented. She folded her arms over her chest and tipped her head to the photo on the mantel. "That's your wife?"

Bo glanced at the photo of Nadine. She sported a grin from ear to ear, because that picture had been taken the day she learned she was pregnant.

"My late wife," he corrected. "She died not long after giving birth."

"I'm so sorry for your loss." It sounded heartfelt, as if the loss had been hers, as well. Strange. "Do you have a son or daughter?"

"Both. I have twins."

She glanced away but not before Bo saw something flicker through her eyes. What, exactly, he didn't know, but it didn't seem to be a normal reaction.

"I remember your name now," she continued. "Wasn't your wife at the San Antonio Maternity Hospital during that hostage standoff?"

Bo let the question dangle between them for several seconds. It was definitely an uncomfortable silence, and if he'd had any doubts that his guest was nervous, he didn't have them after that. "That's right. My wife had the babies by herself while hiding in a nurses' lounge. She had internal bleeding and died."

The lack of emotion in his tone certainly didn't mean there was a lack of emotion in his heart. No. Losing Nadine had been the most difficult thing he had ever faced. If it hadn't been for the babies, he would have shut down and died emotionally right along with her. But he'd survived for their children and because that's what Nadine would have expected him to do.

"So, you had questions about the neighborhood?" Bo asked, changing the subject.

She nodded. "Um, is it safe?"

He thought of the van and hesitated. "I'm a cop. I wouldn't be living here with my children if it wasn't."

Another nod. She moistened her lips. Hell. That mouth was so familiar. Where had he seen it before?

"Are you from San Antonio?" he asked.

"No. Born and raised in Dallas, but for the past two years I've been traveling so much that I don't really have a place to call home."

"No family?"

There it was. Another flicker in her eyes before she glanced away again. "No family."

"You're not a very good liar." Bo hadn't intended to be so blunt, but frankly he was tired of this conversation. For a woman who wanted to know about the neighborhood, she didn't have much interest in it. "Now, why don't you tell me why you're really here?"

She opened her mouth. Closed it. Stared at him. And looked even more uncomfortable. He knew how she felt. Bo was uncomfortable, too.

He stared at her, waiting for an explanation that one way or another he was going to get. He wouldn't let her leave until he knew if she were connected to that van.

He was about to toss that particular accusation at her, when something flashed in his head.

And he knew where he'd seen that face and that mouth.

"I know why you look so familiar," he told her. "The surveillance video at the hospital."

She shook her head. "What video?"

"The one I studied a thousand times after the hostage standoff. A woman wearing green scrubs left the area of the nurses' lounge only seconds before I got there. The hair is different, darker, but the mouth—it's the same."

She didn't deny it. In fact, her body language confirmed it. "I have a problem," she practically whispered. "A serious one."

"Yeah, you do. You left the scene of a crime, lady, and the police want to question you. Hell, *I* want to question you. What were you doing in that nurses' lounge with my wife and newborn babies?"

She stood there, blinking hard as if fighting back tears. "I was a hostage, too. I was trapped there like everyone else on the ward."

Bo hadn't known what answer to expect, and he wasn't sure yet if he believed her. After all, she'd fled the scene, and people didn't usually do that sort of thing unless they were running from the law. But there was something in her voice. Something in her eyes. Some deep pain. Bo understood that and knew she probably wasn't faking it. He'd already determined she wasn't much of a liar.

He went closer to her so he could keep watch with his lie-detector eyes. "You were with my wife?"

"Yes." She sank down onto the sofa and looked at her hands. "After the gunmen stormed into the hospital ward, they fired some shots at the ceiling. People ran. Obviously, there was chaos. And Nadine was in the labor room next to me. Our labors were just starting so we were able to get out of our beds and hide."

Each bit of information was a mixed blessing. For months, he'd wanted to know what Nadine had endured in those last hours, but since she'd never been able to tell him herself, he had been the one to try to fill in the blanks. As a cop, those blanks had been filled with gruesome images. Now, he had the chance to learn the truth. Well, maybe.

If this woman was telling the truth.

Because his legs suddenly felt unsteady, Bo had to sit, as well. He took the chair across from her. "How did you get from the labor rooms to the nurses' lounge?"

"The gunmen were trying to gather everyone into the hall outside the delivery suites. Nadine and I waited until the gunmen were in one of the other rooms, and that's when we left. We used the back hall and followed it to the nurses' lounge."

She fidgeted with the clasp on her purse, finally got it open, extracted a mint and popped it into her mouth. "There was a TV in the lounge, and we were able to figure out what was going on."

Yes. He remembered the TV. It was still on with the volume muted when he got to Nadine. "You didn't try to contact anyone?"

"There was no phone in the lounge, and neither of us had our cells with us. We'd left them in the labor rooms. Then, it wasn't long before the pain made it impossible to try to escape. So, we stayed put…and helped each other."

Just hearing this reopened all the old wounds. The pain. Hell. Several hours before the hostage standoff had begun, Nadine had called him from her routine doctor appointment. Her cervix was dilated, she'd said, and the doctor wanted to go ahead and admit her to the hospital.

Bo knew he should have been there to protect her. And he would have been if there hadn't been a damn traffic accident. That fifteen-minute delay had meant the difference between life and death. Because if he'd been there at the hospital, he could have gotten Nadine the help she needed, and she might not have died from complications.

He pushed aside those regrets and focused on his guest. "Why are you really here? And please don't try to lie and say it's because you're interested in the neighborhood."

She nodded, paused again. "I wanted to talk to you about what happened in the nurses' lounge."

"Good. Because I'm all ears. And while you're at it, why don't you explain why you fled the scene?"

Silence. But that didn't mean she didn't have a response. There was plenty of nonverbal stuff going on. Increased respiratory rate. Her pulse, working on her throat. Bo didn't care for any of it. Nor did he care for her. This woman clearly had some secrets, and he didn't plan for them to be secrets much longer.

He came out of the chair, startling his guest with his abrupt movement. Ms. Cooper jumped to her feet and looked ready to run, but Bo caught on to her shoulders to stop her.

"You will tell me what happened," he insisted. But then he got a sickening thought. "Did you know the gunmen? Were you their partner?"

Her eyes widened. "No."

"And why should I believe you?"

She didn't get a chance to answer. That's because they heard the rushed footsteps.

Both looked in the direction of the sound, and a moment later Rosalie appeared in the entryway of the living room. "Hate to disturb you, but it's important." There was already alarm on her face, but it went up a notch when the nanny noticed their positions. Bo still had her by the shoulders.

"What's going on here?" Rosalie asked.

He turned his attention back to Ms. Cooper. "I'm not sure."

"Well, whatever it is, I hope it can wait," Rosalie insisted. From the other end of the hall, Bo could hear his son, Jacob, babbling and playing. "You said something about a black van when you came in. You thought it might have been following you?"

That grabbed his attention. Bo let go of the woman's shoulders and turned toward Rosalie. "Yes. Why?"

Rosalie aimed her trembling hand in the direction of the front door. "Because a black van just pulled up in front of the house."

Chapter Two

Mattie's heart dropped to her knees.

No, no, no! This couldn't be happening. They couldn't have found her this fast.

Bo reacted like a cop. He whipped his gun from the shoulder holster that was concealed beneath his jacket.

"Go to the babies," he told the nanny. "Call Garrett O'Malley at headquarters. I want a unit out here now." Then he headed for the front door.

Mattie followed him. She eased her snub-nose .38 from her purse and braced herself for the worst. However, she hadn't counted on the worst coming from Bo himself.

He turned around, lightning fast, and with his left hand caught on to her right wrist. Before she even knew what was happening, he tore the gun from her hand.

"What the hell are you doing with this?" he snarled getting right in her face. So close that his body brushed against hers.

Mattie pretended not to notice the contact. "I have my reasons for carrying a gun. And you might need backup if there's danger."

"I don't want or need backup from you. Get in the living room and stay there."

Mattie didn't try to wrestle her gun away from him, not that she would have succeeded anyway. He outsized her by at least seven inches and seventy-five pounds. But despite being outsized, she disobeyed his order.

She went to the front door and looked out one of the beveled glass sidelight windows. Even through the distortion of the bevels and the dusky light outside, she had no trouble seeing that black van. What she couldn't see was who was inside it. The heavily tinted windows prevented that.

"What do you know about this?" Bo asked, joining her. Well, actually he muscled her out of the way and looked out for himself.

"Nothing…specifically. Maybe nothing at all."

That earned her a glare from his narrowed brown eyes. "Then you'd better get into *un*specifics, even if they involve nothing at all."

Mattie tried to keep her chin high, though it wasn't easy. "Later. After we take care of this."

Whatever *this* was.

It could be someone from Witness Protection, or her family, or maybe the men who'd been hunting her. None of these was a good option. Unfortunately, with her luck she didn't think it would be a van of Girl Scouts selling cookies.

From the end of the hall, Mattie could hear the sounds of children playing. Happy sounds. The nanny obviously hadn't frightened the children with her alarming news about the van. That was good. Now Mattie had to make sure it stayed that way. She didn't want the children upset or anywhere near the possible danger.

Despite Bo's grunt of obvious disapproval, Mattie stayed by the sidelight window. "How long before the police unit arrives?" she asked.

"Soon." He slipped her .38 into his jacket pocket. "Once they're here, I'll go out and have a chat with whoever's in that van. And then, Ms. Cooper, I'm taking you to headquarters for an interview and possibly even an arrest for carrying a concealed weapon."

Mattie couldn't go to headquarters, of course. She couldn't risk being seen. If she couldn't convince Bo otherwise, then she'd have to figure a way out of there. But she didn't want to leave. Not with so much unfinished business.

Or with so much at stake.

Bo volleyed glances between the van and her. He had a unique way of making her feel like a criminal.

Unfortunately, that wasn't all.

He also had a unique way of making her feel like a woman.

It probably had something to do with all that testosterone emanating from him. Yes, he was a man. As alpha as they came. Tall, dark brown hair. Oh, and dangerous, too. Not the kind and gentle soul that Nadine had described. But Mattie saw the appeal.

Or rather, she *felt* the appeal.

And she gave herself a good mental tongue-lashing for it. There was no room in her life for Bo Duggan or any other man.

After she had another look to make sure no one was

coming out of that van, Mattie stepped back, putting some distance between her and the hot, glaring cop.

And then she saw it.

The photo on the wall.

She probably hadn't noticed it when she first came in because Rosalie had quickly ushered her to the living room. But Mattie saw it now. It was a picture of two babies.

A boy and a girl.

Both were around a year old. Both smiling for the camera. The boy had dark brown hair and was a genetic copy of Bo Duggan, right down to his already intense eyes.

And then there was the little girl.

Brown hair, as well, but hers was shades lighter than the boy's. Green eyes, not so much intense but filled with curiosity. She was so beautiful.

So precious.

Mattie heard the sound escape from her throat. Part moan, part gasp. A paradox of emotions flooded through her. The unconditional love mixed with the heart-wrenching pain of how much time she'd already lost.

She felt the movement next to her. It was Bo, although she had to blink back the tears just to see his face.

He was scowling.

And worse, he was puzzled and almost certainly on the verge of demanding answers. Mattie wasn't ready to give him those answers just yet. First, she had to lay the groundwork. She had to convince him—somehow—to help her.

"The van," she reminded him, looking back out the window. It was still there. No open doors.

Bo returned his attention to the menacing vehicle, as well, and the silence sliced right through the foyer. "Who's out there?" he asked.

She had to clear away the lump in her throat before she could speak. "I honestly don't know."

"But it's related to you?"

"Maybe. But I don't think so. I've covered my tracks well. Plus, as you said, the van followed you. There shouldn't be a connection between me and you."

Mattie prayed that that was true. It didn't mean it was. Someone could have put one and one together and that would have led them to Bo. And to that precious little girl in the picture.

"Have you been followed before?" Mattie asked.

"No." He was adamant enough about it, but there was something that made her keep pushing.

"You're sure?"

He cursed under his breath. "Someone's been looking into my personal info. And yesterday someone tried to break into my SUV."

"Yesterday," she repeated. Mattie didn't like the timing. Yesterday was when she'd called Bo's house and asked for an appointment to see him.

She caught some movement on the street and spotted the white police cruiser. It came to a stop behind the van.

"Wait here," Bo ordered. But he didn't just order it. This time he snared her gaze, and there was trouble in his eyes. Trouble that dared her to defy him.

Mattie stayed put. Besides, it was possible that

whoever was in that van would want to shoot her on sight. She didn't want to die, and she didn't want bullets coming anywhere near the children.

Much to her surprise, the driver of the van didn't slam on the accelerator and speed away. She watched as the person inside rolled down the window. Bo approached, his gun aimed and ready. The two uniformed officers who got out of the cruiser had their weapons trained on the van, as well.

When the window was completely lowered, she spotted the man inside. Scraggly salt-and-pepper hair. Long, thin face.

He was a stranger.

That didn't mean he wasn't a gun hired by someone who didn't qualify as a stranger. It wouldn't be the first time a gunman had been paid to come after her.

"Is everything okay?" she heard someone ask.

She looked over her shoulder and spotted Rosalie. The sixty-something-year-old nanny with the sugar-white hair was in the doorway of one of the rooms down the corridor. She had the little boy in her arms, his legs straddled around her thin hip.

Mattie's heart lurched, and she waited. Breath held. Hoping to see the other child. And then hoping that she didn't. Not at this moment with the van out there.

"The police are here," Mattie relayed. "Bo should be back soon."

Rosalie nodded and disappeared into the room, where she'd hopefully be safe with the children if bullets started flying.

Mattie forced her attention back on the van. The driver was smiling. His demeanor was almost apologetic. He even laughed about something one of the officers said. Bo didn't share the laugh, but he did lower his weapon, and then he said something to the uniformed officers before turning to walk toward the house.

Mattie opened the door for him but stood to the side so that neither the officers nor the van driver could see her.

"The guy says he's interested in buying the house across the street," Bo announced. "That seems to be the lie of the day, huh?"

"You think he's lying?"

"Maybe. But even if he's not, those are fake plates on his vehicle. He'll need to explain that to the officers." He re-holstered his gun. "And speaking of explaining, let me check on Rosalie, and then I can call someone to stay with her while I take you down to headquarters."

"No." She grabbed his arm to stop him from heading to the nursery. "If you take me there, you'll be signing my death warrant."

He couldn't have possibly managed a more skeptical look. "I'm a cop, not a killer."

"There are others, though, who would love to pull the trigger." Mattie wished she'd rehearsed this or at least figured out the best way to approach what she had to say. Of course, maybe there was no best way.

He shook off her grip and turned, practically trapping her against the wall. "Did you have something to do with the men who took the hostages at the hospital?"

"No. I told you that I was one of the hostages."

"Madeline Cooper," he said as a challenge.

"Mattie," she offered, though she knew this wasn't going to turn into a friendly visit.

"Mattie," he repeated. "Your name wasn't on the list of patients who were in the ward during the hostage standoff."

"Because I left before the police arrived."

"Yeah. I know." His eyes narrowed. "And why would you do something like that?"

Mattie answered his question with one of her own. "Can I trust you?"

"As much as I can trust you," he warned, his eyes narrowing even more.

If she'd had a choice, she would have backed off then and there. But she didn't have a choice. "I was in the Witness Protection Program."

He hesitated only a heartbeat. "I want your case number so I can verify it."

"The number doesn't mean anything anymore. There was some kind of leak, and someone found out my new identity and location. Right before the hostage situation, that someone tried to kill me. I escaped and went to the hospital. The trauma must have triggered my labor. When I checked in, I used a fake name, obviously, and I said I didn't have my insurance card with me."

"You think the ski-mask-wearing SOBs were really after you?"

She shook her head. "No. At least I don't think so." From what she'd read about the case in the past thirteen months, the gunmen had been there to break into the lab and tamper with some DNA evidence. Nothing related to her.

"I couldn't just let the cops find me there at the hospital that day," she explained. "My former boss believes I'm dead, and if they'd learned differently—"

"Who's your former boss?"

She decided to tell him the truth, because maybe this would help her cause. "Kendall Collier."

Those cop's eyes darkened. He obviously recognized the name. "You're not Madeline Cooper. You're Mattie Collier. And two years ago you testified against Kendall Collier."

"Yes." Her boss, her uncle. And also someone who'd gotten involved with an illegal arms dealer and gotten off scot-free because of a technicality. "I have reason to believe that Kendall, or someone else, will kill me if anyone learns I'm alive. That's why I left the hospital."

He made a sound deep within his chest to indicate he was thinking about what she'd said. Processing it. She could see the moment that *the* question came to him. It didn't take long.

"On the video, you didn't have a baby with you. You were alone. What happened to your child?"

Mattie considered several ways she could go about this, but those ways all led to the same inevitable end. It was an end that Bo Duggan was not going to like.

She pointed to the picture on the wall. "My daughter is here with you. You've been raising her. But I've waited long enough, and I want her back."

Chapter Three

Bo hadn't thought there could be too many more surprises today, but he was wrong. He was also obviously dealing with a liar or someone in need of medication.

But Mattie Collier seemed to be lucid.

Well, except for that part about him having her child. There wasn't a chance that was true. No lucid woman would be saying that.

"Nadine had twins," he spelled out for her. "A boy and a girl."

Mattie shook her head. "No. Nadine had a son that I helped deliver. I had a daughter. And when I realized that I had to get out of that hospital or be killed, I knew I couldn't risk taking my child with me."

"So you put your newborn baby in the arms of my unconscious wife?" Bo didn't even try to take the sarcasm and skepticism out of his voice.

"She wasn't unconscious when I left. Tired and sleepy, yes. But conscious. We talked." Mattie huffed and pushed her hair away from her face. "Nadine agreed—she was to tell you about what I was doing. But only you. And then I told her when it was safe, I'd come for the baby."

Bo couldn't even let himself fathom that this might be true. It wasn't. Jacob and Holly were his. They were his life. And he'd already ascertained that Mattie Collier was a liar. The trouble was, he couldn't quite figure out why she'd come up with this particular lie.

Maybe to get his help with her Witness Protection problem?

Perhaps. She was obviously troubled and in trouble. But it seemed an outlandish approach to get his help.

And why did he want to help her?

She'd riled him with her accusation about being Holly's mom. She'd also riled him with her stream of lies and her connections to an alleged lowlife scumbag like Kendall Collier, someone that Bo would prefer not to have introduced into the lives of his children.

Still, Mattie had that vulnerable look about her, and he hoped like the devil that vulnerability was all there was to it. This wasn't a man-woman thing.

Was it?

But then he rethought that question. It couldn't be that. Other than a passing glance, he hadn't noticed another woman since Nadine.

"Do you have any proof whatsoever about what you're saying?" he demanded.

"No. But you can get proof by doing a DNA test on my daughter. I brought the kits with me."

"*My* daughter," he corrected. "Holly is mine. Both babies have O positive blood type—that matches mine."

"O positive is a common blood type." She stepped closer. "I know this is hard for you to accept—"

"It isn't hard, because I won't accept it. But I will ask

why you're doing this. Do you think if you have some kind of emotional hold over me that I'll do whatever it takes to keep you out of the path of your uncle and his hired guns?"

Mattie stepped back as if he'd slapped her. "Even you can't keep me out of Kendall's path. An entire team of federal agents failed. I failed."

"Ahhh. So, by your own admission a dangerous situation still exists in your life. Yet, according to your delusional plan, you told Nadine that you'd come for the baby when it was safe."

He expected to see some anger in her eyes, especially since he'd just caught her in another lie. But there was no anger. Only weariness and fatigue.

She leaned back against the wall. "I have a friend who works in the Office of Vital Statistics in Austin, and she told me that someone is searching through birth records for the time period my daughter was due to be born. That someone is looking for her as a way to get to me, and judging from the records they're searching now, they're getting close to finding her. If I stay in hiding, I can't protect her, and protecting her is my first priority. That's a promise I made to her father just hours before he was murdered."

"Your story just keeps getting better and better," he mocked. Though he wouldn't put it past a criminal like Kendall Collier to commit murder. Bo didn't personally know the man, but from what he'd heard, Kendall was capable of just about anything.

Which only weakened Mattie's story.

"If you're telling the truth," Bo explained, "you

wouldn't be here. A mother wouldn't put her baby in that kind of danger."

"A mother without a choice would have," she countered. "I don't have a choice."

"I beg to differ. You can turn and walk out that door right now." Of course, he wouldn't let her do that. If she was going anywhere, it was to police headquarters for a long hard interrogation.

"I've been living in fear for a long time." Her voice was strained and low now. "I worried that right after the hostage situation, the hospital would do DNA tests on all the babies. I thought my secret would be discovered then."

"How do you know the hospital didn't do tests?" Bo snarled.

"If they had, then you'd know that the little girl in the picture is mine."

She had him there. But some of the babies had been tested, those in the newborn unit that had been evacuated because the gunmen had set a fire near it before they escaped. And the other group that had been tested was those newborns that had been physically separated from their mothers at any time during the standoff.

That hadn't been the case with Nadine.

Bo and the other officers had found her and the babies in the nurses' lounge. Alone. It was obvious Nadine had given birth, and it was equally obvious that she was holding her babies in her arms.

Mattie glanced in the direction of the nursery when one of the babies fussed, but the noise soon stopped.

"Nadine didn't say anything when you got to her?" Mattie asked.

"Not much."

"But she said something," she pressed.

Oh, yes. Nadine had said something. Something that Bo had replayed in his head a million times. Words that he would never forget.

We have to protect her.

Not *them.*

Her.

The comment had puzzled Bo, but he'd dismissed it as the ramblings of a traumatized, dying woman. Nadine had meant to say *them.* The twins. Just as she'd meant to tell Bo that she loved him. But there hadn't been time, and Nadine hadn't had the energy to speak anything else.

"What did she say?" Mattie whispered. She was begging. And there were tears in her eyes, though she quickly blinked them back.

Bo didn't like those tears. They seemed genuine. The real McCoy. Still, he wasn't ready to cut her any slack. Not with what was at stake.

"I'll tell you what Nadine said," he countered, "when you tell me why you're really here."

Mattie was apparently still contemplating that when he saw the movement out of the corner of his eye. Rosalie stepped from the nursery. And she wasn't alone. She was carrying Jacob, and Holly was peeking around Rosalie's skirt.

"Is that van gone?" Rosalie asked.

Bo nodded and went toward her. He didn't want Mattie seeing Holly. But it was too late. She obviously saw the child, because Mattie went in that direction, as well.

He blocked her from moving any closer.

"What's wrong?" Rosalie demanded.

Bo locked eyes with Mattie, but he addressed his comment to the nanny. "Just wait in the nursery."

"You keep dodging the question, Bo," Rosalie answered. "And I think it's time you told me what's going on. I have ears, you know. I can hear what this woman is saying. Well, most of it, anyway."

Bo had no idea what to say to that, and it turned out that an immediate response wasn't required. That's because Holly squealed "Da Da" and toddled toward him. She had just taken her first steps two days before, so when she wobbled, she fell to the floor and crawled toward Bo.

Jacob followed her lead, babbled "Da Da" as well and wiggled and squirmed so that Rosalie let him down. Jacob had been walking for nearly a month now but still had some trouble mastering the carpet in his bare feet.

Holly made it to Bo first. Her loose brown curls danced around her beaming face, and despite everything else going on, Bo's bad mood melted away. He scooped up his daughter in his arms and got rewarded with a sloppy kiss on his cheek. A moment later, Jacob reached him, as well, and both of Bo's arms were suddenly filled with the children he loved more than life itself.

He looked at Mattie. This time, she wasn't successful in blinking back those tears. She reached out, her fingers going straight toward Holly's curls, but it was Rosalie who snagged her wrist.

"You said some powerful things," Rosalie acknowledged. "What I want to know is why you're saying them."

Mattie kept her attention nailed to Holly. "Because it's the truth."

Rosalie met Bo's gaze, and he didn't see the immediate dismissal that he hoped would be there. He kissed the babies again and passed them back to the nanny. "I need to clear this up with Ms. Collier."

Rosalie looked ready to argue, but thankfully she didn't. She pulled both kids into her arms and headed back down the hall.

"I was going to name her Isabella," Mattie said before he could speak. Her voice cracked. "But Holly suits her. It's a good fit."

He didn't want to hear any of this.

"This ends now," Bo quickly told Mattie. "I've already wasted enough time. If you were really Holly's mom, you wouldn't have come here."

"I told you I didn't have a choice. I've been keeping tabs on my uncle and his cronies, and I have reason to believe that Kendall or someone else has made the connection between your wife and me."

There it was. The feeling of being punched in the gut. "And how would he have done that?"

"I'm not sure. Maybe that hospital video. Maybe by talking to eyewitnesses who were able to give him a description of me." She paused. "As I told you, someone has been researching all the babies born around the time my child was due. It's possible Kendall knows that you have my child. And if he knows that, then it won't be long before he comes after her. Because he'll probably try to use Holly to get to me."

Every muscle in his body tensed. Bo couldn't bear the thought of anyone being a threat to his child.

"I still don't believe you," he said, enunciating each word so that she wouldn't misunderstand.

"Just think this through," she countered. "Nadine and you must have known she wasn't carrying twins."

"We didn't. There were no ultrasounds. Nadine had read a lot of articles about ultrasounds, and she was worried they might not be a hundred percent safe. Something to do with the way the high-frequency waves could maybe alter cells. Even though there's no conclusive evidence that an ultrasound would be harmful, Nadine didn't want to take the risk unless it was absolutely necessary."

Mattie cleared her throat. "If what I'm saying isn't true, then why else would I have been in that maternity hospital?"

He could think of a reason. A bad one. Maybe she'd been there to assist the gunmen. But if so, then why hadn't she gone with them?

Or maybe she had.

Keeping an eye on her to make sure she didn't go after Holly, Bo took out his phone, scrolled through his numbers and tapped Sergeant Garrett O'Malley's personal cell.

"Bo, have you got ESP or something, because I was about to call you," O'Malley answered, obviously seeing Bo's name and number on his caller ID. "You're not going to like this, but the guy in the black van hasn't even gotten here, and his lawyer has already arrived. It's Ian Kaplan."

"You know this Ian Kaplan?" Bo asked. He heard Mattie's breath rattle, and she took a step back.

"No, but I ran a check on him as soon as he showed up," O'Malley explained. "Ian Kaplan is expensive and exclusive."

He felt another punch. That was not a good connection. So what did this exclusive lawyer have to do with a van driver with fake plates?

Bo didn't think he was going to like this answer, either.

"Do me a favor, Garrett. I told you someone's been doing computer checks on me, and it flagged firewall markers. The person used a PC in a coffeehouse over on San Pedro. I had someone lift prints from that PC, and they were running the forty or so partials they found. Is that list ready?"

Bo heard Garrett's keystrokes on the computer. "Yeah," the sergeant said a moment later. "Forty-six partials but only two hits."

The odds sucked, especially since the person responsible might not have prints on file in the database. "Is Ian Kaplan one of the hits?"

"No. But there is a name here I recognize. Kendall Collier."

Bo thought his blood might have turned to ice.

"You know, the guy that beat that illegal arms rap about a year and a half ago," Garrett continued. "His own niece testified against him, went missing and is presumed dead, but I'm thinking she went into Witness Protection and they faked her death. So why the heck would an SOB like Kendall Collier be digging into your files?"

Oh, hell.

"I'll get back to you on that," Bo told Garrett.

He shoved his phone into his pocket, caught on to Mattie's shoulders and put her hard against the wall. "I want the whole truth, and I want it *now*."

Chapter Four

Mattie wanted to give Bo the truth he was demanding, but she had no idea what that truth was. That would change. She had to figure out what was going on so she could try to keep her daughter safe.

Her daughter.

That nearly took her breath away. She was so close to her baby. Holly was just up the hall. Mattie wanted to run to her, take her and get as far away from this place as possible. But there were some big reasons why she couldn't do that.

The biggest reason now had her pressed hard against the wall.

Bo was right there, in her face, his gaze drilling into her.

"Your uncle used a computer in a coffee shop to dig into my background," Bo told her, though she didn't know how he managed to speak with his jaw that tight. "I know it was him because we found his prints on the keyboard."

It felt as if someone had punched her. "Oh, God. Kendall's closer to learning the truth than I thought. I'd hoped we'd have at least a day or two."

Bo got even closer. His chest pushed against her so that it was hard to breathe. "A day or two for what?"

"To get Holly to some place safe." Mattie mentally cursed, as well. "If Kendall used a public computer and left his fingerprints, then he wanted you to know he was searching for information on you. Have the computer checked again, because I'll bet he also used it to do searches on babies born the same day as Holly."

His eyes narrowed, his stare became even more intense, but he finally backed away from her. "Why would Kendall want me to know he's doing these things?"

"Maybe because he wants to use you to find me. So he can kill me. Of course, Kendall would never confess to something like that. According to him, he loves me and forgives me for testifying against him."

He stepped back even farther, apparently giving her theory some thought. Finally, Bo groaned and pulled out his phone again.

"Whoever you talk to," she warned, "be careful what you say."

Not that it would matter much at this point. If Kendall didn't know she was at Bo's house, then it was just a matter of time before he did. That's why she had to hurry up this conversation.

Bo dismissed her warning with an ice-cold glance with those intense brown eyes. But Mattie knew he wasn't really dismissing everything she'd just told him. No. Bo was too sensible for that. And while this had to be ripping his heart apart, he would need to get to the truth.

She was counting heavily on that.

Mattie wasn't sure who Bo reached with his call.

Maybe Sergeant O'Malley again. But whoever it was, Bo requested information about her, about her Witness Protection file, and he also asked for the browsing history on the computer Kendall had used. Each request seemed to make him angrier, so Bo was in full stewing mode when he ended the call. However, she couldn't give him the time he no doubt needed to work through his anger and the bombshell she'd just delivered about being Holly's mom. They had too much to do.

"You mentioned Ian Kaplan earlier," she reminded him. "Why?"

He glared at her so long that for several moments Mattie didn't think he would answer. "He's the attorney for the guy in the black van."

Mattie's nerves had already been right at the surface, but that caused the blood to rush to her head. "Then the man in the van is connected to Kendall, because Ian is one of my uncle's lawyers."

Bo studied her. "You know this Ian?"

She nodded. "We worked together a lot when I did some P.I. jobs for my uncle. He's very loyal to Kendall. And Kendall was no doubt sending another message by having him represent the man who was probably sent here to kill me."

"You're a P.I.?" Bo questioned.

"I was. Am," she corrected, since she still had her license. "Much to the disgust of my family. The Colliers aren't big on family members with careers in law enforcement." That was a massive understatement.

"Yet your uncle hired you."

"He did. After my parents died in a car accident five years ago, Kendall sort of took me under his wing. He hired me to do background checks on potential business associates. When I learned one of those associates was an illegal arms dealer, I told Kendall, but he didn't believe me. That's when I contacted the authorities."

"A Collier with a conscience." And it was obvious he didn't bother to tone down the sarcasm.

Mattie couldn't blame him for his attitude. He was right. Her parents had owned several investment businesses that were barely legal. She had known from an early age that they had questionable ethics, but only after she'd become a P.I. and had dug into their backgrounds had she realized just how corrupt they were.

"As you know, I testified against Kendall," she continued, "but he was acquitted."

"Because the FBI didn't have the proper search warrant when they found the incriminating documents."

She nodded, swallowed hard. "And I think because of that, Holly's father, my fiancé, was gunned down when I was six weeks pregnant. The police weren't able to find any proof of who killed him."

Bo blinked, probably because that had struck a still-raw nerve. He'd lost Nadine, the love of his life, and Mattie had lost Brody, the love of hers.

Sometimes, life just plain sucked.

"After someone tried to kidnap me," she continued, "I was placed in so-called Witness Protection. Turns out I didn't get much protection there."

Mattie took a deep breath to regain her composure, and she glanced toward the nursery. "Look, I know you have questions, but honestly they should wait."

The glare turned sharp again. "For what? For you to try to tell me again that Holly is your daughter?"

Obviously, Bo wasn't going to take her word on that, and she didn't blame him. She had walked into his ideal family life and had essentially ripped it apart.

Mattie reached into her shoulder bag. Bo reached, too, lightning fast, and he snagged her wrist.

"You already have my gun," she reminded him. Mattie waited until his grip eased a little, and she extracted the two DNA swabs that she'd bought online.

She saw the argument she and Bo were about to have, but his phone rang, cutting off the angry words that he was no doubt about to fire at her.

Bo let go of her wrist, but he stayed close, still violating her personal space. Normally, Mattie would have put some distance between them, but she wanted to hear his phone conversation, especially when she glanced at the caller ID screen and noticed that it was Sergeant O'Malley again.

"Mattie Collier," she heard the sergeant say. "She's in Witness Protection, but someone hacked into her file. Her identity was compromised."

That didn't soften Bo's glare. "Someone tried to kill her?"

"Well, at minimum someone tried to kidnap her several times, and it's highly likely the culprit had intentions to murder her. The FBI thinks the attempts are connected to her uncle, Kendall Collier. And that brings me to the computer in the coffee shop. You wanted to know what other searches Kendall made…"

Mattie automatically moved closer, so close that her cheek brushed against the back of Bo's hand. He jerked away from her and went to the center of the room where she couldn't hear a word the sergeant was saying.

"Yeah," Bo said to the sergeant a moment later. Then the seconds crawled by. She certainly couldn't tell from Bo's expression what exactly he was being told, but she doubted it would be good news.

While he finished his conversation, Mattie glanced out the window to make sure all was well. There were cars parked in the pristine driveways. Her own vehicle was still in front of Bo's house. Someone was walking a dog. But there were no menacing black vans or possible assassins lurking in the shadows.

Not now, anyway.

But they would come. She was certain of it.

Bo ended the call and closed his phone, but he just stood there, staring at the cell.

"You were right," he finally said. He came back across the room toward her. "Kendall used the computer to search for babies born on Holly's birthday."

Mattie wasn't exactly relieved, because it meant Kendall was closing in fast, but at least now Bo might realize that they both wanted the same thing.

To protect Holly.

"You need to know the truth about her DNA," Mattie pressed. She opened one of the kits and swabbed the inside of her mouth. She put the swab back into the plastic bag and handed it to Bo along with an unused one.

More seconds crawled by, and Mattie could feel her heart in her throat. Everything hinged on this.

Bo snatched the kits from her. "I'll have the tests done, but I'm not giving up my daughter. Got that?"

No. She didn't get that. But now wasn't the time to argue with a father on the verge of losing a child he loved. Even if arguing was exactly what Mattie wanted to do. She wanted her baby in her arms, right here, right now. But her need for her baby would have to wait. Holly's safety had to come first, and since that safety depended on Bo's help, she had to keep this as non-hostile as possible.

"I probably don't have to remind you to keep those results a secret," she said. "Kendall has probably already bribed labs all over the city to alert him to something like this."

"I'll use the police lab," he mumbled. "And I'll make sure the results come only to me."

Well, it wasn't foolproof, especially considering how someone had hacked into her Witness Protection files, but Bo needed these test results so they could move on to the next stage. Plus, he was aware now of the danger and would hopefully be taking massive precautions.

Mattie used the pen and notepad near the house phone to jot down her number. "I obviously use a prepaid cell these days. No way to trace it. But when you find out who the man in the black van is, I'd like to know."

Bo glanced at the paper but gave her no assurance that he would do that. Mattie would give him until noon the following day. If she could wait that long. And if she hadn't heard from him, then she would call him.

"I want you to move Holly and your son to a safe house," she added. "If you can't arrange that for tonight, then ask for officers to patrol the neighborhood." She'd already noticed that he had a security system.

"Don't tell me how to protect my kids," Bo snapped. "I've done all right so far."

"Yes, but you haven't run up against the likes of my uncle."

He looked at her phone number and then the DNA kits before his gaze came back to hers. "The authorities want to talk to you."

"It'll have to wait until I can figure out a way to neutralize my uncle and his hired guns."

"Neutralize?" he repeated, sounding very much like a cop again. "What are you planning to do?"

"After I'm sure Holly is safe, I'll call Kendall and see if I can negotiate a deal with him. I'll tell him I won't testify against him if there's a new trial."

It cut her to the core to make that kind of compromise. After watching her family's dirty dealings, the one thing that Mattie had always sworn was that she wouldn't be like them. But her child was at stake. If she had any hopes of being a mother to her baby, she had to bring things to a peaceful end with Kendall.

"You believe your uncle would adhere to a truce?" Bo pressed.

"No. Not voluntarily, anyway. I plan to appeal to his new fiancée, Cicely Carr. We're old friends, and I think I can reason with her."

"And if you can't?"

Mattie met his gaze head-on. "Then I'll make arrangements to live a new life in hiding." She paused. "And then I'll petition the courts for custody of my daughter."

There. That was the gauntlet she hadn't intended to throw tonight, but a lie wouldn't have worked. Bo would have instantly spotted it and called her on it. At least this way he knew her intentions were, well, motherly.

"You're leaving now," he insisted. And to make sure that happened, he took her arm and began to haul her toward the front door.

Mattie dug in her heels and stopped, whirling around to face him. She landed against him again, body to body. They'd already touched from head to toe, so this was familiar to her now. It was almost like being in his arms.

Almost.

The seemingly permanent glare on his face didn't give her any warm and fuzzy feelings. Neither did his body for that matter. But he did stir something deep within her, and it was a stirring she preferred to ignore.

Mattie stepped back. "Please let me say good-night to Holly."

"Not a chance." He didn't roll his eyes exactly, but it was close.

It was the answer she'd expected, but it still felt like someone had clamped a fist around her heart. "You know I'm telling the truth about being her mother." Mattie didn't try to keep the emotion out of her voice, but she did try to blink back the tears.

Mattie had known she couldn't take the baby with her tonight. Well, her head had known that, anyway. The rest of her was having a hard time walking out that door even though there was no alternative. There wasn't a chance in Hades that Bo would let her leave with Holly. Not now. Probably not without a court order, which she would get.

"If you don't do the DNA test, I'll get a judge to force you to do it," she managed to say.

But there was something new in his eyes. Something

beneath the shock and the pain. Something that made her believe the test would be done. Bo was, after all, a cop, and he no doubt had a need for the truth, even if that truth was too painful to bear.

She needed the truth, too.

Mattie turned, stopped and then eased back around. This time she made sure she didn't run into him. No more touching. It was creating a warmth that shouldn't be there.

"What did Nadine say to you before she died?" Mattie asked.

The muscle in his jaw flexed again, and he glanced at the DNA baggies that he had practically crushed in his hand. "I'll call you with the test results."

Her heart suddenly felt a little lighter. It wasn't nearly as good of a concession as holding her baby would be, but it was a start.

"Your gun," he said when she started to leave. He took it from the waist of his pants and handed it to her. "You have a permit for it?"

She nodded. "Thank you—"

"Don't," he warned. "I don't want you to thank me for anything. I just want the test results to prove Holly is mine, and then I want you out of our lives forever."

Mattie nodded again. "If she's not mine, you'll never see me again." But Mattie knew the little girl was hers. Bo would soon know it, too.

She reached for the door and at the same time looked out the window. Old habits. And this time, the old habit had her hand freezing on the doorknob.

"What?" Bo snarled. But he didn't wait for her to tell

him what she'd spotted. He muscled her aside and had his own look out the window.

"The dark green car," she whispered. "It's parked up the street, about fifteen feet from mine." Mattie was surprised at how calm her voice sounded when inside there was a hurricane of emotions and fear.

Especially fear.

My God. Had Kendall sent someone after her here?

"Does the car belong to one of your neighbors?" She prayed the answer would be yes, but Bo shook his head.

"Could you run the license plate?" she asked Bo, but he was already dropping the DNA bags onto the foyer table and taking out his phone.

He called someone and a moment later rattled off the plate numbers. He also drew his gun. And they stood there together while they kept watch. There was a streetlight, but because the car windows were tinted, Mattie couldn't tell if there was anyone inside. She did know the vehicle hadn't been there earlier.

"You're kidding," Bo mumbled a moment later.

His answer surprised Mattie a little, but there was certainly no humor in that remark. Worse, she saw the car door swing open.

Mattie lifted her gun and waited with her breath frozen in her lungs. The stranger kept his head down, so that she couldn't see his face. But the tall, thin man who stepped from the vehicle had dark hair.

He was also armed.

Even in the darkness she could see the familiar bulge beneath his coat.

He eased his car door shut, as if he didn't want to

alert anyone to his presence, and he fired glances all around him. Mattie stepped back from the window so she'd hopefully be concealed, but she didn't take her eyes off him.

Finally, she saw his face.

And she gasped.

No. This couldn't be happening.

But that thought barely had time to register when the man whipped out a handgun. He didn't stop there.

He came straight toward the house.

Chapter Five

Bo pushed Mattie aside so he could see what had just caused her to gasp.

Hell.

A man was walking full speed ahead toward the house. Bo didn't have to guess who he was or what he wanted.

He wanted Mattie.

Bo had been able to figure that out from what Sergeant O'Malley had just told him. Now the question was, would Bo just hand her over?

As a cop, he was duty bound to do just that, but he was positive Mattie wouldn't go without a fight, and he didn't want a fight in his house with his kids just a couple of rooms away.

This was turning into being one hell of a night.

Bo positioned Mattie behind him, and he opened the door. However, he had no intention of just letting the man barge in. "The car is registered to the federal marshals," Bo let her know. "Witness Protection."

No gasp this time. Mattie groaned and no doubt understood why he'd responded with "You're kidding" when Sergeant O'Malley had told Bo about the license plates.

"I know," she mumbled.

"Larry Tolivar. U.S. Marshal," the man said, pulling back his coat so that Bo could see the badge attached to his belt.

Bo still didn't fully open the door.

"You know him?" Bo asked Mattie.

"Yes. He was the man in charge of my case. And I don't trust him."

That went without saying. Bo wasn't sure he trusted the guy either, but he didn't know exactly why.

Looking all around as if he expected an ambush, Tolivar came to a stop on the porch and reached for the door. Bo held it in place so the marshal couldn't open it any farther.

"Lieutenant Bo Duggan," he said, identifying himself. "How can I help you?"

"You can let me talk to Mattie Collier."

The guy had the attitude of a fed, all right. Some arrogance mixed with an air of authority. Well, Bo had his own damn air of authority, and he didn't exactly want to examine why he felt this stupid need to protect Mattie.

He wanted her out of his house. Away from the kids, especially Holly. And here he had the opportunity to do just that, but he couldn't forget that Mattie had nearly been kidnapped and killed while in protective custody.

"Why would you think Mattie Collier was here?" Bo demanded. It was a reasonable question, especially since he'd bet his paycheck that Mattie had taken some serious security precautions before coming to his house.

Well, he hoped she had anyway.

"She's here," Tolivar insisted. He fired another glance over his shoulder. "And you're to release her to my custody immediately."

"I'm not going with you," Mattie insisted right back.

Bo couldn't fault her for speaking up, but he would have preferred to take care of this himself. He could have sent Tolivar on his merry way and then five minutes later done the same for Mattie. Now he was in some kind of jurisdictional contest with a federal agent.

Or was he?

Tolivar had apparently been an agent at one time, but Bo had no idea if that were still true.

Bo kept his gun ready and took out his phone again. He called Sergeant O'Malley and asked for verification. Before Tolivar could give him an outraged look, Bo used his phone to click the man's picture, and he fired the image off to O'Malley.

"Just double-checking," Bo remarked.

"Check all you want, but the bottom line is that Mattie Collier is coming with me. She's in danger and needs protection."

Mattie moved to Bo's side. "Don't make me laugh. The closest I've come to dying was when I was in your agency's custody. I entered the program voluntarily, and now I'm voluntarily leaving it."

She glanced at Bo, and the confidence that had been in her voice wasn't in her eyes. Those green eyes looked to be on the verge of spilling some tears. She also seemed to be asking for his help.

Great.

Now they were playing allies, when both of them knew they were enemies at heart.

"You can't leave the program," Tolivar insisted. "You'd be dead within an hour."

"I've done pretty well on my own for the past nineteen months."

"But there's a new threat." Tolivar huffed and switched his attention back to Bo. "You have to convince her to come with me."

"Maybe I will if you can explain how you knew she was here."

The arrogance returned to his lean expression, but then he glanced around them again. "Look, it's not a good idea to be standing out here in the open."

"Then talk fast," Bo suggested. "Because I'm not letting you in unless I have confirmation you're who you say you are." He glanced down at his phone. "No confirmation yet. So start talking."

Tolivar's mouth twisted, and he mumbled some profanity. "We've been keeping tabs on Mattie. And you."

Bo went still. "Me?"

The marshal nodded. "We were able to follow Mattie the day she went into labor. We were in the process of dispatching someone to return her to our custody and stay with her while she was in the hospital. Then the hostage situation happened, and we couldn't get to her."

"You knew I was at the hospital?" Mattie asked, her voice trembling a little now.

"We knew." No tremble for Tolivar, but he certainly wasn't as cocky as he had been earlier. Especially when his gaze came back to Bo. "We got access to the security feed, and we deduced that Mattie had been with or near your wife."

Bo let each word sink in.

"We caught just a glimpse of Mattie when she was sneaking out of the San Antonio Maternity Hospital," Tolivar continued.

"How?" Bo demanded. "Because I studied the surveillance tapes, and I didn't see when or where she left the building."

Tolivar glanced away. "I was there, and we had several agents watching. We thought she might try to get out before anyone could find her. And we were right. We got just a glimpse of her coming out of the service entrance."

Bo shook his head. "The cops were watching that entrance."

"Not by then. The gunman had just driven off with a hostage, and most of the other officers, including you, had raced into the building."

Later, Bo would make this moron give an official statement as to why a federal marshal had seen a possible witness escape and hadn't alerted the police.

"As I said, we got just a glimpse of Mattie as she was leaving, but we lost her soon afterward," Tolivar added. "And because we didn't know where she'd gone, we kept looking for flags. You, Lieutenant, were one of those flags."

That hung in the air a few seconds before it hit Bo like a heavyweight's fist. Mattie had a similar reaction, because she gasped and elbowed her way in front of Bo.

"Are you saying—" But she couldn't finish.

Bo, however, could finish. He pushed Mattie back behind him and grabbed on to Tolivar's lapels, pulling the man closer so that Bo was right in his face.

"You knew Mattie had been in the room with my wife?" Bo clarified, though he couldn't stop the anger from raging through him.

"We deduced it after reading through all the notes of the investigation and eyewitness reports." Tolivar's breathing suddenly became uneven. "We knew Mattie and your wife had been in labor rooms next to each other and that they disappeared before the gunmen could round them up with the other hostages. We didn't know exactly what went on between the women, but we thought that eventually Mattie would come to you. Maybe because of something that…happened when she was with your wife."

Bo had to get his teeth unclenched. "Say it, you SOB. Say that you knew Mattie was pregnant when she went in the hospital but didn't have a baby with her when she came out. Say it!"

"We didn't know for sure what had happened," Tolivar insisted.

But they sure as hell had guessed. "You waited, watching, for her to come to me."

Tolivar didn't deny it, and even if he had, Bo wouldn't have believed him. He cursed and wanted to ram his fist into this man's face. And he might have done just that if

Mattie hadn't pulled him back. She couldn't have done that unless Bo had allowed it, but he was so riled that he didn't trust himself to settle for just one punch. He wanted to clean his porch with this guy.

"Just leave," Mattie told the marshal.

Good idea. That way, Bo could try to deal with what he had just learned. Hell. Everything he'd believed about the past thirteen months had been a lie.

Tolivar shook his head. "I can't leave, not until I convince you to come with me."

"You're wasting your breath," she assured him. She reached for the door to slam it shut.

"There's an assassin after you," Tolivar said, blocking her attempt to shut the door.

"Tell me something I don't know." And Mattie tried to shut the door again.

"An assassin who was hired today," Tolivar continued. "This afternoon, as a matter of fact. We have reason to believe he knows about your connection to the lieutenant."

Bo just stared at the man and didn't know whether to laugh or curse again.

Mattie's gaze met Bo's, and he saw the fight in her eyes turn to pure, raw frustration. "I'm sorry. I didn't know."

"And you still don't," Bo quickly assured her. "The marshal here could have made up the assassin story to get you to go with him."

Why the heck he was volunteering that, Bo didn't know. He probably needed his head examined, but by God, he didn't want this swaggering fed to ride roughshod over a woman who had already had enough people run over her.

While he was at it, Bo decided this bozo could be lying about the baby situation, as well. He didn't believe anything that came out of Tolivar's mouth.

"You'll be sorry, and dead, if you don't come back into our protection," Tolivar warned Mattie.

That was the last straw. Bo slammed the door in the marshal's face, locked it and set the security system.

"Is everything okay?" Rosalie called out.

Since Bo didn't know the answer, he settled for saying, "Just stay put. I'll be in there soon."

First, he had to figure out how to diffuse a very big bomb.

Bo kept an eye on Tolivar. The marshal did indeed return to his vehicle, and he sped away. Bo didn't think for one minute that this was the last they would see of him. Tolivar would likely go to his office and return with backup.

Well, maybe.

Legally, there was no way anyone in Witness Protection could force Mattie to return, since she wasn't under any obligation to testify. But that meant Bo had to figure out what to do with her.

"Keep an eye out. See if Tolivar comes back," Bo told Mattie.

She went over to the window, freeing him to keep an eye on the area where his children were. He also took out his phone, and this time he called his boss, Captain Shaw Tolbert. Since Shaw's own wife had also been a maternity hostage, the captain had personal knowledge of what had gone on that day.

Hopefully, not too personal.

Hell. No one in SAPD better have known about Mattie leaving her baby behind while she went on the run.

"Bo," Shaw answered, obviously seeing his name on the caller ID. "I just got a call from a marshal over in Witness Protection."

They worked fast, and that meant Bo had to play catch-up. "Mattie Collier," Bo started. He walked down the hall toward the nursery. "She's here at my house. You happen to know why?"

"If I'm to believe what Marshal Tolivar said, Mattie gave birth to a baby girl and left the newborn with Nadine." The captain paused. "Is it true?"

Bo cracked open the nursery door and peered inside. Rosalie was seated in the rocking chair and had a baby in the crook of each arm, much the way Nadine had been holding them when Bo had found her in the nurses' lounge after the end of the hostage incident.

Rosalie glanced up but continued to read a Dr. Seuss book to Jacob and Holly. There was nothing unusual about that. Rosalie and Bo both read to them a lot. It was part of their nightly routine.

Tonight, it caused his heart to ache.

He'd taken moments like this for granted. He had thought that because he'd endured Nadine's death, there wouldn't be any more nightmares to face.

Well, he might be facing one now.

He couldn't lose his little girl. He just couldn't. It would be like losing Nadine all over again.

"Bo?" the captain said. "Is it true?"

"I'm not sure," he whispered. Bo stepped back and

closed the door so his conversation wouldn't disturb story time or alarm Rosalie.

That obviously wasn't the answer Shaw wanted to hear, because he cursed. "What do you want to do about it?"

Nothing. Bo wanted to send Mattie on her way and pretend this night had never happened. But he couldn't do that. Damn it. He couldn't live his life with his head in the sand, even if that's exactly what he wanted to do right now.

"Mattie just gave me a sample of her DNA," Bo continued. "I can use the cheek swab on Holly. The samples need to be compared."

Compared. That was such a benign word for something that could change his and his family's lives forever.

"I'll have someone pick up the samples tonight," Shaw concluded. "I can log them in under my name so that it won't be connected to you or Mattie. The lab will put a rush on them, and you should know something by tomorrow."

Bo didn't thank his captain because the words would have stuck in his throat. He was already dreading that the tests had to be run, but what he was dreading more were the results.

He took a deep breath to try to steady his knotted stomach, and Bo forced his mind back on the next task at hand. Mattie was still by the front window, and she was volleying glances outside and at him.

What are you going to do? she seemed to be asking.

Bo was wondering the same thing.

"If Tolivar is telling the truth, then there's an assassin after Mattie," Bo informed the captain.

"It's possible. I've been checking her records while we've been talking, and while she was in Witness Protection, her identity was compromised."

"How?" Bo wanted to know. "And who did it?"

"As for the how, someone hacked into the computer database. They don't know who was responsible, but the department believes this goes back to Mattie's uncle, Kendall Collier."

Yeah. He certainly had the most to gain by finding her.

Revenge.

God knows what Collier would be prepared to do to find a niece who had, in his mind, betrayed him.

"Collier's a rich, powerful man," Bo pointed out. "Is it possible he has this Marshal Tolivar on his payroll?"

"It's possible. It would have taken money and resources to hack into the Witness Protection database. Collier has the money, and Tolivar has the resources." Shaw's quick response meant he'd already thought of it. "Let me handle looking into that. In the meantime, we have this situation with Miss Collier."

Yeah, it was a situation, all right. She was looking at him with those sad doe eyes again.

"Mattie needs to be in protective custody," Shaw added.

Bo snapped back his shoulders. "You aren't suggesting we turn her over to Witness Protection."

"No. Besides, I doubt she'd be too eager to go with them."

"You're right about that." It was stupid to feel even

mildly relieved that she wouldn't go back into a system that had nearly gotten her killed. "So, what do we do with her?"

"We protect her," Shaw simply stated. "She did law enforcement a huge favor by testifying against her uncle, and it wasn't her fault that the FBI screwed up the search warrant and got most of their evidence thrown out."

No. It wasn't her fault. And it wasn't his that this mess had been brought right to his home.

"What are you suggesting?" Bo asked.

"Probably something you don't want to do, but hear me out, Bo. Mattie Collier is already there, and until I can make other arrangements, that's the safest place for her."

There went another shot of adrenaline and anger. Because so many objections came to mind, it took Bo a moment to pick which one to verbalize first. "There's an assassin after her and maybe even a corrupt federal marshal. My kids are here in the house."

"Yeah. I know, and as a dad myself, I know your twins are your first priority. That includes Holly."

That knot in his stomach twisted and tightened. Bo knew what the captain meant. If Collier, the assassin or anyone else after Mattie suspected that Holly was her daughter, they might try to take his little girl to get Mattie to cooperate.

Hell.

It wouldn't even have to be true that Mattie was Holly's biological mother. The SOBs would just have to think that it was.

When he looked at Mattie this time, he was sure his

eyes were narrowed to slits. How dare she bring this danger right to his babies.

She shook her head, obviously not understanding the venom he was now aiming at her.

"What are you asking me to do?" Bo questioned the captain. And he held his breath, waiting for the other shoe to fall.

"I'll get to work on a safe house, one under our jurisdiction. One where I can control the security until we can get this all figured out. I would move you now, but this is going to require a lot of work to make sure we're not taking you from the frying pan and into the fire. I want to make the arrangements myself and keep it out of anyone else's hands. Until I can work out everything, I'll send a couple of officers to sit in front of your place in a patrol car. That should deter an assassin or anyone else."

"You're sure about that?" Bo managed to say.

The captain paused. "I'll make things as safe for your family as possible. But in the meantime, Mattie Collier stays there, with you, in *your* protective custody."

Chapter Six

Protective custody.

To Mattie, this arrangement didn't feel so protective, not with Bo's obvious disapproval at her presence in his house. He had made her feel totally unwelcome, and it had started before the conversation with his captain had even ended.

After that call, Bo had grumbled that she would be staying at his house for the night, and then he'd promptly disappeared into the nursery, leaving Rosalie to show Mattie to the guest room. Rosalie had relayed Bo's order for Mattie to stay put in the guest room until morning. In other words, he didn't want her sneaking out to look at Holly.

Of course, she couldn't blame Bo and Rosalie for the chilly reception. Mattie had made a massive mistake by coming to Bo's.

But then, maybe not.

If Kendall had suspected that Holly was her baby, then it was just a matter of time before he would have used the child to get to her.

That didn't make Mattie feel any better.

Her baby was still in danger, and even though she

might be one step closer to proving that Holly was hers, what good would that do unless she could neutralize the danger?

As she'd done many times over the past year and a half, she wished Kendall were in jail where he couldn't be as much of a threat. But since he wasn't, that meant Mattie had to deal with the devil himself. She had to call Kendall and try to negotiate a deal with him.

Her life for Holly's safety.

Of course, there were no guarantees that Kendall would agree or, even if he did, that he would abide by any agreement with her. Plus, Mattie didn't want to die. She had been on the run for so long that fighting for her life was as natural as breathing. Still, if it came down to it, she would turn herself over to Kendall for a guaranteed assurance that Holly would be okay.

Mattie glanced at the clock on the nightstand next to the bed. It was 5:00 a.m. She'd gotten maybe an hour's sleep, and with every sound she heard, she'd reached for her gun. Bo had no doubt done the same, especially since he'd spent the night in the nursery. She knew this because the guest room was next to the nursery, and before the babies had fallen asleep, she'd heard Bo playing with them. She hadn't heard the door open or him walk out.

The sounds of Holly's laughter had filled Mattie with more love than she could have ever imagined. It had also caused her heart to ache. She had missed so much already. Thirteen months was a lifetime when it came to a baby. And her little girl was no longer a newborn but a toddler learning to walk.

Mattie hated Kendall for taking that time away from her.

She glanced at the clock again and groaned softly. A whole two minutes had passed. She wanted the hour to fly by because the quicker the time passed, the sooner she might get to see Holly. Of course, Bo might continue to lock all three of them in the nursery. Or he might usher Mattie out of his house as soon as it was daylight. He wasn't just going to hand over Holly without some kind of court order.

Mattie threw back the covers and got up, since it was obvious she wasn't going to fall back asleep. She took off the loaner gown that Rosalie had given her so she could dress in the green pants and top she'd worn the day before. Since she didn't have a change of clothes, she'd washed her underwear the night before and had hung it on the chair to dry. Her bra was still damp, but it would have to do. At least she had a toothbrush and some toiletries in her bag. Along with her gun.

Being on the run had taught her to be prepared.

Mattie didn't really need to use the bathroom because she'd gotten up just about an hour earlier to do that, but she did need to brush her teeth and freshen up. She grabbed her purse and threw open the door so she could head to the bathroom just up the hall. She didn't get far. She turned and smacked right into Bo.

Suddenly, she was smothered in his arms and against his chest. It didn't take but a split second to register that those arms and chest were bare and that there was a warm, male, musky scent to go along with all those toned muscles.

"Oh," she managed to say, and she stepped back. But

it was already too late. That scent and touch had gotten to her and had seeped right into her body, warming her in places that shouldn't be warm.

Not when it came to Bo, anyway.

Mattie soon realized that touching him was off-limits, but seeing him had the same effect on her. His hair was rumpled, as if he'd just climbed out of bed.

After a long night of sex.

His five-o'clock shadow was now more outlaw stubble. Dark and dangerous. Like the man himself. He wore loose jeans that were slung low on his hips, and it gave her a nice view of the abs to go along with the rest of his nearly perfect body.

Perfect except for the scar on his right shoulder.

It looked like a gunshot wound. And that snapped her out of the hot-body fantasy she was weaving around him.

"What are you doing up?" he growled.

His tone further dampened her fantasy, even though being near him had a unique way of renewing that fantasy.

"I couldn't sleep," she whispered and glanced over his shoulder. The nursery door was closed. "Thank God we had a quiet night." Quiet as in no one had attempted to kill them.

Bo made a sound that was minimally agreeable. "They're still in bed," he grumbled, obviously following her gaze.

Hopefully he hadn't followed her gaze when she'd given his body the once-over. But he obviously had. Mattie realized that when their eyes met. She didn't have a ton of experience with men, but she saw the glimmer of heat.

Involuntary heat, that is.

Bo's mouth turned to a snarl, but even that didn't make him less hot.

"Sorry," he mumbled at the exact moment that Mattie said the same.

They stared at each other, apparently waiting to see which would be the first to put a foot in their mouth.

Mattie decided to go first. "Don't worry. Even if we didn't have some huge obstacles between us, you're not my type."

The corner of his mouth lifted, but it was just as much a snarl as a smile. "Yeah. I'm a cop, and you're from a family of criminals."

She winced before she could hide her reaction. It stung. Always did when people linked her to her scummy family.

"Sorry," he mumbled again.

She tried to shrug. "I did voluntarily go to work for my uncle," Mattie admitted. "So, I deserve that."

He shook his head and mumbled something under his breath. "No. You didn't." Bo motioned toward the kitchen. "Want some coffee?"

She did, desperately. Her brain was screaming for a caffeine fix. But her gaze wandered back to the nursery.

"They won't be up for another half hour or so," Bo let her know. "Rosalie's in there with them now."

Good. So the babies weren't alone. Even though Rosalie had assured her the windows were wired to the security system, Mattie still didn't want to take any chances. If someone tried to break into the nursery, Rosalie would be there to get the children out.

Mattie followed him into the kitchen, placed her purse on the counter and sat at the table while Bo started the coffee. He then disappeared into the adjoining laundry room and a few seconds later came out wearing a snug black T-shirt. End of the peep show, which was just as well.

"So, why did you go to work for your uncle?" he asked. He opened the fridge and took out the makings for breakfast. Eggs, bacon and orange juice.

Mattie's stomach growled, and she realized it'd been noon the day before since she'd eaten. Would Bo let her stay for breakfast, or would he have her out of there before the kids woke up? It wasn't even 5:30 yet, but she had no idea how long Holly and Jacob would stay asleep.

When he glanced back at her, Mattie realized he was waiting for an answer to his question.

"Kendall talked me into coming to work for him, after he'd assured me that he was nothing like my father. He offered me a great salary with medical insurance. Since my fiancé and I were planning on having a child, I thought it was a good idea." She paused. "I obviously thought wrong. My father was a saint compared to Kendall."

Bo made another of those sounds, a cross between agreement and a male grunt, and he poured her a cup of coffee, sliding it across the table toward her.

Since this was the most civil he had been to her, Mattie hated to ruin the moment, but they had things to discuss.

"Did you send the DNA tests to the lab?" she asked.

He froze a moment, turned his back to her and started to make the bacon and eggs. "Captain Shaw had an officer pick up the samples last night."

And that was apparently all Bo intended to volunteer.

"Holly's DNA will be a match to mine," Mattie continued, knowing she was wading into deep, dangerous waters.

He didn't issue one of those grunts this time, but he did aim a glare at her from over his shoulder.

"We've identified the man who was in the black van," he said, obviously ignoring her assertion that the DNA tests would match. "His name is Terrance Arturo. You know him?"

She repeated the name to see if it would jog any memories. It didn't. "No. He works for Kendall?"

"We're not sure. His lawyer hasn't allowed him to say much."

Yes, his lawyer. "Ian Kaplan."

"Just how well do you know him?" Bo pressed.

"I worked with him for months, but I knew him before that. I thought he was a decent guy." Mattie paused again. "I think he had a crush on me or something, because he seemed to be jealous of Brody, my late fiancé."

Now she got a grunt. And silence. The only sound came from the sizzling bacon.

"Nadine said you were, and I quote, 'the best husband in the world.'" Mattie waited for a response but didn't get one. Bo continued to beat the eggs that he'd just cracked into a small bowl. "She talked about you almost the whole time she was in labor."

Even through his T-shirt, she saw the muscles in his back tense. "Did she blame me for not being there to rescue her?"

Oh. So, that's what was going on in his mind. "No. Just the opposite. She insisted that you would come for her. And you did."

"Too little, too late," he mumbled. He set aside the eggs he'd been beating as if they were suddenly too fragile to be in his hands, probably because he had a death grip on the glass bowl. Then he turned around to face her.

"Not too late for Jacob and Holly," Mattie insisted. "And as for Nadine, that wasn't your fault."

"The hell it wasn't." His gaze fired all around the room as if he were looking for someplace to aim the dangerous energy that was a powder keg inside him.

It was a massive risk, but Mattie got up and walked over to him. "Despite the circumstances, Nadine was happy when she gave birth to your son." She reached out, touched his arm.

Bo jerked away from her at first, but when Mattie caught his wrist, he didn't fight it. He just stared at her, and she could see and feel every ounce of the pain that he was experiencing.

"Nadine knew she was going to die?" he asked, his voice barely a whisper.

Mattie shook her head. "I'm not sure." She inched even closer and blinked back the tears that were burning her eyes. "She said you were the love of her life.

The answer to her prayers. She also said you would help me."

Now he tried to pull away, but Mattie held on. "I need your help, Bo. I need you to tell me what Nadine said when you got to her in the nurses' lounge."

For a moment, she thought that was the end of their conversation. He was putting up that wall again. But then, something changed. Bo didn't dodge her gaze. Instead, he looked deep into her eyes.

She was aware of the sounds. The smells. The bacon was either burning or close to it. But the only thing she saw was Bo.

A raw groan tore from his throat, and he pulled her to him, against him. Not a punishing grip. A hug. He pulled her into his arms.

"Nadine said, 'We have to protect her.' And then she closed her eyes and didn't open them again."

"Her," Mattie repeated. "Nadine meant Holly. I told her to ask you to protect my baby."

She held her breath, waiting for Bo to admit that Holly was hers, but the sounds stopped him from saying anything.

It was a giggle. Followed by footsteps.

Bo jerked away from her and moved the bacon off the burner. He pushed past her and headed for the hall just as Jacob rounded the corner. He was wearing only a diaper and a single blue sock.

Even though the little boy was obviously a novice at walking, he was doing a good job making his way to his dad. He had a big grin on his face as if he'd just done something naughty but fun. Mattie found herself smiling despite the tense, heart-wrenching conversation she'd just had with Bo.

"Jacob?" Rosalie called out. "Get back in here."

The little boy giggled and made a beeline for his father. Bo scooped him up his arms and gave him a kiss on the cheek. "Did you escape?"

Jacob babbled something the two males must have understood, because they shared a grin.

A moment later, a harried-looking Rosalie appeared in the doorway. But Mattie's heart sank, because Holly wasn't with her.

"That boy's getting faster every day," Rosalie complained, laughing. "And they both got up way too early this morning."

"Go ahead and tend to Holly," Bo told her. "I'll get Jacob some breakfast."

Jacob's attention landed on Mattie, and he reached for her. "Tiss," he insisted.

Mattie was certain she looked confused, but before she could ask what the little boy wanted, Jacob shifted his weight and practically plunged into her arms.

"Tiss," Jacob repeated, and he gave her a kiss on the end of her nose.

For such a simple gesture, it filled her with more emotion than she would have thought possible. Mattie felt the tears threaten again.

So this was what it was like to have a child.

"Jacob obviously likes to kiss," Bo mumbled, and he pulled out one of the two high chairs that were stored against the wall. "And run around half naked. Come on, son. Time to eat."

That got Jacob's attention, and he went right back

to Bo so his dad could put him in the high chair. Bo sprinkled some dry cereal O's right onto the tray and went back to finish the scrambled eggs.

Bo's cell phone rang, and he pulled it from his pocket and sandwiched the phone between his ear and shoulder so he could continue to cook. His motions were seamless. He'd obviously fallen right into the daddy routine.

"He wants what?" Bo asked, causing Mattie to walk closer. His body language suddenly indicated there was a problem. "You've got to be kidding me."

Mattie tried to listen to the conversation, but it was drowned out by the sound of Rosalie's voice. The nanny was talking to Holly, and she walked into the kitchen with the little girl in her arms.

Mattie froze, unable to take her eyes off the child. Yes, she'd seen her the night before, but not this close. So close she could finally touch those curls. And that's exactly what Mattie tried to do. But unlike Jacob, Holly pulled back, burying her face against Rosalie's neck.

"She's shy around strangers," Rosalie remarked, and the nanny looked to Bo for what appeared to be some kind of approval. But Bo was caught up in his phone call.

Mattie figured that call was important, but she couldn't take her attention off her daughter. She reached out, hoping that Holly would have a change of heart and come to her, but the baby shook her head and grumbled, "No."

Jacob, however, wanted her attention, and he grabbed Mattie's hand, turning her toward him. He held out one of the cereal bits for her to take. She did, and that earned her one of those grins from the little boy.

"Everything okay?" Rosalie asked Bo the moment he ended the call. The nanny put Holly in the high chair next to Jacob.

"I'm not sure." Bo shook his head, and he glanced at Mattie before heading out of the kitchen and into the living room. "Ian Kaplan is out front, and he wants to see you."

"What?" Mattie raced after him and went to the sidelight window of the front door. The sun was just beginning to rise, but there was enough light for her to spot the blond-haired man leaning against the pricey red sports car.

It was Ian, all right.

"How did he even know I was here?" she asked.

Bo walked to her side and stared out the window with her. "He won't tell the officers that."

Mattie was betting either Kendall told him or else Ian had learned it from his new client, Terrance Arturo, the guy in the black van.

"Ian wanted me to give you a message," Bo continued. "He says he can save your life, and all you have to do is walk out there and talk to him."

Chapter Seven

Walk out there and talk to him.

Right. As if Bo would let that happen. But one glance at Mattie, and he knew she was considering it.

"Ian could gun you down on the way out the door," Bo reminded her.

"The two officers are out there. I doubt they'd let him pull a gun." However, she didn't sound completely convinced of that.

Bo tried again. "I don't want to risk a shootout with my kids in the house."

Since he was trying to reason with her, he probably should have said *the* kids instead of *my* kids, but the truth was, they were his. Both of them. And that didn't have anything to do with DNA. It made his heart ache just thinking of the possibility that he might lose a child he loved more than life itself.

Of course, Mattie no doubt loved Holly, too.

Still, Mattie hadn't raised Holly for the past thirteen months. She had no history with the baby. She only had a mountain of danger that might fall down on her at any minute. And because of that danger, Bo needed to move

Jacob and Holly as soon as he got Ian away from the house.

"But what if Ian can put an end to this mess?" Mattie asked.

Bo took out his phone and pressed in the number to the officers out front. "Then he can tell you all about it while he's out there and you're in here."

"Let me speak to our visitor," Bo told the officer when he answered, and he watched as the young cop did just that.

"Lieutenant Duggan," Ian spat out, making it sound like profanity. "I want to see Mattie."

Bo moved Mattie in front of the sidelight window for just a second and then pulled her back. "There, you've seen her. Now, tell me how you knew she was here."

Ian flashed a snarky smile. "Well, the cops in front of your house were a dead giveaway."

"Wrong answer." Bo put some snark in his voice. "Try again."

That at least wiped the smile off Ian's face. "Look, Mattie and I are on the same side here. I just want to make sure she's safe."

"She is. And you dodged the question again. How did you know she was here?"

Definitely no smile now. The man's eyes narrowed. "Put Mattie on the phone, and I'll tell her."

Bo merely clicked on the speaker function. "She's listening."

"Mattie," Ian said after several seconds. "I want to talk to you *in private*."

She looked up at Bo, and he shook his head.

"Ian, what is this all about?" Mattie asked. "Why are you here?"

"Why?" he snapped as if the answer were obvious. "Because I care about you. Because I want to keep you alive. I can do that, Mattie. All you have to do is talk to me."

"I will…if you'll tell me how you knew I was here."

Good for her. Because Bo was certain that information would give him some critical details about Ian— like his motive for this untimely visit.

Ian huffed and shook his head before he responded. "I hired Terrance Arturo to find you."

Mattie's mouth dropped open. "The man in the van that you're representing?"

"Yes. He's not exactly a P.I., but he's done this sort of work for me before. And for the record, he didn't know about the phony plates on the van. He borrowed the vehicle from a friend."

Bo figured that would be easy enough to confirm. "But how did Arturo find Mattie? She's been in hiding."

More hesitation. "Arturo found Mattie through you."

Mattie pressed her fingers to her lips, and groaned softly.

"Explain that," Bo demanded.

"I've been trying to find Mattie all this time, and I hired several people to look for her. I figured she might visit her old friends. Or Brody's grave." Ian paused again. "I also anticipated that she might want to talk to you, since Mattie and your wife were in the hospital the day the maternity hostages were taken. Mattie's got a good heart, and she probably wanted to tell you about your wife's last hours. Am I right?"

Bo didn't answer.

"I mean, why else would she have gone to you?" Ian added. Maybe he was faking it, but there didn't seem to be any smugness in that remark. "I also had some of the other hostages and the nurses from the hospital followed. I figured it was one of the nurses who'd taken Mattie's baby."

Interesting theory, especially since that had happened with one of the other hostages. But did Ian believe that had also happened with Mattie's newborn, or was Ian's explanation designed to try to put Mattie more at ease?

Bo didn't care right now. He only wanted this man away from his home.

"Marshal Larry Tolivar also helped me find Mattie," Ian commented.

That grabbed Bo's attention. "Helped how?"

"Inadvertently." Ian's smiled returned. "The marshal was pressing any- and everyone who knew Mattie to give up her whereabouts, so I figured he'd find her. So, I had him followed, as well."

That was a lot of time and manpower to locate Mattie.

"How can you save my life?" Mattie asked. She glanced over her shoulder when she heard Holly start to fuss. Bo knew that whine. Rosalie was likely wiping the baby's face. But it obviously spiked Mattie's nerves.

"I'll tell you that when I can actually see you," Ian insisted.

Bo was tired of this game and decided to put an end

to it. "Mattie and I will meet you at police headquarters. You can tell her there."

He saw the flash of surprise in Ian's expression, and he expected the lawyer to turn him down flat. But Ian checked his watch. "How soon?" Ian pressed.

"An hour." Bo looked at Mattie, and she agreed with a nod.

"I'll be there." Ian turned as if to get back into his vehicle but then stopped. "Mattie, don't go on the run again. It's not necessary. I've worked out a deal for you. A deal that will keep you safe." Ian handed the phone back to the officer, got in his car and drove away.

"A deal," Mattie repeated. She looked both hopeful and frightened. After all the attempts that had been made to get to her, Bo understood the reaction.

He also understood what he had to do. He ended the call and called his captain. Yes, it was early, but this was too important to wait.

"Tell Rosalie to get the kids dressed and ready to leave," he instructed Mattie.

Mattie must have wholeheartedly agreed with that request because she hurried away. Or maybe she was just anxious to get back in the room with Holly.

"One of the officers at your house just gave me an update," the captain greeted him.

"Yeah. Ian Kaplan was here. Mattie and I are meeting with him at headquarters in one hour. But I want to move the kids before we go."

Bo walked back to the kitchen, where Mattie was trying to coax Holly from Rosalie's arms. Holly would have no part of it, so Mattie ended up taking Jacob from the high chair instead. His son gave Mattie a *tiss* and wound his arms around her neck.

"I thought you'd want the twins away from there," Shaw answered. "So, here's what I need you to do. The two officers at your house will take your nanny, Jacob and Holly to my house. I'm here and I'll stay here for at least the next two hours. Then, Mattie and you can meet with Ian Kaplan. If nothing is resolved in that meeting, then we can work out a protective custody arrangement for Mattie and the kids if necessary."

Oh, it would unfortunately be necessary.

"My advice?" Shaw continued. "Get the kids and Rosalie out of there quickly. If we're really dealing with Kendall Collier, then it's best to start putting up some buffers."

Bo couldn't agree more.

"One more thing," Shaw said before Bo could hang up. "Those DNA test results should be done soon."

Great. Something else to deal with, and the results could be as potentially dangerous as an assassin after Mattie.

Bo ended the call and hurried to the garage so he could open it for the officers. He tossed one of them the keys to the white SUV that Rosalie used. "You'll need to move the infant seats into your patrol car," he instructed. There was a set of seats in both his and Rosalie's vehicles, but the ones in the white SUV were easier to remove.

Bo hurried back to the nursery so he could help Rosalie and Mattie. But the women already had it under control. Mattie was dressing Jacob in denim overalls and a shirt. For once, his son was actually cooperating with the dressing process and was babbling away to Mattie.

Mattie looked up, snagged Bo's gaze. "Where will you take them?"

"The officers will take Rosalie and them to the captain's house."

Rosalie did the snaps on Holly's pink overalls. "I'm guessing this is necessary?" the nanny asked.

"It is." Bo put his phone in his pocket so he could take Jacob from Mattie.

"Because of me," Mattie mumbled. "Bo, I'm so sorry—"

"Don't." And because he sounded so gruff, he toned it down a little. "I believe both Marshal Tolivar and Kendall Collier have been watching me. Eventually, this would have happened."

"Maybe not. If I hadn't shown up…"

Then, Collier might have used Holly to get to Mattie. Of course, that left Bo with a big question—why hadn't Collier tried to use Holly sooner?

Maybe the man hadn't known about Holly's possible connection to Mattie after all? And maybe there was no connection. Maybe the DNA test would prove it. If so, Bo could put an end to the danger and the custody threat in one fell swoop. Mattie could then be on her way to locate her own child.

So why didn't that feel as perfect a scenario as it should have?

Maybe because of that pained look on Mattie's face. She was obviously hurting, and Bo was hurting for her. He wasn't cold and heartless, and with Mattie around, he was getting a constant reminder of the camaraderie that was starting between them.

And of the attraction.

It was there, simmering, creating all sorts of problems for him.

Rosalie grabbed the diaper bag and looped it over her shoulder. Since there was no reason to delay things, Bo took a deep breath and headed for the garage.

"Let's make this quick," he instructed while they were still in the cover of the garage. "I don't want the kids out in the open any longer than necessary."

The officers pulled up into the driveway, directly behind the SUVs, and they opened the doors.

Bo gave Jacob a kiss on the cheek. "Be a good boy," Bo told him. And he pulled Holly into his other arm so he could kiss her, as well.

"Da Da," Holly said, and then poked out her bottom lip as if she might burst into tears. His baby girl did not like to have her routine broken, and she probably sensed that something wasn't quite right.

Bo handed Jacob over to Rosalie, giving him a moment to console Holly.

"It's okay," he whispered to Holly, and he kissed her again. Bo pulled her closer for a hug, and her little arms coiled around his neck. "Daddy will be back soon."

When Bo glanced at Mattie, he saw the tears in her eyes. He mentally groaned. This goodbye was just as hard for her as it was for him.

"Why don't you say bye-bye to Mattie?" Bo prompted the little girl.

Holly's big green eyes were suddenly curious, and

she even managed a slight smile as she waved. "Bye-bye, Ma."

That *Ma* was obviously Holly's attempt to say Mattie's name, but it caused the moment to freeze. Mattie reached for her as if she might yank her right out of Bo's arms. But she didn't. Mattie's hands fell back to her side, and the smile she gave Holly would have melted a heart of stone.

"They should go," Mattie said, though there was little sound to her words.

She turned and went back into the house before Bo could even attempt to comfort her. Which was just as well. He didn't know what to say or do to make this better. Besides, he needed to get the kids out of there.

He took the lead, heading to the passenger's side of the car with Holly. Rosalie went to the other side, and they strapped the twins into the car seats. Rosalie took the seat between them.

"I'll call you after the meeting at headquarters," Bo assured the nanny, and then he kissed the babies one more time.

This wasn't an ordinary goodbye, but he prayed it wouldn't be a long one. He needed the twins far more than they needed him.

Bo stepped back into the garage and watched as they drove away. He waited until the patrol car was out of sight before he closed the garage door and went back inside, expecting to see Mattie.

But he didn't.

He heard the sound of water running and followed it until he found her. She was in the bathroom, door open, and she was brushing her teeth. Her movements were frantic, probably because her hands were shaking.

"I'll do whatever it takes in this meeting to get this all resolved," she promised. She grabbed a brush from her purse and assaulted her hair with it.

Bo went to her, took the brush from her hand. Or rather tried to. She fought him, struggling to hang on to it, all the while tears pooling in her eyes. He could feel the nervous energy radiating from her.

He gave up on the brush and hauled her into his arms.

Mattie put up a token resistance. And then fell apart. The sobs racked through her, consuming her, and Bo knew there was nothing he could say or do except stand there and let her cry it out.

He wasn't sure how long the worst of it lasted, minutes probably, but each minute drilled home that this situation with Mattie was not going to be resolved easily. Somehow, in this already dangerous mix, Bo had started to be concerned about her. Not her situation.

But *her*.

Maybe that had something to do with the way Jacob had taken to her. Or maybe it was this stupid attraction.

As if she'd read his mind, Mattie lifted her head and looked into his eyes. They were too close, of course, because she was in his arms. Her breath met his, and he drew her scent and taste into his mouth.

Oh, man.

He didn't want this.

But apparently the warning wasn't enough, because

he lowered his head and kissed her. Bo instantly changed his mind.

He wanted this.

Her mouth was damp from her tears, and he could taste the salt and her mint toothpaste. That should have been a turnoff, a big red flag that the timing sucked for kissing, but it didn't turn off anything for him. Bo kissed her, keeping it soft and gentle, so he could take in everything her mouth was telling him.

And what her mouth was saying was that she wanted this, too.

Mattie made a soft sound deep within her throat. Part surprise, part pleasure. Almost hesitantly, she put her hands on his chest. First one, then the other. She leaned into him, closer and closer, increasing the pressure of the kiss with each fraction of distance that she erased between them.

The pressure erased the soft and gentle approach, too, and Bo found himself taking rather than consoling. Her taste hit him like a ton of bricks. It had been so long since he'd kissed a woman and had one in his arms that his body was suddenly greedy for more.

He took more.

Bo deepened the kiss, touching his tongue to hers.

The jolt hit him even harder. Man, this was not a good place to go with a very vulnerable woman who had more emotional baggage than he did.

Mattie obviously realized that, too, because she jerked back, an "oh" rushing from her mouth as she took her lips from his. She blinked, stared up at him and repeated the "oh."

Bo repeated it, too. "Sorry," he said, because he didn't

have a clue what else to say. Kissing Mattie was wrong on too many levels to count. He pushed aside the part about how right it'd felt, though.

She fluttered her fingers in the direction of the bathroom. "We should, uh, finish dressing so we can leave for the meeting with Ian."

Yeah, they should. And they would once he could walk. That kiss had aroused him beyond belief.

"What do you think Ian is going to say to you?" Bo asked, hoping a real conversation would get his mind off that kiss and the hard ache in his body.

She shook her head. "I'm not sure. I've had a mixed experience with Ian. After Brody was killed, Ian offered to have me move in with him so he could help me raise the baby I was carrying. I obviously turned him down."

"How did he take that?"

"With cool anger," she readily answered. "I mean, I knew he was upset, but he stayed polite. Why?"

"Just trying to get a handle on what we're dealing with here." And since his thoughts were more sexual than business, Bo moved away from her. "I'll get dressed."

Bo moved but then stopped. "Do we need to talk about what just happened?"

"No." She answered so quickly that it left no room for argument.

Which was a good thing in his mind. Because the kiss shouldn't have happened in the first place. And it wouldn't happen again.

Bo cursed.

He wasn't a man who lied to himself, and he wondered why he'd started it now. If Mattie and he were alone, it would happen again, so that meant he had to work on the *alone* part. If this meeting didn't pan out, then he would see about placing her in someone else's protective custody.

Bo was thankful he'd already showered, and he went to the master bedroom and dressed as quickly as he could in his usual dark work pants and white button-up shirt. He clipped his badge to his belt.

Just as the doorbell rang.

Bo checked his watch. It was a little after 6:00 a.m., hardly the time for visitors. Hell. He hoped Ian hadn't returned. Just in case, he put on his shoulder holster and drew his gun. By the time he came out into the hall, Mattie was already there and looking very concerned. Unfortunately, that concern might be warranted now that the officers were no longer outside.

"Wait here," he instructed. Bo made his way to the front of the house, but instead of going to the door, he looked out the window of the dining room that was adjacent to the foyer.

He saw a delivery truck pulling away.

Then he spotted the package on the front step.

"Who is it?" Mattie asked.

Bo heard her footsteps and motioned for her to stay back. "A package."

"At this time of morning?"

But Bo didn't answer. He knew in his gut that there wasn't time. He turned, barreling toward Mattie, and he pushed her to the floor. It wasn't a second too soon.

The blast roared through the house.

Chapter Eight

Everything seemed to happen at once. Bo dove at her, tossing her to the floor. Mattie didn't have time to react or say anything.

And then there was the deafening sound.

Because she'd been on the run for so long, her first thought was that someone was trying to kill her. She fought to see what was going on, but Bo dragged her toward the laundry room.

Mattie soon saw why.

The front door had literally been blasted from its hinges, and there was smoke and debris whirling through the air.

My God.

She'd been right. Someone had tried to kill them.

Almost immediately, the alarm sounded from the security system. It was a piercing shrill that clamored through the entire house.

Bo pushed her into the laundry room, and he used the keypad on the wall next to the door that led to the garage so he could silence the alarms. Good. They needed to be able to hear what was going on.

He peered out into the hall, probably to make sure

no one was coming through the gaping hole and into the house. He already had his gun drawn, but he took out his phone and called for assistance, both from the cops and the fire department.

"Who did this?" she asked the moment he hung up.

"I don't know, but I will find out."

It wasn't fear she heard in his voice but rather anger. No, not just anger. Rage. Because this attack had happened in his home, where just minutes earlier the babies had been. Mercy. They could have been hurt. Thank God Bo had insisted they go to the captain's house with the officers. They were safe.

She hoped.

"The children," she managed to say.

"The captain is there, and he'll make sure no one gets near them."

Mattie wanted desperately to believe that, but too many bad things had happened for her to be optimistic. Her purse with her gun was in the kitchen, and she wanted to run and grab it so she could hurry to the captain's house.

"We have to go," she insisted.

Bo shook his head. "It might not be safe to leave."

It hit her then. Yes, there had been damage to the door, only the door. There was no fire. No secondary explosion. No attack. And that meant this blast had gone off for only one reason: to get Bo and her running out of the house where an assassin could gun them down.

"But we can't stay here," she whispered, listening for any indication that they were about to be attacked.

"No. Not with that door wide open." He kept watch and reached behind him to take a set of keys from a hook on the wall. "As soon as a patrol car arrives, I'm getting you out of here."

Good. She didn't want to stay. Mattie wanted to go to the children.

The children, she mentally repeated.

Even though Jacob wasn't her child, Mattie felt a connection with the little boy, and she was just as worried about him as she was Holly.

The seconds crawled by, and they continued to wait. It had probably been only a couple of minutes, but it felt like an eternity.

Mattie heard the autumn wind whistle through the opening created by the blast. She heard her own breathing. And Bo's.

But she also heard something else.

Something rattled.

It took her a moment to pick through the other sounds, and she realized it hadn't come from the front of the house but rather the back.

"Someone's trying to get in the back door, into the kitchen," Bo whispered.

That sent her stomach to her knees. God. When was this going to end?

Bo fired glances between the front and the back, and he kept his gun ready to respond in case there was another attack. Mattie could only stand there, listen and wait. She didn't have to wait long.

The doorknob rattled again, this time almost violently, and then there was the sound of wood being splintered.

Someone had kicked down the kitchen door.

And that someone was inside.

"I'm Lieutenant Duggan!" Bo called out. He pointed his gun to the ceiling and fired.

Even though it was clearly a warning shot, the blast sent Mattie's heart pounding out of control. She needed her gun so she could try to defend them, but there was no chance she could go into the kitchen.

"Unlock the door," Bo told her, and he fired another warning shot into the ceiling. Bits of the acoustic tile rained down on them.

Mattie somehow managed to turn the latch, even though her hands were shaking. It obviously didn't help that she'd had experiences with nearly being killed, because the danger felt fresh and raw, just as the day when the gunmen had stormed the hospital.

"Get in the black SUV," Bo ordered, and he muscled her out of the laundry room and into the garage.

The large metal garage door was closed, thank goodness, so that gave them some protection in case there was someone at the front of the house waiting for them. But it would also trap them inside if an assassin came through the kitchen.

Mattie didn't waste any time. She got in the SUV, jumped into the passenger's seat and waited for Bo to follow her. But he didn't. He stayed in the doorway with his gun lifted high.

Had he seen the person who'd broken down the back door?

"Get in!" Mattie insisted. She didn't want him to stay put and be gunned down.

Mattie leaned over, threw open the driver's door and started the engine. Bo slammed the laundry room door and jumped into the SUV. In the same motion, he pressed the garage door opener clipped to his visor, and the large double door began to inch open.

"Put on your seat belt and stay down," Bo warned her.

Somehow Mattie managed to get the belt secured around her. Bo did the same. She slid as deep into the seat as she could but also kept watch of the laundry room door. It sickened her to think of an intruder inside Bo's home, but right now, she only wanted to get out of there.

The moment the garage door was fully open, Bo gunned the engine, and the SUV bolted down the driveway and into the street. She heard the sirens then. Thank God backup had arrived, because she wanted this would-be killer caught.

Mattie lifted her head just enough for her to check the rearview mirror, and she saw the laundry room door open. She caught just a glimpse of the man as he peered out but then quickly slammed the door shut.

She gasped.

"Yeah," Bo said. "I see him. It looks like Terrance Arturo, the guy from the van last night."

It did. But then she hadn't gotten more than a glimpse. If it was indeed Arturo, then that would lead them right back to Kendall. She didn't think it was a coincidence that Ian, Kendall's friend and employee, was also Arturo's attorney and that both had shown up at Bo's less than an hour after she'd arrived there.

While he sped away from the house, Bo took out his phone and pressed in some numbers. "O'Malley," he said a moment later. "No. We're all right. I have Mattie with me, and the twins were already at the captain's house, but I want additional officers dispatched there."

Her heart was practically pounding out of her chest, but that sped it up even more. Bo had assured her that the children would be safe, but if they needed extra officers, then he must believe they could be in danger.

"I just passed the officers responding to the scene," Bo continued, "but I want to get Mattie to headquarters before I come back and assist. Is Terrance Arturo out of jail?"

Mattie couldn't hear the officer's response, but Bo's profanity confirmed that the man was free. Free and responsible for an attack that could have killed them.

Well, maybe.

There had only been enough explosives to take out the front door, but a true killer would have put enough in that package to blow up the entire place. That meant this had probably been a kidnapping attempt.

And she had likely been the target.

"What?" Bo snapped, drawing her attention back to him. "He's there right now?"

Mercy, was he talking about Arturo? Or was there another attacker already at the captain's house? Mattie put her hand to her chest to steady her heart, and she waited and prayed.

"The children are fine," he said, obviously seeing her reaction. "But Terrance Arturo is out of jail, so he could have been responsible for that package."

Anger soon replaced the fear. "And we both know it was Kendall who was behind this."

Bo nodded, his expression as ripe with anger as

hers. "We'll get a chance to ask him all about it. He's at headquarters with Ian Kaplan, and he wants to talk to you."

BO REMINDED HIMSELF that he was a peace officer. A twelve-year veteran of the SAPD and head of a large investigative unit. He couldn't just walk into an interview and beat someone senseless.

But that's exactly what he wanted to do to Kaplan and Collier.

Probably because of them, his home had been violated. Hell, *he* felt violated. And it would take a lifetime or two for him to come to terms with how close his children had come to being hurt. If they had been home and not at the captain's, then God knows what could have happened.

Plus, there was Mattie. Yet another attempt on her life, another nightmare to add to the memories of the ones already there. Mattie and he might be on different sides when it came to Holly, but she damn sure didn't deserve to bear this kind of burden all because she tried to do the right thing.

It was difficult, but Bo kept reminding himself of the *right thing* part. She wasn't responsible for any of this, and even though he hated that the danger had spilled over to his kids, he couldn't fault Mattie. No, the *fault* was inside the interview room waiting for a meeting they'd demanded.

"You're sure the children are all right?" Mattie asked again.

"I'm sure." He'd called both Rosalie and the captain, and both had assured him that all was well.

It was *well* there at the captain's house, but Bo felt anything but well here at headquarters. He needed to get control of his temper before he walked into that room, because this might be the most critical interrogation of his life. Until he stopped the danger that centered around Mattie, his children might never be safe.

"Let me ask the questions," Bo insisted as they walked toward the interview room. He glanced at her. She was pale, and her lips were still trembling a little. "If you're not up to this, you can wait in my office."

She started shaking her head before he even finished. "No. I want to look Kendall in the eye. Ian, too. After what just happened, I want to strangle them both."

Bo felt the same way, and he hoped they both could hang on to their composure long enough to get some answers from these slimeballs.

Bo led Mattie not to the interview room but to the observation area next to it. Through the two-way mirror, they could see Ian Kaplan seated in the far right chair at the metal table. Next to him was a sandy-haired woman wearing a gray outfit.

"That's Cicely Carr," Mattie provided.

Kendall Collier's fiancée. "You said you know her?"

Mattie shrugged. "We grew up in the same social circles and went to the same private school. But I haven't spoken to her in years."

Social circles and private schools. Those were reminders that Mattie was wealthy and had probably had the best privileges that dirty money could buy. But she was anything but privileged now.

Cicely didn't exactly look the privileged part, either.

Her clothes and hair were nice enough, but she certainly didn't scream "old money." She was somewhat of a plain Jane in her dove-gray suit that didn't seem to be tailored for her rail-thin body.

Bo followed Mattie's gaze, which was firmly on the man who was standing behind Kaplan and Carr.

Kendall Collier.

Bo recognized the man with the graying brown hair from the photos of his trial. Unlike his fiancée, Collier was dressed to perfection. He wore a midnight-blue suit that probably cost more than Bo made in six months. But while the suit screamed his social status, the man himself did not. Collier was pale, and even though he was standing, he was not moving, as if trying to conserve his energy. Bo had expected someone arrogant and impatient, but he didn't see any of that.

Bo led Mattie from the observation area and back into the hall. He paused, just long enough to allow her to change her mind, but she only opened the door and went inside.

"Mattie," Ian Kaplan and Cicely Carr said in unison. They got to their feet, and both were smiling.

"It's so good to see you." Cicely Carr came from around the table and wrapped her arms around Mattie.

Mattie went stiff and then eased herself out of the woman's grip. "Cicely, why are you here?"

"To help Kendall mend some fences with you." She looked at her fiancé and gave him a dazzling smile, which he didn't exactly return.

"I thought it would help if you talked to her," Kaplan added.

"The only one Mattie wants to talk to is me," Collier

interrupted. He kept his distance on the other side of the table. "I'm here to bury the hatchet," he added, looking at Mattie.

"Bury it where—in my back?" Mattie snapped.

Carr shook her head. "It's not like that anymore. Kendall's a changed man—"

"Really?" Bo made the interruption this time. "Then who tried to kill Mattie this morning?"

Bo studied each of their reactions. Carr gasped and flattened her hand over her chest. Kaplan had just a flash of surprise—or else he faked it—but he resumed his poker face when he looked at Collier, whose reaction was the strangest of all. He seemed angry.

Seemed.

"Are you okay?" Kaplan asked Mattie. "Were you hurt?" He walked toward her, but Bo blocked his path.

"You think I'm responsible," Collier concluded. He groaned softly and scrubbed his hand over his forehead.

"Kendall didn't do this," Carr protested, turning toward Bo. "He's a changed man. I swear he is." She whipped back to Mattie. "Do you think we would be getting married if he hadn't changed?"

"People marry for all kinds of reasons," Mattie said, her eyes narrowing.

"Yes," Collier quietly said, and he repeated it. "I'm forty-nine, Mattie, and I want to be with my family. That's my priority now."

Carr slid her hand over her stomach. "Our baby is due in seven months, and we want all of this bad blood to end before he or she comes into the world."

Mattie glanced down at Carr's stomach and then at Collier, who only nodded. Bo wasn't sure what to make of the moment. He'd interrogated enough people to know when someone was lying to him, but this didn't seem like a lie. Well, not about the baby, anyway.

"I've sold my business," Collier continued, looking at Bo now. "That'll be easy enough for you to check. There's nothing illegal going on. I've learned my lessons, and in part I can thank Mattie for that."

Mattie lifted her left eyebrow. "Is this for real?"

"Yes," Collier confirmed. Both Kaplan and Carr nodded in agreement.

"I feel as if I've stepped into an alternate universe," Mattie mumbled. Then she hiked up her chin and faced down Collier. "You had my fiancé gunned down."

"Not me." Collier pulled in a long breath. "But it was probably one of my former business associates. I believe they're the ones who tried to kill you immediately after the trial."

"Your business associates?" Mattie challenged, and her eyes narrowed again.

"I want names of these associates," Bo insisted.

Collier lifted his shoulder and slipped his hands into his pockets. "That wouldn't benefit anyone, especially Mattie, and it has cost me a great deal, but I've negotiated a truce with them. There will be no more threats on Mattie's life. She can find her child and bring him or her home."

"For the record," Kaplan added, "Kendall isn't admitting to any wrongdoing. He merely orchestrated a legal transaction that gave an amicable severance of ties to several of his former business associates."

Bo rolled his eyes at the legalese. "And I'm to take your word for this?"

"It's the truth," Carr insisted. She kept her attention fastened to Mattie. "We don't want any more problems, because we want to concentrate on our new life together."

"That's one of the reasons all three of us wanted to talk to you," Kaplan continued a moment later. "We want you to be able to get back to normal. And Kendall and Cicely want you back in the family." He paused a moment. "I'd especially like having you in my life again."

Bo didn't miss that last part. Mattie was right. This guy did have feelings for her, but Bo didn't know if they were real or of the sicko variety. Kaplan could be holding a grudge because Mattie had rejected him. That was often a motive for murder.

Collier's motive was obvious, too. Revenge for Mattie testifying against him. But Cicely Carr...well, she apparently loved Kendall Collier, and that made Bo wonder how far she would go to protect her baby's father. Was her adamancy about a new life just an act, or did her idea of a new life mean Mattie being out of the picture if she didn't cooperate with the game plan?

Mattie huffed and turned to Bo as if to ask what the devil was going on. He didn't know. But he would find out.

"Someone tried to kill Mattie just this morning," Bo reminded them. "If you worked out a so-called truce with your former business associates, then who was responsible for the attack?"

None of them jumped to answer that. Finally, Collier took a step forward. "I doubt you'd believe me."

"Try," Bo ordered.

"You should question Marshal Larry Tolivar."

Bo certainly hadn't expected that name to come up in this conversation. "Why?"

It was Kaplan who continued. "I've been trying to locate Mattie since she disappeared, and I've become suspicious of Marshal Tolivar. I think he's the one who allowed someone to hack into the Witness Protection database."

"You have proof?" Mattie asked.

"Not exactly, but if you dig into Tolivar's financials, you might find hints of a payoff. I believe someone, probably those former business associates, paid him and paid him well so they could access Mattie's files."

Bo didn't like the way Tolivar's name kept popping up. It was time to have the marshal investigated. "Your former business associates?" Bo questioned. "The ones that you won't identify because it'll get us killed?"

"Kendall would tell you if he could," Cicely Carr said as if it were gospel.

"I can't give you names," Collier reiterated. "But when you find the payoff that I believe Tolivar received, that should lead you to the people behind all of this."

He tipped his head toward the door. "Time to go."

"Not yet," Bo insisted. "Explain to me why you'd use a computer in a coffee shop to dig into my background."

Kendall blinked, shook his head. "I have no idea what you're talking about."

"Really?" Bo pressed. "We have your prints."

"Then someone planted them there." He glanced at Mattie. "Someone's obviously trying to keep me in trouble with the law. And with you. Besides, why would I use a coffee shop computer? If I wanted to find out anything about you, I would have used one of my P.I.s. Or Ian."

True. Unless this really was some kind of intimidation tactic. Bo was either dealing with an innocent man or a very dangerous one.

"I've said my piece," Kendall Collier said a moment later. "And now Mattie needs some time to think."

Collier walked out first but not before he reached out to Mattie. She dodged his hand, stepping back. Her uncle nodded and seemed disappointed, but that was the only emotion he showed. Bo made another mental note: have Collier followed and see if SAPD could get authorization for some wire taps. If his shady business associates were responsible for what had happened, Bo wanted them identified and put behind bars, where they could never get to Mattie and the babies.

"Please give Kendall a chance," Cicely Carr whispered to Mattie. "Don't disappoint us."

That caused Mattie to pull her shoulders back, and she was likely about to return fire over Carr's comment, but the woman walked out and hurried after Collier.

Ian Kaplan, however, stayed put. He took out his card and handed it to Mattie. "That's in case you've forgotten my number. We really need to talk. *Alone*," he added, glancing at Bo.

"That's not going to happen," Mattie assured him.

Kaplan flinched as if she'd slapped him. "I'm trying

to help you. That's why I pushed Kendall to put an end to all of this. I want you back in my life."

Well, there it was. All laid out. The lawyer still wanted Mattie. That riled Bo to the core. This moron could be responsible for the danger, and yet he was practically inviting Mattie to his bed.

Bo didn't want to think that what he was feeling was partly motivated by jealousy. But he couldn't totally dismiss that, either. Their kiss had changed things that shouldn't have been changed.

"I can help you find your child," Kaplan continued.

"How?" Bo snapped.

Kaplan shot him an irritated "get lost" look, but his expression softened when he turned his attention back to Mattie. "I can have an entire team of P.I.s out searching for the baby. All you have to do is say that you want my help."

And jump in his bed.

Bo felt his mouth bend into a snarl. "Specifics," he spelled out to Kaplan. "When you're ready to give specifics, Mattie and I will be ready to listen."

Kaplan's snarl matched Bo's. "Mattie and I can talk without you."

"No, we can't," Mattie spoke up. She huffed and pushed her hair away from her face. "Look, Ian, I'm not sure I even trust you, so we're not on the same side. And I'm not going to have any private conversations with you."

The color drained from the lawyer's face. "You're choosing Bo Duggan over me? Over your own family?"

"Bo protected me this morning. He put his life in danger for me. So, yes, I'm choosing him over you."

Kaplan sputtered out a few syllables before he finally seemed to regain his composure. "Call me when you change your mind." The man practically ran into Bo as he hurried out.

Mattie immediately leaned against the wall. Maybe it was the adrenaline catching up with her, or maybe this meeting had just drained her, but Bo held her because she looked ready to slide straight to the floor.

"I didn't expect this," she mumbled.

Neither had he. Bo slipped his arm around her waist and eased her to him. Her heart was pounding so hard, he could feel it against his chest.

"You think your uncle could be telling the truth about wanting a truce?" Bo asked.

"I don't know." She dropped her head onto his shoulder and gave a weary sigh. She leaned against him as if it were the most natural thing in the world.

It certainly felt natural, and that set off huge alarms in his head. He couldn't get this close to Mattie. But he didn't move, either.

"I just want the danger to be over," she whispered.

Bo was about to agree when he heard the footsteps. He pulled away from Mattie, but not before Captain Shaw Tolbert appeared in the doorway. His captain blinked and obviously noticed the close contact between Mattie and him.

"Rough meeting with her uncle," Bo managed to say, but explaining himself wasn't high on his priority list right now. "Who's with the children?"

"Several officers. Don't worry. They're safe."

"But for how long?" Mattie asked, her voice filled with emotion.

"For as long as it takes," the captain assured her. "I watched most of the meeting through the two-way. I already have someone working on a background check for the marshal, and I'll see what I can do about getting a search warrant so we can look through Kendall Collier's recent business records."

Good. The ball was already rolling.

"Cicely's family might be the business associates that Kendall was referring to," Mattie volunteered. "I don't have any proof, but her family is a lot like mine, and they've had dealings with Kendall in the past."

The captain and Bo exchanged glances. This hadn't come up in the original trial. They knew that Collier had received funding for the illegal arms deal, but the Justice Department had never been able to identify the source of that funding. Maybe it was Cicely Carr's family.

Or Carr herself.

"So what about their marriage?" Bo asked Mattie. "Is that legit?"

Mattie shrugged. "Could be. Even though Cicely is eighteen years younger than Kendall, she's always had a thing for him. Plus, I think her family always tried to push them together, but I had no idea that Kendall even thought of Cicely as a prospective partner. He usually goes for the flashier, more glamorous type."

Bo gave that some thought. "Maybe he's marrying her to appease her family and make peace with them."

"I'll look into that, too," the captain volunteered. He turned to Mattie. "Bo and I have to start making some security arrangements. A safe house for the twins," he clarified. "Why don't you wait in my office while we're doing that?"

She looked at Bo, and he nodded, only because the captain had *suggested* it. "Since you didn't get a chance to eat this morning, I'll have someone bring you some breakfast. And when the captain and I are done, I'll come and get you."

"My office is just up the hall." The captain pointed in that direction.

Mattie gave another hesitant glance before she walked away.

"Okay, what's wrong?" Bo immediately asked. "Did something happen to the twins?"

"No. Nothing like that." Captain Tolbert glanced out into the hall as if to make sure no one was listening. "I thought you might like to hear this without Mattie around."

A lot of bad things started to go through his mind. "What?"

The captain took out a piece of paper from his jacket pocket and handed it to Bo. "These are the results of the DNA tests we ran on Holly and Mattie."

Chapter Nine

Something was wrong. Mattie could feel it, and better yet, she could see it on Bo's face.

Bo was doing everything he should be doing—making the final arrangements for a safe house, checking on the investigation into Cicely's family and Marshal Larry Tolivar. He was even doing the paperwork about the explosion. From the moment he'd collected her from the captain's office and moved her to his, he'd been dealing with nonstop calls and questions.

What he hadn't done was look her in the eye.

And that meant something was wrong.

Mattie nibbled on the sandwich and chips that one of the uniformed officers had brought her, and she waited for an opening to question Bo about what had put him in such a mood. She even listened to the way he responded to the callers, but she couldn't hear anything specific that she didn't already know.

Was this about the kiss at his house and the embrace in the interrogation room?

Maybe.

Bo could be dealing with some guilt over what he was feeling for her and his loyalties to his late wife. Mattie was certainly dealing with some of that, too, but Brody had been dead nearly two years now. While a part of her would always love him, being on the run had taught her that life was too short to live in the past. She really wanted a chance at living in the present and planning a future.

"The safe house is nearly ready," Bo relayed to her when he finished his latest call. "It shouldn't be more than another hour at most. Setting up furniture and food for the twins is taking more time than we anticipated."

Of course. And that led her to something else that was on her mind. "Will I be at the safe house with all of you?"

There. She saw the flicker in his jaw. Something was definitely wrong, and that caused her heart to ache. Mercy, was he planning on sending her somewhere else just so she wouldn't be around Holly?

"You'll come with us," he mumbled and continued to stare down at the paperwork he had positioned in front of him.

The relief was instant. "Thank you. I know that couldn't have been an easy decision for you to make, but I really appreciate—"

"The captain got the DNA test results back," Bo blurted out.

Mattie's pulse was suddenly thick and throbbing. She dropped the rest of the sandwich onto the wrapper and stood. Just getting to her feet was an effort. She felt as if all the bones in her body had crumbled on the spot.

Oh, God. This was why Bo had been dodging her gaze.

"And?" she prompted, though speaking was an effort, too. Everything inside was on hold, waiting.

"The test was a match." Bo looked at her now, and he stood, as well, facing her. "Holly is your biological child."

The breath whooshed out of her, and Mattie heard herself make some kind of sound. Part gasp, part sigh, but mostly it was a sound of relief. Even though she'd never doubted it, that precious little girl was hers.

When she started to laugh, she pressed her fingers to her mouth. She wanted to celebrate, jump for joy and shout it out so the world would know.

Holly was her baby.

But her joy went south when she saw Bo's expression. She'd never seen anyone in that much pain.

"I'm sure Nadine intended to tell you," Mattie said. But it was the wrong thing to say, because Bo only shook his head. Maybe there was no right thing to say in a situation like this.

Mattie walked closer to him, reached out and caught on to his hand. He pulled back, or rather tried to, but she held on. "I can't say I'm sorry about the test results. But I am sorry for what this is doing to you."

He glanced around as if he might tear out of the room. Or curse. Or yell. Or do a dozen other things to vent the emotion he was feeling. But he simply groaned and dropped back down into the chair.

"I didn't know," he mumbled. "I swear, I didn't suspect a thing until you showed up yesterday."

Mattie believed him. Nadine hadn't lived long enough to tell him the truth, and Mattie hadn't been in a position to try to claim her child.

She still wasn't.

"I can't just give her up," Bo insisted, his voice and face now tight with anger. "I can't just hand her over to you."

"I know." And it took every ounce of her courage to say that.

Bo blinked and stared up at her. "Then what the hell are we going to do?"

She gave his hand a gentle squeeze. "We're going to take the children to the safe house. We'll protect them, and when we know who's responsible for the danger, we'll work out what needs to be worked out."

That didn't appease him as she thought it would. He jerked away from her and cursed. "I'm the only father she's ever known. The only thing that needs to be worked out is for her to stay with me."

Mattie couldn't totally dismiss that. Bo had been part of her daughter's life since day one. "Holly loves you." She tried to keep her voice calm. Hard to do with the anger and emotion radiating from Bo. "I wouldn't dream of cutting you out of her life. I think we can work out visitation—"

"I don't want damn visitations!" he shouted. "I want my baby girl."

When he got up and bolted for the door, Mattie just grabbed him and held on. That put them body to body, of course, and they stood with her back against his closed office door and with Bo against her. The energy between them was so dangerous and strong that it frightened her.

But she wasn't scared of Bo.

Mattie was more frightened of her own reaction.

She had no intentions of giving up her child to this man, to anyone, but she couldn't deny this pull between them. It was too strong.

"Don't," Bo warned, but she had no idea what he was specifically warning her about.

Maybe she was giving off a signal of her intentions. And her intentions were apparently to kiss him, because that's what she did. Mattie came up on her toes and put her mouth to his.

Bo was stiff at first, and she thought he might pull away again. But he didn't. He ran his hand into her hair and jerked back her head so he could deepen the kiss. It was brutal and punishing, his mouth pressing hard and desperate while his body did the same to hers.

He didn't stop there.

He grabbed both her wrists in his other hand and pinned them against the door. He pinned her, too, giving her all his weight.

And all his anger.

While the kiss raged on, the middle of his body ground against hers. In the back of her mind, Mattie considered that she should be stopping this. Anger and kissing shouldn't be mixed, but with Bo, the mixture worked just fine. Yes, she was reeling from the news about her daughter. Yes, she was worried about the danger.

But she was also aroused beyond belief.

She wanted Bo, and she wanted him now.

Her body was on fire, and the kisses and body contact made her feel like a pressure cooker ready to go off. Until that moment, she hadn't been sure that Bo and she would become lovers, but she was certain of it now.

But *now* would have to wait.

She tore her mouth from his at the exact moment that someone knocked on his door. Bo stepped back, repeated some profanity and stared at her as if he couldn't believe what had just happened. Mattie was having trouble believing it, too, but she hoped it would happen again. And that made her very stupid. She shouldn't be playing around with Bo. No. He was too dangerous for that.

She moved to the side and tried to level her breathing before he threw open the door. It was the captain, and he gave them the same look as when he had caught them embracing in the interview room several hours earlier.

"I told Mattie," Bo admitted.

"And?" the captain asked when Bo didn't add anything else.

"We'll work it out." Bo seemed to issue that as some kind of challenge to her and to himself. "Are you here about the safe house?"

The captain shook his head. "I need you to come down to my office. Larry Tolivar just showed up, and he'd like to talk to both of you. Especially you," he said, looking at Mattie.

Well, Mattie wanted to talk to him, too. She wanted the truth about Kendall's accusation that the marshal had sold information about her in the Witness Protection Program.

"By the way, Tolivar already knows we're digging into his background," the captain explained. "And he's not very happy about it."

"He'll be even less happy about it when he talks

to me." Bo started down the hall, and the captain and Mattie followed.

She considered asking the captain to postpone this little chat. After all, Bo was dealing with the fact that Holly wasn't his daughter. Hardly the time to be interrogating a suspect, but Mattie knew she stood no chance of stopping him. He needed somewhere to aim the emotions brewing inside him, and he might as well aim them at Tolivar.

The marshal was indeed in the captain's office, and he was pacing.

"Still alive, I see," Tolivar grumbled.

"Yes." She made sure her voice didn't waiver. Hard to do with everything she'd been through in the past twenty-four hours. "SAPD's taking good care of me."

Tolivar made a grunt of disagreement and aimed his glare at Bo. "You're having me investigated. Bad idea, Duggan. You don't want to play games with me."

"You're right. No games. I just want some answers. Did you send an explosive device to my house this morning?"

"I won't dignify that with an answer," Tolivar snarled.

"But you will," the captain insisted. "Answer Lieutenant Duggan's question."

That earned the captain a glare. "No. Of course not. I'm a peace officer, just like you, except I'm not some local yokel. I work for the federal government, and Mattie is in my protective custody."

"Not any longer," Bo said. "She left the program. I called your boss and let him know that about two hours ago."

Mattie hadn't heard him make that call, but then he'd

apparently made some before he moved her into his office. Good. She didn't want any association with Witness Protection or this man.

"Kendall Collier's hired someone to kill you," Tolivar insisted. "Investigating me or leaving protective custody isn't going to stop that."

"It might if we learn you have a connection to him," Mattie quickly pointed out. Suddenly all eyes were on her. "Kendall and perhaps someone close to him are the only ones who would have wanted to know my new identity and location. And you would have had access to it."

Tolivar aimed his index finger at her. "Someone hacked into the system. If you want to start assigning blame, then look to your uncle. He paid someone to do it, and it wasn't me."

"Then who?"

"Somebody close to Kendall Collier. Maybe his lawyer, Ian Kaplan, or maybe one of his hired henchmen."

"Funny," Bo remarked. "Kaplan said you were responsible for hacking into those files."

Tolivar flinched, obviously not expecting that. "Then he's lying through his teeth."

Bo shrugged. "Somebody is. That's why we're investigating anyone associated with this case. If you've got nothing to hide, then why don't you give us access to all your computer and financial records?"

The room got so quiet that you could have heard a pin drop.

"I don't share personal information with local cops,"

Tolivar finally barked. "And my advice is to back off, or I'll bring some heat down on SAPD."

The captain put his hands on his hips. "Is that a threat, Marshal?"

Maybe it was the steely look in the captain's and Bo's eyes, but Tolivar seemed to back down. "I just want to do my job and keep Mattie alive."

"She's no longer your job," Bo countered immediately. "In fact, you have no reason to be anywhere near her. Got that?"

The staring contest started, and Tolivar even took some steps so he'd be in Bo's face. "Yeah, I got that, Lieutenant. And when somebody blows her brains out, don't come crying to me."

With that, the marshal muscled his way past them and headed out.

"I want him followed," Bo said to the captain.

"Legally, we can't do that." The captain watched the marshal walk away. "But there's nothing that says I can't have an officer in Tolivar's general vicinity. I'll get someone on him." He took out his cell and made a call.

"Thanks." Bo put his hand on the small of Mattie's back and got her moving toward his office. They hadn't gotten halfway there when Bo's phone rang.

She held her breath, as she did with all the calls he received, but she always thought of the children. Of the danger. And Tolivar's visit had drilled home just how close that danger could possibly be.

"Everything's there?" Bo asked the caller. Whatever the answer was, it caused his forehead to bunch up. "Yeah. I'll tell her."

When Bo hung up, Mattie tried to brace herself for more bad news. "What now?"

It took him several moments to answer. "The safe house is ready. The twins... The children," he corrected, "are already en route." He motioned for her to follow him, and they reversed direction. "There's a car waiting to take us there so we can be with them."

It hit Mattie then as she was following Bo up the hall. This wasn't about the danger or the investigation. It wasn't even about the move to the safe house. It was about what would happen at the safe house.

"Yes," Bo said, as if he could read her mind.

Tear sprang to her eyes, because Mattie knew that soon, very soon, she would finally have her baby in her arms.

Chapter Ten

Bo felt sick to his stomach. Since Nadine's death, he'd worked so hard to give his children a normal, happy life. Hell, he'd worked to give himself that, as well.

Now everything was unraveling.

Mattie had DNA on her side. Ironic that a test he'd used to get convictions for killers and rapists was now a test that could cause him to lose his little girl.

He checked the rearview mirror again, something he'd done a lot on this half-hour drive. He had to make sure no one was following them, and that's the reason he'd driven all over the city. The safe house was only about ten minutes from police headquarters, but for safety reasons, he hadn't taken a direct route.

"It's going to rain," Mattie mumbled, looking out the car window and up at the sky.

Yeah, the clouds were heavy and gray, which suited his mood to a T.

"You think it'll storm?" she asked. Mattie had a firm grip on the remote control for the safe-house garage, and she'd had that grip on the small device since they'd picked it up earlier from police headquarters.

"I don't know." And he was more than a little

surprised they were discussing the weather when they were just minutes from arriving at the safe house. Minutes away from Mattie taking the next step to claiming Holly. "Why?"

"I'm scared of storms," she answered.

He gave her a flat look. "You have a killer after you, Mattie. I think a storm is the least of your worries."

She nodded. Nodded again. And didn't say anything for several moments. "How are you handling this?"

Bo nearly laughed. "How do you think?"

Her gaze slid over him. "You look calm."

"Well, yeah. Looks can be deceiving. I've spent the last half hour trying to figure out how to stop this from happening." He paused. "I can't stop it, can I?" he added in a hoarse grumble.

"No." Now, she paused. "I wish Nadine had been able to tell you the truth that day. Something more than 'Protect her.' There's no way you could have known what she meant by that."

Bo wasn't sure he wanted to open this can of worms, but he couldn't just let it go, either. "Did you know Nadine was dying when you left?"

"No. We were both weak from our deliveries, and we both kept nodding off. But when I left her, she was very much alive."

But already dying from the internal bleeding. Mattie couldn't have known about that. Nadine probably didn't, either. If she had, Nadine would have found a way to leave him a note or something.

"Nadine loved you very much," Mattie added.

Yes. He never doubted that. But that didn't make her

death hurt any less. And now losing Holly was another cut, another wound that would never heal.

Bo pulled into the driveway of the safe house and took the remote from Mattie so he could open the garage door. There was another unmarked car with two officers parked just up the street, but now that he had arrived, they would probably leave. There wasn't enough manpower to devote three officers to protecting Mattie, but with the security measures in the house itself and his own abilities, Bo prayed he could keep everyone safe.

"It looks like a typical suburban house," Mattie remarked. She tapped her fingers on the armrest, apparently impatient that it was taking so long for the garage door to fully open. "You're sure it's okay to be here right in the heart of the city?"

"Hiding in plain sight is the best way." He hoped. This particular place had a For Rent sign out front, and SAPD had used it before as a safe house for holding witnesses.

"Don't the neighbors suspect anything?" Mattie wanted to know.

"No. We had a cop posing as a property manager go around and tell everyone that this place would be for short-term rentals." Still, that didn't mean Bo wouldn't be on guard. After all, the children were inside.

"Wait until the garage door closes before you get out," Bo warned her. He pulled inside the garage, turned off the engine and hit the remote control again to shut the door.

Mattie looked as if she were preparing for a sprint, and the moment the door closed, she was out of the car.

She raced to the entry, but as Bo knew it would be, the door was locked.

"Hurry," she insisted.

He unlocked the door and stepped back. Mattie ran inside. He followed her and hoped this wouldn't be traumatic for Holly. Bo already knew it would be traumatic for him.

Mattie hurried through the kitchen and into the living room. No kids. But he heard laughter coming from one of the bedrooms, and they headed in that direction. Rosalie was sitting on the floor playing building blocks with the kids. Thankfully, Mattie didn't go barging in. She held back, waiting, watching and crying.

Yeah, there were tears in her eyes.

Rosalie looked up, a smile on her face, but that smile faded when she spotted Mattie. "What's wrong?" she immediately wanted to know.

Even though Holly and Jacob were way too young to know what any of this meant, Bo didn't want to tell Rosalie in front of them. He motioned for the nanny to join him in the hall.

"Da Da!" Holly and Jacob called out in unison. Bo went into the room, scooped them up in his arms and gave them each a kiss. He kissed them like this every day, but today felt bittersweet.

Rosalie stood, hesitantly, and Bo put the babies back on the floor so he could step outside the room with Rosalie. Mattie stayed in the room and eased down on the floor, as well. She didn't get too close, but Jacob noticed his new *playmate*. He grabbed one of the plastic building blocks and brought it to her.

"Ta Ta," he said, meaning "thank you."

When Mattie smiled and repeated it, Jacob brought her even more of the blocks. Soon, Holly joined in on the game, but she wasn't nearly as adept at walking as Jacob. She wobbled and would have fallen if Mattie hadn't caught her in her arms.

The moment seemed to freeze.

Holly giggled and looked at Mattie. Bo could feel the love and emotion radiating from Mattie. This was the moment she'd no doubt dreamed about, a moment that had probably kept her alive and fighting.

The moment was a nightmare for Bo.

Holly had no idea that this woman was her biological mother, but she would soon grow to love Mattie. And that meant he would lose his baby girl.

"It's true?" Rosalie said softly. "She's really Holly's mother?"

"It's true," he managed to say.

"Tiss," Jacob announced when Mattie stacked some of the blocks. But he kissed Holly's cheek first and then he kissed Mattie's. A moment later, Holly did the same.

When Holly's lips touched Mattie's cheek, Bo heard Mattie make a sound deep in her throat. It matched the love that was in her expression. And that's when he knew. Mattie wouldn't put up with this arrangement for long. She would no doubt demand custody as soon as she could.

Rosalie looked up at him. "What are you going to do?"

"I'll fight to keep Holly." But he didn't think it was a fight he'd win.

Still, he would fight. There was no other alternative.

He couldn't just let Mattie rip Holly from his life, and even though she'd spoken of visiting rights and such, he didn't want that, either.

He wanted his daughter.

Bo wanted the life he'd had before Mattie had walked in and turned it upside down.

Mattie glanced back at him, as if to say she was sorry, but how could she be? She literally had everything she wanted in her arms.

"How long will we be here?" Rosalie asked.

Bo didn't take his eyes off Mattie and the children. "I'm not sure. Probably at least a day or two." He was being optimistic. The investigation was complex, with a lot of possibilities for things to go wrong.

Rosalie patted his arm in motherly fashion. "Find the person after Mattie," she reminded him. "And then you can get on to this business of the heart."

"Like I said, I'm not giving up Holly."

"I didn't mean that." Rosalie didn't continue until he looked at her. She touched her fingers to his chest. "I mean the matter of your heart."

Bo shook his head. "What are you talking about?"

Rosalie huffed. "It's as plain as the nose on your face that you're attracted to Mattie. She's attracted to you, too. It's also plain to see that you're both fighting it. My advice? Don't fight it anymore. Things might be easier to work out if you're loving and not snarling at each other."

Bo was sure he scowled. "Are you saying I should get involved with Mattie so I can keep Holly?"

"No. I'm saying you should get involved with Mattie

because you want her. The custody issue would just be an added benefit."

He didn't curse because he wasn't sure he could keep the kids from hearing.

"Just think about it," Rosalie added and headed for the kitchen.

She left Bo there to stew. Yes, he was attracted to Mattie. Hell, he got aroused just thinking about her, and he kept getting a very vivid image of her naked and in his bed. Her legs wrapped around him while he buried himself deep inside her.

But that wasn't going to happen.

Was it?

That question hit him damn hard.

If they kissed again, it just might happen whether he intended it to or not. Wanting Mattie overrode his common sense, and that meant he needed to solve this case so he could concentrate, as Rosalie had put it, on matters of the heart.

He stepped farther back into the hall and took out his phone so he could call Sergeant O'Malley for an update. Mattie glanced back again, probably when she realized he was calling someone. Her left eyebrow lifted to ask if everything was okay. Bo just nodded. She nodded back and gave him a brief smile.

And Bo wondered when the hell things had gotten so easy between them that they could communicate without words.

"O'Malley," Bo greeted when the sergeant answered. "Tell me you have some good news. Any good news will do."

"Well, it's news all right. I'll let you decide whether

it's good or not. We have our techs digging through the financials for Cicely Carr's family. If they were involved in the illegal arms deal with Kendall Collier, then it's not there in the records. Carr, however, is a different matter."

"What do you mean?" Bo was definitely interested in the information, but he also didn't take his attention off Mattie, whom Jacob had coaxed into stacking blocks with Holly and him.

"She withdrew a good portion of her trust fund about the same time the illegal arms deal took place, and we can't find where that money went."

"Why didn't this come up during the FBI investigation?" Bo asked.

"Because she hid the deal through several layers of corporate red tape. Besides, the FBI was focusing on her parents, not her."

So, Cicely Carr could have given or loaned money to Kendall Collier. Was that now the reason Collier was marrying her? To keep her quiet?

"There's more," O'Malley continued. "This is the part that might be good or bad. I'm looking at the whole arms deal with a fresh eye, and Collier might have been telling the truth about his involvement. He honestly might not have known he was investing in illegal weapons. Before this incident, he'd done business with the dealer, Armand Brier, and it appears that Brier bundled the arms deal along with other investments."

"Then why did the FBI pursue Collier?" Bo asked.

"Because he did try to cover it up after he learned about it. That's about the time Mattie came into the picture. She found the documents, heard some of Collier's phone conversations and maybe thought he'd honchoed the deal."

Hell. So maybe Mattie had gotten herself in scalding hot water by testifying against a man who wasn't the primary player. "But someone killed Mattie's fiancé and tried to kill her," Bo pointed out.

Bo checked to make sure Mattie hadn't heard that, but her attention stayed firmly on the kids.

"Yeah," O'Malley agreed. "My theory is that the initial attacks were orchestrated by this Armand Brier. He probably wanted to do away with Mattie or anyone else who could have sent him to prison for the arms deal."

"Then, why didn't Brier go after Collier?" Bo wanted to know.

"I'm not sure. Maybe they came up with some sort of compromise. After all, Collier would have gone to prison, too, because he did cover up the deal after the fact."

Yes, but that wasn't nearly as bad as what Brier had done. Of course, Bo wasn't about to cut Collier any slack. "So you think Brier sent that explosive to my house?"

"No," O'Malley quickly answered. "Brier was found dead about four months ago. He was shot and killed near his office in London. An apparent robbery gone bad."

Or else Collier had eliminated the one man who could send him to jail. Now he might be out to eliminate Mattie just so he would have the assurance and maybe a little revenge.

"Thanks for all of this," Bo told O'Malley. "I'll talk to Mattie about Cicely Carr and see if she knows anything that can help with the investigation. And I'll tell her about Brier's death, of course."

"There's more," O'Malley said before Bo could hang up. "We followed Tolivar as the captain requested, and we saw something odd. He's meeting with Ian Kaplan right now, as we speak."

"Kaplan?" Bo said that loud enough that it caused Mattie to look at him. He held up his finger in a "wait a second" gesture to let her know he'd fill her in. "Let me guess. Tolivar is ready to beat Kaplan to a pulp because Kaplan told us that Tolivar is the one who's after Mattie."

"Not exactly. I don't know what's going on, but this meeting isn't what we expected."

Confused, Bo shook his head. "What do you mean?"

"I'm sending a picture to your cell," the sergeant explained. "In this case, a picture's worth a thousand words."

Bo pressed the button to open the image, and he watched as it loaded on to the tiny screen. Bit by bit, the image became clearer.

"Hell," Bo mumbled.

What was going on?

Chapter Eleven

Mattie was not a happy camper.

Here she should be spending the rest of the day with her daughter, but instead she was at police headquarters again. She could blame Larry Tolivar for that.

And Ian.

She studied the photo on Bo's phone. A photo of Tolivar and Ian, two men who were supposedly ready to throw each other under a bus with one accusing the other of wanting her harmed. Yet that wasn't the case in the photo. They were shaking hands and smiling as if a friendly meeting were normal for them.

Maybe it was.

"I've known Ian for years," Mattie told Bo as they walked toward the interview room where Ian was waiting for them. She handed Bo his phone. "But until I went into Witness Protection, I'd never seen Tolivar. Never heard Ian mention him, either."

"Well, they're pretty chummy in that picture," Bo snarled.

Yes, they were. And that's the reason Bo had called Ian the moment he'd seen it and demanded that he come to headquarters to answer some questions. Bo had called

Tolivar, as well, but the marshal hadn't answered his phone. So that meant Ian would be providing any initial information about the encounter.

In other words, this might be a total waste of time.

Still, Bo had to investigate the meeting between the two suspects, and even though Bo had insisted that she could stay at the safe house, Mattie had decided to come anyway. The sooner she got to the bottom of what was happening to her, the sooner she could get on with her life.

And her life was with Holly.

Soon, very soon, she'd have to figure out how Bo fit into the picture. Or if he fit in at all. He was still reeling from the news of the DNA test, but he also might be gearing up to battle her in court. They might find themselves enemies if they weren't already. Too bad this was one enemy that she wanted in an entirely different way.

Mattie wanted more of those hot, out-of-control kisses. She wanted Bo to take her just as those kisses had suggested he might. Hard and fast, where she didn't have to think about the consequences. She'd spent too many months planning and plotting. Running and hiding. And now what she wanted was to spend time with her daughter.

And have sex with Bo.

She felt her face flush. Felt her body go warm in anticipation of what parts of her were suggesting. Of course, her brain was telling her to back off, and she probably would. But she was secretly hoping Bo would take this to the max.

"You okay?" Bo asked, stopping outside the interview

room door. "You're flushed, and you're breathing funny."

"Oh." She quickly tried to fix that. Talk about wearing her heart on her sleeve.

"Oh?" Bo questioned.

Since she didn't want to verbalize anything right now, she didn't answer. She just stared back.

"Oh," Bo finally said, and he huffed. "Yeah. We'll deal with that later."

"How?" she blurted out. Great. Now, she'd just opened a box that should be left closed.

The corner of his mouth lifted and he crushed his mouth against hers for just a split second. "How the hell do you think we'll deal with it?"

No smile this time. He glanced around as if to make sure no one was around to hear what he was about to say. "Just in case you overheard Rosalie and me talking earlier, I want you to know that how we deal with this heat has nothing to do with how we deal with Holly."

"Why would it?"

"Exactly." He made a grunt of agreement. "Rosalie thinks we'll be more amicable to each other if I'm... well...having sex with you." It sounded as if those weren't the words he wanted to use. He likely had something much more crude on the tip of his tongue.

"Amicable," she repeated. Mattie blushed. That wasn't the word she would use, either. "It would be very..." And here she tried to figure out the best way to put it. "Satisfying."

"Hell," he mumbled and then added something much harsher. "When and if I get you in my bed, I won't be aiming for something just satisfying and amicable. I figure if we're going to screw up our lives, then it might as well be something to remember."

All right. That stole her breath away as only Bo could do. He gave her another of those crushing kisses on the mouth that in no way qualified as a peck, then threw open the door to the interview room.

Ian smiled when he spotted her, but that smile evaporated when his attention landed on Bo. Or maybe what caused his smile to fade was that he might have sensed the sexual energy between Bo and her. Mattie was certain they looked guilty of something.

"I didn't know if you'd come," Ian told her.

"I wasn't sure I would, either." She tipped her head to the photo on Bo's phone. "But I really wanted an explanation for that."

When Ian looked at the picture, his face dropped, and he gave a weary sigh. "You have this all wrong," he insisted, thrusting the phone back in Bo's hand.

"Really?" Bo challenged. "Why don't you tell me just how wrong I have it, because you see, you and the marshal look like old friends."

"We're not," Ian snapped, and he repeated it when he shifted his attention back to Mattie. He stared at her a moment and scrubbed his hand over his face. "Look, I decided to play nice with Tolivar because I want you to be safe. I don't want you hiding out with the cops. Especially this cop," he added, tossing a glare at Bo.

Bo stepped closer, violating Ian's personal space. "So what did you learn from playing nice?"

Ian's glare softened, and he sighed again. "Nothing that I didn't already know, but I think Tolivar is willing to keep talking to me. He thinks I'm just Kendall's flunky, so maybe he'll let something slip when he's spouting off how much he wants to take Mattie back into custody. I want him to admit that he planted Kendall's fingerprints on that coffee shop computer. I want him to give me any information that'll help me put him behind bars."

"You really think Tolivar is dirty?" Bo pressed.

"You bet I do. It makes sense, too. He would have had the expertise to plant Kendall's fingerprints. He could have sold the info in the Witness Protection files and made it look like a hack job."

"Of course, that brings us right back to Kendall. Or you," Bo added. "You two are the ones who wanted to find Mattie and had the strongest motive for paying someone to give you her whereabouts."

"I won't deny that," Ian admitted.

Bo paused, obviously waiting for more, but it didn't come. "Are you admitting you paid Tolivar to hack into the Witness Protection database?"

"You know I can't admit to that." He looked at Mattie when he spoke. "That would be a felony. But I will say I was desperate to find you, and I knew you'd want to be reunited with your daughter."

It was as if all the air went out of the room. Mattie sucked in her breath. "You knew I had a daughter," she accused. "And you knew where she was."

Ian stepped around Bo and reached out to put his hand over her shoulder, but Mattie moved away before that could happen. Ian glanced away, mumbled something and then finally nodded. "Yes."

"How did you find out?" Mattie demanded.

"By having some of my P.I.s follow Larry Tolivar.

He's like a pit bull. He just wouldn't let go of it, so I had him followed. One of my P.I.s spotted him breaking into Lieutenant Duggan's SUV, so I figured this might be connected to him."

"Wait," Bo said when Ian was about to continue. "Your man saw the marshal break into my SUV and you didn't report it?"

"No reason. The guy didn't take anything. He just swabbed the infant car seats and taped them down for hair samples."

There was only one reason Mattie could think of that someone would want to do that—to get a DNA sample. She wasn't sure the Justice Department had her DNA on file, but she was betting they did.

"After the marshal went to Duggan's house, I put one and one together," Ian explained. "After all, the lieutenant has two babies who are the exact age that your child would be."

Mattie looked at Bo to see if he was buying this. Maybe. Ian was making a good argument.

"You're positive you didn't know about my baby until yesterday?" she asked.

Ian looked her straight in the eyes. "I swear. Mattie, if I had known where your baby was, I would have tried to get her for you."

Bo cursed, and Mattie touched him to stop him from grabbing Ian and putting him up against the wall. She couldn't stomach the thought of Ian trying to take Holly. Bo was obviously having trouble with that, as well.

"You would have tried to get her," Mattie repeated. "Ian, I don't want you involved in this. And I especially don't want you trying to take my child."

He tried to touch her again, but this time Bo batted the man's hand out of the way, using far more force than necessary.

"Am I interrupting anything?" someone asked. The door was ajar, and someone pushed it fully open. It was Cicely Carr. "I asked at your office," she said to Bo. "And they told me you were here."

Cicely volleyed glances at all of them, and her forehead bunched up. However, Mattie figured she'd heard at least the last part of the conversation and knew what had prompted the uncomfortable silence.

"Why are you here?" Cicely asked Ian. She didn't seem pleased that her fiancé's attorney was at the police station again.

"Mattie and I had some things to clear up," Ian snarled. He grabbed his briefcase from the table. "But it's useless. She doesn't trust us, Cicely. She only trusts this cop here."

Cicely smiled, and Mattie wondered if anyone could be that sappy sweet and still be genuine. "Of course she trusts us. We're practically family. Mattie just needs some time, right?"

Mattie huffed. "What I need is proof of who's trying to kill me."

"Well, you can cross Kendall and me off that list. And Ian," the woman added after a long pause. "That's why I wanted to see you again. To tell you that all of this digging into my family's records isn't necessary. I'll tell you anything you want to know, because Kendall and I have nothing to hide."

Bo took the woman up on that offer. "Did you give

Kendall the money for his part in the illegal arms deal?"

"Cicely," Ian said as a warning. "You don't have to answer that."

"But I will. If it'll make Mattie realize we're on her side now." Cicely squared her shoulders and turned to Bo. "Yes, I gave Kendall the money, but neither of us had any idea it was for illegal arms. And no, my parents weren't involved. I gave Kendall money from my trust fund. So there, you can stop digging and stop asking questions. We're all on the same side now."

"So you keep saying," Mattie mumbled. "But the bottom line is someone killed Brody." Her voice cracked a little when she said her late fiancé's name. "Someone tried to kill Bo and me just this morning."

Cicely gave a long sigh and kept her gaze on Mattie. "What will it take to convince you that Kendall wasn't behind any of that?"

"What will convince me? Finding proof that someone else did it."

Cicely paused a moment and then gave a crisp nod. "All right. Let me see what I can find out."

"Don't," Bo warned. "If you're truly innocent in this, then your questions could get you killed. Someone wants to silence Mattie permanently, and this person might not like you trying to finger him."

Cicely paused again. "That's a chance I have to take. For Kendall. He wants Mattie back in his life. Other than me and our unborn child, she's the only family he has left. Family's important to him now."

Mattie folded her arms over her chest. "Why now?

Kendall's never shown once ounce of family concern for me. What happened to make him change?"

"I happened," Cicely said, hiking up her chin. "Kendall fell in love with me, and love changed him. Love, and our baby." She slid her hand over her stomach.

Ian cleared his throat, drawing everyone's attention back to him. The attorney just stared at Cicely. "You might as well tell them the rest."

"The rest?" Bo demanded when Cicely didn't answer.

"Kendall is dying," Ian announced.

Well, Mattie hadn't seen that bombshell coming. Apparently neither had Bo, because he looked surprised, suspicious even, but not especially concerned.

"Kendall's not dying," Cicely corrected. "But he does have aplastic anemia. It's a blood disorder where the body doesn't make enough red blood cells. He's on medication, and we're searching for a bone marrow donor. Once he has the bone marrow transplant, he'll be fine."

"But so far, there's been no donor match," Ian explained.

"Is that what this is all about?" Mattie snapped. "Kendall wants me to be a donor?"

"You're not a match." Ian, again. Cicely was just standing there sniffing back tears. "You were already in the National Bone Marrow Registry, so we checked."

That was true. She'd become a registered donor years ago when a friend had needed a marrow transplant.

Mattie got a really bad feeling about this. "But my child could be a match."

Cicely didn't say anything. She just kept sniffling. However, Ian finally nodded.

Mattie cursed, and she turned so quickly that Bo had to catch her or she would have fallen.

"Get out of here," Mattie demanded.

"We don't want to hurt the child," Cicely insisted. "We just want her tested to see if she's a match."

"And you thought the best way to do that was to kill or kidnap me?"

"We didn't do those things," Cicely practically yelled. "We only want the baby."

"Well, you're not going to get her." Bo kept his voice calm, though Mattie didn't know how he managed it. Since he already had hold of her, he got her out of the room.

"You can't let Kendall die!" Cicely shouted. "I love him, and I won't let you do this to him."

Mattie ignored Cicely's ranting, but she heard every word. And every word was motive for why someone had tried to blow up Bo's home. That perhaps hadn't been a murder attempt but a kidnapping. If Cicely or Kendall had her, then that would get them one step closer to her baby and the bone marrow that Kendall apparently needed to live.

"We need to get back to Holly," Mattie mumbled.

Bo obviously understood that, and that's why he was hurrying down the hall with her. "We need to be careful, though. They could have told us about the bone marrow so that we'd rush back to the safe house. I can't do that. I have to make sure they aren't following us."

"Of course. I wouldn't put it past them."

He led her out of the building, but he didn't go to

the unmarked car that he'd left in the parking lot. "We have to switch cars," he let her know. "If Cicely Carr or Kaplan had someone watching the parking lot, they could have seen us drive up, and then they could have planted a tracking device on the vehicle. It wouldn't have been easy to do, but it might have worked if their hired help was wearing a fake cop's uniform."

That caused her breath to race. "And a tracking device would have led them straight to Holly."

"That's not going to happen." He took her to the motor pool garage and checked out another vehicle.

"Do you think your uncle's in love with Cicely?" Bo asked as they got in the new vehicle.

"I doubt it." She lifted her shoulder. "I could be wrong, though."

"And she could have gotten pregnant to give him a chance at getting another bone marrow donor."

She nodded. "True. Plus, there's the fact that they can't be forced to testify against each other if they're married."

And it would probably work. Of course, if there was no new evidence against Kendall, there likely wouldn't be another trial anyway, especially with the arms dealer already dead.

Mattie didn't say a word until they were out of the parking lot and on their way. "Maybe this means Kendall no longer wants me dead."

"Maybe."

He kept watch in the side and rearview mirrors. So did Mattie. No one pulled out of the parking lot with them, but there were plenty of people in the area. Some in parked cars on the streets. Some milling around. One of them could have been hired to watch for them.

"Maybe?" she questioned.

He hesitated a moment. "If you're dead, then as your next of kin, Kendall could petition to get custody of Holly."

"Oh, God." She rammed her fingers through her hair and repeated it. "I have to draw up a will naming you as her guardian. And I have to let Kendall know that killing me won't get him Holly."

"You could also let him think you'll cooperate with the bone marrow test."

Her gaze flew to his. "What do you mean?"

"If you tell Kendall that you'll have Holly tested, then that buys us some time. We're close to figuring all of this out, Mattie, and we just need to give Kendall a little something so that he backs off."

She gave that some thought. "But what if it's not Kendall who's after me? What if it's really Marshal Tolivar?"

Then he and Mattie could have even bigger problems. Tolivar could come after Mattie, maybe to silence her, maybe to kill her, and Kendall and his cronies could try to take Holly.

"Oh, God," Mattie mumbled again.

Obviously, Bo knew what they were up against. And right now, Mattie just wanted to get back to the safe house so they could protect Holly.

Mattie huffed when they caught the red light just one block up from headquarters, and she checked around them again. Nothing seemed suspicious or worth mentioning to Bo.

"If I let Kendall think I'm going to cooperate and have Holly tested, what next?" Mattie asked. "Do I actually go through with the test?"

Bo didn't answer. Mattie followed his gaze and saw that Bo had zoomed in on a man who was about twenty feet away and walking toward them. The guy was wearing a baseball cap slung low over his face and a raincoat. While there was indeed rain in the forecast, the garment, and the man, gave Mattie an uneasy feeling.

"You think he could be a problem?" Mattie asked, just as the light turned green.

Mattie held her breath, waiting for the car in front of them to move. But that didn't happen. The vehicle still didn't budge when the cars behind them started to honk their horns.

That's when Mattie knew they were in trouble.

Bo grabbed Mattie and pushed her lower into the seat. Good thing, too. Because the man whipped out a gun from beneath his raincoat.

And he fired right at them.

Chapter Twelve

Mattie heard the blast. Thick and loud, it echoed through the busy street. Despite the fact that it sounded exactly like a car backfiring, she knew that wasn't the case.

The sound was a gunshot.

"Stay down!" Bo shouted, drawing his gun from his shoulder holster.

Mattie wanted to remind him to stay down, as well, but the next shot drowned out her voice. The windshield shattered, cracking and webbing, except for the gaping hole in the center.

A hole caused by a bullet.

That put her heart in her throat. Mercy, they were literally out in the open and right in the shooter's line of fire. The next bullet proved that. It ripped through what was left of the windshield and dropped a chunk of safety glass right onto her.

Bo tossed her his phone. "Press the first number and tell them we need help."

Mattie had no idea how she managed to press the button to make the call. Her hands were shaking violently.

"O'Malley," the officer answered.

"Someone's shooting at us." She looked up at the street signs. "We're on St. Mary's." Though she couldn't see the cross street.

"I'm on the way," O'Malley assured.

"Get down!" Bo called out, and it took her a moment to realize he wasn't talking to her but to the half dozen or so pedestrians on the sidewalk. Most were already ducking for cover or running.

All except the tall man wearing a raincoat. Although she couldn't see his face, something about him was familiar.

"I can't return fire," Bo said. With his gun still at the ready, he ducked down. "Too many people."

That didn't stop the gunman, though. He fired another shot into the car, and Mattie heard it slice through the door right next to her.

Bo cursed and jammed his foot onto the accelerator, plowing their vehicle right into the car ahead of them. There was no driver inside. Maybe he'd run the moment the bullets started firing as the other drivers had done. Or maybe it was more sinister than that. This guy could have been in on this attack. Either way, since there were vehicles on three sides and the gunman on the remaining side, it meant they were trapped.

An image of Holly flashed through Mattie's mind. Mattie and her baby might never get to know each other, and that broke her heart. But what broke it even more was that both Jacob and Holly could become orphans if Bo and she couldn't get out of there.

She cursed because she didn't have her gun with her. She could grab Bo and try to run for cover, but the gunman was better positioned. Even though the car wasn't much protection, it was better than being out in the open where they could be gunned down.

"Enough of this," Bo mumbled, and he took aim and fired. Not at the man but into the air so that it wouldn't hit any innocent bystanders.

Through the side window, Mattie saw the gunman dive to the sidewalk, joining the others already there.

She wanted to cheer. The danger wasn't over, not by a long shot, but at least Bo's shot had caused the gunman to stop shooting. Mattie doubted the lull would last long.

Bo didn't waste any time. He gunned the engine again, his front bumper grinding against the much larger car in front of them. Finally, it moved, but not enough to give Bo room to maneuver them out of there.

Mattie kept her attention focused on the gunman, and she nearly screamed when she saw him lift his head from the sidewalk.

And his gun.

"He's going to shoot again," she tried to warn Bo. But it was too late.

The gunman fired. The bullet slammed through the car and right into the seat, less than an inch from her arm. The next one went into her headrest.

Well, it was clear which one of them the gunman wanted dead. This attack was for her, but the gunman probably didn't care if he killed Bo in the process.

Bo cursed and hit the accelerator again, ramming into the other car. It worked. The jolt sent the car forward and finally gave Bo the opening he needed. He jerked the steering wheel to the left. With the tires squealing and the bullets continuing to blast through their car, Bo got them away from there.

"O'Malley's on the way," Mattie relayed to him. She tried to brace herself for more of the shots, for the deafening deadly blasts.

But they stopped.

Bo grabbed his phone and made another call. Unlike her, he was able to give a more specific address and a description of the gunman. He also requested an ambulance in case any of the bystanders had been hit.

Mattie didn't sit up, but she lifted her head just enough that she could see the side mirror. And what she saw had her just as frightened as the prospect of more bullets coming their way.

"The gunman's running," she practically shouted.

She didn't want him to escape. Mattie wanted the cops to arrive right now and arrest him. Then they could force the man to tell them who'd hired him. That information was critical, and once they had it, then this danger might finally end.

"Don't let him get away," Bo told the officer on the other end of the line. He continued to maneuver the car through the busy streets, quickly putting some distance between them and the gunman.

"He wanted me dead," Mattie mumbled.

"Yeah." Bo reached up and tore away what was left of the safety glass. "But we're going to get him."

She latched on to that promise and continued to watch. And pray. Mattie hoped he didn't have some way of following them and launching another attack.

Or…

"We need to get to the children now," Mattie blurted

out. She suddenly had an overwhelming need to make sure that that wasn't where the gunman was headed next.

"We can't go to them. Not now."

Mattie frantically shook her head, ready to argue with him. She had to make sure the children were okay.

"This could have all been a ruse," Bo explained. "While we were pinned down, someone could have put a tracking device on the car."

"I didn't see anyone do that." But she couldn't say with 100-percent certainty that it hadn't happened.

"There was a lot going on," he went on while he maneuvered the car through the side streets. "And it's too big of a risk to take. We can't compromise the location of the safe house. Plus, we can't drive into the neighborhood with the car shot up like this. It would draw attention to us, and we don't need that."

Mattie knew this was all true, but each moment she was away from the kids was agony. It obviously was for Bo, as well, because he took out his phone again and made another call. This one he put on speaker.

"Rosalie," he said the moment the nanny answered. "Is everything okay?"

"Yes, but I was about to ask you the same thing. The officer here with us just got a call that something had happened to Mattie and you?"

"It was probably a case of wrong place, wrong time," Bo lied. "But we're all right."

Another lie. Mattie was shaking and wasn't sure she could stop. But she was also relieved. Rosalie and the children were safe.

For now.

She wanted to tell Bo to have another officer sent out, but that might not be smart, either. Heck, the person after them could be watching headquarters for just that sort of thing. Bo was right. Best to return to the station and regroup. And get another car.

"I'll phone you from headquarters," Bo assured Rosalie. "I'll also be tapping into the security feed at the house…because I want to take a look at the babies. I think Mattie would like that, too."

Yes. She would. Right now, just seeing them would help soothe her.

"Do you see anyone following us?" he asked Mattie right after he ended the call.

"No. But with all the traffic, it's hard to tell." Then what Bo did really sunk in. "You don't think the gunman will follow us to police headquarters and start shooting at us there?"

He didn't answer her right away. "We'll be careful when we get out at the parking lot."

Oh, God. This might not be over.

It seemed to take a lifetime, but they finally reached the headquarters building. Bo parked the bullet-riddled car next to the side entrance, and true to his word, he hurried them inside.

No one fired shots at them.

Several officers asked how they were, and Bo gave them a clipped answer that they were unharmed. He didn't stop, however. He got them to his office, and while he rang Rosalie he used the laptop on his desk to tap into the safe house security system. Mattie soon saw the children sleeping in their cribs.

"What happened?" Rosalie whispered, and she went

into the hall, probably so she wouldn't wake the children. Since Bo had the call on speaker, Mattie had no trouble hearing the woman.

"Someone fired a few shots at us after we left headquarters."

Because she was still in camera range, Mattie saw the stark fear on the woman's face.

"But it's all right," Bo assured her. "As soon as we can, Mattie and I will be back. In the meantime, just stay inside and keep everything locked up. The officer is still there with you, right?"

"In the living room. He hasn't left the house."

"Good. Make sure it stays that way." There was a tiny beep from his phone. "Rosalie, I have another call coming in, but I'm going to keep the security feed on for several more minutes."

So he could keep watch. Mattie was thankful for it. Just seeing both children, safe and sleeping, made her breathe easier.

"O'Malley," Bo said when he took the other call. "What's going on?"

"We're in pursuit, but we have an ID. One of the officers recognized him. It's Terrance Arturo. Gotta go. I'll call when we have him."

Terrance Arturo. That turned her blood to ice. "Didn't they arrest him?" she asked.

Bo nodded. "But they had to release him."

Mattie squeezed her eyes shut a moment. "Arturo works for Ian and therefore Kendall."

Bo nodded again, and he slipped his arm around her waist. "When he's caught, I'll question him. If Ian or Kendall ordered this hit, then I'll get the truth from

Arturo." Bo eased her closer to him. "You should sit down. You're shaking."

Yes, she was, and since Mattie wasn't sure she could stand much longer anyway, she slid to the floor, using the wall to support her back. Bo took the laptop and slid down right next to her, but they were only there a few seconds when Mattie heard something on the security feed from the safe house. It was Jacob. He'd woken up and was starting to fuss.

Rosalie immediately went to the little boy, picked him up and started to rock him. Bo zoomed in on that tiny precious face, and it brought home exactly what was at stake here.

Their children.

"If Arturo isn't caught," Mattie whispered, "I'll call Kendall and start the process to make him think that I'll help him, that I'll have Holly tested as a possible bone marrow donor."

Bo didn't say anything, but that got his jaw muscles working. It was a decent backup plan, but he obviously hated the idea as much as she did. She didn't want Kendall even speaking her daughter's name until she was sure he wasn't the one trying to kill her.

Jacob lifted his head from Rosalie's shoulder and looked directly into the camera.

"Hey, grumpy," Bo teased his son. Bo touched his fingers to the screen.

"He can hear you?" Mattie asked.

"No. The audio feed is one-way. We can only hear them. It's for security reasons so that if someone manages to get access to the security system, they won't be able to backdoor their way into the police computer."

That made sense, but she would have liked the little boy to hear their voices.

"He looks so much like you." She studied the tiny face still staring at them as if he knew they were on the other end of that camera. "I didn't see it so much when he was born, because I didn't know what you looked like then, but I see it now."

"You held him when he was born?" Bo asked.

"Yes. I guess you could say I delivered him. I cut the cord with a pair of scissors I found in the nurses' lounge. Nadine had done the same for me about a half hour earlier when Holly was born." Mattie lifted her shoulder. "Maybe that's why I feel so close to Jacob, because I was there with him right from the start."

The pain and tension returned to Bo's face, and she was sorry she'd brought it up. He took a deep breath, kissed the top of her head and then slipped his left arm around her so he could pull her to him. Until they pressed together.

Like a real couple watching their family.

Mattie stiffened at that thought and cursed herself for even thinking it. It didn't matter how many kisses they'd shared. It didn't matter how hot the attraction. He wasn't looking for a wife, because she doubted he'd gotten over Nadine.

"Thank you." Bo whispered the words so softly that it took her a moment to figure out what he'd said. Before she could ask him what he was thanking her for, his phone rang again.

"It's O'Malley," he relayed to her. His phone was no longer on speaker, so Mattie couldn't hear what the sergeant was saying.

"How did that happen?" Bo asked, his voice rough and filled with the tone of the profanity he didn't use.

"No," Mattie mumbled. Please. She didn't want any more bad news.

She started to imagine the worst—that Arturo had learned the location of the safe house, and he was on the way there. She got to her feet in case they had to hurry out of there.

Bo stood, as well. "You're sure?" he asked O'Malley.

Bo obviously didn't like that response, either, because this time he spat out the profanity he'd held back earlier. "Bring him in. I want to talk to him."

That gave Mattie some hope. Had they actually caught Arturo? But those hopes were soon dashed.

"Arturo's dead," Bo let her know the moment he ended the call.

Part of her was relieved. The man wouldn't be coming to the safe house, and he couldn't make another attempt to kill her. "So we don't know who hired him?" she asked, already knowing the answer.

Bo shook his head. "He died on the scene without saying a word."

There was something he wasn't saying. "Died? How?"

"A shootout. Arturo was running a street over from where he attacked us, and when he was confronted, he tried to shoot his way out of it. Or so it seems."

"What do you mean? Did someone from SAPD shoot him?"

"No." And those jaw muscles stirred again. "Marshal Larry Tolivar killed Arturo."

"Tolivar? Why was he there?"

Bo shook his head. "I don't know, and it might take a while before we find out. Tolivar's not saying anything until his legal rep from the Justice Department shows up."

Chapter Thirteen

Bo practically rammed the keys into the ignition of the new unmarked car, the replacement vehicle for the one Arturo had shot to hell the day before. He was not in the right frame of mind to be questioning two suspects. One who was also a federal marshal and the other suspect, Kendall Collier, who might be behind all of this.

But he didn't have a choice.

While Bo would have preferred to stay at the safe house and have a long, relaxing breakfast with Mattie, Rosalie and the kids, this part of the investigation was too important for him to pawn it off on anyone else. Still, spending time with Mattie and the kids sounded like heaven.

And that troubled him a lot.

Lately, Mattie was part of every image that he had about his immediate future. She was there. Helping with the kids. Talking to him. Adding something that hadn't been in his life for a long time. Yes, a big part of that *something* was sexual attraction, but he had the feeling that it could be a lot more than just that.

And that scared him.

Because to accept Mattie into his life meant he had

to give up the old feelings he had for Nadine. Bo wasn't sure he was ready to do that.

"You okay?" Mattie asked, putting on her seat belt.

No. He wasn't. But Bo kept that to himself. Instead, he nodded, started the car and opened the garage door so he could back out.

"Your last chance," he mumbled. "You can stay here, and I can question Kendall and Tolivar on my own."

"I'm going," Mattie insisted. "I wouldn't have called Kendall and asked him to come to the station if I didn't plan to be there. He wants to talk to me, and I want to talk to him."

He checked her eyes to see if there was any doubt. There wasn't. But there was fatigue, and he was sure it was mirrored in his own eyes. It'd been a long night, and Mattie was likely still reeling from the shooting the day before—even though she managed to look amazing in the loaner purple dress that had been brought to the safe house for her. Thankfully, Bo kept several outfits in his office and had been able to use one of those, because he hadn't wanted to risk going back to his own house to get anything.

Because he thought they could both use it, he leaned over and put his mouth to hers. Bo had intended it to be something quick. Just a kiss of reassurance, but it was as effective as an hour of good foreplay. His body always seemed primed and ready when he was around Mattie.

"Do you think having sex would make us think better, as in clearing our heads?" The corner of Mattie's mouth lifted, and it made him wish she would smile more often.

Of course, they didn't have a lot to smile about at the moment.

"Don't know about the thinking part," he drawled, kissing her again. "But it'd make us feel a hell of a lot better."

Since that wasn't a joke, Bo decided to end the torture and get to headquarters. Plus, it wasn't a good idea for them to be sitting in a garage kissing, especially when they had to discuss some things before they talked to their suspects.

"You shouldn't be in the room when I talk with Tolivar," Bo said, and he continued even over her objection. "You can listen in and watch. You can even feed me questions if you think I'm missing something, but I have to do this interrogation by the book. We don't want his legal rep to step in and pull him away from our jurisdiction."

"They can do that?" she asked. No sign of that smile now. Reality was hitting her again.

"They can try." But Bo wanted to keep this within the SAPD so he could continue to have Mattie in his protective custody. If the feds took over the case, God knows what they would try to do in the name of protecting her.

"And now for Kendall," Bo said, moving on to their next problem. "I got a call about him this morning when you were in the shower. It's true. He really does have aplastic anemia. It's similar to leukemia, and he's stabilized with meds for now. But the only chance at a cure is a bone marrow donor."

"Holly," she mumbled.

"Holly," Bo confirmed. "Kendall could be so desperate to see if Holly's a match that he could be pretending to be a changed man." But Bo had to tell her the rest. "Or it could be for real. He did indeed sell his business, and he's had no recent association with anyone shady."

"That doesn't mean he's changed."

"No. But there's more. He's apparently working with the feds, the very people who arrested him for the illegal arms deal."

"He's what?"

Bo understood her shocked reaction because it was the same one he'd had when the captain told him the news. "The Justice Department won't give us details, only that Kendall is cooperating with them by giving them information about some of his former business associates. It's my guess that this deal will give him immunity, clear his name, and in turn the Justice Department will get to make some arrests."

She huffed. "And Kendall will go free."

Yes. And that could be a major problem, if Kendall was indeed the one who wanted Mattie dead. It might mean that Bo had to bargain with the devil, with Kendall, if there was any hope that Mattie would have a normal life. And her normalcy was necessary for Holly's.

Bo parked in the secure lot directly next to the headquarters building, and when they were done, he wouldn't use the same car to return to the safe house. He wanted to put as many layers of security as possible between this would-be killer and the children.

He led Mattie toward the interview room with the intention of starting with Tolivar, but he spotted Kendall in the hall outside his office. The man was alone, without his attorney or his fiancée. Kendall was leaning the back of his head against the wall, and he had his eyes closed. For just a brief second, Bo saw the man's fatigue, and Kendall no longer looked like the threat that he might possibly be.

That made him even more dangerous. He could be playing the part of a wolf in sheep's clothing.

"Kendall," Mattie said, practically snapping out his name.

Kendall's eyes flew open. He didn't offer them a smile or anything else friendly. "You wanted to see me."

Bo ushered them into his office so they'd have some privacy.

"I want to know the truth," Mattie said without even waiting until they were fully inside.

"The truth," Kendall repeated. "I wonder what that is myself."

Bo rolled his eyes. "Could we cut the existential BS and get to the facts? Mattie and I want to know what you're really up to. And then you can tell us if you hired Arturo to try to kill her."

"I didn't hire him," Kendall said calmly. "But I can't rule out that someone did because they thought in some kind of warped way it would help me."

"Because if I'm dead, you'd be my daughter's next of kin," Mattie jumped in. "Well, I did an online will last night, and I've named Bo as her legal guardian. So, if I'm dead, you won't get your hands on her or her bone marrow."

Kendall nodded. "Good."

Surprised, Bo glanced at Mattie who obviously shared his reaction. "Good? Why?" she pressed.

"Because I don't want anyone with a reason to kill you. I know you don't believe that, but it's true."

"You're right," Mattie countered. "I don't believe that."

Bo wasn't sure he did, either, but it left him with a question. "Who would kill Mattie in order to help you?"

Kendall shrugged as if he might not answer, but he finally said, "Cicely. She wants me to live. That's why she insisted she get pregnant."

"You don't want the child?" Bo questioned.

Now, there was some emotion. Something flared through his eyes, but Kendall quickly concealed it. "I want the child," he insisted. "It's the mother I'm having second thoughts about."

So he didn't want to marry Cicely, but since she was carrying the baby that could ultimately save his life, Kendall was stuck with her. But Bo didn't feel sorry for the man. After all, Kendall could be the man who wanted Mattie dead.

"And then there's Ian," Kendall added after taking a deep breath. He looked Mattie straight in the eyes. "He could want to kill you for a different reason." He tipped his head to Bo. "And you're that reason."

Mattie made a sound of total disbelief. But Bo didn't. "Ian is jealous of me," Bo stated. "You think he's jealous enough to want me dead?"

"Maybe he wants both of you dead. Since he can't have Mattie, it's possible he might not want anyone to have her." Kendall paused. "I've been going over all of this for months. I didn't kill Mattie's fiancé, so that means someone else did."

Mattie folded her arms over her chest. "And you think that someone is Ian?" She didn't wait for him to answer. "You're suggesting an old friend of yours could be guilty of some serious crimes, and you're apparently willing to do the same for your soon-to-be wife."

"If they're guilty, I want them to pay."

"Yeah," Bo grumbled. "And if they're arrested, then the guilt isn't on you."

"Believe what you will," Kendall said softly. He opened the door and started to leave.

But instead he practically ran into Cicely.

The woman looked as startled as Kendall did. But Bo saw something else in the depths of her eyes. She was angry. Had she heard Kendall's accusations?

"Why are you here?" Kendall asked Cicely.

"Because I love you. Because I was worried about you."

He didn't respond to that. He merely kissed her cheek. It was as chaste as the look he gave her. "I have an appointment. I'll see you at lunch." With that, he strolled away.

But Cicely didn't budge. "Did you agree to have your daughter tested for the bone marrow match?"

"No," Mattie answered.

"No?" It seemed as if all the breath left Cicely's body. "But why not? How could you have turned down Kendall at a time like this?"

"Kendall didn't ask," Bo informed her. And even if he had, the answer probably would have been no.

"He didn't?" Cicely was obviously dumbfounded. "He was supposed to ask." She shook her head. "But you'll agree to do it, right?"

"Bo and I will have to give that some thought," Mattie insisted.

"Thought? What's there to think about? You have a chance to save him, Mattie. You can't refuse. He's your own flesh and blood."

"He might have killed Brody," Mattie reminded her.

Cicely opened her mouth as if to vehemently deny that, but she closed it. She stood there for several long moments, apparently trying to figure out what argument she could give that would make Mattie change her mind.

"Don't you dare ruin my one chance at happiness," Cicely finally said, her voice clogged with emotion and with tears in her eyes.

Bo stepped closer, and he made sure the scowl on his face was a good one. "Is that a threat?"

Oh, Cicely clearly wanted to say that it was. But she was too smart for that. "No threat," she finally said.

Cicely reached into her purse and pulled out a business card, which she handed to Mattie. "Call me if you change your mind. Oh, and there's this…" She pulled out a small black jeweler's box that she gave Mattie, as well.

Mattie opened the box and Bo saw the diamond ring inside. Mattie shook her head. "What is this?"

"Ian found it in Brody's desk after he was killed. Apparently, Brody planned to give it to you."

"Oh." And that was all Mattie said.

Cicely shrugged. "I didn't think it was a good idea to give it to you, but Ian disagreed."

Mattie eased it into her pocket. "Thanks." And

judging from her expression, she wasn't sure if it had been a good idea. It had definitely brought back some memories, and he could see the proof of that in her suddenly sad eyes.

"Think about having the test done," Cicely insisted. She walked away, hurrying in the direction where they'd last seen Kendall.

"Are you okay?" Bo asked Mattie.

She paused a moment. "I'm fine. The ring was just a surprise. When Brody proposed, he didn't have a ring yet. He said we would pick it out together, so I didn't know he'd even bought one." If she wanted to add anything to that, she dismissed it by clearing her throat and tipping her head to an exiting Cicely. "After conversations like the one we just had with her, I don't think we're any closer to the truth than we were when all of this started."

"Maybe." Bo waited for her to bring up the ring again. She didn't. So he decided to move on. "But we do have a lot of facts. Somewhere in all of that, there's the truth." But he was certainly beginning to suspect Cicely more and more. "Any reason Cicely would have been the one to have your fiancé killed?"

"Not directly." Now she paused. "But if she thought she was protecting Kendall…"

No need to finish that, because Bo was convinced that Cicely would do anything for Kendall. After all, she probably got pregnant to give him a possible bone marrow donor.

"I need to do the interview with Tolivar," he reminded her. "You can watch from the observation room and just text me if you have any questions."

They headed in that direction, but before they made it there, Bo saw his captain and Tolivar making their way up the hall toward him.

"There's been a change of plans," the captain volunteered, and judging from his sour expression, this wasn't a good change for them.

Like his expression, Tolivar's stare was cold and hard. "My rep advised me to speak with my boss before I answer any of your questions."

Mattie huffed, and that was exactly how Bo felt. However, he didn't direct his comments to Tolivar but to his captain. "He shot and killed a man here in the city. It's our jurisdiction, and he should have to answer questions."

"Normally," the captain snarled.

"What the captain means is that Terrance Arturo was a suspect in a federal investigation. I was in pursuit of him when he took those shots at you. When he ran, I went after him. He turned, tried to kill me, so I took him out. Just as I'm trained to do."

"Yeah. But in doing so, you took out an assassin that someone had hired. By killing him you prevented us from learning the identity of his boss."

"I also saved him from coming after you again," Tolivar said directly to Mattie.

She nodded. "I'm grateful for that, but by killing Arturo the danger didn't end for me."

"No," Tolivar agreed. "And that's why I wanted you back in my custody." His expression turned even harder. "But you've made your bed. Now you can sleep in it."

When the marshal started to walk away, Bo caught on to his arm. "What the hell does that mean?"

"It means I don't give a rat's you know what about Mattie, you or your situation. I was just trying to do my job, and look where the hell it got me." He threw off Bo's grip and walked away.

"What did he mean by that?" Mattie asked.

"Tolivar was suspended about a half hour ago," the captain explained.

"For shooting Arturo?" Bo wanted to know.

The captain shook his head. "We're not sure, and the Justice Department isn't talking. I'm thinking they want to pull him in because he botched this case."

Hell. Bo hoped that didn't mean some kind of cover-up. He wanted details about why Tolivar had been right there when Arturo launched that attack.

"Do we have any surveillance footage of the shootout between Arturo and the marshal?" Bo asked.

"We're working on it. If we get it and if it shows Tolivar acted improperly when he killed Arturo, then somehow I'll haul his butt back in here."

Well, that was a start. "What do we do about Tolivar in the meantime?"

"Stay out of his path," the captain warned. "And watch your backs, because I wouldn't be surprised if Tolivar tried to get some revenge."

Chapter Fourteen

Mattie winced when the lightning shot through the sky. The storm had finally rolled in around midnight, and it wasn't showing any signs of letting up.

The thunder came, a low rumbling growl, and the rain pelted against the windowpanes. Thankfully, those were the only noises she heard. The safe house was quiet, and despite the storm, the children were sleeping. Rosalie had insisted on staying the night with them in the nursery, and even though Mattie had volunteered, as well, Bo had convinced her she should get some rest.

Right.

She was exhausted, and she'd managed to doze a little. Cat naps. If she could get her brain to settle down, she might get some honest-to-goodness sleep. But her thoughts kept going back to the danger. To the engagement ring she'd tucked into the dresser drawer. To the whole custody issue with Holly.

And to Bo.

Especially Bo.

There was another jolt of lightning, and Mattie resisted the urge to pull the covers over her head. That's what she would have done when she was a kid, but tonight she was already too warm, as if her skin were too tight. She recognized the feeling.

It was a pull, deep inside her. Probably some primitive response, she reasoned.

But the bottom line was she wanted Bo.

He was just next door, one room over, and she wanted to go to him. To climb into his bed with him. And do exactly what her body wanted her to do.

Mattie could only imagine what it would be like to be taken by a man like Bo. He always seemed right on the edge between danger and reason. Between being out of control and taking control.

What would it be like to have him inside her?

Moving, taking and not asking permission for whatever he chose to do to her?

Mattie could almost feel it, and it took the breath right out of her. She pressed her arms over her breasts, trying to stop the tingling that was making its way all over her body.

She saw movement through the open doorway of her room. Heard the footsteps. And then saw Bo. He was naked. Well, almost. He wore a pair of loose boxers that rode low on his hips. And he was aroused.

The boxers didn't hide that.

Was she just dreaming? Mattie was afraid so. She wanted to reach out and touch him, but he would no doubt disappear. So instead of trying to touch and losing the moment, she took her time, savoring the sight of him.

Outside the window another bolt of lightning slashed through the night and sent a spray of light over Bo's body. He was like something out of a fantasy.

All man and muscle.

His chest strong and welcoming. His face set in that expression she'd come to know so well. He looked ready to devour her.

Mattie smiled, still sleepy but now very alert. And very hot. "Are you here to devour me?" she asked, chuckling.

"If that's what you want," he drawled. He dropped his cell phone on the nightstand.

She froze. That didn't sound like a dream response. That sounded like the real thing.

Mercy.

If he was real, then no one deserved to look that good.

He stared at her, his eyes narrowing slightly. "I thought you'd be scared."

"I was." She swallowed hard. Not because she was afraid of the storm or what he might do next. Mattie was afraid he might go away.

But he didn't.

Bo reached down and jerked back the covers. She still had her hand on her breasts and probably looked like she was groping herself. However, she didn't have time to dwell on that. He moved forward, putting his knee on the bed. The mattress shifted with his weight, turning her toward him.

He leaned down, his mouth hovering over hers. His breath kissing her. He shoved aside her hand and put his own palm on her breast. "This is the only time I'll ask this—do you want me to leave?"

"No." She couldn't answer fast enough.

She reached for him, but Bo beat her to it.

His mouth came to hers, but not with the hard pressure she'd expected. No. He was almost gentle. Almost. His mouth barely touched, and it was the same with his tongue. But there was nothing gentle about his body. His muscles were all corded as if he were fighting a fierce battle with himself.

With that same surprising gentleness, he moved the kisses to her cheek. To her neck. And then to her breasts, kissing her through the flimsy fabric of her cotton gown. Each touch of his mouth jabbed at the ache in the center of her body. Each time he ran his tongue over her nipples, the ache pierced through her until she arched her hips, looking for some kind of relief.

He cursed when she brushed against his erection.

Bo stared at her, his eyes hot and burning now. He grabbed her gown and pulled it over her head, sending it flying to the floor. He cursed again when he saw her panties and quickly rid her of those, too. He stripped them off her legs, but in the same motion he lowered his head and kissed her right in the center of all that heat.

Now Mattie cursed.

And when she arched her back, it wasn't to seek relief. This wasn't relief. His mouth was torture, and it nearly sent her straight to a climax.

She didn't want this to end so soon. She wanted it to last all night, but she would settle for at least a few more minutes. That wouldn't happen if he continued to kiss her there.

Mattie gripped his shoulders, pulling him up to her. More torture. Both of them were misted with sweat, and it created some sweet friction, with his firm male body sliding against hers.

"Could we do this now?" she asked, but it wasn't really a question. She fought to get his boxers off and then tried to position her body so that she could take him inside her.

But Bo had his own positioning ideas. He kissed her hard and rough this time. Just the way she wanted. The gentle foreplay had been nice, but she didn't want nice now. She wanted this hot alpha cop that she'd been lusting after for days.

Bo didn't disappoint. He latched on to her right leg, hooking it around his back. He did the same with her left one, and that put his hard sex right against hers.

Yes! Talk about living out a fantasy.

He kept kissing her, kept pressing his chest against her. And then he went inside her in one long stroke that filled her until she thought she might scream. She wasn't a screamer, but she might make an exception for this.

Her breath was gone, so she couldn't tell him how good it felt. She couldn't tell him that she was on fire. But Bo apparently knew that, because he moved in her, sliding against the right place to make that fire turn into an inferno.

Mattie fought to hang on, but the heat was too much. The need was too much.

And Bo knew exactly what he was doing.

He drove inside her, over and over again. So it didn't take much. A few of those strokes. Another kiss. And Mattie felt the gold light explode inside her head. Maybe it was the lightning. She doubted it, though. That gold light was from Bo. And she latched on to it. She latched on to him.

And she let herself shatter.

HELL.

That one word kept repeating through Bo's mind. He was in trouble.

Being with Mattie had been far better than his expectations, and he'd expected something pretty damn amazing.

Because his body wasn't on fire right now and had just been sated, he wanted to dismiss this visit to her bed as bad judgment. He could have even lumped it together as a reaction to all the stress they'd been under.

Yeah. "Stress sex." Good name for it.

Hell.

He wasn't even sure it'd been just sex. It felt a lot more like making love, and that caused him to mentally curse again. He knew better than to get involved with Mattie. She already had too much to deal with, and now he'd added himself to the things she had to work out. Because she was no doubt trying to put this in its proper place just as he was doing.

He braced himself for the talk. The one where she would make him feel like dirt for adding this wrinkle to her life.

But she didn't say a word.

Mattie made a sound of sleepy pleasure, a sort of low feminine moan, and her eyes drifted closed.

She fell asleep.

Bo stared at her, watching her face, waiting. But after a few minutes, it was clear she wasn't in the mood for talking.

Relieved, and a little confused, he rolled off her so his weight wouldn't crush her. Without opening her eyes, she adjusted, wiggling her body against him until she was on her side facing him, her breasts squished against his chest.

She made another of those sounds of sleepy pleasure.

Maybe because she was thinking about her late fiancé?

That put a scowl on his face. Because he sure hadn't been thinking about Nadine when he'd been inside Mattie.

He was right back to mumbling *hell* again.

Bo pushed her hair from her face and brushed a goodnight kiss off her forehead.

"Bo," she mumbled, using the same tone as her sleepy pleasure sounds.

The way she said his name, it went through him like a shot of expensive whiskey. Smooth and warm. It made him want to take her all over again. And he might have done just that.

If his phone hadn't beeped.

He had changed the ring tone so it wouldn't wake everyone if he got a midnight call. And that's apparently what he'd gotten.

Bo reached over, retrieved his phone and checked the caller ID screen. It was Sergeant O'Malley and therefore a call he had to take.

He got out of the bed, moving away from Mattie's warm body. His own body protested the loss right away, and he promised himself he would go back to her when he finished.

"Don't give me bad news," Bo whispered to the sergeant. He went into the adjoining bathroom so he could talk.

"Not this time. We just got a call from a tech over in

the Justice Department. Because of the nonstop attempts to kill Mattie, they've been working night and day to see if they can figure out who hacked into the Witness Protection database."

"And?" Bo asked.

"And we have a winner. It's Terrance Arturo."

Arturo. A dead guy who used to work for Kaplan and Collier. "Is there proof?"

"Just some notes found in Arturo's apartment. Don't worry. We'll keep digging. The captain's here, and he just brought in Collier, Cicely Carr and Kaplan for questioning. Tolivar's boss has agreed to bring him, as well."

Since it was midnight, he was betting all of them were especially riled with the timing and the subject of this interrogation. "I'll get dressed and get down there."

"No. The captain says for you to stay put. But he thinks by morning, he'll know who was behind the attempts to kill Mattie and you."

Chapter Fifteen

The voices and sounds woke her.

Mattie's eyes flew open, and she was stunned to see that it was daylight. The rain was still spattering against the windows, but there was no hint of lightning or thunder. The worst of the storm had passed.

She glanced at the clock and couldn't believe the time. It was 8:00 a.m., and even though that was still early to a lot of people, it obviously wasn't for Jacob and Holly, because it was their voices she was hearing.

Mercy, she hadn't expected to sleep at all, much less for eight straight hours.

She threw back the cover and caught Bo's scent still on the sheets. On her, too. It made her feel all warm and golden again. But then she sighed. Yes, it was great sex, but Bo was probably having trouble coming to terms with it. Mattie was surprised to realize that she wasn't having doubts or issues. It was crystal clear to her.

She cared deeply for Bo and wanted him in her life.

However, working that out was an entirely different matter. Bo might not be ready for an emotional entanglement, especially since he already had enough entanglements in his life.

She took a quick shower and dressed in another of the loaner outfits that she grabbed from the closet—a dark red cotton dress and a pair of black flats. Mattie slapped on some makeup and tried not to think about how awkward it would be to face Bo. She only thought about facing Jacob and Holly and hoped she wasn't too late to share breakfast with them.

Mattie hurried into the kitchen and came to a stop. Bo was at the stove cooking, his back to her, and he had his phone anchored between his ear and shoulder. Rosalie was wrestling with Jacob, trying to get him strapped into the high chair. Holly was already in her chair, and the little girl gave Mattie a bright smile.

These were the things she'd dreamed of seeing for the past thirteen months, and here was her baby, right in front of her.

Jacob smiled, too, when he saw her and quit struggling with Rosalie, who quickly put him in the chair.

"Sorry about all the noise," Rosalie said, "I was trying to keep them quiet."

"I'm glad they woke me." Mattie wouldn't have wanted to miss this for the world. She went closer and helped Rosalie put some dry cereal bits on the trays. Mattie knew this part of the routine. The kids would eat the cereal while Bo prepared a hot breakfast. This morning, it was oatmeal. Bo was stirring a pot of it on the stove as he added some brown sugar.

"He's been on that phone since the kids got up," Rosalie remarked, dishing up some of the oatmeal into two different bowls.

The nanny handed Mattie one of them after adding

some milk to cool it down. Apparently, she was going to get to feed her daughter this morning.

But Mattie gave some of her attention to Bo. She couldn't tell who he was talking to, but judging from his stiff body language, it was about the investigation.

Mattie pulled up a chair and gave Holly the first spoonful of oatmeal. Most of it made it into her mouth. However, Holly took part of that bite into her hand and squished it around her fingers.

All right. So breakfast would be messy. But fun. Holly babbled with each bite and even offered Mattie some from her fingers. Mattie gladly sampled it and then did the same for Jacob, who obviously wanted to be included.

She loved them both so much and wondered just how much it would break her heart if she couldn't have all of them—Bo, Holly, Jacob and even Rosalie—in her life.

Bo ended the call, closing the phone and shoving it into his pocket. He looked ready for work in his black pants and white dress shirt. He'd even shaved, making her wonder if he'd gotten any sleep whatsoever.

"Sorry I didn't get up sooner," she said to him. She'd been right about the awkward part. "I slept like a rock."

He smiled a little, just enough to ease some of her anxiety and to renew the heat that always flared whenever she was around him.

"That was my captain on the phone," he explained, the smile fading. "When they searched Arturo's apartment, they found notes that indicate he's the one who hacked into the database of the Witness Protection Program."

She tried not to react, because Holly was only inches away, but it was impossible to keep her emotions totally in check. Arturo. He had been the one who had started the spiral of danger that had ultimately caused her to leave Holly in the hospital with Nadine.

"Any idea why he outed my location and identity?" Mattie asked.

Obviously sensing the seriousness of the conversation, Rosalie took over feeding duties, and Mattie stood so she could face Bo.

"Arturo probably did it for money. There's about twenty thousand dollars of unaccounted funds in his bank account."

So, for twenty grand he had compromised the lives of her and Holly. If he weren't already dead, Mattie would have gone after him for that. Of course, that left her with the big question. "Who paid him?"

Bo shook his head. "Still trying to figure that out. Detectives have been going through his apartment all night, and they found a key that appears to be to a safety deposit box. They're trying to figure out now where the box is located so they can get into it."

Good. Because maybe there was proof of his boss's identity, and that meant Bo could soon make an arrest.

"The captain had Kendall, Cicely and Ian all in for questioning," Bo added.

"During the night?"

"Most of the night," he clarified. "He just released them about a half hour ago."

Well, Mattie would hear about it, that was for certain. They were all probably fuming, especially since none of them thought the police had a right to consider them suspects. "What about Marshal Tolivar? Did the captain manage to question him, too?"

"Not yet. But he's having a meeting first thing this morning with Tolivar's boss."

More good news, because maybe they would finally get the truth about the marshal. "So we have to go back to headquarters?" Mattie asked.

"Not just yet. I thought you deserved a quiet morning."

Holly chose that moment to let out a squeal when she couldn't get a glob of oatmeal out of her hair.

"Time for baths," Rosalie announced. She put the oatmeal bowls aside, and Bo helped her get the children out of the high chairs.

"Need help?" Mattie asked the nanny.

"No thanks. Bo and you probably have some things to discuss anyway." Rosalie smiled in such a way that Mattie wondered if the woman knew what had happened between them last night.

Rosalie carried the babies out, one snuggled in each arm, and just like that, the kitchen went from being very noisy to totally silent. Since Mattie wasn't sure what to say, she settled for pouring herself a glass of orange juice and sitting on one of the bar stools at the counter. Bo poured himself some coffee.

And the silence continued.

"Sorry I fell asleep on you last night," she mumbled.

More silence. And then he walked toward her and

dropped a kiss on her lips. "Actually, I was the one on you." He smiled, and that made everything instantly better.

"I was worried about you," she admitted. "I wasn't sure how you'd handle the after part."

"I wasn't sure, either," Bo admitted. "But I decided—"

His phone rang, and both of them cursed under their breath. He glanced at the caller ID screen before he answered. "O'Malley," he greeted.

Mattie figured this call was important, but she hated that the sergeant hadn't waited several more seconds so she could have heard what Bo was about to say.

"He did what?" Bo asked, his voice suddenly as intense as his expression. "Why?"

Mattie couldn't hear a word of what the sergeant was saying, but she wasn't getting a good feeling about this. Mercy. What was going on now?

"Does the search warrant cover that?" Bo asked, and a moment later he huffed. "All right." He paused. "I'd rather not do it that way, though."

Bo met Mattie's gaze, and she could tell he was trying to reassure her, but it wasn't working.

"Let's go with Plan B," Bo continued, still talking to O'Malley. "Yeah, that with heavy security. Oh, and you said she'll need a photo ID that the bank officials will verify with their security service. No fakes. This needs to be a real ID in case it has to stand up in court. No repeats of what happened with the federal investigation into Collier's case. Someone needs to print her another copy of her driver's license."

It was impossible to tell exactly what was going on

from just hearing Bo's side of the conversation. Were they talking about her?

"Okay. That sounds good," Bo finally said to O'Malley. "We'll leave just as soon as an officer arrives to stay here with the kids."

She set her juice aside. "What's wrong?" Mattie asked when he ended the call.

Bo scrubbed his hand over his face. "The key they found in Arturo's apartment was indeed for a safety deposit box at a bank downtown."

"And the search warrant doesn't allow you to search that deposit box?" She'd been able to gather that much from what she'd heard.

"No. It's a foreign bank, and they're insisting the search warrant isn't valid because there are two names on the account. Arturo's and yours."

Mattie was so glad she wasn't holding the juice glass, or she would have dropped it. "Mine? Why would Arturo put my name on his deposit box?"

Bo shook his head. "We might not know that until we get a look at what's in that box. This bank's going to stonewall a search warrant for hours, but you should be able to get into the box right away."

She was already getting to her feet, but she was also trying to figure out why this had happened. "How soon will the officer be here?"

"He's already out front. We had a car patrolling all night, so he was just up the block." Bo walked around the counter. "I'll tell Rosalie what's going on."

Mattie followed him so she could say goodbye to the children. Hopefully, this wouldn't be a long trip, and maybe, just maybe, there was something in that safety deposit box to tell them who was trying to kill them.

Of course, they could get more than that. Mattie remembered what had happened the last time they were downtown.

Arturo had tried to kill them.

She and Bo kissed the children and headed out to the garage once Bo let the other officer inside. Mattie didn't voice her concern until they were in the car.

"What if this is a trap?" she asked. "What if Arturo set it up so that if he were killed, then this would draw me out in the open?"

"I thought of that. That's why we're going with Plan B. We'll send in a female detective wearing a hat and dark glasses. I'll be with her. The idea is if anyone is watching, they'll think it's you."

"And where will I be?"

"Safe with two detectives in the building next door to the bank. If all goes well, then we'll take you into the bank so you can get into that box."

"With my newly printed driver's license?" she questioned.

"Yeah. No repeats of what happened with Kendall. Evidence that would have convicted him was thrown out because the FBI didn't execute a proper search of his office and files. I want to be able to use anything incriminating in that box to make an arrest and to prosecute this SOB."

Mattie couldn't agree more. She nodded. "Let's do this."

Bo nodded, too, but he didn't move. He sat there, looking at her. And then he leaned over and kissed her.

It was smooth and gentle. Probably for reassurance. But Bo's kisses only reassured her that she wanted him. They did the opposite of calming her down.

"Hold that thought," he mumbled against her lips. "And tonight, I want you to come to my bed."

Like the kiss, that invitation warmed her to the bone. So, it wouldn't be just a one-night stand between them, but Mattie didn't want to think beyond that. One step at a time.

Without taking his eyes off her, Bo started the engine, and he pressed the remote control on the visor to open the garage door. Mattie braced herself for another kiss, another assault on her senses. She wasn't, however, prepared for her door to fly open.

It happened so fast, she didn't have time to think or react.

Something came flying at her. A canister of some kind.

And it exploded.

Chapter Sixteen

Bo caught just a glimpse of the person dressed all in black, and in that glimpse he saw the silver canister that the guy hurled into the car.

That glimpse was all Bo got.

Something began to spew from the can, and it created an instant fog. Bo's eyes watered to the point that he couldn't see, and he began to cough uncontrollably. Tear gas.

Beside him, he heard Mattie coughing, as well. And struggling. She seemed to be fighting something, though Bo couldn't tell what. He drew his gun and reached for her, trying to pull her closer so he could try to protect her. What he couldn't do was shoot, because he had no idea where to aim. For all practical purposes, he was blind.

Bo blinked hard, trying to focus, and he used his left hand to open his door. The garage door was already open, and he was hoping the ventilation and the falling rain would clear out the tear gas. But it wouldn't happen immediately. And that meant he somehow had to get Mattie out of there.

Still coughing and unable to catch his breath, Bo

latched on to Mattie's arm and pulled hard, trying to yank her out on his side of the car. It didn't work, and Bo knew why.

Someone was trying to pull her out the other side.

Bo hadn't seen the person, probably because the guy had stayed low and slipped in the moment Bo opened the garage door. Of course, it hadn't helped that Bo had also been kissing Mattie, and that had given this SOB the time to launch an attack.

Later, Bo would curse himself for the lapse in judgment. But for now, he had to save Mattie. He also had to pray there was just one attacker. Because if there were others, he might not be able to stop this.

Whatever *this* was.

If it were an assassination attempt, then why hadn't the guy just shot them when he had the chance? Why not just shoot now? That was yet something else he'd have to figure out later.

Bo pulled harder, trying to drag Mattie toward him. She still didn't budge, but he heard her gasping for air and struggling. She was fighting the guy, but like Bo, she probably couldn't see a thing, and without air in her lungs, her fight would be weak at best.

Bo considered yelling out to the officer inside, but that was too big a risk to take. This could all be a ruse to get inside the safe house so that someone could kidnap Holly. Bo couldn't take that risk, and he knew without a doubt that Mattie wouldn't want him to take it, either.

Since this tug-of-war wasn't working, Bo stumbled from the car and tried to pull in as much fresh air as he could. The tear gas had created a thick, misty fog in the car itself, but it wasn't confined just to the car.

It was all around, making him wonder if their attacker had opened another canister on the garage floor. If so, this had been a well-planned attack. But it left him with one nasty question.

How had this person found the location of the safe house?

Bo had locked the door that led from the garage into the house. He was sure of that. He was also sure that the officer would have reset the security alarm. But alarms weren't going to help them if this guy decided to get inside the house.

Bo somehow managed to stay on his feet, though each breath and each step were a struggle. Still, he didn't give up. He had to get to the other side of the car so he could help Mattie.

He made it to the back of the car, using the vehicle itself to help support his weight. Without it, he would have dropped to his knees and given in to the coughing fit.

Bo tried to shout out a warning, but that failed, too, so he lifted his gun and took aim at the dark figure that was trying to drag Mattie out of the car. When there was a break in the mist, Bo saw something else.

The guy was wearing a military-style gas mask.

"Stop!" Bo finally managed to say.

But the person didn't. Their attacker grabbed Mattie's hair and pulled her partially out. In the same motion, he put a gun to her head.

Mattie was still struggling, still trying to say something, and pulling back. She was trying to get away from the person with the gun. But Bo only concentrated on the guy wearing the gas mask. It could be Tolivar, Ian or Kendall. Hell, it could even be Cicely.

Or a hired gun.

Whatever the case, this situation was as dangerous as it got, because the person was using Mattie as a human shield.

"Let her go," Bo tried to say.

The guy clearly had no intention of doing that. Bo expected him to try to run.

He didn't.

With the gun still pressed to Mattie's head, the guy said something to her. Something that Bo couldn't hear, but whatever it was, just like that, she stopped struggling.

Hell. What was going on?

That question didn't stay unanswered for long. Because the guy crawled over Mattie.

"Stop!" Bo yelled again.

But it didn't do any good. The guy got behind the wheel and threw the car into Reverse.

He came right at Bo.

Bo had to dive, fast, out of the way, so he wouldn't be run over. He hit the concrete floor hard, landing on his shoulder. The pain shot through him, but he somehow managed to hang on to his gun.

For all the good it would do.

He still didn't have a clean shot.

With the tires squealing and kicking up smoke, the gunman peeled out of the garage and driveway. He was getting away.

With Mattie.

Bo's eyes were still watering, so he couldn't see

clearly, but he took aim at the rear tire. The blast would no doubt alert everyone inside, and he prayed the officer would keep everything locked up and secure.

Bo fired, and the bullet ripped through the tire. But it was too little, too late.

Because the driver gunned the engine and sped away despite the flat tire.

He tried to blink away the rain and the remnants of the tear gas, and he started running. Somehow he had to get Mattie out of that vehicle. God knows what this man was planning to do to her.

Bo fired another shot at the other rear tire. This time, the bullet hit the rim. He saw the spark of metal against metal, and Bo's heart went to his knees.

The gunman just kept on going, quickly eating up the distance between Mattie and him. Bo saw her terrified expression before the car disappeared around the corner.

MATTIE COULDN'T CATCH her breath, and she felt on the verge of a panic attack. The tear gas or whatever had been in that canister was responsible, but she knew she had to fight off the effects or she was going to die.

She caught a glimpse of Bo in the mirror and watched as he fired another shot. He was aiming for the car's tires, she was sure of that. But even though at least one tire seemed to be damaged, the driver wasn't stopping.

Mattie reached for the door handle. Her captor was driving fast, and the car was shaking from the now-flat tire, but she couldn't wait and hope that he would slow down. She had to get out of there now before he managed to get her away from Bo and the safe house.

"Move and I'll shoot," the man growled. She heard him but didn't recognize his voice. Of course, he could be disguising it. "If I have to kill you, I'll go back for your kid."

Mattie froze. She couldn't stop herself from reacting to that threat. Maybe because her adrenaline and anxiety levels were through the roof. Logically, she knew that Bo would do whatever it took to keep this goon from getting anywhere near Holly.

But Bo could die trying to protect her daughter.

She'd caught a final glimpse of Bo before the gunman sped away. He looked enraged. Mattie was furious, too. How had this man gotten close enough to kidnap her in broad daylight?

Her head was pounding now, and the sound of the tire slapping against the asphalt didn't help. She needed to think clearly, but instead she was a mess. Her eyes and throat were on fire, and she couldn't pull in a decent breath.

"Who are you?" she asked, but even saying just those few words caused her to cough almost uncontrollably.

"That's not your concern. Right now, the only thing you have to do is sit there and shut up."

No. She needed to do a lot more than that. Bo would try to come for her, Mattie was certain of that, but she couldn't count on him or anyone else reaching her in time. She had to save herself.

"Where are you taking me?" she demanded. Mattie looked all around her to see if there was anything inside the vehicle that she could grab and use as a weapon.

Her purse was on the floor. She might be able to hit him with it.

"I said shut up," he snarled.

He ripped off his gas mask and tossed it onto the back seat. Mattie got a good look at him then. He had dark brown hair and eyes.

And he was a stranger.

He'd been hired to kidnap her. Maybe even to kill her.

Mattie's heart sank. If this had been Kendall, Ian or Cicely, she could perhaps reason with them. Perhaps even with Tolivar. But how did you reason with a man who was likely doing this for money?

"Whatever you're being paid, I can pay you more," she tried.

The man jammed the gun against her head. "I said shut up."

So much for her attempt to bribe him. Mattie cleared her throat after another round of coughing and kept watch, waiting for a chance to escape.

He drove out of the subdivision and took a right on the main highway. She knew it would eventually lead them to the interstate, where there'd be lots of traffic. Certainly someone would see the gun pointed at her head or the flat tire and report it to the cops. There was also the fact that they were in an unmarked police car.

It probably had GPS tracking.

The relief flooded through her. Bo would be able to find her. But she still wasn't giving up on her own attempts to escape. She would just need to wait until the driver was distracted. A few seconds was all she needed. And she could open the door and jump out. He would fire at her, of course, so that meant she had to pray that she wasn't injured in the fall. She would need to be able to run.

Each second that he drove clicked off in her head, and she finally saw the sign for the interstate.

But he didn't take it.

The gunman drove right past it and took a right turn. He drove about a mile before he came to a stop behind a dark blue truck. This wasn't a residential area but rather a street lined with warehouses that were spaced far apart. There wasn't another person in sight.

He turned to her and jammed the gun even harder against her head. "I'm only going to say this one time. Cooperate or you die. I get paid whether I deliver you dead or alive."

Mattie had no idea if that were true, but if his boss didn't mind her dead, then why hadn't he just killed her in the garage? He certainly had had the element of surprise and could have fired a couple of shots before she even knew what hit her.

So, who wanted to keep her alive?

And why?

"Come on," the gunman insisted. "We're getting in that truck."

Oh, God. If he managed to get her in that vehicle, then there might not be any way for Bo and the cops to track where he was taking her.

"I said come on," he growled.

He latched on to her hair again and dragged her across the seat toward him. The pain shot through her. So did the fear. He was a lot bigger than she was. Stronger, too. Plus, he had a gun, and she didn't. But Mattie knew she couldn't give in to that fear.

She had to do something now.

She'd had some martial arts training when she became a P.I., and she would rely on that. She prayed it would be enough. If she could just get away and run back to the main highway, someone would be able to help her.

With the gunman still pulling at her, Mattie went limp.

Because he had hold of her and because he was so strong, she went flying at him. Mattie lowered her head and aimed for his chest. She rammed into him, sending them both crashing to the rain-slick pavement.

She tried to get up, but he used his strength to keep her pinned to the ground.

"Stop it," he growled right against her ear. "Or I make one phone call. Just one. And a sniper will start shooting in the safe house. He won't stop until he's killed everyone inside. Got that?"

Mattie stopped struggling. Yes, she wanted to live. She wanted to raise her daughter, but she couldn't risk Holly, Jacob and Rosalie's safety so that she could live. That's the reason she had walked away from the hospital thirteen months ago. She hadn't waited this long only to put her baby right back in danger.

"That's more like it." He got up and jerked her to her feet.

The rain whipped at them. It was coming down harder now, and she hoped that would slow him down a little.

It didn't.

He didn't waste any time. With a firm grip on her, he

hurried to the truck. It was unlocked, so he opened the door and crammed her inside. The moment he was in, he pressed the button to engage the locks. That's when Mattie noticed she didn't even have a lock on her side of the truck. The lock button and the door handle itself had been ripped off.

She was trapped.

The gunman started the engine and jammed his foot on the accelerator. The truck bolted forward, the tires digging into the mud on the soft shoulder. But that barely slowed him down. He raced down the side street and past the warehouses.

Mattie watched the side mirror as they sped away. When the unmarked car was no longer in sight, she knew her chances for rescue had just gone from slim to none.

Chapter Seventeen

The wipers slashed across the windshield, clearing the rain that was coming down hard now, but it wasn't clearing it fast enough for Bo. He needed to hurry, and the rain and slick roads were slowing him down.

So was the GPS tracker.

He was getting the tracking feed from a computer at headquarters, and it was being transmitted to his phone. But it seemed to be moving at a snail's pace. The red blip on the screen was cruising along, only to disappear for a few seconds. When it popped back up, it was blocks ahead of where he'd been on the previous image. If the transmission had a delay at the wrong time, he might miss a turn and have to double back.

His heart was pounding hard enough to hurt his ribs. The tear gas was still giving his eyes and throat some problems. But those were all minor annoyances. The only thing that mattered now was getting to Mattie in time.

From the moment he'd seen the gas-masked goon driving off with her, Bo had had a split-second debate with himself. Part of him wanted to rush after Mattie, but he also knew he had to keep the children safe. He couldn't be sure this wasn't a trick to draw him away from the house. That's why he'd taken the time to call for other officers, not for his own backup, but he wanted a team of detectives guarding the house. When he was certain they were on their way and only minutes out, he'd jumped into the officer's unmarked patrol car and sped after the gunman and Mattie.

He had to get to her in time.

God knows what this kidnapper had in mind, but Bo didn't think the outcome would be good for Mattie.

Was Kendall or Ian behind this? Or Cicely? Maybe they planned to hold Mattie captive so that she would agree to have Holly tested as a bone marrow donor. That seemed extreme, but these were people who had dealt in extremes before.

Bo cursed when the blip disappeared again. His chest was pumping now, and every nerve inside him was primed and ready for a fight. What he needed was his opponent, and for that to happen he had to see where the gunman was taking Mattie.

The red blip jumped back onto the screen, and Bo saw the getaway car's turn. Hell. He had to slam on his brakes and then hope like the devil that he didn't go into a skid. He'd be of no help to Mattie if he crashed. He took the turn on what had to be two wheels, and fought with the steering wheel to regain control.

Then his phone rang.

That cut the tracking feed images.

He saw the captain's number appear on the screen, but Bo only wanted it to go away so he could get back to finding the car.

"I need you off the line," Bo said, answering the call.

"I know. Because you're getting the GPS coordinates. But I can give them to you while I see if I can talk you into waiting for backup."

"Not a chance. I'm finding Mattie."

"That's what I figured you'd say, but I had to try. Keep going straight. The car's just ahead." The captain paused. "It's not moving, Bo."

That nearly knocked the breath right out of him. If the car wasn't moving, that meant God knows what could be happening to Mattie.

The gunman could be trying to kill her.

Bo slammed his foot on the accelerator and spotted the car on the side of the road. He tried to see what was going on inside, but the rain made that impossible. He pulled up behind the car, slamming on his brakes, and he jumped out before his vehicle even stopped moving.

He drew his gun, took aim and approached the car.

His heart dropped.

Because the car was empty.

Empty!

He hurried back to grab his cell phone. "She's not here. No one is." Bo glanced around at all the warehouses. There were dozens of them, and the gunman could have taken her in any one of them.

Except why would he park back here, a good twenty yards from the nearest one? Why not just park closer?

"I have officers on the way there to look for her," the captain told Bo.

Bo heard him but didn't respond. That's because something caught his attention. Something off on the shoulder of the road, dug into the mud.

Tire tracks.

And they were very recent, because the rain hadn't washed them away yet.

The gunman had ditched the unmarked car and moved her to another vehicle. Bo cursed. There was no way to follow her now.

Or was there?

The road was just two lanes and fairly narrow, so he hurried to the other side. No tracks there, which meant the gunman hadn't made a U-turn and gone back out to the highway. He'd driven straight ahead.

"Get the officers out to Industrial Road," Bo told the captain. He raced back to his car, got inside and gunned the engine. "And see if you can get any kind of surveillance feed from one of these warehouses. Based on those tire tracks, I think we're looking for a heavy vehicle, probably an SUV or truck."

"We're on the way," the captain assured him. "But we'll do a silent approach. All unmarked cars. We don't want this guy panicking."

Neither did Bo. Because that was the fastest way to get Mattie killed.

"Where does this road lead?" Bo asked.

"Nowhere. It's a dead end. But there are two smaller roads that feed off it. One is about a half mile up on your right. The other, about a mile to your left. The one on the right just leads to more warehouses, but the one on the left will take you back to the highway."

And the gunman could be on either.

If Mattie's attacker planned to kill her right away or hand her over to someone else, that could happen in one of the more remote warehouses. However, if he wanted to get her out of the area, then he would head back to the highway because that in turn would take him to the interstate. If the gunman made it that far, it would be next to impossible to find Mattie.

Bo shoved his phone in his pocket so he could concentrate on the drive and so he could keep his gun ready. He flew past the warehouses, taking notice of each of the parking lots. There were some semis, but he was pretty sure he wasn't looking for that type of vehicle.

He slowed down when he approached the turn on the right. The turn that would lead to more warehouses and a dead end. It wasn't the turn he thought the gunman would take.

But Bo saw the dark blue truck.

It was the right size to have made those tire tracks in the mud, and it was parked at an odd angle in the side parking lot of one of the warehouses. Next to it was a black car.

His gut told him Mattie was in one of those vehicles.

Bo didn't slam on his brakes because it would make too much noise and possibly alert her kidnapper. Instead, he came to a stop and backed up so he could turn into the road. He didn't speed, though it was next to impossible to keep himself from doing just that. Bo wanted to make it look as if he were headed there on business. Maybe as a worker at one of the warehouses. He wanted the element of surprise on his side.

As Bo approached the truck, he kept his focus straight ahead, but he studied the truck from the corner of his eye.

Mattie.

He was both relieved and terrified to see her in the

cab of the truck. She was alive, but the guy had a gun jammed against her head.

It took everything inside Bo to keep driving. If he stopped now, the gunman would likely just shoot her point-blank. Bo had to figure out a way to stop that from happening.

He turned into the parking lot of the next warehouse. He couldn't see the truck from that angle, which was good, because it meant the gunman couldn't see him. Bo jumped out of his car and started running toward the back of the warehouse. His best bet was to try to sneak up on them.

The rain beat at him, and he had to wipe the drops from his face just to see. Still, he didn't slow down because his gut was telling him something else—he didn't have much time.

It seemed to take forever, but he finally reached the far corner of the warehouse. He stopped and peered around the corner.

Hell.

He was right about not having much time. The gunman had Mattie out of the truck, and he was dragging her toward the parked black car. Someone was already inside that vehicle, but Bo couldn't see the person's face.

He could certainly see Mattie's and the gunman's faces, though. Mattie was frightened, but she was also fighting to stop herself from being taken to that black car. But the gunman was fighting, too. He kept his weapon pointed at her head while he muscled her toward the other vehicle.

The trunk of the black car popped open. Someone

inside had obviously used an interior button to do that. And the trunk was where the gunman was trying to force her to go.

"Stop fighting me!" the man yelled. He slammed his gun against the side of Mattie's head. He was a stranger. And about to be a dead one.

The rage roared through Bo, and even though he knew the person in the car could take a shot at him, he couldn't just stand there and let Mattie be beaten by this thug.

Bo came out of cover and took aim so he could fire a warning shot over the gunman's head. He wanted nothing more than to put a bullet in this guy, but Bo couldn't risk that with Mattie in the man's grip.

He fired the shot, and just as Bo had hoped, her attacker pivoted in Bo's direction. What the man didn't do was let go of Mattie. He slung her in front of him.

"Drop you gun and let her go," Bo ordered.

For a split second, Mattie's eyes met Bo's. The rain was sheeting down her face, and she was pale, but he saw something he hadn't seen earlier when she was in the other vehicle.

Determination.

She wasn't going to just stand there and let this kidnapper kill her.

Mattie threw her weight to the right, landing with a thud against the black car. And even though her attacker didn't let go of her, there was just enough space for Bo to get off a clean shot.

He took it.

The gunman aimed his weapon at Bo. He wasn't

nearly fast enough. Bo double tapped the trigger, sending two bullets right into the man.

Her attacker dropped to the ground, his weapon skittering across the wet concrete.

He watched the guy on the ground to make sure he wasn't faking his death. Bo didn't want this SOB going for the gun. But he also had another matter: the black car.

"Move away from the car," Bo told Mattie.

But it was already too late.

The car door flew open, and someone inside grabbed Mattie and dragged her into the car.

Chapter Eighteen

It took a moment for Mattie to register that someone had hold of her and had pulled her onto the driver's seat. She was literally sitting on someone's lap. Her attention had been on the gunman. The man who'd kidnapped her and threatened her life.

He was now dead on the ground.

Bo had shot him. Bo had saved her.

She hadn't had time to feel the relief or run to Bo. Because someone had her again.

Mattie fought to break free of the grip, but then her new attacker pressed something over her face. A cloth. And because Mattie was already breathing hard, she drew in the sick-sweet smell.

Chloroform.

She recognized the scent from a case she'd worked on early in her career. Someone was trying to knock her out.

Mattie rammed her elbow against that someone and made contact. The person gasped and loosened the grip just a little on the cloth. Even though Mattie was already feeling the effects of the drug, she elbowed the person again and again.

Until her attacker dropped the cloth.

However, she didn't have time to get out of the car because an arm curved around her neck, and someone jammed a gun against her head. Again.

"Mattie?" Bo called out.

He was moving closer to the car, and he had his gun aimed. Mattie could see that much, though her vision was blurry. Everything was swimming in and out of focus. Including her ability to concentrate. She cursed the chloroform and her attacker. She needed a clear head if both she and Bo were going to get out of this alive.

"Move and I'll kill him," her attacker growled against her ear.

It was a man, and even though her head was too fuzzy to recognize the hoarse whisper, she understood what he was threatening. He would kill Bo.

Mattie stopped struggling. She stopped fighting. She just sat there and drew in some deep breaths, hoping it would help her think better.

What could she do to stop this?

Bo walked closer, and he didn't take his attention off her and her attacker. He stepped to the side of the car, by the open door, and his eyes widened when he looked inside.

"Let her go," Bo warned.

Was he talking to another hired gun, or was that recognition she saw on Bo's face?

"Step out of the car and put down your gun. You're not going to get away with this," Bo tried again.

"I already have," the man fired back.

She lost what little breath she'd managed to regain.

That's because Mattie recognized the voice. This wasn't a hired gun or a stranger.

It was Ian.

Ian was the one holding the gun to her head. And he was no doubt the one who'd hired the dead man to kidnap her from the safe house.

"How did you find me?" she asked.

"The ring."

She was surprised that he gave an answer, any answer. But she shook her head. "What ring?"

"The one I had Cicely give you. Your old engagement ring. Well, a fake one, anyway. Brody didn't leave that in his desk. I bought it and put a tiny tracking device in the bottom of the box. It worked. It led me right to you."

Ian moved his mouth closer to her ear. "I would have had my man there sooner, but I got held up at police headquarters and couldn't call him. I was there most of the night. If not, this would all be over by now."

Over. Oh, God. "What do you want?" Mattie asked.

Ian brushed a kiss on her cheek. "I want you, of course."

His words and the touch of his mouth on her skin turned her stomach. Was he insane, or was this some kind of sick attempt to help Kendall?

Mattie looked at Bo to see what she could read from his face. But he was all cop now. He had his gaze pinpointed on Ian. She wanted Bo to shoot him or do whatever it took to stop this, but Bo couldn't do that because Ian had positioned her in front of him.

"Stop right where you are," Ian said when Bo took

another step closer. "If you move, Mattie dies. If she moves, you die. Your choice."

Some choice. Mattie didn't intend to let that happen.

"Backup will be here soon," Bo informed him. "They'll do a silent approach, no sirens. So you won't even know they're here until they're already in position. Let's end this now before they arrive."

Ian laughed. "I can only imagine what your idea of ending it is. I'm sure you've already gotten into Arturo's safety deposit box so you know what's going on."

But they didn't know, because they hadn't gotten into the box yet. What was Ian talking about?

Mattie tried a different approach. "What do you want from me?"

Because Ian's chest was right against her back, she felt him stiffen. "I want what I've always wanted—you. I love you, Mattie. I always have."

Oh, yes. He was crazy. But knowing that didn't help the situation. Insane people couldn't be reasoned with, and God knows how Ian was planning to show her how much he'd always loved her.

"Before supercop here got in the way, I was just going to take you with me," Ian added. He was angry now and pressed the gun harder into her temple. "No one would have gotten hurt, and it wouldn't have come down to this."

"This?" she repeated. "You're trying to kidnap me."

"No. I knew if we spent some time alone, you'd see that I was the man you really loved. Not Brody. And definitely not this cop."

"Listen to what you're saying," Bo challenged. "You

say you love her, but you're ready to kill her. That doesn't make sense."

"Yes, it does." His voice was different now. An eerie calmness replaced the anger. "Because if I can't have her, no one can. Mattie's always been mine."

Bo took a step closer, and from the corner of her eye Mattie saw the dark green car approach. Backup, no doubt. She didn't doubt the cops would try to get themselves into a position to end this, but Ian still had the gun pointed to her head. And since he was crazy, he could kill her and then try to end his own life.

Maybe Bo would live, and that would mean Jacob and Holly would have at least one parent.

She felt Ian move a little, and she glanced back. He'd seen the dark green car. He knew there wasn't much time before this would escalate or he would have to surrender.

Mattie feared surrender was the last thing on Ian's mind.

"Let her go," Bo ordered again. "Right now, you'd just be charged with kidnapping. You're a lawyer. You know you can pull an insanity plea. You can walk away from this and just get time in a mental facility."

Even though she hated the thought of Ian being out in just a few years, that was better than any alternative she could come up with.

"True. I could do that," Ian conceded. "If it weren't for that damn safety deposit box. I swear I didn't know Arturo was smart enough to cover his butt that way. Too bad. Because his attempt to protect himself means my plan is all screwed up. I can't pin any of this on Kendall or Tolivar. I have nothing to lose."

She looked at Bo, who shook his head. Obviously, he didn't know anything about this, either. But it sounded as if that safety deposit box contained some kind of information that would incriminate Ian.

"Ian, what did you do?" Mattie demanded.

"What didn't I do?" Ian countered.

Ian had the seat already pushed all the way back, and he began to maneuver her deeper inside the car. He also tipped the gun away from her head.

And he aimed it at Bo.

"And it was all for you," Ian whispered to her. "Before this is over, you might appreciate that. You might learn to love me the way I love you."

"Never."

It might not be wise to make him angrier than he already was, but Mattie figured she had to do something. Ian was trying to get them into a position so he could drive away with her. And shoot Bo. If she could just get Ian to move the gun, just a little more to the right, then she could ram him with her elbow again and not risk him getting a shot off in Bo's direction.

"Never is a long time," Ian growled. He gave her another adjustment. She was still in his lap, but now she was behind the wheel. Mattie glanced down and saw the keys already in the ignition. "I can change your mind. Where I'm taking you, all we'll have is time."

That made her skin crawl.

"First, though," Ian added, "I have just one tiny piece of unfinished business."

He meant Bo. Ian was going to try to kill him, and Bo wouldn't be able to return fire, because despite the new position, she was still in the way.

What she was about to say was risky, but anything at this point was risky. "I could never love you, Ian. I'm in love with Bo."

Since her attention was fastened to Bo, she saw him blink, and he was no doubt asking himself if she meant it.

She did.

It was the worst possible timing, but Mattie realized it was the truth. She was in love with Bo.

"You're in love with him?" Ian snapped. He put the gun back to her head. "You're lying."

"No. I'm not." And the truth was there, right in her voice. She could hear it. Bo could, as well.

And obviously so did Ian.

Ian yelled, a feral sound that pierced through her right ear, and she felt his arm tense.

He was about to pull the trigger.

Mattie drew back her elbow and rammed it into his belly as hard as she could. But it was too late.

The shot blasted through the car.

THE BLOOD RUSHED to Bo's head when he saw what was about to happen. He shouted for Mattie to get down, but the sound of his voice was drowned out by the bullet that Ian fired.

A thousand things went through Bo's mind, none good. He had been a cop long enough to know that a point-blank shot was usually fatal.

He raced to the car, to the tangle of bodies, and he was terrified of what he might see there. In that moment, that one horrible moment, Bo was aware of just how much Mattie meant to him.

He couldn't lose her. It couldn't be too late to save her.

Bo shifted his angle to the side, and he saw her moving inside the car. Thank God. She was alive. That didn't mean she wasn't hurt, though. It was the same for Ian. There was still a fight going on between Mattie and him, and Ian still had his gun.

Bo wanted to reach inside and try to pull Mattie out, but he couldn't take the chance. He couldn't tell if Mattie was somehow restraining Ian's shooting hand. If he wrenched her from the vehicle, that might give Ian the perfect opportunity to fire another shot.

And this one might be fatal.

Bo was aware that backup had arrived. From the corner of his eye, he saw them making their way toward him. They had their guns drawn, ready to help, but no one could help right now. He watched the struggle, trying to figure out how to get Mattie out of there alive.

She twisted her body, her head whiplashing against the seat. Ian had shoved her, and in that shove, he had created just enough space for Bo to see that Mattie had a death grip on Ian's right wrist. That prevented Ian from shooting directly at Mattie, but that meant he could use his left hand to punch her. And that's what the man was doing.

Ian landed a punch right to Mattie's face.

No amount of willpower and training would have stopped Bo at that point. He couldn't stand by and watch Ian beat her to a pulp.

Bo holstered his own gun so he could use his hands, and so Ian couldn't use it against him if this fight got worse than it already was. Bo was ready for *worse*. He was ready to kill this guy with his bare hands.

It was a tight fit, but Bo managed to reach into the car. Ian must have seen him coming because he started to fight harder, and he rammed his fist into Mattie's jaw again. Somehow, she held on to to his wrist.

And Bo helped.

He latched on to the gun itself. He couldn't wrench it from Ian's hand, but it freed up Mattie to move back.

"Get out of here!" Bo told her.

Bo cursed when Ian got in another punch, this one landing on the side of Mattie's head. She cursed, too, and fought to get away. Because they were all crammed into the small space between the seat, the console and the steering wheel, there wasn't much room to maneuver.

Ian turned his head and sank his teeth into Bo's hand. The pain shot through him, but Bo didn't let go because that was the hand he was using to try to control the gun.

"You sick piece of slime!" Mattie yelled at Ian. She caught hold of Ian's hair and rammed his head against the console.

That stopped the biting, but Ian came after Mattie again. Before the man could punch her again, Bo caught Mattie's arm and slung her out of the way. She landed behind him somewhere, and that meant he could grab Ian with both hands.

Bo dragged him from the car.

"I'll kill her!" Ian shouted. And he kept shouting it while he tried to bash his gun against Bo's head.

Bo's anger level was beyond dangerous, and that last attempt to kill Mattie pushed him over the edge. Bo slammed Ian face first against the car.

Ian gasped and wheezed for breath, and Bo couldn't believe it when the SOB tried to aim the gun.

At Mattie.

Ian was going to try to shoot her.

"Get down," Bo told Mattie.

Just as Ian pulled the trigger.

Bo didn't look back to see where the shot had landed, but he prayed Mattie had gotten out of the way in time. He put all his anger and attention on Ian. Bo rammed his full weight against Ian's back, and he bashed the man's right hand against the car. When Ian still held on, Bo whacked his hand again.

And again.

The gun finally dislodged and went crashing onto the ground. Ian gave up, too, and sagged against the car.

"Mattie, are you all right?" Bo asked, and he held his breath.

"I'm okay."

Well, she sure as hell didn't sound okay, so he glanced at her. Mattie didn't look okay, either. Her mouth was bleeding, and she had a cut on her cheekbone. God knows how many bruises she had on her. She was pale and shaking, but she hadn't been shot. Bo thanked God for that, because Ian had had several chances to shoot her.

Bo tipped his head, and the other officers moved in. He waited, holding Ian in place, until one of the officers kicked Ian's gun out of the way, and the other officer came in to cuff the man and read him his rights.

Bo watched, hoping like hell that Ian would try something. He wanted the moron to come at him again so he could pulverize him.

"Don't," Mattie whispered. She touched Bo's arm and rubbed gently. "Let it go."

"Can you?" Bo snapped. The emotion was still raw and angry and roaring through him.

"Yes. Because Ian doesn't matter. He'll go to jail for the rest of his life. You and I, on the other hand, are free. No more danger. We can spend the rest of our lives with Jacob and Holly."

With just those words and her touch, she soothed him and lessened his anger over Ian's attack. She reminded Bo of what was really at stake here.

Ian cursed, apparently upset that Mattie could find a silver lining so soon after the hell she'd just been through.

Ian stopped cursing, and much to Bo's surprise, he laughed. "Don't go planning any happily-ever-afters, Mattie," he spat out. "Because once you listen to what's in that safety deposit box, you're not going to be able to live with yourself."

Chapter Nineteen

Mattie stared at the safety deposit box that Captain Tolbert placed on the center of the table in the crime lab. She hadn't expected the police to bring the entire box so it could be analyzed, but here it was.

Like a rattlesnake coiled and ready to strike.

"Ian was probably lying about what's inside there," Bo assured her.

He slipped his arm around her and pressed a kiss to her forehead, just above the bandage. The stitches she'd gotten just a half hour earlier were starting to sting now, and she felt achy and bruised from the fight with Ian. Yet, those were minor things. Bo and she were alive, the children were safe, and Ian wouldn't be able to hurt them anymore. The only thing left to deal with was the box and what might be inside. Oh, and of course, there was Bo.

She needed to deal with him, too.

"We got the court order," the captain explained. "So, it's open. I first had it tested to make sure there were no explosives or booby traps. There weren't. So I had a look inside while you two were with the medics."

Mattie's gaze whipped to the captain's so she could

see if there were any hints of what she was about to face. He was somber. His expression seemed to say, "I'm sorry."

She took a deep breath, leaned over the stainless steel table and opened it. There were papers, a small tape recorder and a gun.

"What is all of this?" Bo asked, tightening his grip on her.

"Terrance Arturo obviously didn't trust Kaplan, even though he was working for him." The captain took out the first piece of paper and handed it to Mattie. "He explains that Kaplan hired him to break into the Witness Protection files so he could find you. There are numbers for the offshore account where Kaplan deposited the money, and Arturo even tells us how to trace the money back to Kaplan."

Well, that certainly wasn't bad news. "And the gun?"

"According to Arturo, it was the weapon he used to kill your fiancé. We'll run ballistics, but we're pretty sure it'll be a match." He paused. "Arturo says Kaplan's prints are on the gun because he's the one who gave it to Arturo."

So it was yet more proof that would keep Ian in jail for life or maybe even get him the death penalty.

"I've gone through the papers," the captain continued, "and from what I can tell, Kaplan set up Collier in that illegal arms deal. Your uncle did try to cover it up afterward, so he's not completely innocent, but all the attempts to kidnap and kill you came from Kaplan."

"Kendall's innocent?" Bo asked, sounding as surprised as she was.

"Almost. He threatened Mattie so she wouldn't testify against him, and that's why she was placed in Witness Protection, but there's no proof that he would have actually killed her. The real threat was Kaplan all along. I think Kaplan set things up to make it look as if Collier wanted her dead."

"But you said Collier tried to cover up the arms deal," Bo pointed out.

"Yes, and he might have to face charges for that. But we might be able to cut him a deal if he'll testify against Kaplan."

Which he would be a fool not to do. Kendall might be ruthless in business, but he wasn't stupid.

"What about Marshal Tolivar?" Bo asked.

"Innocent, too. There's proof in these papers that Kaplan set him up, as well."

Mattie shook her head. How could one man have tried to ruin so many lives? Worse, he'd nearly succeeded.

Mattie glanced at the last item in the box. "What's on the tape recorder?" she asked the captain.

The captain paused as though unsure how to give her the bad news.

"I'll listen to it," Bo volunteered. "I can summarize what's on it." He kissed her forehead again. "Rosalie will be here with the kids any minute and you can spend time with them in my office."

It was a generous offer. She did want to spend time with Jacob and Holly. And Bo. But she had to know what was on that tape.

Mattie stared at the captain. "Ian said I wouldn't be able to live with myself after I listen to what's in the box."

The captain mumbled some profanity. "He is obviously a psychopath. He created a vile situation, and when it didn't work out the way he wanted, he blamed you. You have nothing to feel guilty about, Mattie."

"What's on the tape?" she insisted.

The captain glanced at Bo first. "It's a recording of Kaplan meeting with your fiancé, Brody. Arturo's in the room."

"Arturo recorded it?" Bo asked.

Captain Tolbert nodded. "Kaplan offers Brody a deal—leave Mattie, move out of the country, and Kaplan will let him live. Brody tells Kaplan that he won't leave, that he won't hurt Mattie that way. That's when Kaplan orders Arturo to kill him."

Even though Mattie hadn't been there, she could almost see it. Ian had probably thought Brody would jump at the chance to live, but he had chosen her instead.

And Brody had died because of it.

Bo cursed under his breath. "Don't you dare let Ian get to you like this." Bo no doubt saw the tears in her eyes. "Ian and Arturo killed Brody. Not you. This isn't on you."

As if to convince her of that, Bo kissed her. It wasn't a peck of reassurance like the others. This was a real kiss. It shouldn't have made any difference in what she was feeling.

But it did.

Bo pulled back and lifted her chin to meet her eye-to-eye. "If Ian had offered you the same deal today, to give up the person you love or die, would you take it?"

Mattie didn't even have to think about this. "No."

"Neither would I. Because love is worth fighting for. And yes, sometimes it's worth dying for."

"Like today," she whispered. She had certainly been willing to die to stop Ian from killing Bo.

"Brody didn't have a chance to fight for his life. Ian took that away from him. But don't let Ian take away anything else. Don't let him stop you from reaching out and taking what's right in front of you."

The tears returned to her eyes, because Bo was right. The person she loved more than life itself was standing right in front of her.

And that person was Bo.

"The past is the past," Bo said, as if still trying to convince her. "Yes, part of you will always love Brody. Part of me will always love Nadine. But this is now, Mattie. This is the present and the future, and I want to spend that present and future with you."

The captain cleared his throat, reminding them that he was still in the room. She'd forgotten all about him, mainly because the only thing she could see and feel right now was Bo. He'd said just the right thing to put things into perspective. She couldn't let a deranged man like Ian ruin her chance at happiness by trying to weigh her down with old baggage. Baggage Ian had created.

"Maybe I should just step out for a couple of minutes," the captain mumbled.

Neither of them stopped him.

"You told Ian you were in love with me," Bo continued. "Is it true?" But he didn't wait for her to answer. "I need it to be true."

Mattie came up on her toes and kissed him. "It's true."

He smiled against her mouth. "Good. Because I'm in love with you, too."

Everything inside her turned to warm silk. How could anything feel this right, this perfect? She had only known Bo a few days, but she knew she wanted to spend the rest of her life with him. She was about to tell him that, too, but he kissed her again, and her world tipped on its axis.

He pressed her against the stainless table, in the sterile, cold room that was suddenly warm and welcoming.

Bo must have heard the sound at the same moment she did because he pulled away from her and went to the door through which the captain had just exited. But it wasn't the captain returning. Mattie recognized that sound.

It was Holly, and she was giggling.

Mattie hurried to the door and saw Rosalie making her way down the hall toward them. Jacob was toddling across the glossy tiles, and since he looked ready to fall, Rosalie had a hand on him. In the crook of her other arm was Holly, who was apparently laughing at her brother's antics.

"Hope we're not interrupting," Rosalie said. She leaned down and placed Holly on the floor, as well. "But they were ready to take your office apart. Figured they'd do less damage down here."

"You're not interrupting," Bo volunteered. "I was just about to ask Mattie to marry me, but it's probably better if I do it in front of all of you, anyway."

Mattie felt her mouth drop open. But she also felt the love race through her. The moment had already been perfect, but Bo had found a way to make it even better.

Bo reached down and picked up Holly when she made her way toward him, and he kissed her on her cheek. He passed her to Mattie so she could do the same. The little girl smiled, pressed both of her chubby hands to the sides of Mattie's face and gave her a big kiss.

"Ma," Holly announced.

Obviously not wanting to be left out of the action, Jacob strung together several Ma Mas, and he tugged at Mattie's dress. Mattie bent down and scooped him up, as well.

Rosalie smiled and blinked back tears. "Well? Seems you owe Bo an answer about that marriage proposal."

"My answer is yes," Mattie whispered. Just for Bo. But then she repeated it, louder, so the children and Rosalie would hear.

Rosalie clapped and wiped the tears from her face.

Jacob picked up on the clapping and did the same. Holly soon joined him for the celebration. Even though they were too young to know what her yes meant, they obviously knew this was a happy time for their new family.

Mattie's arms were already full, but she managed to turn to Bo so she could kiss him the way she wanted. A kiss to let him know that their future would always be filled with love. Like now. Forever.

* * * * *

GENUINE COWBOY

BY
JOANNA WAYNE

First published in Great Britain 2012
by Mills & Boon, an imprint of Harlequin (UK) Limited,
Eton House, 18-24 Paradise Road, Richmond, Surrey TW9 1SR

© Jo Ann Vest 2010

ISBN: 978 0 263 89509 4

46-0312

Harlequin (UK) policy is to use papers that are natural, renewable and recyclable products and made from wood grown in sustainable forests. The logging and manufacturing processes conform to the legal environmental regulations of the country of origin.

Printed and bound in Spain
by Blackprint CPI, Barcelona

Joanna Wayne was born and raised in Shreveport, Louisiana, and received her undergraduate and graduate degrees from LSU-Shreveport. She moved to New Orleans in 1984, and it was there that she attended her first writing class and joined her first professional writing organization. Her debut novel, *Deep in the Bayou,* was published in 1994.

Now, dozens of published books later, Joanna has made a name for herself as being on the cutting edge of romantic suspense in both series and single-title novels. She has been on the Waldenbooks bestseller list for romance and has won many industry awards. She is also a popular speaker at writing organizations and local community functions and has taught creative writing at the University of New Orleans Metropolitan College.

Joanna currently resides in a small community forty miles north of Houston, Texas, with her husband. Though she still has many family and emotional ties to Louisiana, she loves living in the Lone Star state. You may write Joanna at PO Box 852, Montgomery, Texas 77356, USA.

To my good friends Patsy and Hill, who are always there when I need them for golf, fun or just to talk. They are part of the reason I LOVE living in Texas. And to my marvellous editor who keeps me on track.

Chapter One

"Mommy! Mommy! Don't let him get me!"

Eve Worthington jerked awake at the sound of her young son's voice and then dodged the agile body that propelled itself from the floor into the middle of her bed.

She gathered Joey into her arms. "Did you have a nightmare, sweetie?"

"A man was in my room. He was going to hurt me."

"It's okay, Joey. There's no one in the house but you and me. You're safe. I won't let anyone hurt you."

She kissed the top of Joey's head and let her lips linger in the soft blond hair that smelled like sunshine and springtime. She held him close, her hands splayed across his back until the shudders stopped.

It had been two years since he'd lost his father to a drive-by shooting mere blocks from their Dallas home. He'd been almost four years old at the time, independent and curious, a ball of energy who was eager for any adventure.

Now he seldom made it through the night without

waking screaming, in the throes of a nightmare. He held tightly on to her hand whenever the two of them left the house. Even at the neighborhood park that he loved, he didn't want her out of his sight, especially if there was a man around. When she'd tried to enroll him in kindergarten, he'd become so distraught, she'd decided to hold him back a year.

She was a psychiatrist. She should know how to help Joey get past this, know how to make him feel safe. Her mentor and favorite professor, Edgar Callen, claimed she was simply too close to the situation to be objective.

Edgar was probably right but her own fears went much deeper than even he knew. Her three years of working with prisoners in Texas correctional institutions had left their scars even before she'd lost her husband.

Her friend Miriam, whom she seldom saw anymore, also a psychiatrist, believed that Eve had become far too protective of Joey. Miriam was likely correct in her assessment as well. But Joey had been through so much that Eve couldn't help being overly cautious with him.

"Can I sleep with you, Mommy?"

"You'll be more comfortable in your bed. I'll come and lie down with you until you fall asleep."

"I don't want to go back in there."

"We'll turn on all the lights and look around. When you see your toys and stuffed animals, you'll know the bad dream wasn't real."

"It seemed real."

"I know it did. Nightmares are like that, but there's nothing in your room when the light is off that's not there when the light is on."

She scooted to the edge of the bed, then threw her bare feet to the floor, just as a streak of lightning zig-zagged across the night sky. Joey stood on the mattress and wrapped his short arms around her neck.

She picked him up, noting, as always, how light he felt in her arms. He was small for his age and a difficult eater, constantly complaining of stomach pains. The pediatrician had ruled out any medical reasons for them.

Once back in his room, they spent a good half hour making sure every toy was in place. By the time he'd settled in his bed with his stuffed lion, a light rain was slapping against the window and low rumbles of thunder growled in the distance.

Eve snuggled beside her son until he fell asleep, though she doubted he'd sleep soundly with the storm kicking up outside. There was little use to go back to her room only to be dragged from bed again.

She climbed out of his bed stealthily and turned down the quilt on the spare twin bed in Joey's room. Finally, Eve drifted into a sound sleep. When she opened her eyes again, it was half-past six. Amazingly, both she and Joey had slept through the rest of the night.

She stretched and turned to check on her son. He'd kicked off his covers, but his lion was still clutched tightly to his chest. She listened to his gentle breathing, watched the steady rise and fall of his chest and felt a tightening in her throat.

Moving quietly so as not to wake him, she climbed from the bed and walked to the bedroom door, lingering to look back at Joey. If only he always looked as peaceful as he did this minute.

Padding to the rear of the house, she started a pot of coffee, pausing when she was done to stare out the kitchen window. The thunderstorm had given way to a calm dawn, but water puddled the lawn and dripped from the few leaves that clung stubbornly to the lone oak tree.

Eve went back to her bedroom for her slippers before walking almost to the street to retrieve the plastic-wrapped copy of *The Dallas Morning News*. When she'd worked, reading the newspaper had been a luxury reserved for weekends and holidays. Now that she'd become a full-time mother to her troubled son, it was part of her morning routine.

Stripping away the wet wrapper, she tossed it into the trash and spread the paper on the kitchen table as the odor of fresh-perked coffee filled the room. The headlines dealt with the wrangling between local politicians. She ignored it and skimmed the rest of the page before flipping to an inside section.

Her breath caught as her focus centered on a black-and-white photograph at the top of the page. The caption beneath the picture gave her chills.

Orson Bastion had escaped from the Texas State Penitentiary at Huntsville, Texas.

Eve sank into the chair as her mind dragged her into the past. Her home phone rang, startling her back into the present. She checked the caller ID. Gordon Epps, the prison's warden. She lifted the receiver.

"I just read about Orson's escape," she said, saving him the trouble of trying to break it to her gently.

"I was afraid of that. Are you okay?"

"I've had better mornings. When did he escape?"

"Sometime during the night. He was first missed at the 2:00 a.m. security check. One of the security patrol found the guard pulling night duty on Orson's wing dead. He'd been strangled."

"Orson's calling card. Are you sure he escaped the premises?"

"Relatively sure. We've spent the night searching and there's no sign of him. Speculation is that he somehow rode out with the trash."

At least he was with his own kind.

"He took the guard's gun, so we know he's armed."

"And there's no doubt he's dangerous," Eve added. "He could be anywhere by now."

"Law enforcement officers across the state have been notified. With any luck, he'll be back in custody in a matter of hours. Still, I wanted to give you a heads-up."

"You don't think he'll come after me, do you? I haven't had any dealings with him in two years. He must have a lot worse enemies than me to get even with."

"I suspect Orson's only interested in saving his own hide now. He's likely keeping a low profile and hightailing it out of the state as fast as he can."

"I hope you're right."

"If you're worried at all, Eve, you could always go spend a few days with Troy Ledger. His ranch is not that far away, and I know he'd love to see you."

"How is he?"

"Adjusting well to freedom. He's reunited with his son Dylan and they're working his old ranch."

"Then I doubt he'd be thrilled about my running to him at the first sign of trouble."

"Just a thought. How's the boy?" Epps asked.

"Joey's making progress, but still experiencing a lot of anxiety and separation issues."

"I hate to hear that. I've got to run, Eve, but if there's anything I can do, give me a call. And think about paying a visit to Troy. If Orson is stupid enough to seek revenge against you for your testimony at his parole hearing, he'd never think of looking for you at the home of a former inmate accused of killing his own wife."

If Orson was stupid enough to come after her... But Orson wasn't stupid. She'd seen the results of his intelligence testing. He bordered on genius. That didn't mean he wasn't evil to the core. And he *had* threatened to get back at her for fouling his early parole attempt.

Orson's threat echoed in her mind. She had no doubt when he'd hurled it at her that he'd meant every word. So how could she convince herself that he wouldn't come after her now?

"I appreciate the call, Gordon."

"Okay, and keep me posted if you decide to leave home. If you stay, you need to alert the police that Orson could show up there. Demand protection. Promise me you'll do that."

"I'm not sure the Dallas Police Department responds to citizen demands."

"Then go see Troy for a few days. He'll understand

and you're surely not afraid of him. You've said yourself that you'd never met a prisoner whose innocence was as compelling as Troy's."

She had been convinced of his innocence, had even made a statement to the press on his release that she'd trust him with her life and the life of her son.

She'd meant the words at the time. But was she ready to put them to the test?

Did she dare not?

...far through...the...

Chapter Two

The frosty late November air had a bite to it, and the
wind stung Sean Ledger's face as he ducked through the
door and into the cozy barn. He was up early and raring
to go to work. He had a feeling this just might be the day
he made some real headway with Go Lightly.

He'd been at Cahill Horse Farm for just over six
months and Go Lightly was still a challenge. The horse
had racing in its blood and was fast enough to be a threat
in any of the major races for two-year-olds.

Until the starter fired his shot and the gates opened.
Then Go Lightly bucked and fought the jockey, as if
he were being asked to run along a track planted with
land mines. Ted Cahill was about ready to give up on
the animal. Sean wasn't.

He just needed more time, and fewer distractions—
compliments of Tom's wife.

Women. Sean didn't understand them and doubted he
ever would. Give him a horse any day. Sean could get
into a horse's mind, figure out what had frightened it or
killed its spirit. Given time, Sean could usually bring a
horse around.

Women, on the other hand, were beyond comprehension. As far as he was concerned, they weren't just from another planet, but from another galaxy. And they were welcome to it.

He pushed the irritating thoughts aside and tuned into the life pulsing in the barn. Suzy pawed at the pile of hay at her feet, threw back her head and snorted.

"Good morning, old girl." Sean reached over and scratched the long nose. "You don't like being ignored, do you?"

Suzy snorted again and stretched her head over the stall door so that she could rub against the rough denim of Sean's jacket.

Thunder threw back his head and neighed loudly, then kicked his back feet, protesting any- and everything. Aptly named, he was the most high spirited of all the quarter horses at Cahill Farms. He'd been a winner in his day, and he knew it. The past glory earned him the right to be a contrary sire.

The stud settled a bit, almost gloatingly, when Sean turned his attention to him. Sean shrugged out of his denim jacket and hung it on a peg near the door. Leaning against a support post, he pulled a folded envelope from his shirt pocket. He removed the letter, the latest from his brother Dylan. After reading through it, Sean reread the last paragraph.

"You'd love the Texas Hill Country, Sean. Pay us a visit, if only for a few days. Give Dad a chance. You won't be sorry."

Troy did not share Dylan's confidence that he'd like returning to the ranch. And as for giving Troy Ledger a chance, those days were long gone. When he was a kid, he'd had his father on a pedestal so high the man would have needed a parachute to come back to earth safely.

Troy Ledger hadn't utilized a parachute or a safety net. He'd nosedived off the perch into the pool of blood that had soaked Sean's brutally slain mother.

"Is that a love letter?"

Sean turned at the seductive voice, nodded to Sasha Cahill, then folded the letter and stuffed it back in his pocket. "Far from it."

"I'll bet you left lots of broken hearts back in Kentucky when you came to work for my father."

Not a subject he was interested in pursuing, especially not with his boss's seventeen- going on twenty-one-year-old daughter. "Don't you have school today?"

"Teacher Institute day. You don't mind my company, do you?"

"I'm paid to work, not socialize."

"I love watching you interact with Go Lightly. Your voice and the way you touch him makes me wish I was an emotionally scarred racehorse you were out to save."

Oh, good grief. It was bad enough that Sasha's mother came on to him like a dog in heat. Now Sasha. If it was something in the water, Ted Cahill had best dig his family a new well.

"You're not a horse." She was a spoiled brat, though he refrained from saying so. "Why don't you take Suzy out for a ride? She could use a good workout."

"Horses aren't the only animals that need a whisperer, Sean."

The whisperer label was one Sean had never encouraged. It sounded like magic and tended to make people expect miracles. Sean was not a magician. He walked away, heading toward the back of the horse barn where he had a small office.

"Please come riding with me, Sean. I hate to ride alone. You know Mom's worthless before noon and Daddy's gone for the day."

Her voice had that breathless quality that made her sound like a hormonally charged adolescent trying out for the role of Lolita. If he was her father, he'd ground her until she was past the pimple stage.

Sean shook his head. "Sorry, *kid,* I have work to do."

He strode past the horses, stepped into his office and closed the door behind him. Had there been a bolt, he'd have locked it. The idea of owning his own quarter horse farm sounded better by the day, and he probably had enough money saved to pull it off if he still took on a few private clients who owned problem horses.

He tossed his hat to the top of a stack of unopened cardboard boxes and plopped onto the worn chair behind the metal desk. Remembering the letter, he pulled it from his pocket and dropped it into the top drawer to be answered later—with a very succinct "no."

Forging a relationship with a father he hadn't seen since the day the man received a life sentence for murdering his mother didn't hold a lot of appeal for Sean. Release on a technicality didn't wash away the man's sins.

The door to Sean's office squeaked open. He groaned.

When he finally looked up, Sasha's jacket was dangling from a crooked finger. Her chest was bare, her firm breasts pointing at him as if daring him to resist temptation.

He took a deep breath—and the dare. "Put your jacket on, Sasha. You're too smart, too pretty and way too young to be playing this stupid game. Don't devalue what you are inside by throwing yourself at me or anyone else."

She leaned against the rough-hewn doorframe. "Look at me, Sean. You'll see I'm old enough."

Sean stood and grabbed his Stetson. When he reached the door, he picked up Sasha at the waist to move her out of his way. The crazy kid threw her legs around him and pressed her bare breasts against his chest.

He heard footsteps and cringed as he looked up to find Laci Cahill staring at him. The old adage "If looks could kill" had never seemed more apt.

Laci propped her hands on her hips. "Well, this explains a lot."

"This is not what it looks like," he assured Sasha's mother.

Laci's irate glare made it clear that she didn't believe him.

Thankfully, Sasha had dismounted his hips at her mother's appearance and was pulling on her jacket at a speed that he'd previously only seen her exhibit when texting messages on her touch-screen cell phone.

Laci stepped inside the office. "Go to your room, Sasha."

Sasha scooted past him without a glance.

"Why bother with the old mare when you have the filly?" Laci snapped.

"I'm here to train horses, Laci. That's all, and I definitely didn't initiate that scene you just walked in on."

"Do you expect me to believe that?"

"I can't control what you believe, but I'm telling you the truth."

"Stay away from my daughter, Sean. If I ever catch the two of you in another compromising position, I'll not only see that Ted fires you, but that you never work as a trainer again. Do I make myself clear?"

"Crystal clear."

In fact, a lot of things were clear right now, mainly that he couldn't work in this type of strained environment. "I'll pack my things and be off the Cahill property by noon."

"What's that supposed to mean?"

"You don't have to worry about watching me every second or firing me. I quit."

Laci grabbed his arm. "That's not necessary. I know how Sasha is. This isn't the first time she's pulled something like this."

Talk about changing horses in midstream. A minute ago, Sean was to blame for everything. Now it was Sasha. A man could get dizzy trying to keep up.

"I'll leave Ted the names of a couple of guys he might want to interview for my job," Sean said. Older men who hopefully wouldn't be subjected to seduction at every turn. "And don't worry, I'll leave you and Sasha out of my explanation for leaving on such short notice."

"You're making a mistake, Sean. There's not a trainer

in the state who wouldn't salivate at the thought of going to work for Ted Cahill."

"And now one lucky applicant will get to drool all over his work shirt." Sean tipped his hat and walked away. Amazing, how a man could start out a day with great expectations, only to have it blow up in his face.

Sean went back to the desk and pulled his brother's letter from the drawer. Dylan's written words weighed heavy on his mind as he retrieved his worn jacket and walked back to his small cabin to gather his things. Maybe a trip to the Texas Hill Country wasn't such a bad idea after all.

It would be good to see Dylan again and finally meet his brother's new wife—before Dylan's dreams of idyllic marriage evolved into reality.

Or maybe that kind of luckless romance was reserved for Sean.

Chapter Three

Troy Ledger turned off the TV and walked back to his small kitchen, taking his half-empty plate with him. He'd just caught the tail end of the six o'clock news, and that had been enough to kill his appetite.

Orson Bastion had escaped from the pen and taken out a guard in the process. Talk about a brutal reminder of his prison life. Impulsively, his hand moved to the scar on his cheek.

His thoughts moved to Eve Worthington. The news of Bastion's escape had to be frightening for her. If he had her phone number he'd call her. But best that he didn't have it. For all he knew, she'd left the area by now.

Troy washed his plate, rinsed it and stood it in the drainer. He reached for the skillet he'd used to fry a slice of ham for his sandwich and immersed it in the hot, soapy water. The old dishwasher needed replacing, but there wasn't much need for a fancy machine when a man lived alone.

His son, Dylan, and Dylan's new wife, Collette, had moved out of the old family house and into their starter ranch house two weeks earlier. They needed their privacy. They were only a good horse ride away, but Troy missed them a lot more than he was willing to admit.

Troy and Dylan had built the newlyweds' house themselves, with lots of suggestions from Collette. She was quite a woman, even reminded him of Helene a little. Not that he needed a reminder of Helene. She was seldom far from his mind and never out of his heart. Never had been. Never would be.

But the last few months of working with his son on the house and the ranch they were getting up and running again had meant more to Troy than Dylan could possibly realize. Seventeen years in prison had robbed Troy of much of his five sons' childhood and all of their adolescence. They'd grown from boys to men without him. Dylan was the only one of the five who'd shown any interest in having Troy back in his life. He prayed that would change one day, but he couldn't count on it.

Troy finished the dishes and dried his hands. It was only six in the evening, but he was exhausted. Working from sunup to sundown did that for a man. Fatigue didn't bother him. The prospect of spending another night alone in the rambling old house did.

He could handle the days, but alone at night, memories of Helene haunted his mind. He could hear her laughter, sweet and melodic, filling the house as she interacted with their rambunctious sons.

He could smell her fragrance, like a bouquet from the garden she'd pampered like one of their children. He could see her on Sunday morning, her dark, shiny hair dancing about her shoulders, leading them all to church whether they liked it or not.

But the most devastating memories came when he crawled into the bed he'd once shared with Helene. It had taken him weeks to even enter the master bedroom, had taken weeks more before he could bear sleeping in the bed.

Even now, three months later, he couldn't stretch out between the sheets without his arms literally aching to wrap around her and feel her warm, loving body cuddled against his. Some nights the pain was all but unbearable.

He leaned against the sink as the memories swelled inside him. The gentle ache in his chest erupted into heated stabs that threatened to slice his heart into pieces.

The images swirling in his head darkened as the nightmare he'd lived over and over for almost two decades took front and center: Helene's body in a pool of blood, faceup, her head against the hearth, her beautiful locks of hair matted with crimson.

The pain became blinding and this time much too physical. Troy clutched his chest as he stumbled backward, falling against the scarred wooden table. Each beat of his heart was agony.

Then reality checked in. This was more than grief. He was having a coronary attack.

There was a knock at the door as he tried to drag himself to the phone. The door was unlocked, as it usually was on the ranch. He waited, hoping it was Dylan.

But there was no reason to think his son would return tonight.

He heard a child's voice, or maybe he was hallucinating.

He fell over a chair and the crash reverberated through the house.

"Troy, are you in there? Are you okay?"

The voice was female, vaguely familiar. He tried to answer, but all he managed was a guttural moan.

"Troy, what's wrong?"

He looked up and into the eyes of Eve Worthington. Now he was certain he was hallucinating. The last person who'd be coming to his rescue was the young psychiatrist who'd worked so hard to pull him from his emotional shell while he was in prison.

"Please tell me what's wrong. Is it your heart?"

His response was choked by the pain.

"Hang in here with me, Troy. I'm calling an ambulance."

The room began to spin. He tried to focus on Eve, only to have her disappear in a swirl of darkness.

He wouldn't die. He couldn't. Not until he found Helene's killer. He would not fail her again.

"WHAT'S WRONG WITH HIM, Momma? Is he dying?"

"Shh, Joey. He's sick. We have to help him."

Troy muttered something unintelligible. She leaned in closer so that she could hear him better.

"Dylan," he gasped. "Call Dylan."

Dylan—the son Gordon Epps had mentioned. "I'll get him," she said, her fingers already punching in 911 on her unfamiliar cell phone. Once she was assured medical help was on the way, she glanced around the room and spotted Troy's cell phone on the kitchen table.

She left Troy's side long enough to get it. It took only a second to find Dylan's number amidst Troy's limited contacts. He answered on the second ring.

"What's up, Dad?"

"This isn't Troy, but I'm with him. I think he's having a heart attack. I've called an ambulance, but he's asking for you." The words tumbled out of her mouth. She wasn't even sure she was making sense.

"Who is this?"

"I'm just a friend who happened to drop in. Troy's in a lot of pain and barely conscious."

"I'll be right there."

"I'm scared, Momma. Let's go home."

She looked at her son. "We can't go yet, sweetie." She held out a hand and he inched toward her, clearly frightened of Troy.

"Eve." Troy's speech was clearer, but sweat beaded on his brow and his breathing was still labored.

"I'm right here, Troy."

"Orson…"

"Yeah." She cradled Troy's head in her arms. "He's escaped."

"Dangerous… Stay safe."

"I will." Even in the panic of a heart attack, Troy was worried about her. That was so like him. Thank God, she'd shown up when she did.

Joey tugged on her arm. She tried to pull him down beside her, but he backed away. "Is that a bad man?"

"No. He's my friend."

The words didn't convince Joey, and she couldn't do much to make him feel safe until the emergency was over. Fortunately, the door flew open minutes later and a good-looking man in jeans rushed in, still pulling on his shirt. An attractive woman with flaming red hair followed right behind.

She stood and moved away so that they could squeeze in beside Troy. "I'm Eve Worthington, an old friend of your father's. I just—" The scream of an approaching ambulance drowned out the rest of her words.

Dylan took over from there and the next few minutes passed in a blur of activity. Joey began to tremble as the house filled with strangers and medics who worked quickly to get Troy onto the gurney and into the ambulance. Eve held on to his shaking hand, tugging him out of the way and giving assurances as best she could amid the chaos.

Both Dylan and Collette Ledger were so engrossed in their concern for Troy that they simply accepted her explanation as being an old friend without question. It wasn't until Dylan had thanked her profusely and rushed to follow the ambulance to the hospital that she had a minute to reflect on her own situation.

It wasn't good. Once she'd realized that the police weren't taking concerns for her and Joey's safety seriously, she decided to take Gordon's advice and pay Troy a visit. She really hadn't thought beyond that.

For the first time since she'd arrived on the scene, Eve really looked at Collette Ledger. Even in sweatpants, she was striking, with thick red hair that fell in loose curls about her shoulders and a faultless complexion.

Eve suspected they were near the same age, though Collette could easily be a few years younger than her thirty-one years.

"I'm so thankful you dropped by," Collette said. "I hate to think what might have happened if you hadn't shown up when you did."

"I'm glad I was here, too," Eve said. "Believe me, my timing is not usually that good."

"You're not from this area, are you?"

"No. I live in Dallas."

"I didn't think I'd seen you around town before. How do you know Troy?"

"From prison."

"Really? Prison."

"I was his psychiatrist."

"You don't look like a psyche. Not that you looked like an inmate. I mean..."

"It's okay," Eve assured her. "We're both a little shaken now."

"That's for sure. I don't know what your experience with Troy has been, but I'm guessing it was good, or you wouldn't be here."

"I'm very fond of him," Eve said.

"So am I, Collette agreed. "He's difficult to get to know, but once he opens up to you, you can't help but like him. And no matter what anyone says, I know he didn't kill his wife. Dylan realizes that, too."

"I agree," Eve said.

"I'm glad we're on the same page here. Troy didn't mention that you were stopping by tonight."

"I was going to surprise him," Eve said. Shock him was more like it. And ask him if she could stay with him a few days. That was out of the question now. There was no reason to get into any of that with Collette, though.

"I'll be going now," Eve said. "There's nothing more I can do here except get in the way."

"Where are you going?"

An excellent question that Eve couldn't honestly answer. She'd had no backup plan. Eve quickly considered her options. "Joey and I are on our way to visit friends in Austin," she lied.

Joey tugged on the hem of her shirt. "You said we were going to a ranch."

"We did. This is it. Now we're off to the rest of our adventure."

"There's no need to rush off," Collette said. "If you're half as shaken as I am, you're in no shape to drive. And I could really use the company. I hate the thought of waiting alone for news about Troy. I'll make coffee."

"Coffee sounds good. And I do think I'm still in a bit of shock."

Collette filled the pot with water from the tap and spooned the grinds into the filter. "I'm so worried about my father-in-law that I can barely measure the water."

"Troy's tough. If anyone can pull through a heart attack, it's him," Eve said, unconsciously falling into the psychiatrist role. Not that they were certain Troy had a heart attack, but it had certainly appeared to be a coronary trauma.

"Have you had dinner?" Collette asked. "I'm not sure what Troy has in his fridge, but I have leftover roast beef and gravy at my house, or I could make you a salad. And I'm sure we could rustle up the makings of a peanut butter and jelly sandwich at either house, if Joey would prefer that."

"Thanks, but we've had dinner." Joey had eaten half a sandwich and a few apple slices in the car. That qualified as a major meal for him. As for herself, she hadn't eaten anything all day except a half slice of toast and a few cashews she'd munched in the car. Her stomach had been in no condition for food after the morning's call from Gordon. Her insides were even shakier now.

"What's your son's name?" Collette asked. "You probably said already, but it didn't register in the bedlam."

Eve rested her hands on his shoulders. "This is Joey."

"Hi, Joey."

The boy mumbled a hello, his eyes downcast.

"Joey. I like that name," Collette said. "Would you like to watch TV? I can probably find the cartoon channel if you'll help me."

Joey nodded, but scrunched himself against Eve's leg as if Collette had threatened a time-out.

"He's shy around strangers," Eve said, wishing that was all that kept him glued to her.

"Can't blame him for being a little cautious, considering what we've been dealing with tonight. Why don't you get him settled in the family room? I'll bring the coffee when it's brewed."

"Thanks."

Joey clung to her leg, his thin fingers digging into the fabric of her trousers as he shadowed her to the couch. By the time she found a channel he liked, Collette was returning with the coffee, a glass of milk and two oatmeal cookies that appeared to be homemade. Collette set the milk and cookies near Joey.

He mumbled a thank-you, and smiled timidly, staring at Collette from beneath his dark lashes. Eve experienced another wave of uneasiness that bordered on panic. They would have been safe here, even if Orson did still have the crazy notion of coming after her. It was certainly the kind of thing that a manipulative, revengeful person like Orson would do. Now her only option would be a stuffy hotel, and even taking Joey to a park would involve risk.

She and Collette moved to chairs near the window, still in Joey's sight, but not so close that he'd hear every word, even if he had been listening. Fortunately, he appeared lost in a cartoon.

Eve supplied the most basic facts about her relationship with Troy—that he had become a friend as well as a patient when she had served as his therapist during his incarceration. She'd stopped working at the prison two years ago and hadn't seen Troy since that time. She felt remiss for not getting in touch with him sooner.

"I wish everyone saw Troy as you do," Collette said. "Too many people around here still see him as a murderer. Troy never complains, but I know the suspicions and mistrust take their toll. I think it hurts him most that his sons have avoided seeing him since his release— except for Dylan, of course."

"Troy always talked a lot about his sons."

"He will be so sorry he missed visiting with you."

The conversation turned to less stressful topics. Ranch life. The house Dylan and Collette had just built. Helene's treasured courtyard garden that Collette had restored with Dylan and Troy's help. Life in the small town of Mustang Run.

When Colette's phone rang, Eve was surprised to see that an hour had passed since the ambulance had sped away with Troy inside.

Collette pulled the phone from her pocket and checked the caller ID. "It's Dylan."

The tension seemed to melt from Collette's features as she talked, allowing Eve to breathe easier. She stood and took their coffee cups to the sink, giving Collette a little privacy. For once, Joey didn't follow.

Collette was smiling when she joined her in the kitchen. "They're still running tests, but Troy is responding to treatment and meds. He's conscious and talking."

"Thank goodness."

Moisture brimmed in Collette's eyes. "It would have been so sad if Troy had lost his life just when he was finding it again. I just hope his other sons give him a chance the way Dylan has."

"Maybe tonight's incident will open their eyes," Eve said.

"I wouldn't bet on it, but I'm sure Dylan will let them know about it. Anyway, Dylan said Troy remembers that you were here, and he's asked about you."

She'd almost hoped he wouldn't remember. He didn't need to waste his energy worrying about her.

"He seems to be under the impression that you're in some kind of trouble," Collette said.

"I'm sure I didn't say anything to give him that impression."

"Still, Dylan says he seems anxious to see you. I know this is an imposition, but is there any way you could make a quick trip to the hospital in the morning? It would mean a lot to him."

"I'm not sure." She wasn't even sure she'd stay in Austin. Perhaps the best thing now would be to just go home and rely on the police for protection.

"You could stay the night," Collette said. "Then you wouldn't have to drive these unfamiliar country roads in the dark."

"You mean stay here at the ranch?"

"Sure, there's lots of room," Colette said. "It's not fancy, but it's comfortable. I'd invite you to stay with Dylan and me, but unfortunately we haven't furnished the guest room as yet."

Staying here was the perfect solution. Even if Orson was still planning revenge, he wouldn't show up here. And by morning Orson might be behind bars again.

"I suppose I could stay tonight," she said, trying not to sound too enthusiastic. "If you're sure Troy won't mind."

"After you saved his life? Not that he'd mind anyway. I'll help you get your things out of the car and show you to the guest rooms. All the beds have new mattresses and linens, so you can take your pick."

"I can manage the luggage. I'll just bring in an over-night bag."

"Then I'll straighten the kitchen. Oh, but first give me your cell phone number in case I need to get in touch with you about Troy. That way you won't have to bother picking up the house phone if it rings and answering a hundred questions if someone calls for Troy. And I'll give you my number in case you need something in the house that you can't locate."

Eve was hesitant to give Collette her phone number. The phone was new, temporary, bought with cash at a convenience store to make certain Orson could not use it to track her down. It had been purchased right after she'd gone to the bank and withdrawn five thousand dollars so that she wouldn't have to use her credit cards.

The only one who had the phone number was Gordon Epps—and the ambulance service, if they bothered to check their incoming call records.

But surely Collette could be trusted.

Once they'd exchanged numbers, Eve took her car keys from her pocket and started to her car. Joey jumped off the couch when he saw her pass with her keys in hand.

"I'll be right back, sweetie. You can keep watching TV. I'm just going to the car to get our luggage."

"What about our adventure?"

"It's late, and I'm very tired. We'll spend the night and get an early start in the morning."

"I don't want to spend the night here. I wanna sleep in my bed."

"Your bed is all the way back in Dallas. Besides, this is your first visit to a real ranch."

"And in the morning, I'll show you the cows and the horses," Colette said. "Do you like horses?"

"I think so. I never got close to one," he said, hurrying to keep up with Eve as she started toward the car. "But I need to go home."

Eve stooped and hugged him. "It's going to be okay, Joey. You'll like it here, and I'll sleep next to you."

"Promise?"

"I promise."

The howl of coyotes in the distance and the forlorn hoot of an owl greeted them as they stepped onto the porch. Dark shadows jumped out at her as she took the creaking steps to the walk. Weirdly, she had a chilling feeling that someone was watching her.

It was just the isolation of the ranch and the fear that stalked her. She couldn't give in to it. Yet the icy trepidation stayed with her until she and Joey were back inside the well-lit house.

She'd be safe here. To believe otherwise in the face of the facts would be letting Orson Bastion win the battle of minds without him ever making a move against her.

She was tougher than that.

THE CREAKS AND RASPS of the rambling old ranch house set Eve's nerves on edge. Surprisingly, the same had not been true for Joey. He'd fallen asleep mere minutes after she'd tucked him into a twin bed at the end of the long hallway.

Once she was sure he was sleeping soundly, Eve left

him to brush her teeth and wash and cream her face in the nearby bathroom.

Thoughts of Orson continued to plague Eve's mind as she slipped into her cotton pajamas. Of all the inmates she'd counseled, he'd been the only one she dreaded having to talk to—even before the night he'd left no doubt that he could kill her without a second's remorse.

Joey was still sleeping soundly when she returned to the bedroom, but anxiety was buzzing inside Eve like a horde of angry bumblebees. Knowing sleep wouldn't come quickly, she went back to the family room and turned on the TV.

The local news was coming up next. Great. If they'd just announce that Orson Bastion had been recaptured, her nightmare could end and she could not only get a good night's sleep, but actually look forward to seeing Troy in the morning.

She shed her slippers and stretched out on the brown leather sofa while a string of commercials aired. Finally the screen switched to the newsroom of a local channel.

"Stay tuned for breaking news concerning escaped convict Orson Bastion."

Eve tensed and waited. When a sophisticated blond anchor appeared, the grim expression on her meticulously made-up face guaranteed the news would be disturbing.

"A young woman was fatally strangled after being kidnapped from a Dallas shopping center this afternoon. Her car was found deserted a few hours later. Police suspect that escaped prisoner Orson Bastion may have been involved in the death."

Eve clutched a throw pillow to her chest and fought off a bout of nausea. Orson had killed again, which was exactly what she'd testified he'd do if he was released from prison.

He'd exhibited so many behaviors consistent with that of a psychopath, especially the lack of emotional involvement with others. The only thing that was missing was the fact that he didn't have a real history of criminal behavior; or, if he did, she hadn't been made aware of it.

He was in jail for killing his stepbrother in an act of rage. He'd only received a charge of second-degree murder. Orson had been twenty-eight years old at the time. He was forty now.

Eve flicked off the TV. She didn't need to hear more. Gordon had said Orson would never look for her at the Ledger ranch, but what if Gordon was wrong? Still, this was likely the safest place on the planet, at least for the time being.

If Troy were here, she'd likely feel totally safe, but she was alone in this rambling old house, without so much as a weapon to protect her son.

She walked to the kitchen, checked the drawers and took out a carving knife. Just in case. Not that she'd need it. Still, knife in hand, she wandered back into the den just as streams of light flicked across the window. The low hum of an engine purred and then stopped.

Someone was here, parked in the driveway.

Surely not Orson. He couldn't have found her this

quickly. Yet adrenaline pumped through her leaving her shaking so violently she had to hold the knife with both hands.

Heavy footsteps clumped across the wooden porch. Eve fought the rising panic. She had to stay calm. She could do this. She had to do this. If the man outside the door was Orson, a lock would never deter him.

She stood so that she'd be behind the door if it opened, poised to bury the blade of the knife in Orson's back the minute he stepped inside—if it was Orson.

She heard the flick of a key in the lock. If the person at the door had a key, surely it wasn't Orson. The knob turned, the door opened and the intruder stepped across the threshold.

His breathing was deep and sharp. His voice echoed though the room.

"The day of reckoning has finally come."

Chapter Four

The voice proclaiming the fatalistic message was masculine, husky. Unfamiliar.

The intruder reached for the door and slammed it shut, leaving her and the knife in full view.

Her knees buckled and her breath rushed out in a whoosh. This wasn't Orson. Instead, it was hunk of a cowboy who reeked of strength and power.

Before she could say anything, he grabbed the arm holding the knife, yanked it over her head and shoved her against the wall. She struggled to push him away, but she might as well have been flailing against a brick wall. A brick wall with broad shoulders that smelled of musk and forest glens.

"Take your hands off me," she sputtered.

"After you tell me what the hell is going on here."

"I thought you were someone else." Her relief drowned in a rush of confusing awareness, as the man's breath heated a spot just below her right earlobe. His masculinity was staggering. She gasped and gulped for air.

"Who are you?" he demanded.

"I'm a friend of Troy's. Now back off before I—"

"Before you what, come at me with a knife?"

She writhed and tried again to break free, but he strengthened his hold on her wrists and kept his body pressed against hers.

Finally, she shifted so that she was staring straight into the depths of his dark eyes at extremely close range. Something jumped inside her, an eruption of emotions that under the circumstances made no sense at all.

His hold loosened, as if whatever had left her quaking had affected him as well. "I'll take that knife," he said. "And then you can tell me who you are and why you're defending my father's house like it was the Holy Grail."

Anxiety swelled again. This didn't add up. "You're lying," she said. "I met Troy's son earlier tonight."

"You may have met Dylan. I'm Sean, the mild-mannered offspring with a cool head. Lucky for you."

She saw the resemblance now. He looked even more like Troy than Dylan did. The same slightly squared jawline. The same classic nose. Only, Sean was years younger than Troy, and so ruggedly handsome that he could have been a soap opera star. And he was still so close that he could probably feel her heart beating.

Collette had said that Troy's other sons were estranged from their father. But then Dylan must have called them when he left for the hospital. Maybe his having a heart attack had gotten through to at least one of Troy's other sons.

"If you talked to Dylan, he must have told you I was here," she said, still trying to make sense of this.

"He mentioned a friend had found Dad. He didn't say you were staying here. In fact, he made a point of telling me the house would be empty and the spare key was under the flowerpot next to the door. So what are you doing here?"

"If you'll release me, I'll explain." She wouldn't, of course, but she'd tell him all he needed to know.

"Deal. As soon as you let go of the knife."

She exhaled sharply and released her killer grasp on it. Before he moved away, his right hand slid slowly down her left arm. Awareness vibrated through her.

"Mommy! Mommy!" She made a quick return to the harsh reality of the situation, as Joey's high-pitched calls echoed down the hallway.

"My son," she said. "He has nightmares."

Sean cocked his head to the side and arched his brows. "Your son. A husband? A daughter? Exactly how many people are in this house?"

"Just my son, Joey, and me. I don't have a husband and Joey's an only child."

She was babbling in her relief. Whatever complications Sean presented would be minuscule compared to what she'd have faced had it been Orson instead of Troy's son who'd showed up tonight.

"Momma!" The cry had become more hysterical.

"I'm coming, sweetie."

She hurried away without further explanation, grateful to break away from Sean Ledger and get her emotions back under control.

In the two years since Brock's death she hadn't once felt the pangs of attraction for another man. She'd begun to worry that she never would. Now was not the time for fate to turn up the heat.

SEAN WATCHED EVE WORTHINGTON hurry down the hall and disappear into what had once been his bedroom. She was the last thing he'd expected to find when he pushed through the heavy door of his childhood home.

Before encountering her, his head had been swimming in a thick fog of memories. The good, the bad and the tragic had immersed him so deeply into the past that his feet had felt like lead when he climbed the steps to the porch.

Nothing like a woman about to plunge a knife into your back to smack you back into the present. *But what in the hell was a woman and kid doing here?*

Dylan had written several times about their father and the fact that he was settling into the life of a rancher. Not once had he mentioned that Troy had a lady friend—one young enough to be his daughter. If he had, Sean would have never come home again.

He'd been only thirteen years old when his mother was murdered in this very house. His world had been destroyed that day. Then, when his father had been accused of the crime, Sean literally wanted to die.

When his brothers were asleep that night, he'd taken one of his dad's guns and actually placed the barrel of it into his mouth. He might have pulled the trigger if his imagination hadn't played ghostly tricks on his mind, probably an easy feat, considering his shaky emotional state.

He saw his mother that night as clearly as he saw

the weapon in his hands. She'd stepped into the room and taken the gun from his shaky hands. It had fallen to the floor without a sound. He'd tried to hold on to his mother, but she dissolved like a warm breath on a frosty morning.

He never told anyone about that, had tried to block it from his own mind. But there had been many nights when those memories were so vivid that he could feel the chill of the evaporating vapor and taste the cold metallic bitterness of the gun barrel.

He shouldn't have come back here. Returning to Willow Creek Ranch had worked for Dylan, but there was no way Sean would ever mend fences with his father or become totally convinced of his innocence.

He'd visit his father in the hospital in the morning, but then he'd be on his way. In fact, he should probably apologize to Eve Worthington for barging in on her and leave right now, before he looked into those gorgeous, haunted eyes of hers again.

He started down the hall after Eve, hating the memories that the house awakened. He stopped near the doorway where she'd disappeared. Her voice was soft and reassuring when she talked to her child, yet there was a shudder of fear in its depths, likely the same fear that had initiated her waiting at the door with a knife.

She'd thought he was someone else, obviously someone she was deathly afraid of. A stalker? An ex-husband? A betrayed lover?

None of his business and not his problem. He was running from woman trouble, not looking for it.

He stopped, just out of sight of Eve and her complaining son.

"I wanna go home."

"It's too far to drive back to Dallas tonight. Besides, you don't want to miss the fun of seeing the horses, do you?"

"What if I don't like horses?"

If she was from Dallas, then why hadn't Dylan realized she was spending the night? Perhaps he'd just forgotten with all that was going on with Troy. Still, it was odd he hadn't remembered it when he told him to make himself at home. Sean turned and walked back to the kitchen.

He opened the refrigerator and pulled out a beer. He'd barely swallowed his first swig when his cell phone rang. It was Dylan. Sean didn't bother with a hello. "What the hell have you gotten me into in now?"

"I take it that means you've arrived at the ranch and met Eve Worthington."

"I met her all right. She threw me a welcoming party, only instead of balloons, she was wielding a knife."

There was a short pause in the phone conversation in which Sean overheard a muttered thanks from Dylan.

"Sorry, bro," Dylan said. "One of the nurses just brought me a cup of coffee. What's this about a knife?"

"Dad's houseguest took me for an intruder and came at me with a kitchen knife. I had to take it away from her."

"Still fighting off the women."

"You're smiling, aren't you?"

"Maybe just a little. Why'd she have a knife?"

"She thought I was someone else."

"Probably believes all that bunk about the house being haunted."

"Our house is haunted?"

"So some of the locals say. Anyway, I'm sure Eve's fear was no match for your Ledger brawn and charm. Apologize to her for the confusion."

"As soon as you explain why you failed to warn me the house was occupied."

"I just found out myself. I called Collette to tell her you were in town, and she said she'd persuaded Eve to spend the night. That's why I'm calling, hoping to give you fair warning. Collette is calling Eve, probably has her on the phone now."

"A little after the fact."

"You know, you have to take some of the blame," Dylan said. "You could have called and said you were coming *before* you reached Mustang Run. Then we could have avoided the surprise element."

"I wasn't sure I'd actually go through with the visit, until I saw the city limits sign."

Even after he'd made the call to Dylan, he still might have turned around and driven the other way if Dylan hadn't told him about Troy's coronary attack.

"Why are you still at the hospital?" Sean asked. "You said you were leaving for the night the last time we talked. Troy's not having any new problems, is he?"

"No. Dad's resting now. The cardiologist on staff stopped by the room. He says the prognosis is good for a complete recovery, though nothing is guaranteed. I'm heading that way now. Do you need anything?"

"A few answers. What's the deal between Dad and Eve?"

"Hard to say. The situation being what it is, I haven't had a chance to get the full story from either of them. Apparently, they became friends when she was his prison psychiatrist a few years back. She said she was just passing through tonight and decided to stop in and see him. Just in time to save his life, I might add."

"Then they're not a romantic item?"

"Man, Sean. Where did you get an idea like that? She's our age. She has a kid, probably a husband as well."

"There is no husband. And what did you expect me to think? I show up, and she's here in her pajamas."

"In her pajamas, huh? That must have spiced up the knife removal routine."

"I was defending, not groping."

"Whatever. But don't read any more into this than is actually there. Eve said she was passing through. No reason not to believe her."

"Then she didn't mention that she was in any kind of trouble?"

"No, but now that you mention it, Dad seemed anxious about not getting to talk to her."

"Did he say why?"

"No. He's been pretty much incoherent all night, first from the coronary trauma and then from the meds."

"Okay. We'll talk more when I see you."

"I'm dead tired. Do you mind if we put off our reunion

until morning? Collette and I will come down and cook you, Eve and the boy an old-time ranch breakfast."

"Sounds like a winner. I guess I can round up some linens and a pillow around this place?"

"Take your old room. The beds are made."

"And occupied."

"Then avoid temptation and find another room."

"There is no temptation involved."

"Then just make yourself at home. And, Sean, I'm really glad you're here. It will mean a lot to Dad."

Sean doubted that. He said a quick goodbye.

Once he'd finished the beer, he checked the rest of the fridge's contents. Choices weren't bad.

He found bread in the pantry and made himself a ham and cheese sandwich, then poured a tall glass of milk to wash it down. Halfway through the meal, he heard the soft patter of footsteps in the hallway.

He looked up as Eve joined him in the kitchen. She'd pulled a pale blue robe over her pajamas. That did nothing to hide the fact that she was a damned attractive woman.

She looked around the kitchen, her gaze focusing on the sandwich fixings he'd left on the counter.

"Help yourself," he said. "Bread's fresh and the ham is good. There's plenty of beer, or milk if you're a purist."

"I'm not opposed to cold beer, but a glass of milk sounds better tonight."

"Something to soothe the savage beast."

A blush flushed her cheeks. "I'm not ordinarily so

savage. I'm a city girl. I guess I let the isolation get to me."

"Looked like a little more than that to me."

"Look, Sean, I'm really sorry about the knife incident, but can we just forget about it now?"

"Subject closed." For the time being. "There's hot chocolate mix in the pantry."

She nodded. "That sounds even better. Can I make a cup for you?"

"Sure. Why not?"

She turned back to face him, and her straight, shiny brown locks seductively bounced around the bottom of her chin. Much *too* seductively.

He finished off his sandwich and wiped his mouth on the paper towel he'd been using as a napkin, just as she started to the table with two steaming mugs of cocoa in hand.

"Sorry, but I didn't find marshmallows," she said.

"I suspect Troy is not a marshmallow kind of guy," Sean said. "But then, you evidently know him much better than I do."

She stared into her cup for a moment and then lifted her eyes to meet his. Hers were the color of warm cognac, vibrant even in the fluorescent light from the overhead fixture.

"I was Troy's prison psychiatrist for a couple of years."

"Dylan told me. He called while you were calming your son."

"Collette called me as well. She explained everything. I'm truly sorry for intruding on your homecoming."

"Actually, I'm more the intruder. You were the invited guest."

"It's your home."

"*Was* my home. When I was thirteen. I've hung my hat in a lot of places since then."

"Nonetheless, Joey and I will clear out of your way in the morning."

"Don't leave on my account. It's a big house, and I don't plan to be here long."

Her shoulders squared. "You should. You owe it to your father to get to know the man he is today."

He bristled a bit at the preachy tone, especially when she had no idea what she was talking about. "Do you always offer your opinion to people you've just met?"

"No," she admitted. "I seldom give advice at all anymore."

Her shoulders and voice fell as if he'd sucker punched her. It gave him no pleasure. "It's okay," he said. "My dad and I have issues."

She merely nodded, leaving lots of questions in his mind about just what his father had told her about him and his brothers. Had Troy played her, fed her what he thought she'd like to hear in order to make an impression on her? Or had she just dug around in his mind and come up with her own conclusions?

She finished her hot chocolate, stood and carried her empty cup to the sink. Once she rinsed it, she turned back to him. "Again, I'm sorry for the knife incident, and I wish you and Troy the best."

He watched her walk away, her slim hips swaying just enough to make her exit interesting. He thought again of the way her body had felt pressed against his. For a minute back there, he'd had the crazy urge to kiss her.

The urge surfaced again, and he wondered what she'd do if he followed her to the bedroom door and kissed her good-night.

Probably come at him with a knife while he slept.

He'd leave well enough alone before he became as lust-craved as Laci Cahill. With one big difference. He wasn't married—and had no intention of ever playing the matrimony game.

EVE PULLED THE COVERS about Joey and leaned close, letting her lips brush his forehead. Asleep, innocence was etched into his youthful face. If only she could give him that simple purity of joy back again, instead of dragging him back into the ominous threat of peril.

Trepidation played havoc with her breathing as she backed away from Joey's bed. What if that had been Orson at the door tonight? What if he'd been the man who'd pinned her to the wall with his brute strength? The truth shuddered through her.

There would have been no way she could have protected Joey.

But it hadn't been Orson Bastion. It had been Sean Ledger, whose hard, unrelenting strength held her captive. Yet, the minute she'd realized he wasn't dangerous, it had been attraction, not fear, she'd felt at his hands.

Eve slipped out of her robe, draped it across the one chair in the room and then dropped to the twin bed opposite Joey's. She slid beneath the crisp sheets and pulled the quilt over her as confusing thoughts tumbled through her mind.

The dread that had chilled her before Sean's arrival had disappeared. The rambling old house no longer made her uneasy. If anything, she felt protected. Sean made the difference.

Yet, she couldn't start relying on him. Tomorrow might bring anything. Tonight she needed to get some sleep.

Her eyelids grew heavy, and she turned over to stare out the window and into the darkness, and the scatter of stars that studded the sky.

Her mind flashed back to Sean and a rush of heat crept inside her.

Surely not desire, she told herself. Not in this situation. If she felt anything at all for Sean, the attraction stemmed from pure relief that he wasn't Orson Bastion.

If he had been, she'd be dead.

But Orson was still on the loose.

SOMEONE WAS IN THE HOUSE. Eve could hear him breathing, smell the odors of sweat and cheap aftershave, see his shadow coming nearer.

She clutched the knife and felt the sear of pain and hot, sticky blood gushing into her hand. When she looked down she saw that the handle was missing and the blade had sliced into her palm.

Her brain began to clatter. Eve jerked awake and sat up in bed. The clattering wasn't in her brain, but was coming from the bedside table where her cell phone was vibrating against the old wood.

She glanced at the clock as she grabbed the phone to quiet it before it woke Joey. Five minutes before six in the morning was extremely early for a call from either Gordon or Collette, and they were the only two who had her number.

The vibration in the palm of her hand mirrored the state of her nerves as she whispered hello.

"It's Gordon. Is this Eve?"

"Yes." The urgency in his voice told her this was not a good-news call.

Chapter Five

Eve tried to steady the phone in her shaky hand as she untangled herself from the bed covers.

"I can barely hear you," Gordon said. "Are you okay?"

"I'm fine."

"Where are you?"

"Hold on."

She slid her legs over the side of the bed and padded into the hall, quietly closing the bedroom door behind her before resuming the conversation. "I'm sorry, Gordon. I should have called you and let you know I was all right. I took your suggestion. I'm at Troy Ledger's ranch in Mustang Run."

"Thank God for that. Troy is the one man who'll understand your situation. How is he?"

"He's in the hospital." She told him how she'd arrived to find him in the throes of an apparent heart attack.

"Good thing you showed up when you did," Gordon said.

"I'm taking that as a good omen, but I'm still worried about Troy."

"Are you alone in Troy's house?"

"Not exactly. Troy's son Sean is here."

"You mean Dylan?"

"No, it seems I wasn't the only one who showed up at the ranch unexpectedly last evening. It's complicated."

"Sounds that way. The good news is you're safe and don't have to worry about Orson showing up at your house."

And yet she could hear the alarm in Gordon's voice. "Is there news about Orson?"

The long pause sent her pulse spiraling.

"This could mean nothing, Eve. There's no conclusive proof that Orson is even still in Texas."

"Don't beat around the bush. Just give me the truth."

"Okay. I don't know if you've heard, but a young woman was killed yesterday in a carjacking, and the police seem to think Orson might have been involved."

"I caught just the basics on the evening news last night."

"Then you know the car was deserted a few miles from where you live."

"No, I didn't realize that." A new wave of uneasiness wrecked havoc with her control. For all she knew, Orson might have already been to her house looking for her. Had she been there…

She forced herself to breathe. "Is there more?"

"Reagan Conner has been trying to get in touch with you."

"Reagan Conner? Should I know who that is?"

"He's the homicide detective investigating the murder."

"Why would he contact you?"

"To see if I know anything to help them locate Orson. He questioned me about former inmates that Orson might try to hook up with for help in getting out of the area. I gave him a few names, but also told him about the threats on your life."

"Did Detective Conner mention that I'd called the police department yesterday and told them I could be a target?"

"Yes. He wanted my take on the threat Orson made to you, but for the record, he thinks you're overreacting. He's convinced Orson's only concern will be avoiding capture. Nonetheless, he says he's been trying to reach you."

"Did you give him this number?"

"No. You asked me not to give it to anyone, and I wouldn't go against your wishes without asking first. I think you should call him, but handle it anyway you want. Just don't go home until Orson is back in prison, or the cops are certain he's out of the area."

"Thanks for the heads-up that he was near my neighborhood. You can be sure I won't go home until I'm convinced it's safe to do so."

Not that she had any idea where she would go, now that she couldn't stay here.

"Just hang tight," Gordon said. "Every cop in the state is on the lookout for him. He'll be behind bars soon."

"I'm counting on that."

In the meantime, Orson was disrupting every aspect

of her life. If she didn't have Joey, she'd just buy a gun and take her chances with the monster back in Dallas.

But she did have Joey. Violence had torn his life apart once. Now she not only had to protect him, but see that he was not traumatized again.

Once they'd said their goodbyes, anxiety scratched along her raw nerves like the claws of a wildcat. She drooped against the wall and buried her head in her hands, massaging her temples, as if that would stimulate her brain into making a decision as to what she should do next.

"Is there a problem?"

Sean's voice startled her. She turned to find him a few feet away, shadowed in the moonlight that filtered into the house. He was wearing jeans, still unsnapped at the waist. No shirt. No shoes.

She fought an impulse to throw herself into his strong arms and stay there until the quaking inside stopped. After the knife episode, surely he'd think she was nuts. She managed to keep a ragged hold on her composure.

"How much did you hear?" she asked.

"Enough to know it wasn't good news."

"Good news seldom comes at daybreak, does it?"

"Not often. Anything I can do to help?"

"No, but thanks for asking."

"I'm a good listener. Actually, I'm not," he admitted, "but I'll make a stab at it, since we're both awake anyway."

"Believe me, you don't want to get involved in this."

"In that case, can I offer a shoulder to cry on?"

"That's the most tempting offer I've had in days." Maybe years, but she wouldn't go there. "But crying wouldn't help."

He propped a hand next to her shoulder, leaning against the wall, not pinning her in as he'd done before, yet so close she could feel the titillating warmth of his body.

Maybe it was just the act of standing this close to a half-dressed hunk when the sun hadn't even peeked over the horizon, but she seemed to be forgetting how to breathe.

"Who did you think I was when you came at me with the knife?" Sean asked.

"I don't know. A burglar, I guess. Didn't we go over this before?"

"Are you sure you're not running from someone?"

"That's a ludicrous idea."

He cupped her chin in his right hand, tilting her head so that she had to meet his piercing gaze head-on. "I know fear when I see it, Eve. Even in people."

"I'm not afraid," she lied. "I'm concerned about a friend. That's all. I'm really tired and I'd like a few more hours sleep before I have to get up."

"Have it your way. If you change your mind, I'm in the room right across the hall. And remember, you don't have to rush off in the morning just because Troy isn't here. I'm not going to seduce you or try to take advantage of you, you know."

Intentional or not, she was already being seduced.

Apparently all it took in her current state of mind was a gentle touch and a wallop of masculinity.

But even if she was attracted to Sean, she couldn't stay. Troy had enough problems, without having to worry himself with her. In fact, even visiting Troy in the hospital would be a mistake. She wouldn't get into that with Sean, either. She'd just get up in a few hours and clear out.

It was the only sensible and considerate thing to do.

Yet, it was all she could do not to run after Sean and take him up on the offer of one of his broad, muscular shoulders to cry on, as she watched him walk away.

SEAN SOAKED UP HIS remaining cream gravy with the last bite of his second biscuit. "Eggs, steak, hash browns, gravy and biscuits. Now, that's what I call a breakfast."

"Takes a hearty breakfast to keep a cowboy going," Dylan said.

"You've definitely synced into this ranching lifestyle," Sean said.

"Does that surprise you?"

Sean nodded. "Yeah. Lost my bet with Wyatt. I said you'd never last a week back in Mustang Run."

"So you and our older brother were betting on my falling out of the saddle. Too bad I didn't get in on any of that money."

"I'd have changed my bet if I'd known you'd luck into meeting a gorgeous woman who makes heavenly biscuits." Sean tipped his coffee mug toward Collette.

She smiled and tossed her head, so that her wild halo of red hair resettled around her shoulders. "Thank you. You are now officially my favorite brother-in-law."

"Only because you've never met the others," Sean assured her.

Sean wiped his mouth on the plaid napkin and leaned back in his chair. The others were through eating, though all five of them continued to linger at the marred kitchen table. Everyone's plates except Eve's and Joey's were empty. Joey had eaten half a biscuit and a few bites of scrambled egg. Eve's food was practically untouched.

She seemed distracted, troubled. He was still certain she was running scared, but she clearly didn't want his help. Fine, she wasn't his problem. He should just let it go at that.

"I'm heading into the hospital as soon as we finish here," Dylan said. "Why don't you ride in with me, Sean? I want to be there to see the look on Dad's face when he sees you for the first time in seventeen years."

Sean dreaded the moment. The last time he'd seen his father, the judge had just issued the sentence of life in prison. Sean had been sitting in the courtroom with his brothers and his grandparents. His grandfather had lifted a fist a victory. His grandmother had cried and proclaimed justice had been served, but it wouldn't bring back her beautiful Helene.

The heartbreaking disappointment of that day was firmly implanted in Sean's mind. Until then, he'd prayed for a miracle that would prove his dad hadn't killed his mother.

His prayers had died along with a large part of his

heart that day. All he'd gotten in answer was an almost blank stare from his father before the security officer led him away.

Not once in all the years since had his father reached out to him; so why the hell would Troy Ledger give a damn about seeing him now?

He drained the last of his coffee. "I'm not sure that the shock of seeing me would be the best medicine for Troy in his condition. Maybe I should just postpone the reunion for a few days."

"I think having you there is exactly what Dad needs," Dylan protested. "Besides, I don't trust you to stick around long before the neigh of a distant horse lures you away."

"I haven't even checked out the neighs on this ranch yet. I could stay around here and do that this morning."

"Where is the hospital?" Eve asked.

"It's Carlton-Hayes Regional Hospital, near Austin."

"Not my favorite place," Collette threw in.

"Collette had a life-and-death experience of her own there," Dylan said.

Eve ceased the restless worrying of her coffee mug's handle. "What happened?"

"Explanation not fit for childhood consumption," Collette said, nodding toward Joey. "But the bottom line is, Dylan saved my life."

"Then she had to marry me," Dylan teased. "Collette's driving into the hospital a little later. You can wait and follow her in, Eve. That way Collette can introduce Joey to her favorite horses before you leave."

Eve hesitated before responding to the suggestion, but not long enough to convince Sean that she'd ever considered accepting his invitation to stay on at the ranch.

"Great idea," Eve said. "I'll follow Collette to the hospital and then be on my way. I'll get my things together as soon as I help clean up the kitchen."

Sean stared at Eve. Her shoulders were straight, her face and eyes showing only minimal signs of the emotional upheaval that had her quaking in the hallway mere hours ago. Only the tight muscles in her neck and her nervous fidgeting gave her away.

"Sean and I will clean the kitchen," Dylan said. "You three go out and enjoy the morning on the ranch. Joey, if you ask just right, Collette might even take you for a ride on Starlight."

Sean should let it go at that. Troubled horses were his forte, not stubborn, scared women.

He stood and gathered a few dishes to carry to the sink. Eve gathered the serving platters. When she left to go back to her bedroom, Joey, as always, tagged along beside her. The two of them on their own, about to go on the run again.

Sean waited until she was out of earshot. He could kick himself for what he was about to do, but he did it anyway. "I hate to disappoint you, bro, but I'm driving Eve to the hospital. Not to fear, though. I'll be certain you're there for the father/prodigal son moment."

Dylan looked puzzled. "Am I missing something here? Eve just said she would follow Collette in."

"She still will. I'll just be with her."

Dylan rubbed his freshly shaved chin. "Something tells me that knife removal routine must have been even more intriguing than it sounded."

"Let's just say it was eye-opening. It's mere suspicion at this point, but I think the shapely angel who came to our father's rescue last night might be in some trouble of her own."

"That would explain Dad's reaction to her visit," Dylan said.

"Interesting that Dad would know of her trouble, since it sounds like they haven't been in touch in years," Sean commented.

"Perhaps they have a mutual friend."

"Could be."

Dylan squirted some liquid detergent into the sink and turned on the water. "Just be careful. Good-looking women and trouble are a recipe for disaster."

Sean gave his brother a playful punch to the arm. "Who would know that better than you?"

"Exactly. So, on second thought, forget everything I said and go with your instincts."

Sean left his brother with the dishes and went off in search of Eve. He found her in the bedroom, zipping the overnight bag she'd thrown onto the bed and engrossed in conversation with Collette and Joey.

"Can my momma go with us?" the boy asked Collette.

"You don't need me to go see the horses," Eve encouraged. "You could go with Collette and I could pack, load the car and be ready to go when you get back. And,

Collette, I'd rather he not ride one of the horses this trip. He's had no experience."

"Whatever you say," Collette said, "but Starlight's extremely gentle, and I would have let him ride with me. I'd never let him do something dangerous."

Joey climbed onto the bed and scooted close to Eve. "What if we get lost and Momma can't find us?"

Collette sat down on the edge of the bed next to Joey. "I promise we won't get lost. I live here and I take care of the horses every day. That's my job on the ranch."

"Do horses bite?"

"Don't worry. I'll only introduce you to the friendly horses. I'll make certain they don't bite you," Collette assured him.

"You're such a big boy that you don't need me to have fun," Eve urged her son.

Joey looked as if he was being forced to choose between a stomachache and a smashed toe.

The kid reminded Sean of himself years ago. After his mother died and Troy went to prison, he'd suffered severe anxiety attacks. It had taken him years to get beyond them. And there really was no reason Eve had to be in that big a hurry to leave the ranch.

"I'd like to see those horses, too," Sean said. "Why don't the four of us just march down to that barn together?"

Joey grinned as if he'd just been offered gummy bears for breakfast. Eve gave Sean a stay-out-of-this look.

Nonetheless, a few minutes later they were treading the worn path from the house to the horse barn and the fenced pasture beyond. To Sean's surprise, Joey walked next to him.

"Watch the mud," Eve cautioned Joey when they approached a low spot. "You only have one pair of shoes with you."

Tennis shoes, Sean noted. "You need a pair of boots," he said. "A cowboy can't be worried about a little mud."

"Yeah, Momma," Joey agreed. "Cowboys have to get muddy."

Sean stooped low. "Climb on my shoulders, pardner, and I'll give you a ride over the muck."

Joey looked to his mother for approval. When she nodded, he grinned again and climbed aboard. Sean had worn jackets that weighed more.

"Can I feed the horses?" Joey asked.

"Sure," Collette said. "Like I said, that's usually my job, but I can sure use some help. And once you feed them, they'll really love you."

"Horses treat most people well, as long as you respect them and teach them what you expect from them," Sean said.

Even when he'd been Joey's age, Sean had loved horses, especially Sinbad. It had been storming the night he was foaled, the thunder so loud it had rattled the horse barn as if it were kindling.

Sean's mother had insisted Sean stay inside, but his father had changed her mind. "A boy should see his own horse come kicking into the world," Troy had said.

Old memories of life on the ranch attacked without warning, and a violent churning rumbled in Sean's gut. The images grew painfully vivid. His dad teaching him to ride. Sean playing with his brothers on sunny afternoons. Him sneaking his first smoke behind the woodshed.

Stealing his first kiss in a clump of bluebonnets just past the old corral. Penny Rich. He hadn't thought of her in years. She'd been fourteen, with long, blond hair and budding breasts. He'd been twelve, with braces.

That same spring, he'd broken his right leg while practicing his calf roping for the first local rodeo of the summer. His mother had rushed to him, a look of pure panic in her dark eyes. Mom. Always there.

Until she wasn't.

Sean's knees all but buckled beneath him as the memories intensified. The ache that he'd spent years burying suddenly felt like a suffocating noose around his neck.

He should have never come back to Texas.

Only two things kept him from leaving right now—a woman who needed his help whether she admitted it or not, and the young boy who desperately needed her alive and well.

JOEY CLIMBED ON THE SLATS of Starlight's stall. With a little encouragement from Collette, he reached over and gingerly ran his fingers through the mare's mane.

Eve watched in amazement. Joey's curiosity about the horses no doubt had a lot to do with his fervor, but still, this kind of engagement with strangers was an auspicious accomplishment for him.

Even more surprising was the way he'd climbed on

Sean's shoulders. He'd even questioned where Sean had gone when he didn't enter the barn with them. This from a kid who was still wary of the postman.

Joey looked back at her to make sure she was still nearby. She waved and smiled.

"A budding cowboy. All he needs is a hat and a saddle."

She turned at Sean's voice. "I thought you'd deserted us."

"I needed a minute to wrap my head around being back at the ranch," he admitted.

Naturally he would. She'd been so caught up in her own problems, she hadn't given much thought to what this homecoming must be like for Sean.

He stepped over to the nearest stall, crooned a few words to a gorgeous roan and then turned back to her. "I need a ride to the hospital. Whenever you're ready to go, no hurry."

The statement caught her off guard. "Your brother wants you to ride with him."

"I told him to go ahead without me. I'll catch a ride back with him if need be. Is that a problem for you?"

"If this is because you're worried about me, you needn't be."

"It's not you I'm worried about." Sean raked his fingers through his thick, dark hair, only to have an unruly lock fall back over his forehead. "I just want to make sure you're not stealing the knives."

It was clear that Sean could see right through her and her flimsy lies. But why did he care?

More importantly, how was she going to convince

him she didn't need his help, when his offer became more tempting by the minute?

But she'd have Joey as a chaperone on the drive into town. That would ensure she didn't give into any crazy urges. And once they got to the hospital, she'd make some excuse to leave without seeing Troy. Sean would take her for an ungrateful wench, but that was far better than having Troy ask her about Orson in front of the others, and dragging his whole family into her problems. At least it would be better for them.

Hopefully, it wouldn't be a major mistake for her.

ALYSSA COLEMAN PEEKED THROUGH a slit in the blinds and into the glaring sun outside the front window of her San Antonio apartment. The unmarked car pulled up right on schedule and two men got out.

She figured the taller one to be Detective Reagan Conner. He walked and looked like he'd sounded on the phone. Authoritative. No-nonsense. Tough as nails.

Still no match for her brother.

Both men stopped on the drive where her son Nick was shooting baskets. Nick laughed at something they said and then preened a bit as he sank the next shot. She didn't have to worry about Nick telling them anything. He'd never heard of his uncle Orson. She planned to keep it that way.

She stepped to the door and opened it the minute the bell rang. The two men flashed police IDs and she invited them inside. She wasn't intimidated by them. They'd threaten, but they were saints compared to what she'd grown up around.

She had no idea where her brother was hiding out, but she knew he'd be in touch with her again. He needed something from her, and he knew she'd be too afraid not to do as he asked.

She'd like to help the detectives. She'd like to stop her brother before he killed again. She really would.

But she liked living, so the good detectives would have to rely on their investigative abilities.

SEAN SQUEEZED EVE's duffel into the crammed trunk of her compact car. The contents looked more like Eve and Joey were off for an extended vacation, not a quick trip to visit friends as she'd indicated. The three suitcases could simply indicate she was a clotheshorse, but there were also two large shopping bags of books and toys for Joey, and a boxed video gaming set.

He rearranged a few things and took the liberty of snooping. A large zippered carry-on bag shoved all the way to the back held used Christmas decorations. A stuffed reindeer, a dancing Santa, a set of musical bells and a child's wooden nativity set. Tomorrow was only December first.

His suspicions multiplied and his anxiety level soared. His first instincts that she was on the run held even more credence. Possibilities ran rampant through his mind. Was she dealing with a stalker? A spurned lover? An irate ex-husband?

Or had she broken the law? Did she even have custody of the kid? And who had called her this morning at dawn?

He put everything back in place and closed the trunk.

She wasn't a troubled horse that he could lock up in a stable or fence in until he could figure out what was going on in her head. If she was hell-bent on leaving, there wasn't a lot he could do to stop her.

For all he knew, she might be meeting up with some secret lover who was just dying to take care of her. But if that were the case, why had she been so distracted and nervous at breakfast? And even when she'd been watching Collette take Joey for a ride around the small corral, she'd practically jumped the fence when a rabbit had hopped out of the tall grass behind her.

Sean turned as the front door of the house slammed shut. Joey settled on the top step with his Game Boy and a juice box that Eve had evidently brought with them.

Fighting the growing frustration, Sean went back into the house to grab his hat and a glass of water. He stopped when he spotted Eve standing behind the sofa in the family room. Her fingers dug into the cushioned back of the couch, and her expression was grim.

A picture of a guy who looked like your average tattooed bodybuilder stared back at him from the TV. The picture disappeared and the station's anchorman appeared in its place.

"Escaped convict Orson Bastion is still on the loose and should be considered armed and dangerous. It is quite possible that his appearance has been altered.

"If you see him or someone you think might be him, contact authorities immediately. Do not approach him on your own."

Orson Bastion. There had been lots of talk of him on Sean's truck radio yesterday. He'd escaped from the

same institution where Troy had been held. Sean had
wondered then if his father knew the man. Judging from
the intensity of Eve's focus, he'd say she definitely knew
the escapee.

He muttered a curse under his breath as the truth hit
him like a blow to the gut.

Eve picked up the remote and turned off the TV.
When she started to walk away, Sean blocked her
path.

"We need to talk, Eve." And this time he'd settle for
nothing less than the truth.

Chapter Six

"What's your connection to Orson Bastion?" Sean demanded.

"Keep your voice down, please. You'll upset Joey."

"Then start talking. And skip the lies."

She took a deep breath and exhaled slowly. "He was an inmate at one of the prisons where I worked as a therapist."

"The same one Troy was in," Sean acknowledged. "Were you his therapist?"

"That information would fall under doctor/patient privilege."

"What happened between you and Bastion?"

"Nothing happened."

"And yet seeing him on TV practically sent you into fright convulsions."

She looked away, avoiding eye contact. "Orson's a vicious, unrepentant killer. I just hate to think what he might resort to in order to escape capture."

An unrepentant killer, as compared to his father, who she evidently saw as repentant? Only, that wasn't the case. Troy had never admitted to killing Sean's mother, so there was no way he could have come across as repentant, unless Eve knew something Sean didn't.

"Look at me, Eve. I only want the truth. Why did you really come to Willow Creek Ranch last night?"

Eve raised her chin, but hugged her arms around her chest protectively. Shadows haunted the depths of her eyes, and her trying to be tough only made her appear that much more vulnerable. And made it that much more important that he get the truth from her.

"I've told you why I'm here, Sean. I was in the area. I thought it would be nice to surprise Troy with a visit and see how he's adjusting to his release."

"On the same day Orson Bastion was released from prison. Interesting timing."

"And at the same time Troy was having a heart attack," she reminded him. "At least my stopping in unannounced worked for Troy. Now, can we just drop this and drive to the hospital?"

He shook his head. "Not until you stop feeding me bull."

"You have far more important things to worry about than me, Sean Ledger. Your father is in the hospital. That should take precedence over everything else for you."

He wasn't buying it. He couldn't. The fear he saw in Eve Worthington was too real. "Did you come to Troy for protection from Orson?"

"No. No, of course not," she murmured. "I don't need protection." Stress added a tremor of desperation to her voice. She unwound her arms from her chest and started to walk away.

Sean grabbed her arm. Awareness sizzled though him like the sputter of hot bacon grease. He hated the effect she had on him, but that couldn't influence what he had to do.

"Tell me the truth, Eve. If not for your sake, then for your son's. Is there some reason Orson Bastion would come after you?"

She shuddered and swayed as if she were losing her balance. He pulled her into the circle of his arms to steady her.

Eve sighed, but this time she didn't pull away. "Okay, Sean. You're not going to give up until I tell you the ugly truth, so here it is—I testified against Orson at his parole hearing." Once she started, the explanation tumbled out in a rush. "I believed that if he got out, he'd kill again and again. He swore he'd make me pay."

"So you *are* on the run from Orson Bastion."

"Yes. I know it's probably paranoid of me to think Orson Bastion would give me a thought when he's running for his own life. But Gordon Epps, the prison warden, called me yesterday and suggested I ask your father to let me stay on his ranch until Orson was returned to the prison."

"Why Troy?"

"Because Troy's a man you can count on. I know that and Gordon knows it. And Gordon believes that the Willow Creek Ranch is the last place Orson would expect me to be."

"Because Troy is a former inmate."

"Exactly."

"Why didn't you just go to the police for protection?"

"I called them. I didn't feel they were taking the threat Orson made against me seriously. But it doesn't matter. I shouldn't have come here. I realize that now. Even if Troy were well, he doesn't need me and my problems when he's trying to get his own life back together."

"Showing up when you did likely saved Troy's life."

"And I'm glad for that, but his heart attack is all the more reason I can't ask him to let me stay here. I don't think I should even visit him in the hospital."

"Where do you plan to go?"

"I don't know. This has all become extremely complicated. I just know that I have to keep Joey safe."

"Where's Joey's father?"

"He died two years ago."

Sean decided not to ask for details. Knowing too much about her personal life would break down barriers that he needed to stay in place.

"You shouldn't have to face this alone, Eve."

"I don't have a lot of choices."

"You have one." His arm tightened about her waist, and his muscles hardened, along with his resolve not to let this become personal. "Stay at the ranch. You'll be safe here."

She pulled away. "That wouldn't be fair to you or Troy. The two of you need time to reconnect without worrying about me."

"The reconnecting bit will either happen or it won't.

Whether you and Joey are here will have no bearing on it."

She took his hand. The touch surprised him and sent a new bundle of confusing emotions coursing through him.

"I appreciate the offer," she said. "More than you know. But suppose we're all wrong and Orson does show up here? You can't even imagine what this monster is capable of."

"I worked with horses considered unbreakable for three summers while I was at the university, Eve. Orson can't be tougher than some of the disturbed stallions I tackled. And I've been the top marksman three years running in my National Guard unit. I think I can handle Orson if he's fool enough to show up in Mustang Run."

Her hand relaxed in his. "Stay on the ranch," he coaxed. "Joey can get lots of fresh air and sunshine. You can sleep through the night without worrying about defending yourself with a kitchen knife."

"What about Dylan and Collette?"

"What about them?"

"Don't you think you should get their approval before bringing the possible target of a madman onto the ranch?"

"If they have a problem with it, I'll let you know, and we'll go somewhere else—together. Trust me with this, Eve. I won't abandon you and Joey."

"Why?" she whispered. "Why are you so determined to become my protector?"

"Because a man who'd turn his back on a woman and kid in trouble isn't really a man."

"You, Sean Ledger, are a lot more like your father than you may ever admit."

He seriously doubted that. "Does that mean you'll stay?"

"For now. I can't promise beyond that."

Not the guarantee he wanted, but he'd deal with that issue when the time came. Other issues couldn't wait. "Now that I know what's going on, I think we need to call off our visit to the hospital. No use to risk anyone recognizing you and linking you to Troy."

She stiffened. "See, it's happening already. I'm coming between you and your father."

"I haven't seen the man in seventeen years," Sean said. "A few more days can't make that much difference."

"He's had a heart attack. No matter the prognosis, he could have another one. And even if he doesn't, your visit will mean the world to him. I won't stand in the way of that."

"So, do you have a better idea?"

"Don't use my name in front of anyone at the hospital. And I'll only go this once."

Sean decided to choose his battles wisely with Eve. This one would hit low on the priority level. Even if Orson was reckless and downright stupid enough to still be in Texas, it was unlikely he'd be hanging around a busy hospital.

The fact that Eve was staying on at the ranch was victory enough for now. He'd passed the first hurdle of the day. The second was facing Troy Ledger. He had little hope it would turn out nearly as well.

THE LARGE DOUBLE DOORS to the hospital slid open and Sean, Eve and Joey stepped inside. Having Joey in the backseat of his double-cab pickup had put any talk of Orson off limits. An uneasy silence had settled between them, giving Sean far too much time to think.

He hadn't lied. He'd have offered to help any woman and kid in legitimate trouble, but his feelings of concern for Eve were all mixed up with his uncanny attraction to her. It was not the normal kind of attraction to a good-looking woman, but a sensual onslaught every time he was near her.

It was the knife incident, he decided. Adrenaline and testosterone had formed a formidable alliance when he'd pressed against her, roaring though him with the ferocity of a mad bull. He'd been conscious of her every curve, deliciously aware of her breasts and hips when they'd pushed against his strained muscles.

That had been the fuel that had originally fanned the attraction. It went beyond that now.

He watched her as she walked toward the elevator, hips swaying, shoulders squared, silky hair bouncing. Her hand was clasped with Joey's. She was the perfect mix of spunk and warmth, obstinate yet seductively vulnerable.

And he was going overboard here. She was a woman in trouble. He'd offered his protective services. That was it. Start thinking differently, and it would lead to nothing but trouble.

He and women didn't mix—at least not for long. They wanted more than he had to give. He'd proved that twice before. Only a fool would jump into the path of a kicking horse.

Okay, so he was lousy with analogies, too.

Now that they were inside the hospital, even the temptation of Eve couldn't alleviate the anxiety generated by his inevitable confrontation with his father. Just as he'd promised, Sean had called ahead to alert Dylan of their arrival.

When they reached Troy's room, Dylan and Collette were waiting for them in the hallway. Dylan smiled in anticipation and the dread rolled in Sean's stomach.

Cold. Calculating. Brutal. A murderer.

Sean had heard those words and worse, used by his mother's family over and over through the years to describe Troy. The unmarried uncle who'd become Sean's guardian had hated Troy even more than his grandparents—if that was possible.

At some point, Sean had separated the Troy Ledger they talked about with such hate from the man he'd known as Dad. For all practical purposes, his father had died the day Sean gave up hope of Troy proving his innocence.

Could there be even a fragment of forgiveness inside Sean for the man inside Room 212?

"You guys go in first," Eve said. "Joey and I will wait here with Collette."

"But you'll go in later, won't you?" Dylan asked.

She nodded. "Just don't mention my name in front of any of the staff. I'm traveling incognito this visit."

Dylan looked puzzled.

"Just go with it," Sean said. "We'll explain later."

"I'll hold you to that." He clapped Sean on the back. "Now let's get this show on the road."

Eve stepped in close. "Just give Troy a chance, Sean."

Dylan pushed the door open and stepped inside.

"The moment of reckoning," Sean muttered for the second time in as many days. A moment he'd probably live to regret.

Troy looked up as Dylan walked into his room. "I thought you'd gone home. Ranch won't run itself while you're up here catering to me."

"I have somebody with me that I think you'd like to see."

Troy pushed himself up so that he sat higher in the bed, and waited, expecting it to be Eve Worthington that followed Dylan in. He hated for her to see him like this, but he needed to talk to her, what with that bastard Orson Bastion on the loose.

It wasn't Eve.

Troy stared at the visitor, sure the meds were playing a trick on his mind. He blinked rapidly, his chest as hard as a lump of red Texas clay.

"It's Sean, Dad. He got in last night."

"I know." The words came out like they'd been pushed across sand. "I recognize him from the picture you showed me." Troy wrapped the fingers of one hand around the bed's side rail and extended the other hand toward Sean. "Hello, son."

"Hi. It's been awhile." Sean took a few steps into the room, but ignored the offered hand.

The invisible gap that separated Troy from Sean became palpable. It was more than the years that separated them. It was all the talks they'd never had, the doubts and suspicions and the pain they should have worked through together.

But Sean was here. That was more than Troy had expected, maybe more than he deserved. "Dylan tells me you're a horse whisperer, one of the best in the business."

"I'm a trainer. I've had good luck with troubled horses. The whispering reputation isn't my choosing."

"You were always good with horses," Troy said.

The memories crashed down like blocks of ice, freezing time, weighing him down. His eyes began to sting, and Troy closed them, not wanting Sean to see this weaker side of him.

"Yeah. Horses seldom disappoint you."

"Remember Sinbad?" Troy said, ignoring the sarcasm. "He didn't like for anyone but you to ride him."

"Yeah. I remember Sinbad."

"Did you stop by the ranch?" Troy asked.

Sean nodded. "I spent the night there last night. Didn't have a chance to see much of it yet, but what I saw evidences the hard work you and Dylan have put in on it."

"Collette, too," Troy said. Talk of the ranch was easier for him. "She's a hard worker, that girl. And she loves working with the horses."

"All that and a great cook, too," Sean said.

"And gorgeous, with great taste in men," Dylan added, no doubt trying to ease the tension that filled the tiny room.

Troy shifted and tugged on the hospital gown that always seemed to bunch up in the most uncomfortable of places. "Dylan tells me you've never been to the post."

"No, but came close a couple of times," Sean admitted. "Escaped the noose before the marriage nuptials got underway."

"You'll know when the right woman comes along."

"I'm not looking."

Didn't matter. Troy hadn't been looking either, but once he'd met Helene, he'd have turned his life upside down to get her to marry him.

Dylan leaned on the foot rail. "The cardiologist doesn't want you to have too much company, Dad, so I'm going to duck out and let the two of you visit for a few minutes."

"Thanks, and you don't have to keep driving all the way up here to check on me. I'm going to be fine. Won't be much help at the ranch for a few weeks, but I'll get there."

"Then you'd best talk Sean into staying on a month or so. A little fence-fixing with the peons will help me out and do him good."

Sean pulled a chair next to the bed and settled into it. Troy hoped he wouldn't start asking a bunch of questions about the past. He'd go there with him someday, but he'd rather it not be today. He was weaker than he wanted his sons to know.

Sean raked his hair back from his forehead. Strange

how much he looked like the kid Troy remembered when he did that.

Sean leaned in close. "What do you know about Orson Bastion?"

Sean was dead serious now, his face drawn into tight planes and angles. Any resemblance to the kid from seventeen years ago vanished.

"Why do you ask?" Troy asked.

"He escaped from the prison in Huntsville. I figured you might have known him."

"I knew him all right. For starters, Orson is smart, conniving, manipulative and cunning—with the black heart of a devil."

"Sounds as if you knew him well."

"Better than I wanted to."

"I hear Eve Worthington also knew him well."

Sean had whispered the name, as if he thought the walls might overhear. Even in Troy's weakened state, he juggled the fact and came up with the only sensible conclusion.

"I take it you met Eve. Was she still at the ranch when you arrived last night?"

"Yes to both questions. She says Orson Bastion threatened to kill her for testimony she gave at his parole hearing."

"Yeah, and I have no doubt that he meant it. Where is she now?"

"Just outside the room, with Dylan and Collette. Her son is with her."

"I'd like to see her."

"You will, but first we need to square away a few

things. I've asked her and her son Joey to stay at the ranch until this psycho is captured—just to be on the safe side. I'll stay, too, of course."

"So you've offered to be her bodyguard?"

"I guess you could say that, though evidently she and Gordon Epps think she won't really need one as long as she's at the Willow Creek Ranch."

"That explains why she showed up last night. And I agree. I don't suspect Orson would ever think to look for her there."

"I haven't had a chance to discuss this with Dylan," Sean said.

"Dylan will be fine with it. Collette will, too. She knows what it is to need protection from a madman. And if anyone deserves a break, it's Eve. She's a giver, like your—" Troy stopped himself. Better not to bring up Helene until he and Sean were on more solid footing with each other.

Yet there was something about Eve that reminded him of Helene. That was the reason he'd let down his guard with her, had talked to her at length about what losing Helene that way had done to him. He shared his heartbreak with Eve, when he'd never been able to discuss that with anyone else.

"I think it best if only the family knows that Eve and Joey are on the ranch," Sean said. "And I don't want you to mention her name to any of your friends or the hospital staff."

"I agree," Troy said. "But if Orson decides to track Eve down, he'll find a way to do it. The only thing that will stop him is a bullet. Just so you know what you're getting into."

"I can handle myself, and a gun."

"I never doubted it." But just in case, Troy planned to be in between Sean and Orson if it came to that. He'd failed Helene. He wouldn't fail their son.

Which meant that he had no time to spend flat on his back in a hospital bed. He'd have to recover. Fast. Before Orson found a way to make good on his threat.

THE FEAR WAS DROPPING AWAY from Eve like needles falling from pine trees. It had been four days since Orson's escape, and no more deaths had been attributed to him. The police now believed he was in Mexico.

She hummed as she spread a glob of chocolate frosting over the top of her freshly baked cake. If Orson had moved on, that meant she was out of danger.

Which also meant she had no real reason to stay on at the ranch. So why wasn't she excited at the prospect of going back to Dallas?

She smoothed more frosting around the sides of the three layers. The cake looked good. The test would be in the tasting. It was the first time she'd ever made a cake from scratch. The recipe had come from the internet. She wasn't about to admit to Collette that her culinary talents were pretty much nonexistent.

Her repertoire consisted of grilled chicken or fish, a baked potato, salad and of course the perennial peanut butter and jelly sandwich. And an occasional pizza delivery.

Sean and Dylan on the other hand, were beef men.

Ranching gave a cowboy an appetite, Dylan had claimed last night, when he and Sean had grilled huge sirloins for dinner. Even Joey's appetite had improved in the three days they'd been here, though he only picked at the peas, butterbeans, squash and other veggies that Collette cooked on a nightly basis.

Joey wandered in from the living room, where he'd been watching TV. "Is that for a birthday?"

"No. The cake is for a homecoming."

"What's that?" Joey dragged a chair to the counter and climbed into it, resting on his knees for a closer look at the cake.

"Do you remember Mr. Ledger?"

"Uh-huh. He was sick."

"Right, but he's feeling better now and he's coming home from the hospital this afternoon."

Joey looked upset. "This is Sean's house."

"No, Sean is Mr. Ledger's son, but he doesn't live here. He's only visiting, as we are. This is Mr. Ledger's house."

"He should stay at the hospital."

"He's a nice man, Joey. You'll like him."

"What if I don't?"

"You like Sean. I'm sure you'll like his dad."

Eve sensed the anxiety building in her son. His fear of strangers, especially men, made life almost overwhelming for him at times.

She smoothed the last bit of frosting. "Do you want to lick the spoon?"

"I guess."

Talk of Troy's homecoming had sucked the enthusiasm

right out of him. She handed him the spoon and gave him a hug. "It's going to be fine, Joey. And we'll be going home soon."

She was about to set the empty frosting bowl in the sink when Sean swung through the kitchen door. He dropped a package on the counter beside Joey.

"Looks like you got mail, pardner."

Apprehension stole Eve's breath. No one should know Joey was here. She snatched the package away before Joey could open it.

"It's okay. Let him have it," Sean said, tapping his finger on the address label.

It had been mailed to Sean from a Western store in Austin. She released her wrestler's grip on the package and let Sean take it from her and give it back to Joey.

She should have known Sean wouldn't have blown their cover or given Joey anything that could prove dangerous. No wonder Sean had kept his distance from her the last few days. Fear and paranoia had turned her into an untrusting control freak.

Joey climbed out of the chair and took his gift to the kitchen table.

Sean pulled out his pocket knife, cut the tape and walked back to the counter. "Cake looks good."

"Thanks. Hopefully, it's also edible."

"I'm sure it will be. Chocolate cake is my favorite."

Now she *really* prayed it was edible.

Joey studied his package, turning it around at different angles, as if it were a puzzle he was trying to solve.

"Open it," she urged.

"Men like to take their time," Sean said. He reached for the frosting bowl, raked his finger along the edge, collecting a mouthful of the creamy confection.

He started to taste it, then poked the laden finger in her direction, stopping an inch from her lips.

Her pulse accelerated. She parted her lips and he slipped his finger inside her mouth, then she wrapped her lips around it and sucked.

The sweetness of the frosting was no match for the delicious tingling sensation that vibrated all the way down to her core.

She wanted to return the favor, but didn't trust herself to carry it off with the same nonchalance that Sean had. He returned his finger to the bowl, this time tasting the frosting himself.

Sean licked his lips appreciatively. "Wow. You have been holding out on us in the cooking department."

"Better hold the praise until you've tasted the cake."

He smiled and hooked his thumbs in the back pockets of his jeans. "Nothing topped with chocolate frosting can be bad."

A blush heated her cheeks as she walked over to the table where Joey had finally torn the paper from his package. He reached inside and pulled out a black felt Western hat, a miniature version of the one Sean wore.

Joey ran his fingers over the brim, making the full circle before plopping the hat on his head. He adjusted it the way he'd seen Sean do his. Then he pulled a shoe box from the package.

"Boots," he said, lifting the cover.

"For keeping your feet dry," Sean said.

Joey grinned as he took them out one at a time, holding them up and examining them as if he were an art dealer and they were expensive relics.

Satisfied that they were the real thing, he sat down with them in the middle of the floor and kicked off his tennis shoes. He struggled with getting his foot into the new leather.

Eve stooped to help him, but Sean took her arm and tugged her back to a standing position before she could lend a helping hand.

"I was just going to—"

Sean silenced her with a finger on his lips and a shake of the head. A few minutes later, Joey's feet were fitted snugly into his new boots and he was beaming in triumph and excitement. The hat was knocked askew as he stood, but he straightened it himself and swaggered around the room.

"I'm a cowboy," he said.

"You sure are," Eve said. "A very handsome cowboy."

Joey walked over to Sean with just a trace of his usual shyness. "Thank you."

"You bet, buddy." Sean high-fived him. "Want to go see what the horses think of your new gear?"

Joey looked back at Eve. "You come, too, Momma."

"I'd love to, but I think from the sound of that car in the driveway that Mr. Ledger has arrived."

The mood of the room switched from carefree to

somber in less than a heartbeat. Joey took off his hat and put it on the table. Sean stiffened, his face drawn, as if waiting for a firing squad.

The man was amazing with Joey, but apparently he had no expertise at dealing with his own emotional issues. *That could explain,* Eve thought, *why a man as wickedly tantalizing as he was single.*

Nonetheless, Troy Ledger was home and it was long past time for the two men to deal with seventeen years of mistakes, regrets and a murder case that had stolen much of their lives.

And time for her to get out of their way.

THE NIGHT WAS PITCH-BLACK, the light from the moon and stars blocked by layers of clouds that promised rain by morning. Orson Bastion hunched behind the lonesome tombstone, waiting to make certain there was no one around to see him when he said his final farewell.

The branches in an old oak tree a few feet away creaked and groaned as they swayed in the wind. A funeral dirge that never quit. A sentry to watch over the legions of bones that would never rattle again.

Unsurprisingly, he was the only one at this forsaken cemetery in the wee hours before dawn. No one was following him. He'd outsmarted them all. It was exhilarating how easy that was to do.

Orson crept from behind the tombstone and walked the few steps to the grave of Lydia Bastion. Died at the young age of fifty-eight. She'd been only eighteen when he was born.

She was the only woman he'd ever loved, yet he hadn't

been there when she put a gun to her head and pulled the trigger. Alyssa said her brains had been scattered about the garage like confetti.

He dropped to his knees and dipped his head until the top of it kissed the grassy earth. "Goodbye, Mother. I'm sorry that I wasn't the boy you wanted me to be. You loved me, anyway. No matter what I did, you loved me."

Drops of rain began to fall as Orson walked away from the grave for the last time. He climbed the fence and made his way to the nondescript black compact car he'd left in a patch of overgrown shrubs.

Reaching beneath his shirt, he touched the butt of the pistol in his shoulder holster. Most of the guys he'd met in prison liked heavy-duty arms. A pistol and a razor-sharp hunting knife were all Orson had ever needed.

That and his strength. He could squash a man with his foot or break a neck with his bare hands. Tonight all he'd need was the pistol. He'd done his research well. There would be no screwup.

Anticipation rocked though him. He started the engine and pulled onto the road.

Just a few more scores to settle. Revenge would be quick and sweet. And then he'd disappear south of the border for good. A free man, living the life he deserved.

Chapter Seven

Eve woke to the distant rumble of thunder. The room was dark and the house possessed an eerie predawn stillness that crept under her skin. A chilly draft passed over her, as if a cool hand had brushed her skin. For a second she imagined someone in the room, silently watching her.

She sat up straight, and the sensation passed as soon as she comforted herself with the sound of Joey's rhythmic breathing. Still, pinpricks of apprehension stung along her nerve endings.

In the bright light of day, she could almost convince herself that Orson Bastion was truly out of the country and out of her life for good. But here in the shadowed darkness, reality merged with memories, and if she let herself, she knew she'd sink into the past, into the horror that she didn't like to think about and never talked about.

Moving as quietly as she could, she threw her feet over the side of the bed and slid them into her slippers. Stealing from the room, she stepped into the long hallway.

Sean was just across the hall, and the door to his room was ajar. She hesitated, listening to his breathing, thinking of his body stretched out in the double bed. She wondered what he'd say if she took the initiative and crawled in beside him and curled her body around his.

Her good sense checked in quickly. He'd think she was nuts—or desperate. The latter probably wouldn't be that far off base. It had been two years since Brock's death, months more since she'd slept in the arms of a man. Not that she'd given her lack of sexual satisfaction that much thought until now.

Which meant this was merely a situational attraction evoked by Sean's status as a protector. Her reaction to him would level off as soon as she felt safe and secure, and the proximity issue no longer applied. Any decent psychiatrist would come to that same conclusion.

Unfortunately, resorting to psychiatric labeling and self-diagnosis didn't erase thoughts of Sean stretched out on his bed. Eve tiptoed down the hallway for a glass of cool water that would soothe her throat and hopefully tone down the unwanted desire.

When she reached the family room, the front door was slightly ajar. Her heart slammed against her chest.

"Is that you, Eve?"

Troy. She sighed in relief, thankful that she hadn't gone for a knife to attack a man in his own house for the second time this week.

"It's me." She went to the kitchen, filled a glass with water from the tap and joined him on the porch, closing the door behind her. "How did you know it was me?"

"Years of nothing to do but listen to approaching footfalls. The monotony of prison life fosters a multitude of useless skills."

"I suppose. Are you feeling okay?"

"A little tired. That's it."

"But you were having trouble sleeping?"

"I always do. I see the sun come up lots of mornings from this same spot. But that's okay. I love the freedom of just walking out that door anytime I choose."

"Seventeen years of paying for a crime you didn't commit, but it's all behind you now, Troy."

Troy dropped to the top step and stretched his long legs out in front of him. "Not everyone is as certain of my innocence as you are."

She leaned against the support post. "Are you talking about Sean?"

"Him, and others. He's the one most on my mind now."

Eve hadn't gotten the chance to visit with Troy alone this afternoon. Dylan and Collette had stayed through an early dinner, and then Troy had gone back to the master bedroom to rest. She hadn't wanted to disturb him.

Sean had barely spoken to his father, except to ask a few questions about the ranch. The strain between them had added layers of tension to what should have been a restful continuation of Troy's recovery. She was certain having her and Joey there for protection from an escaped convict hadn't helped either.

So, even if it came during the wee hours of the morning, she was glad to have this time alone with Troy.

"Sean just needs time to get to know you," she said.

"He has years of indoctrination about your guilt to put behind him. He's here, and that's what's important."

"His staying has little to do with me. Not that I'm not grateful he had the good sense to stop you from running off on your own. I sure didn't need to have to go looking for you in my weakened condition. Nonetheless, he'd be on his way by now if it weren't for you."

"Did he tell you that?"

"Not in so many words, but I see it in his eyes and in the way he backs out of a conversation with me before it gets going. I don't blame him. I should have pulled myself from the crushing grief and battled harder to prove my innocence. I should never have given up trying to contact my sons just because Helene's family fought me on it."

"Are you still obsessed with finding Helene's killer?"

"I don't think of it as an obsession, but yes. It's what kept me going all those miserable years in the pen. Her killer not only took her life years too soon, he stole her from me and from our sons.

"And for what? The few dollars we had in the house or to satisfy some inner demon? I'll never rest until I find him and see that he pays."

Eve dropped down beside Troy and put her hand on his arm. "You truly loved her, didn't you?"

"I still do." The words were all but swallowed by his pain.

Eve had difficulty comprehending a love that strong. "You must have been true soul mates."

Troy managed a smile. "Not unless 'soul mates'

means opposites. We were nothing alike. She came from an influential, wealthy family. I was a loner who worked enough odd jobs to pick up entry money for the rodeo. She had class, read poetry, always had fresh flowers and scented candles in the house.

"I lived in worn jeans and dusty boots, drank beer from the bottle and thought there should always be a fiddle in the band. But I swear, I was so in love with her that even after five sons it was sometimes dizzying just to watch her walk into a room."

"Those are the things you should tell Sean."

"He'd still believe what he wants to believe. Everyone does."

Thunder rattled though the clouds and the first large drops of rain began to pelt the walk. It was the same weather they'd had on her last night in Dallas. The night before fear had sent her running to Troy and indirectly to Sean.

"Rain's setting in," Troy said. "I say we try to get a few more hours sleep before the day starts in earnest."

They walked back into the house together. Troy closed and locked the door while she started down the hall.

"I'll be right behind you," Troy said. "I just need a glass of water to take another dadblamed pill. Hand me your empty glass and I'll put it in the sink for you."

"Thanks."

A few steps later, she heard whispering. Joey. And Sean. Joey must have wakened while she was on the porch. He'd probably called for her and she hadn't heard him.

She paused in eavesdropping range.

"I've had nightmares, too," Sean said. "In this very room. This is where I slept when I was a kid."

"Did you call for your mother?"

"Sometimes."

"What did she tell you?"

"That the dark was a cuddly black blanket that God gave the world so that we can sleep. Otherwise little boys would never want to go to bed."

"Did she hug you?"

"Yep. She was the best hugger in the whole world."

"My momma's a good hugger, too."

"I'll bet."

Eve was spellbound by the scene their words created. There were so many sides to this hunk of a cowboy who could tame wild stallions and comfort small boys.

She could come with all the psychological theories she wanted, but if she didn't leave here soon, she was going to fall hopelessly in love with him.

Both Joey and Sean looked up as she stepped into the room.

"Where did you go, Momma? I called you, but you didn't come."

"I'm sorry, sweetie. I stepped onto the front porch with Mr. Ledger for a breath of fresh air, and I didn't hear you."

"Sounds cozy," Sean said.

If the idea wasn't so ludicrous, she'd have sworn there was a tinge of jealousy in his tone.

Joey scratched his big toe. "It's okay, Momma. Sean heard me."

"I see." She was also bewitchingly aware that Sean was wearing nothing but partially zipped jeans that he'd probably grabbed and wiggled into at Joey's first call.

Joey reached for his stuffed lion that he'd left at the edge of his pillow. "Me and Sean are cowboy buddies."

Eve pulled up the covers and tucked Joey in. "That's nice, cowboy, but I think you should go back to sleep now, so Sean can do the same."

"Okay. Thanks, Sean."

"You bet, buddy."

Eve gave Joey a peck on the cheek and then followed Sean into the hall and to the door to his bedroom. "You have quite a way with my son. It usually takes him much longer to warm up to a new man."

"Does he have to do that often?"

"It depends on where we go and who we run into."

Sean trailed a finger up the sleeve of her pajamas, letting it linger at her neck. "I was referring to your suitors. Do you date a lot of different men?"

"Me? None. I haven't been with anyone since my husband died."

His thumb rode her neck and tangled in her hair. "But you do like men?"

Her heart skipped crazily, leaving her positively giddy. "I like some men," she murmured, trying for nonchalance.

"Good."

His free arm encircled her, and he pulled her close. His eyes were dark and mesmerizing. His lips were dangerously close. "I didn't mean I like—"

Sean stopped her protestations with his lips on hers.

Eve closed her eyes and let the thrill of him zing through her. She was so lost in the moment that she'd totally forgotten about Troy still being up, until she heard his footsteps starting down the long hallway. Still, she felt cheated when Sean released his hold on her body and her lips.

"Sleep tight," he whispered, disappearing into his room before Troy reached them.

She stumbled to her door, stepped inside and leaned against the bed railing until she caught her breath.

Eve's heart was beating so erratically, she wondered if her pulse would ever return to normal again.

She wouldn't even try to analyze that.

WHEN EVE WOKE, the sun was beating through the window, the threatening storm of last night having moved on without ever fully developing. Eve knew that for a fact. She'd been awake for the intermittent rain.

Amazed and disturbed by the way an impetuous kiss affected her, she'd been unable to fall asleep for what seemed like hours. In a few weeks, she'd turn thirty-two. That was far too old for this type of infatuation with a man she barely knew.

Even with Brock, she'd insisted on moving slowly. Too many of her friends had gotten married in a fever, only to have the relationship cool down after the marriage. Her and Brock's relationship hadn't cooled down. It had run into an iceberg.

Joey was still asleep, though she knew that wouldn't

last long. The clock said 8:15. Sean would likely be off somewhere on the ranch with Dylan by now. With Troy home, he surely wouldn't feel he had to stay so close.

She hoped Sean wasn't around. That was the problem with a kiss. It changed a relationship completely.

She shrugged into her robe, desperately needing that first cup of coffee. The enticing odor wafted down the hallway. So did the sounds from the TV. She tied her robe tightly and kept walking.

She heard the click of the remote as she reached the end of the hall. And then she saw Sean, fully dressed, one boot on the hearth, his expression hard and strained.

"Is something wrong?" she asked.

"Sit down," he said. "I'll get you a cup of coffee." If his mannerisms hadn't said enough, his tone said the rest.

"Is it Troy? Did he have another attack?"

"Troy's fine. He had an early breakfast and went to his room to read the morning newspaper, fortunately without catching the morning news."

A shudder rocked through her. "It's Orson, isn't it?"

"Yeah. He's not in Mexico."

"Are they sure?"

"No absolute proof, but last night's murder has his name written all over it."

Eve collapsed onto the sofa, bracing herself for what would come next while Sean stepped into the kitchen. He came back with two cups of black coffee. He handed her one and dragged over a hassock, sitting on the edge so that he faced her up close and personal.

She took a sip of the coffee, needing the restorative power it usually provided. This time it lacked that effect. "What happened?" she finally asked.

"According to the news, the homicide detective who had originally cracked the case and arrested Orson Bastion for the brutal beating death of his stepbrother was murdered at his home last night. Police are speculating that Orson is behind the murder."

"Was it a shooting?"

"No. I'm guessing a simple gunshot wound to the head is not Orson's style. The detective was stabbed repeatedly before finally having his jugular sliced."

"I'm not speculating," Eve said. "Orson killed him. I'm sure he did."

"If he's guilty of everything they say, that brings his total for the current killing spree up to three," Sean said. "The prison guard, the woman whose car he stole and now the detective. You were right to fight his early parole."

"We'll never know for sure. Maybe if he'd gotten that break, his anger might have diffused."

"Don't waste time second-guessing yourself with that monster. Men like that don't change just because someone does them a favor. You made the right decision. It's the system that made a mistake in letting him escape."

Being right gave her no pleasure and certainly no reassurance.

Sean curled his hands into fists. "Frankly, I'm tired

of sitting around waiting for the bastard to make a mistake."

His vehemence worried her. "What does that mean?"

"Just what I said. All the police seem to do is wait for Orson to attack again. That's not my style."

"This isn't your fight, and you're not a cop."

"It's my fight if I make it my fight, and as for the police, they don't seem to be getting anywhere."

"What do you think you can do?"

"I want to learn everything I can about Orson Bastion. The more I know, the better chance I have of figuring out his next move before he makes it."

"He's not one of the horses you're used to working with, Sean. You can't micromanage him with theory. I know. I'm the psychiatrist here."

"Your being his psychiatrist is one of the things that will help make this work. I want to know all you know about this man, and don't give me that client privilege crap. If he represents a danger to himself or others, you can talk. So start talking."

This was happening too fast. She hadn't even had a chance to digest the latest gruesome crime. But Sean was right about the law. If the patient was deemed an imminent threat to himself or others, the rules of confidentiality didn't apply.

Orson Bastion wouldn't be worried about his privileges. His actions guaranteed that, if he was recaptured now, he would live the rest of his life in prison. She was certain he had no intention of going back to that life.

Not that Orson had ever leveled with her about anything when he was in therapy. He'd played mind games, said what he thought she wanted to hear. He'd known she was hired by the state to assess him, and he expected her to give him a glowing recommendation for early parole.

What she knew about the evil that festered inside Orson came from her own intuition rather than what he'd actually said. And from what other inmates had said about his cruelty when he was sure no guards were around.

She sipped her coffee and then placed the mug on the table beside her. "I don't know where to start."

Sean reached over and took her hands in his. "Tell me what made you so sure that given the chance Orson would kill again."

SEAN WAS A SEETHING BUNDLE of nerves since hearing the news of last night's murder. It was clearly a revenge killing by a man who'd gone over the edge. Successfully taking out the detective exponentially increased the chance that he'd come after Eve.

Sean had no intention of letting the psycho anywhere near the ranch or her.

"I should start at the beginning," Eve said.

Sean got the impression that she was putting off the worst of her explanation, but there was time. He wouldn't push as long as he felt she was giving him the truth.

"When you counseled Orson, did you see him in his cell?"

"No, I saw him in a room designated for that purpose. There was always an armed guard right outside the room whenever I was working professionally with a subject."

"Did you see all the inmates?"

"No. I was hired by the prison to specifically conduct assessments, usually before prisoners were given more freedom within the institution or when they were up for parole. Occasionally, I was asked to assess and make recommendations for prisoners who were considered at risk for suicide."

"How many times did you see Orson?"

"Probably a dozen or more."

"Sounds like a thorough assessment."

"Orson and a few other convicts, including Troy, were part of a one-time, special study I conducted to determine the effects of prison life on the morale of convicts who were serving sentences of over ten years."

So that's how she'd become such good friends with his father. Ironic, that the study involved a prisoner who made her fear for her life and another whom she'd come to for protection.

"So what made Orson different?"

"The way he talked about the murder that had sent him to prison."

"What kind of things did he say?"

"He blamed everything on his stepbrother, said he'd intentionally driven him over the edge. Orson claimed he hadn't meant to hurt the guy and yet it was reportedly one of the goriest crimes ever committed in that county."

"How long did he serve before he was up for early parole?

"Ten years and a few months. He was convicted of murder two because his defense attorney convinced the jury that his rage was linked to a drug he was taking for migraines."

"Exactly how did he kill his stepbrother?"

"He was waiting for the man when he got home from work that night. He beat him to death with the jack from his wrecked car. Pictures from the crime scene were so gory that two of the jurors got sick and had to leave the room after viewing only a few of them. The judge declared the prosecutor had shown enough to make his point."

Eve clutched her stomach as if thinking of the pictures was making her sick as well.

"Did you see the photographs?"

"Yes, and the images will haunt my mind forever."

And Sean was insisting she dredge it all up again. "That's enough for the time being."

"There's more you should know," Eve said, "and I'd just as soon get it all out now."

He got up from the hassock and sat beside her on the couch. He'd sworn after last night's kiss that he'd keep a safe physical distance between them, but this morning's developments voided those vows.

He snaked an arm around her shoulders.

Eve shifted so that she could see his face, but didn't move away from his touch. "Three weeks after Orson's failed parole hearing, he tried to kill me."

Fury burrowed inside Sean. Was there no end to the misery this man had caused her? "Where were the guards when this happened?"

"Who knows? Orson had been playing the system, had been a model prisoner in the months leading up to the parole hearing, had even claimed to have found religion. As a result, he'd been made a trustee. That offered him a lot more freedom inside the walled area."

Her shoulders tensed and Sean could only imagine the horror creeping back into her consciousness.

"I had finished for the day and was walking back toward my office, my mind already on the upcoming weekend and a planned trip to the zoo with Joey. Orson stepped out from nowhere and planted his meaty hand over my mouth before I had a chance to call for help. He dragged me into a small recreation room that was no longer in use and locked the door behind us. I managed to get in one swift knee to the groin before he slammed my head against the wall so hard that I lost consciousness. When I came to, he'd ripped all the clothes from my body."

Sean's muscles tightened as if wound with girded steel. "The son of a bitch."

"He didn't rape me," she added quickly, "but I'm sure that was his plan."

"What stopped him?"

"A prison work crew returning to the cells passed by and one of the inmates caught a glimpse of Orson through the window. I got out my one and only scream seconds later when Orson kicked me in the stomach.

"An inmate bolted from his group and smashed a fist though one of the windowpanes. Instead of giving up and running away, Orson tightened his hands around my neck and squeezed. With his strength, he would have easily broken my neck had the inmate not managed to open the broken window and come flying at him."

Eve turned to face him and rested her hand on his thigh. "Your father was that inmate, Sean. Knowing the guard might shoot him for bolting and running, he still came to my rescue. Not even knowing who had screamed, he risked his life to save the victim. The jagged scar on his face came from a shard of broken window glass."

For years Sean had heard nothing but horror stories of how his father had brutally murdered his mother rather than lose her. Now he tried to wrap his mind around Troy as a brave prisoner willing to risk his life for a stranger.

The confusing images refused to jell.

Yet, if Troy hadn't gone to Eve's rescue that day…

The clunking sound of stamping footfalls shook him back to the present. He stood as Joey swaggered into the room, rubbing the dregs of sleep from his eyes with his little fists. He was still in his pajamas, but he was wearing his new boots and hat.

"Am I too late to help feed the horses?"

"You might be," Eve said.

"You shoulda woke me up."

"I have an even better idea," Troy said. "Why don't we take a trail ride on the horses and rustle us up a Texas cowboy breakfast."

Joey smiled and crawled up on the couch, taking the spot next to his mother that Sean had just vacated. "What's a cowboy breakfast?"

"You'll have to wait and see."

"Can Momma go, too?"

"I don't know," Sean said. "Can she cook?"

Joey shook his head. "Not cowboy food."

"Oh, well, I suppose we can take her with us anyway." As if he'd ever had any thought of leaving her behind.

"Mighty thoughtful of you hombres," Eve said as she gave her son a quick hug.

She smiled for the first time this morning, and the simple gesture lit up the room. Sean would do what he had to in order to keep her and Joey safe. That was a given.

Losing his heart would be a risk he'd just have to take.

Chapter Eight

Eve should have had zero appetite after news of the detective's murder. But cooking over an open fire after a brisk gallop to Willow Creek had left her famished. And thanks to Dylan and Collette, the task of cooking had been an easy one.

Dylan had delivered in his truck all the food and cooking equipment they'd needed, and had it waiting when they'd arrived at the perfect picnic spot. Their new house was only a hundred yards or so downstream and just over a slight ridge. Sean had pointed out the roofline before they dismounted.

Her stomach growled as the odors teased and tantalized her tastebuds. She spooned the spicy concoction of chorizo, scrambled eggs, melted cheese and salsa onto the fried tortillas, while Sean poured hot coffee for them and milk from a thermos for Joey.

Joey looked a bit dubious when she handed him his plate. "Is this really what cowboys eat?"

"When they can get it," Sean said, "especially if they can eat it outside on a brisk morning."

"What's brisk?"

"Cool weather, when you need a light jacket like you have on right now," Eve said.

She knew her son might not touch his trail-ride breakfast, but he'd loved the ride over the rolling hills and down the wooded trail to the creek. He'd ridden with Sean on a majestic quarter horse named Gunner. She'd ridden Starlight. The gentle mare was a good choice, since it had been years since Eve had been horseback riding.

Fresh air, the sound of Joey's innocent laughter, and the beauty of the countryside had been the perfect antidote for the dark mood that she'd been drowning in earlier. Not that it had changed everything. Danger was still waiting around the next bend.

Sean spread a blanket on the grass, a few feet from the muddy creek bank. Eve straightened the back corners before sitting down on it, taco and coffee in hand.

Sean joined her, sitting far enough away that there would be no incidental brush of arms or shoulders. She wondered if that were an intentional decision so that she'd realize last night's kiss was no more than a natural reaction to a sensual moment. Or maybe he'd never given the kiss another thought.

Joey wandered toward a log that stretched to the water's edge.

"Watch where you're walking, Joey. It's muddy there."

From the corner of her eye she noticed Sean wince, as if she'd done something wrong. But she was only looking out for her son.

Joey turned back to her. "But I've got my boots on." He waited to see if she'd change her mind.

"Right." She gave in. "You've got your boots on."

Joey grinned and marched right through the deepest mud, on his way to the inviting log. He straddled it and set his paper plate on a dry spot near his feet.

"I'm not always this protective," she said to Sean. "At least I don't think I am. It's just that this ordeal with Orson has me too anxious to think straight."

"That's understandable."

"But you still think I need to give Joey more freedom."

"You're the expert."

"My friend Miriam thinks I hover over him. But his anxiety is real. A mother should protect her son."

"I'm not arguing with you."

Nevertheless, she knew he agreed with Miriam. Eve bit into her taco and the flavors exploded in her mouth. "Wow. This really is good."

Conversation ceased while she finished her breakfast. By the time she had, Sean had gone back for seconds. Joey, on the other hand, had pulled all the ingredients from his tortilla shell except a few bites of scrambled egg. The rest he'd tossed into the trees where a couple of black crows were noisily devouring the scraps.

Eve lay back on the blanket, the back of her head cradled in her hands, her eyes feasting on Sean. He was as hot a guy as she'd ever seen, but he was far more than the sum of his physical attributes.

"How is it you know so much about kids?" she asked.

"I used to be one. Besides, if you're talking about the mud thing, guys of every age like riding horses and getting dirty."

"You'd make a great father. Why is it you never married?"

"Long-term relationships lead to complications."

"And you like your life simple?"

"Doesn't everyone?"

"Marriage works for some people. Look how happy Dylan and Collette are."

"Is this a proposal?" he teased.

"I was just making a point," she said, turning away so that he couldn't see the blush that was burning her cheeks. "And you didn't answer my question."

"I guess I just like doing things I'm good at."

Right now, Eve couldn't imagine anything Sean wouldn't be good at.

He finished his taco, set his plate aside and leaned back, propping himself up with an elbow. She looked into his dark, piercing eyes and her thoughts strayed into dangerous, erotic territory.

Wrong place. Wrong time. How could she feel even the slightest surge of passion after news of last night's murder? Yet her mouth ached to feel his lips on hers again.

Perhaps the latest research studies had been correct. Danger was a powerful aphrodisiac.

Her cell phone rang, destroying the moment. She checked her phone. "It's Gordon Epps."

"Probably just wants to make certain you heard the morning news."

Minutes later, any lingering feelings of desire vanished down the dreaded rabbit hole of more bad news. She was sitting up straight now, her resolve to remain calm pushed to the limits.

"Gordon heard from Detective Reagan Conner again," she whispered so Joey wouldn't hear. "This time he said it's urgent that I contact him. It's a matter of life and death."

Sean took her hand in his. "Anything to do with Orson Bastion is a matter of life and death."

ONCE THEY ARRIVED BACK at the house, the tension quickly swelled to volatile proportions. Fortunately, Collette was there visiting with Troy and she lured Joey to the protected courtyard garden on the pretense of needing his help in hanging some Christmas lights.

Eve insisted that Troy join them in the kitchen for the heated discussion.

"Homicide detective or not, he's still just a cop in my book," Sean protested. "If you let him know where you are, there's no guarantee that information won't get leaked to the press."

Eve absently straightened the edge of the tablecloth with her fingers. "The press knows nothing about my connection with Orson Bastion."

"You can't count on that," Troy said, backing Sean. "Orson is the lead story on every local news channel. Reporters are digging into everything they can find about his life. I'll be surprised if my run-in with him doesn't make the news."

"All the more reason I need to contact him," she

said. "Just not from the ranch. We'll have to call from somewhere outside the Mustang Run area, just in case he's able to track the call."

"He'll track the call," Troy said. "Count on it. That's why he gave Gordon a specific line for you to use when calling him."

"Cop or not, I don't think you should let Detective Conner know where you are," Sean insisted.

Eve stood and paced the floor.

Troy worried the scar at his temple. "Why not call your brother, Wyatt, Sean? He'll have suggestions for how this should be handled."

Eve tried to remember what Troy might have told her about Wyatt. She drew a blank. The stress was getting to her.

"Wyatt's a homicide detective in Atlanta," Sean explained. "One of the best. And Troy's right. Wyatt will know how to handle this."

Eve wondered how Troy felt about Sean never calling him Dad. She shot him a look. If it bothered him, he gave no sign.

"I don't know why I didn't think of Wyatt first," Sean continued. "I'm betting he has access to an untraceable line, and he doesn't have to use the Ledger name."

"You can trust Wyatt," Troy assured Eve. "He won't do anything to give away your location. He definitely came through for Dylan when Collette was in danger."

"Then let's call him," Eve conceded.

She tapped her fingers against the wooden tabletop as Sean made the call. The easy phone camaraderie matched what Sean shared with Dylan. Troy was the odd man out. Her heart went out to him. Surely, given time, Sean would see that his father could never have killed his beloved Helene.

If not, they'd both be the loser.

WYATT ANSWERED ON the third ring. "If you're calling with trouble, hang up."

"That kind of day?" Sean asked.

"You know it. I'm thinking of chasing a job wrestling alligators. It would have to be easier. How's Troy?"

"Improving every day. But I need a favor."

"Sorry," Wyatt said. "I won't come down and rescue you from family life. You're on your own."

"This has to do with a woman."

"Even worse."

Sean gave Wyatt the scoop in as few words as possible.

Wyatt responded with a couple of well-chosen curse words. "First Dylan, now you. Are there any women in Texas who don't need protecting?"

"Probably, but I'm just concerned with the one now," Sean said. "Is there any way you can make that call to Reagan Conner without the Ledger name coming into play?"

"I can do better than that. I can connect Eve to him through a line that it will be impossible for him to trace or track the location of."

"The wonders of modern technology," Sean said.

"Yeah. Too bad the criminals can afford it before we get it. Give me the number Conner said to use. I'll get him on the phone and then give you a call back at this number."

By the time Sean had explained the plan to Eve, the call came through. Sean took her hand and squeezed it. "Remember, I'm right here, and no matter what Conner says, I have your back."

Eve took the phone and identified herself to the detective.

"I'm glad you called, Mrs. Worthington. I've been trying to get in touch with you for several days. I've left countless messages on your phone."

"I'm out of town."

"I assumed that, but the department is concerned for your safety."

"The department didn't sound all that concerned when I contacted them the day after Orson Bastion escaped."

"I'm sorry for that misunderstanding, but under the present circumstances, I assure you that I'm prepared to offer you protection twenty-four seven, if you return to Dallas. I'll even send an escort to pick you up and drive you back here."

It didn't add up, Eve thought. Conner seemed too eager to help. "I appreciate your offer, but I prefer to take my chances on my own."

"That's not smart, Mrs. Worthington. Not for you or your son. I would have preferred not to frighten you with this, but you leave me no choice."

"No choice in what?" she asked, growing even more nervous.

"We have credible evidence that suggests that Orson Bastion may be planning to kill you."

Her stomach roiled. "What kind of evidence?"

"I can't reveal that, but like I said, it's from a credible source. I think you're in real danger. That's why we're willing to make certain you're protected if you return home."

"And suppose you can't?"

"We can do a better job than anyone you can hire for that purpose. And if you're working on the assumption that Bastion won't hunt you down wherever you are, you're putting yourself and everyone around you at extreme risk."

Everyone around her. Like Troy and Sean. She knew both of them would take on Bastion to save her and Joey, but at what cost?

"I'll consider your offer," she said.

"Think too long and Bastion may take it out of your hands."

Once the connection was broken, she filled Troy and Sean in on the details of the conversation. Sean became increasingly agitated.

Finally, he slammed his right fist against the table. "The detective isn't worried about you, Eve. He just wants you back in Dallas to use you for bait. He'll have his men there twenty-four seven all right, but they'll be there to arrest Bastion when he shows up to kill you."

Which might be the only way to stop him, she realized. But there was a major drawback. "I can't risk exposing Joey to the danger or to the sight of violence."

"It's too risky for both of you," Sean said. "You're in the safest place you can be. And that's settled."

"It's *my* decision," she said, not sure why she was angry with him, except that he was taking over and that her emotions were so raw she was suddenly fighting back tears.

"Do you want to leave and go back to Dallas?" Troy asked.

"It's not a matter of what I want. If I stay, I'm dragging all of you into danger. I've known that all along, but hearing it from the detective makes it even more imperative that I leave the ranch."

"I don't take Bastion or his threat to kill you lightly, Eve." Troy propped his elbows on the table and waited until she met his gaze. "But I'm not afraid of him, either. You're not only welcome to stay here until he's apprehended, your being here would save me a lot of worry."

"I appreciate that."

Sean rolled his eyes, as if it irritated him that his father had played the situation a lot cooler than he had. He pushed back from the table. "So, are you staying here or running back to Dallas?"

She shook her head. "I need time to think."

Sean's phone rang again, no doubt Wyatt calling to check out the status. She slipped out of the room. She'd heard enough. Now she just wanted to see her son. He had to be protected at all costs, and she could not afford a mistake.

No matter what Troy, Wyatt, or even Sean thought, in the end, her son's safety was her responsibility. But if she could protect him and help in Bastion's apprehension, it would be a win-win for everyone.

"HOW ABOUT PASSING THOSE pork chops?"

"This sweet potato casserole is the best I've ever tasted."

"Glad you requested macaroni and cheese, Joey. I don't remember when I've had that last."

"Eve gets credit for that."

"And I did it without a box," Eve said.

Collette had invited them all for dinner, and conversation flowed like it might on any ordinary night. For Sean, though, it was anything but. Tension churned inside him. He hadn't spoken directly to Eve since the afternoon's phone call to Detective Conner. He couldn't even think straight, what with her considering going back to Dallas and marching right into the hands of a madman.

Wyatt had agreed with him that Eve was being set up as bait. He'd stressed that that didn't mean she wouldn't be protected. But setting a trap for Bastion would still put Eve's life on the line. Plans could be fouled, and even the best of cops made mistakes.

Sean could not let her go back to Dallas until Bastion was behind bars. Only, if she made up her mind to go back, how in the devil was he supposed to stop her? Kidnap her himself?

Maybe that wasn't such a bad idea.

He studied her across the table while she ate. Unlike him, she was engaging in conversation with the others, even smiling at times. But the dark circles around her eyes, the strain to her facial muscles, and even the stoop of her shoulders revealed that the growing threat of danger was weighing on her.

And still, he ached to just carry her off somewhere and…

And what? Finish what he'd started last night? Kiss her senseless? Make love to her?

All of the above, he silently admitted.

He was falling for Eve. Hard. Under normal circumstances, those feelings would likely have him running for his life. Who was he kidding? He had nothing to compare this to. He'd never felt like this about another woman. And that included the two he'd thought himself in love with.

Desire rode him hard and he looked away, determined to focus on the conversation and make it through this meal.

"How was that trail ride this morning?" Dylan asked.

"Awesome." Joey moved the casserole around with his fork. "But riding the horse with Sean was the best fun. And wearing my new boots. I got them real muddy, but Sean showed me how to clean them up."

And if Sean's agonizing over Eve wasn't enough to deal with, he had Joey to think about. Joey had lost his father. Losing his mother to a psycho killer would destroy him. Who knew that better than Sean?

Yet, here he was sitting at the same table with Troy Ledger. Troy wasn't the man Sean remembered running to as a kid. He wasn't the man who'd taught him to ride, played ball with him and his brothers on Sunday afternoons, let him jump from his shoulders at the swimming hole. He wasn't the man who'd stood beside him and told him it was okay to cry when his dog died from a rattlesnake bite.

Troy was older, hardened, and the easy laugh that Sean remembered never came.

But was he the man that Sean had heard about time after time over the last seventeen years? Was he a heartless, brutal killer who'd killed Sean's mother rather than let her escape the marriage?

Dylan was convinced that Troy was innocent. Sean might reach that same conclusion one day; but until he did, he couldn't just act as if the stranger at the table mattered in his life.

The truth was, he couldn't deal with Troy, Eve or family now. "Dinner was great," he said, "but if you guys will excuse me, I have a few things I need to take care of back at the house."

But before the night was over, he'd have to speak privately with Eve and talk some sense into her before it was too late.

"TAKE ALL THE MAGAZINES you want," Collette urged. "I think there's even a few Hollywood gossip sheets in the mix, in case you want to know who's sleeping with whose ex."

"And lots of books on photography, I see," Eve said, picking one up and thumbing through it.

They were back in Collette's bedroom, looking for some fluff reading material. All Troy had at the house were ranching periodicals, and articles on winter feed for beef cattle read like a foreign language.

Not that she expected to really get her mind around any article tonight.

"Do you take a lot of pictures?"

"Constantly," Collette said. "That's what I did for a living before I met Dylan. I kept my studio in town, but I mostly concentrate on creative imagery now, instead of weddings and parties. I still do family and personal photographs on occasion."

"Then you still work?"

"Yes, but mostly from the ranch. It makes a great natural setting for family photos. In fact, I have several appointments scheduled next week. Christmas brings out the need to preserve memories for posterity."

"I can't believe we're already in December."

"And the next few weeks will fly by. I just sprang for adorable Mr. and Mrs. Santa suits. You'd be surprised how many folks love the quirky for their Christmas card shots. You should dress up in one and let me take your picture with Joey, not that you'd even be recognizable in the wig and padding that go with it. Hey, we might even get Sean to pose in the Santa suit, as long he could wear his boots and cowboy hat."

"If we drugged him and tied him down first." Eve laughed in spite of the anxiety that never let up. But she was in no mood for Christmas photos. Orson and peace on earth, goodwill to men were not compatible. "How much do you know about my situation?" she asked.

"Everything Sean has told Dylan," Collette said. "My husband and I don't keep secrets from each other. Orson

Bastion sounds beyond evil. I hope they capture him soon."

"So do I, but in the meantime, are you sure that you and Dylan are okay with me bringing my problems to your doorstep?"

"Absolutely. I brought mine here before you did. Dylan was a lifesaver in the most literal sense of the word. When things settle down for you, I'll share the gritty details. For now, just know you're in good hands with the Ledger men."

"But it was different for you and Dylan. You were in love. Sean barely knows me."

Collette dropped to the floor beside Eve and the basket of magazines. "Don't tell me you haven't noticed that Sean looks at you like you're a bowl of whipped cream that he's dying to dive into?"

A slow burn crept to Eve's cheeks. She hadn't noticed the way Sean looked at her, but if Collette had, then she'd surely noticed the way Sean affected her. Memories of last night's kiss vibrated through her.

It was positively insane for her to experience this kind of desire with all she had to face.

She picked up another magazine, only to find herself staring at a picture of the Ledger ranch house plastered across the cover.

Beyond the Grave

"Oops, forgot that one was in there," Collette said. "Ignore it. It's all hype and hyperbole anyway. And not good bedtime reading for you right now."

But Eve couldn't bring herself to return *Beyond the*

Grave to the stack. She thumbed through it until she found the cover page story.

The opening lines made the hairs on the back of Eve's neck stand on end.

"Does the ghost of the wife of Troy Ledger still inhabit the house where she was brutally murdered? Does she still walk halls at night, looking for her sons so that she can tuck them into their beds? Or is she there waiting on her killer to return?"

"Who wrote this?" Eve said. "And why?"

"It's nothing," Collette said. "Really. Pay the article no mind. The editors of the publication are friends of mine. Sounds weird, I know, but they're great gals who just happen to believe in the paranormal and in making a living from it."

"Did you take the pictures?"

"No, but as a favor to me, Troy gave them permission to take all the photos they wanted of the house and gardens and to do the story. They're really trying to make a go of the magazine, and the story on the Ledger house did give them a giant boost in sales."

Dylan tapped on the open door and stuck his head inside. Joey was a step behind him, holding on to a bag of wood scraps that Dylan had given him earlier to use as blocks.

"I'm going to drive Troy back to the house. I think that big construction project Joey had him working on wore him out."

Joey skipped over to where Eve was sitting cross-legged on the floor. "We used the blocks to build a ranch with a place to ride horses and everything," Joey said. "And we made a bridge to go over Willow Creek."

"So that's what's kept you quiet for so long?"

"I can drive you two home later if you want to visit a while longer," Dylan offered.

"No, I need to get Joey to bed, and I'm a bit tired myself. It's been a long day."

Eve grabbed the stack of magazines she'd put aside, stood and started to the door with Joey a step behind.

Collette followed them out to the truck.

"Thanks for everything," Eve said as she climbed into the backseat with Joey.

"You're welcome. Come back tomorrow and I'll take some shots of you and Joey down by the creek. Maybe we can get one that's frame worthy."

A picture to take home with her to remind her of the week she'd spent on the run. Only, she wouldn't need a reminder.

If all went well and Bastion was caught and returned to prison, the terror would pass, she told herself. The heated memories of Sean would haunt her forever, especially if she never got to finish that kiss. Depending on the plan brewing in her mind, that might have to be tonight or never.

And never was much too long to wait.

Chapter Nine

Eve lay on her back in the twin bed, staring at the ceiling and feeling totally alone as she let the plan take shape in her mind.

The most difficult part would be leaving Joey at the ranch with Troy and Sean so that he'd not witness any violence. He'd be anxious with her away, but not as traumatized as if she'd left him before he'd developed a case of hero worship toward Sean. Sean might be furious at her for leaving, but she was certain he'd keep Joey safe.

She'd go back to Dallas alone. When Orson made his move, the police would arrest him. Orson would return to prison instead of continuing his killing rampage. And it would all happen without Joey being exposed to violence and without putting the Ledger family in danger.

Orson was likely already watching her house, waiting for a chance to make good on his death threat. But he wouldn't show his hand until she was on the scene.

He'd rely on his intellect, have what he thought was a perfect plan to kill her without getting caught. Why wouldn't he feel confident? He'd killed three times since his escape. He carried no guilt. He had no conscience.

But this time Detective Reagan Conner and his team would be there waiting on him. They'd stop him before he could kill her, and then it would all be over.

Unless… Unless any one of a dozen things went wrong.

Suppose the police didn't act fast enough. Suppose Orson really was too cagey to be apprehended again.

One mistake and she could be dead, and Joey would be left without one living family member to take care of him.

Doubts expanded into new avenues of dread. Apprehension rattled inside her like a nest of venomous snakes. She knew what Sean's answer would be to the dilemma, but still the need to talk to him about it swelled to a painful ache.

Or maybe it wasn't talk she needed at all. She touched her mouth, and anticipation heated her lips and curled around her fear.

She was trembling when she reached the door to Sean's bedroom. It was ajar as before. She tapped lightly.

No answer. No sound of his breathing. No sounds coming from his room at all. She stuck her head inside. The bed was still made. There was no sign of Sean.

She hadn't seen him since Dylan had driven them home, but his truck had been parked in the driveway at the side of the house. She'd assumed he was in his room. Obviously she'd been wrong.

Disappointment crept though her in fatiguing waves

as she padded back to the bedroom she shared with Joey. Too unsettled to sleep and not wanting to wake Joey, she picked up the stack of magazines and carried them to the family room. The house was unsettlingly quiet as she flicked on a lamp and nestled into a corner of the leather sofa.

The journal on top was seriously out-of-date. She reached into the stack and made a random choice, not realizing what it was until she'd placed it in her lap.

Beyond the Grave. She hadn't intended to bring that one with her. A chill settled in the room as she thumbed through the magazine, found the article and began to read. If there were facts to be discovered, they were concealed in the darkly evocative narrative.

The Ledger house had a reputation as being haunted. Strangers told of seeing a woman in white out by the gate when they'd pass it at night. She'd try to wave them down as if she needed help. If they stopped, she disappeared.

Others who had dared venture inside the gate claimed to have seen a woman standing at one of the house's many windows. Speculation was that the woman in white was the ghost of Helene Ledger waiting for her five sons to come home. Others believed she was there to make sure that her husband never returned to the house where he'd killed her.

In all fairness, all the writers really attested to was that the house had a warm and welcoming feel to it and that Troy Ledger's new daughter-in-law was totally convinced of his innocence.

The article included several pictures of the courtyard

garden that Collette and Joey had decorated for the upcoming holiday this afternoon. It was said to be Helene's creation and one of her favorite respites before her murder.

The garden had now been lovingly restored to its former beauty. If the ghost of Helene Ledger was still on the scene, the writers were certain her days would be spent there, even if she did roam the hallways at night.

Creepily grotesque, yet weirdly sentimental. Throw in a dollop of unrequited passion for a fascinating stranger and you'd have Eve's life in a nutshell.

She didn't believe in ghosts or goblins or any other paranormal elements. But her psychiatric training and experience had taught her that the mind could mold any fear or fantasy into a virtual reality.

If Helene's ghost were real, it would surely be furious with Eve for bringing danger into the Ledger home.

Her eyelids grew heavy. Eve reached for a nearby throw, pulled it over her and snuggled against the back of the couch. Her head came to rest on her folded arms, and the magazine dropped to the floor.

An icy draft filled the room. Eve shivered and opened her eyes as a strange, vaporous shape floated past her and hovered above Joey's bed. The vapor formed long, sinewy bands that wrapped around Joey like tentacles.

Eve rushed over and tried to beat them off him, but her efforts met with inhuman resistance.

"I'll watch over him. He's cradled in love."

Eve jerked awake as the words echoed in her mind as if they'd traveled through a deep canyon. A cold sweat dampened her pajamas and they clung to her like a second skin. She sat up straight and took gulping breaths to clear her mind.

There were no remnants of a ghostly vapor. She wasn't even in the bedroom where Joey was sleeping. But her conscience had found a way to get through the hurdles she'd erected in her mind.

Joey would be safe here at the ranch without her. She'd go back to Dallas. Detective Conner would get his man. Her world would return to normal.

Normal, but without Sean Ledger in it. She ached to go to him now, beg him to hold her until her nerves steadied.

But if he held her in his arms, she'd never find the strength or the will to leave him. That left nothing to do but go back to her own bed. Alone.

She'd tell Sean and Troy of her plans the first thing in the morning.

SEAN STAMPED THE MUD OFF his feet and climbed the back steps. He'd slept very little last night and woke up with the sun. Hating to disturb the others at that ungodly hour, he'd moved through the house as quietly as he could, made a pot of coffee, and taken a cup outside with him.

He'd taken a brisk walk, got his blood circulating and still dreaded the thought of stepping back inside the house. He and Troy had found no meeting of the minds. They hadn't even come close.

They wouldn't, as long as neither of them took the lead in bringing up his mother's murder. They sidestepped the subject like it was a cliff they'd fall over if they got too close.

Worse, he was losing it with Eve, letting his frustration turn him into a drill sergeant. But she wasn't helping any. She didn't have to look so damned irresistible or sway so seductively when she walked. Or return his kiss with a passion that left him dizzy with desire.

If he let himself, he'd fall so hard it would take a team of horses to right him. He'd even start believing he could actually make a relationship with her work, when experience had taught him it was a mistake to even try.

The only thing going well was his relationship with Joey. Sean could read Joey the way he read a troubled horse. The boy reacted honestly and without thinking about his every move. He wanted independence, yet his dependence on his mother got in the way of his claiming it.

What Sean couldn't decipher was exactly how or why Joey had become so fearful, though he knew a traumatic experience could do that to a kid.

Like coming home from school and finding your mother lying dead in the living room, her hair matted with blood. Sean pushed the gruesome memories back into the crevices of his mind as he stepped through the back door. He took off his Stetson and tossed it onto an empty chair.

Troy was sitting at the kitchen table, reading the morning newspaper and sipping his coffee. He nodded and kept reading.

Sean stared at the jagged scar that punctuated his

face from his temple to his cheek and he recalled the story Eve had told him.

Troy was not the fallen hero from his youth. Nor was he the heartless monster his mother's family had claimed.

Sean refilled his coffee mug and joined Troy at the table. "Can we talk?"

TROY FOLDED THE PAPER and pushed it aside. He'd been expecting this ever since Sean had arrived. Still, he wasn't prepared. Explaining meant revisiting the pain.

It meant saying things that should never have to be said. It meant facing head-on the revulsion that Sean had never really tried to disguise.

"I guess now's as good a time as any for you to say what's on your mind," Troy said.

"Do you remember me?" Sean asked. "I mean really remember me and not just that I'm one of your sons that you dismissed from your life for seventeen years."

"I remember you. When I was around, you took every step I did until you started school. Even as a tyke you loved horses. I brought a saddle in the house and you'd sit in it and act like you were riding. 'Yee-haw' was practically the first word you said."

The first word had actually been "Momma." Troy's chest tightened at the memory. Sean was their second son. He'd been born just a year and a half after Wyatt.

It had been a difficult pregnancy for Helene. Not that she'd ever complained, though Troy had given her plenty of reason. He worked sunup to sundown trying to get the ranch up and running so that he could make enough money to pay the note on the land.

Ranching was all he knew. That and rodeo, and he couldn't afford a wife and kid on his rodeo winnings.

Helene was used to luxuries. With Troy she'd gotten calluses and kids. Her parents had never forgiven him for that. Troy figured this was not the kind of information Sean was interested in.

"You were a heck of a baseball player," Troy continued. "Your team won every game that last year...." The last year before Helene had died. Troy hadn't meant to go there, but it was out there now, hanging in the air, waiting to sting like an angry wasp.

Sean looked him straight on. "Did you kill Mother?"

The answer screamed inside Troy, but yelling it out loud wouldn't make much difference. He'd told the truth from day one. People made facts of whatever they chose to believe.

"You must have made up your mind about my guilt or innocence a long time ago," Troy said.

"I had lots of help."

"From your mother's family?"

"And from a jury."

"I'm not going to knock your mother's family, Sean. They never approved of Helene marrying a poor rancher, but they loved her very much. And they stepped in and raised all of you boys when I couldn't. There's no way I could ever repay them for that, not that they'd want or take anything from me.

"As for the jury, I can't even really blame them for convicting me on circumstantial evidence. I didn't do a lot in my own defense. A big part of me died the day your mother did. I shut down mentally and emotionally."

Troy forced himself to look Sean in the eye, hoping for some sign of understanding, if not forgiveness. The stare he got in return was unrelenting.

"I let all of you boys down, Sean. I let Helene down. I can't change that now, but I'll never forgive myself. But for the record, I did try to get in touch with you through the years. Your grandparents convinced me that you didn't want to hear from me and that forcing myself on you would just make matters worse."

"They were right," Sean admitted. "I had never planned to see or talk to you again."

Yet here he was. Troy was thankful for even that.

"I'd like to believe every word you said," Sean said. "I'd like it more than you know. But just wanting to doesn't make that happen for me, not the way it happened for Dylan."

"It didn't happen that fast for Dylan, either. We went through some tough times. But I can't change any of the past."

If he could, Helene would walk through that door right now, and her smile would make his heart sing.

"Just don't let the past mess up your mind and keep you from finding happiness with someone you love," Troy said. "You don't have to take a chance on me, but take a chance on you."

The silence grew heavy, and Troy was thankful when it was broken by the ringing of Sean's cell phone. He'd said what he could. The rest was up to Sean.

He'd turned into a man's man. Good. Honest. Brave.

Helene would be proud of him.

And knowing what a matchmaker she was, she'd no doubt be pushing him into the arms of Eve Worthington right now. In fact, Troy kind of liked that idea himself.

He stepped out of the kitchen, leaving Sean privacy for his call.

"DID I WAKE YOU?" Wyatt asked.

"Unfortunately, no."

"A restless night?"

"And a worse morning. Tell me, Wyatt, do you think there's a chance that the whole lot of Mother's family misjudged Dad and that he really is innocent?"

"To tell you the truth, nothing seems black and white to me anymore. Dylan sees one shade of gray. You see another. Dakota and Tyler were so young back then, I'm not sure they remember enough to form a judgment."

"I know why Tyler hasn't come around. He's fighting in Afghanistan."

"And Dakota's chasing a championship buckle in the Canadian rodeo circuit," Wyatt said. "What's your point?"

"I was just wondering why you haven't made a visit to the Willow Creek Ranch."

"Doesn't rank at the top of my to-do list right now. I've got killers to get off the streets of Atlanta—not to mention the hottie model who either pushed or watched her prominent sugar daddy fall out of a penthouse window last night."

"Are we still talking about Troy, or is that your way

of telling me that you were too busy to check out Orson Bastion?"

"I managed to dig up a few specifics. I'm just not sure they'll help you."

"Hit me with them."

"His mother's name was Lydia Cantrell, though she'd gone back to calling herself Lydia Bastion before her death. She killed herself a couple of years back, supposedly because of Orson's failed parole attempt."

"Was she married?"

"Not at the time. Her third husband, Sam Cantrell, left her after Orson beat his son to death with a carjack."

"Guess he figured the 'till death do us part' clause didn't extend to a son's murder as well," Sean said. "Does Orson have any living family?"

"A sister named Alyssa Coleman. Divorced. One son, Nick, age eleven. She lives in San Antonio."

Wyatt read off the address and Sean scrawled it on a napkin he grabbed from the kitchen counter, though he was certain Orson wouldn't be hanging out there.

"Where does Alyssa work?"

"A bakery/coffeehouse a few blocks from where she lives. She looks like an aging goth girl. Heavy dark makeup around the eyes. Spiky hairdo. Jet-black hair."

"You have her picture?"

"Found it on her Facebook page, so she might have deliberately chosen a weird snapshot."

"I'll look her up."

"But don't get any crazy ideas about questioning her, Sean. Anything I tell you is strictly to help you figure out how to keep Eve Worthington and her son away from Orson Bastion. You do not want to go up against him. He'll make those wild horses you're so fond of seem like puppy dogs."

"Gotcha."

"If I find out anything else, I'll let you know. In the meantime, no heroics. Death will not become you."

"No heroics," Sean promised. Unless Orson Bastion left him no other choice.

But neither would he sit around and do nothing until Eve gave in to Detective Reagan Conner's pressure and became bait for a madman.

ALYSSA WOKE WITH A splitting headache. Orson had always given her headaches, though in the old days they were usually caused by his slamming a fist into the side of her skull or shoving her into the wall.

She'd tell her mother when she got home from work, but it had never helped. Orson would deny everything and Lydia would believe his lies. As far as Alyssa's mother was concerned, Orson could do no wrong.

"Well, he's doing wrong now, Mom. He's killing innocent people and he's dragging me into his sordid games of revenge. And he's using your only grandson to blackmail me into doing his dirty work."

Alyssa picked up the silver frame that held the picture of her and her mother and threw it against the wall. The glass cracked and shards went flying about the room like cutting rain.

Lydia had helped make Orson into the monster he'd become. She'd let him get by with anything. Given him anything he'd wanted, even money for illegal drugs. He'd been her prince. Alyssa had been the miserable pauper, starved for even a smidgen of her mother's attention.

Alyssa didn't care anymore. All she cared about was Nick. He was a good kid. Not like Orson.

The piercing ring of the cell phone Orson had furtively supplied her with sent her head into orbit. She cradled her head with her right hand as she took the call.

"Did you get the money?"

"I tried, but no one will lend me that much," she replied. "I got behind on all my credit card bills when I was out of work. My credit score bottomed out. I told you that."

"I'm parked in front of Nick's school, Alyssa. I think it's time he meet his uncle."

"No. Leave him alone, Orson. Please, leave him be. I've got half the money. I'll give you that and get the rest tomorrow. Please don't touch Nick."

"I never said I'd hurt him. I'll just take him with me when I leave the country. Teach him to be a man. Just because you're my favorite sister."

His taunting laughter made her stomach roll.

"I'll have the money."

She had one last option—Frank—a loan shark who charged abominable rates of interest and would end up with her car and half of every paycheck. She'd be lucky if he left her with enough money to buy groceries. They'd likely be forced to live on the streets. And even at that, there was no guarantee that Frank would lend her that much.

She should have killed Orson herself, years ago, while he slept. The world would have been a better place.

Chapter Ten

Eve pulled her jeans jacket tight, glad she'd grabbed it when Sean had suggested a quick walk while Joey helped Collette feed the horses. The wind was howling this morning, the wind-chill factor making it seem colder than the forty-plus degrees the outside thermometer read.

She'd known from the insistence in his voice and the intensity in his eyes that this wouldn't be a pleasure walk. She'd been right, though she hadn't expected the topic of their conversation.

Eve slowed her pace. "I never heard that Orson's mother had committed suicide," she admitted, "but I can see how that, coupled with the failed parole attempt, might induce rage in a man like Orson."

"Rage that led to his attacking you three weeks after his mother's death."

"So you'd already considered the correlation between the incidents?"

"Yeah. It makes sense in a sick sort of way," Sean said, "especially if he was close to his mother."

"He talked about her during the therapy sessions,"

Eve admitted. "I got the sense that she was an enabler who contributed to his failure to accept responsibility for his actions."

"I thought psychopaths were born," Sean said, "and Orson sounds like a psychopath to me."

"The nature-versus-nurture argument is unimportant now, where Orson is concerned, but I'm not certain he's a true psychopath. He was twenty-eight when I found any evidence that he'd first been in trouble with the law, and that was when he murdered his stepbrother. Usually, psychopaths start showing signs of poor behavior control that get them in trouble with authority figures much earlier in life."

"Brand him what you want. The most important thing for me is keeping him away from you and Joey." Sean stopped walking when they reached the woodshed. He took Eve's hand and tugged her to a spot where the dilapidated structure blocked the worst of the wind.

His touch tangled with her emotions—heat against ice, desire against frustration.

"I know I came on strong last night, Eve, but you going back to Dallas with Orson still on the loose is too big a risk. There is no reason for you to leave the ranch. You're safe here."

"But for how long?" She leaned against the rough wood and propped one foot on the wall behind her. "Everyone predicted Orson would be back in prison by now. He's not. If he's really after me as Detective Conner said, then he'll find me. One way or another, he'll track me down unless he's stopped first."

"You said yourself that he'd never think to look here.

And if he does, you have me, Troy and Dylan to protect you."

"With Orson, that might not be enough."

He brushed a windblown lock of hair from her face. His fingers lingered on her earlobe and his nearness consumed her. She tilted her head and met his gaze. His eyes were compelling, liquid depths she could drown in.

Unless her intuitive abilities had completely deserted her, the same urges that were buzzing through her were affecting him, too. He dropped his hand from her face and looked away.

"There's more, isn't there?" she asked.

"A little, but probably not important."

"What else did Wyatt tell you?"

"Orson has a sister living in San Antonio."

"Really? I had the impression he was an only child."

Eve listened to the facts about Alyssa Coleman. The decision was made even before Sean finished the explanation.

"I'm going to San Antonio and talk to Alyssa," she said.

"No way." Sean's muscles bunched, making his virile protectiveness even more pronounced.

"I have to talk to her," Eve insisted.

"What's the point? I'm sure the cops have already questioned her. Obviously, they didn't learn Orson's whereabouts from her, and there's no reason she'd tell you anything she didn't tell them."

"Maybe not intentionally, but if I can talk to her face-to-face, I may be able to figure out if Orson is still on his killing spree as Conner thinks, or if he's left the area or the country altogether."

"And you plan to just come out and ask her these things? 'Hi, Alyssa. I hear your brother is out to kill me for blocking his parole. Want to get cozy and tell me how he's doing and where he's hiding out?'"

"She might want to tell me. For all I know, she could be just as afraid of him as I am. In any case, I need to talk to her. I won't even tell her who I am. It's not likely Orson carries my picture around in his wallet to show at family reunions."

"The cops may have a picture of you supplied by Detective Conner, and they'll be watching Alyssa's house just in case Orson is stupid enough to show up there."

"Then I'll visit her at work."

"There's no guarantee the cops aren't watching her there, as well."

"I'll go incognito."

"In what? Sunglasses and a hat?"

"Collette has a Mrs. Santa suit I can wear. The customers will think I work at a department store. Even Santa won't know me from the real thing."

"What about Joey?"

"I'm sure Collette will watch him for a few hours. He won't like my leaving him, but he's used to Collette and Troy, and even Dylan now. You saw how easily he left me to go feed the horses."

"I don't like it," Sean said.

"You can go with me or not, Sean. That's your choice. But I am going."

"I don't get it. Why take this risk when you don't have to, Eve? Why can't you just let me protect you?"

She linked her arm with his, craving his strength and needing him to understand.

"The longer Orson remains free, the greater the chance he'll find me. Even if you and Troy kill him before he hurts anyone, the violence will touch Joey. I can't let that happen—not if there's even the slightest chance I can do something to stop it."

Sean pulled her into his arms and held her so tight she could feel his heart beating against her chest. When he finally released her, he tangled his fingers in her hair at the nape of her neck.

"Okay, Mrs. Santa. Go get ready and I'll load the sleigh."

"Ho, ho, ho." But she wasn't laughing on the inside.

EVE REARRANGED HER short white wig, pulling the wiry strands of fake hair from beneath the fur collar. Visiting Alyssa Coleman might be a good idea, but this costume was not.

"How much farther?" she asked when they entered San Antonio.

"It should be right in this area."

"What's the name of the shop?"

"If Wyatt mentioned the name this morning, I missed it, but we're near her house, so we have to be near the shop."

"That could be it," Eve said, pointing to a green awning on the right side of the street.

Sean slowed and pulled to the curb. A sign on the

walk outside the door announced that eggnog lattes and gingerbread coffees were the specialties of the day.

"You'll fit right in, Mrs. Santa, though with that pot belly, I'd lay off the calories."

"Not funny." She checked her reflection in the visor mirror one last time. "You have to admit I was right about being unrecognizable, though."

"I expect Dasher and Dancer to show up any minute."

"There are no reindeer in Texas."

She wrestled with the yards of red velvet while Sean held the door. A passing car honked. She looked up and waved cheerily. She might as well get into the spirit of the costume.

Sean followed her up the short walk and through the door. They were met by delightful odors of coffee and treats baking in the oven. A display counter was filled with muffins, tarts, cookies, pies and layers of fresh gingerbread.

To Eve's surprise, the few patrons inside paid her and her costume little attention. Most were working at computers. A middle-aged woman was reading, and two young mothers were deep in conversation while their babies slept next to them in their infant seats.

To Eve's dismay, there was no sign of Alyssa, not if she still looked anything like the snapshot of her Sean had found on the computer. Even bypassing Austin traffic, it had taken them over two hours to get here, and it might all be for nothing.

A perky blonde stepped to the counter. "What can I get for you?"

"Just black coffee for me," Sean said.

She smiled and leaned over the counter provocatively, providing a glance of her assets. Eve wasn't surprised. A female of any age would have to be blind not to notice and get turned on by Sean.

"Is the coffee for here or to go?" the blonde asked.

"For here."

"In that case, have a seat anywhere and a waitress will be right with you to take your order."

Eve chose a table toward the back, so that the overhang from her bulky skirt wouldn't trip passing customers. A couple of minutes later, an equally vivacious and friendly waitress showed up at their table. Eve ordered a caramel latte, iced. She was perspiring under the costume.

"Is that all?" the waitress asked after she'd taken their orders. "The blueberry muffins are fresh out of the oven."

"Sure smell good," Sean said, "but I'll pass. Is Alyssa working today?"

"She's in the back, on break. Do you want me to get her for you?"

"If you don't mind."

"No problem."

Eve leaned toward him as the waitress hurried away. "That was smooth."

"You wanted to talk to Alyssa. I'm just trying to help."

She had wanted to see her. She still did—only, now that they were here, she had no idea how to handle the confrontation.

Alyssa joined them and surprisingly slid into a chair next to Sean as if she were expecting him. Her expression was strained and the dark circles beneath her eyes made her look as if she hadn't slept for days.

She spread her hands on the table. "Did Frank send you?" she whispered.

Sean nodded.

If he was Frank, Eve wasn't the only one going incognito.

"Did you bring the money?"

He nodded again.

Eve had no idea what was going on.

"All five thousand dollars of it?"

"Just like you asked for."

Alyssa scanned the shop nervously. "We can't make the exchange here in the open."

"We can go to my truck. It's parked in front."

She shook her head. "I'll go to the ladies' room. Follow me in there and we'll make the exchange. Don't worry. Once you step through the arch, no will see which door you go in. And it locks."

Sean hesitated and Eve finally realized what was going down. Alyssa had mistaken Sean for someone else and he was playing along, hoping to get information about Orson.

"Not so quick," Eve said, keeping her voice low. "Before any money changes hands, we have to know where Orson is hiding out."

Alyssa's face turned ghostly white. "That wasn't part of the deal."

"It is now," Sean said.

"I don't know where he is. He'd never tell me that. I've agreed to all your demands. But I have to have that money." She started to shake, then looked to see if anyone was watching. "Please. I'll do anything you say, but I must have that money."

The woman was scared to death. Eve was certain that Orson was behind that fear. "I have the money with me," she said. "I'll follow you to the bathroom."

Alyssa walked away and Sean grabbed Eve's wrist. "What are you doing? I'm not sure what this is about, but we've pushed it as far as we can."

Eve stood, her skirt bouncing about like a red parachute until it knocked over a chair. This time people did turn to look. Eve took that opportunity to break loose from Sean.

"I'm giving her the money. Pay our tab and I'll meet you in the truck."

"You've lost your mind."

"Probably."

Sean caught up to her before she reached the bathroom door. "Crashing the ladies' restroom is a first for me, but Alyssa is the sister of a madman. You are not going anywhere with her without me."

Eve stepped inside, took the money from her oversize handbag and counted out fifty one-hundred-dollar bills while Sean watched. It was all the money she'd taken with her when she left Dallas, but she couldn't think of any better way to spend it.

"Take care," Eve whispered to Alyssa as she walked out of the ladies' room. "And stay safe."

She and Sean hurried through the shop and out the door.

He put a hand to the small of her back. "You just handed a woman you don't know five thousand dollars for, oh, let's see—zero information."

"And the money will go straight to Orson. And when it does, hopefully a cop will be there to make the arrest. I've given Detective Conner the bait he wants. All he has to do is trail Alyssa, and when she hands Orson the money, the cops nab him."

"That was fast thinking on your part," Sean admitted.

"About as fast as you becoming Frank. Now, how about getting Wyatt on the phone so he can put me in touch with Detective Conner?"

"Who knew Mrs. Santa was a detective at heart?"

"Who did you think squeals to Santa when you've been naughty or nice?

ONCE EVE HAD FINISHED her conversation with Detective Conner, she yanked off the wig and the hat and tossed them into the backseat. "The detective didn't sound all that appreciative," she said as she began wiggling out of the suffocating costume.

Sean cursed the traffic that forced him to keep his eyes and attention on the highway. "What did he say?"

"That I should not have gone to see Alyssa and that I was interfering with police business. Then he thanked me for calling."

In seconds, Eve had stripped down to pair of black

slacks and a white T-shirt. Sean stole a look. Even in that she looked sexy, especially with the tips of her bare nipples outlined beneath the thin fabric.

"What did the detective say when you told him you expected to get your money back?"

"That he couldn't guarantee anything. Bottom line, he still thinks the surest way to apprehend Orson is for me to return to Dallas."

"An invitation that you surely turned down."

"That's when I told him that I thought I'd done my part. The rest was up to him."

Sean reached across the back of the seat and ruffled her hat hair. "You're pretty amazing."

"I thought you'd never notice."

"Seriously, you've held together great through all this. I can see now why Troy thinks so highly of you."

"He's your father, Sean. Would it be that difficult to just call him 'Dad'?"

"More difficult than you can imagine."

Sean plunged into his own thoughts while Eve put through a call to Collette to check on Joey. Eve was a great mother.

Like his mother had been. He had trouble remembering her face these days. Instead, the images were confused with the dozens of pictures of her his grandparents had kept on display.

What Sean remembered about her were moments, prisms of love captured in time. Her hair falling about his face when she kissed him good-night. Her voice when she sang along with the radio. How she'd stay up with him when he was sick and read him stories.

How she'd cried with him when Sinbad had gotten sick and they'd thought he might have to be put down. Mom had been love.

Troy had been his hero, a man's man, the guy Sean had always looked up to. Making his father proud of him had been the greatest feeling in the world.

And then it had all come crumbling down into a pile of ash that still poisoned his mind. So, yes—it was impossible to look at the man and call him "Dad."

And dwelling on this would get him nowhere.

"How's Joey?" he asked, once Collette was off the phone.

"Collette says he keeps asking when we'll be home, but I talked to him, and he seems fine. A little anxious, but fine."

"Then what do you say to stopping for a quick bite? It's two hours past my lunch time."

"I could eat," she said. "But I'm not dressed for the occasion, and I'm definitely not putting that velvet monstrosity back on."

"Not likely anyone would recognize either one of us, now that we're nowhere near Alyssa Coleman, but I was thinking we'd just find a fast-food drive-through. There are several listed for the next exit, and there's a rest stop a couple of miles down the freeway. We can just pull off the road and eat there."

"I could go for a burger and fries."

Sean pulled into the exit lane. Ten minutes later they were parked beneath a couple of spreading oaks. He lowered the windows and breathed in a huge gulp of fresh air. The wind had died down since morning, and there wasn't a cloud in the sky. It was a perfect hill country December day.

Except that Eve still had a dangerous escaped convict who wanted her dead. If she hadn't, she wouldn't need his protection. He'd never have met her. He wouldn't be sitting here now, thinking how much he'd like to kiss her until the hunger inside him melted away.

"Why did you come back to Mustang Run, Sean?"

"I'd quit my job. Dylan had been after me to visit the ranch, so I started driving in this direction. The next thing I knew, I was here and you were coming at me with a knife."

And the desire she'd awakened in him that night was about to push him over the edge of reason now.

"Did you live with your grandparents after your mother died?"

"I lived with my uncle Bill. He was a confirmed old bachelor who taught high school history. He didn't talk much, read too much and hated Troy for killing his baby sister."

"Was he good to you?"

"He wasn't mean. I felt alone a lot. But he paid for me to have horseback riding lessons, and as soon as I was old enough, I started working at a riding stable near our house. I spent as much time there as possible. That might have something to do with my interacting better with horses than with people."

"You do just fine with some people," Eve assured him, "especially with Joey."

"He's a good kid."

"I know, but I can't help but worry about him. He

never talks about his father's death anymore, and he's gotten much better. But I hate to even imagine what it would do to him to face that kind of violence again."

"I didn't realize his father had died a violent death."

"Brock was killed in a freakish drive-by shooting two years ago. We'd never had anything like that in our neighborhood before, and we haven't had one since. The police decided it was random, or possibly a case of mistaken identity."

Eve wrapped her arms around her chest, shrinking inside herself. He ached to hold her, but the timing didn't seem right.

"That must have been incredibly hard on you and Joey."

She nodded her head. "Joey was with him. Miraculously, he wasn't hit."

"He saw his father killed?"

"At close range. Blood from the gunshot wound dripped all over his shoes."

Poor kid." But it explained why Joey clung so to his mother and why he was shy and fearful around strangers. And why she was so fiercely protective of him. Sean had needed reassurance like that when *his* mother died and he'd been much older than Joey.

"You must miss Brock very much," he said. It wasn't a question.

"I hate that Brock was killed and that Joey lost his father, but the sad truth is that Brock and I were getting a divorce. He was leaving me for an aerobics instructor at the gym where he worked out."

The man had to be crazy to even think of leaving Eve.

"A philandering husband murdered in a quiet, upscale neighborhood," Eve continued. "As you can imagine, it caused quite a stir. For a few days, I think I was even considered a suspect in the murder, so I know how devastating that can be."

Eve shifted to face Sean. "It must have been a million times worse for your father. He was convicted of killing a woman he worshipped."

If *Troy was innocent,* Sean thought.

"I left my position with the prison system after Brock was killed, so that I could be with Joey full-time. He needed me at home, and I'd already decided to find a new job. I didn't think I'd ever feel comfortable again at the Huntsville facility, after Orson's attack."

The facts bucked around in Sean's mind. "How long was it before the attack that your husband was killed?"

"Two weeks to the day."

"And no one ever questioned whether or not Orson was behind Brock's murder?"

"Orson was in prison. There was no way he could have killed him."

"That doesn't eliminate the possibility that he had someone else do it for him, perhaps someone he'd met in prison."

Eve wadded her napkin, crushing it in her hands. "If that's true, then even back then Orson had just methodically and determinedly set out to destroy me."

Sean could not let that happen. And he simply couldn't fight his need for her another second.

He leaned across the seat, tugged her towards him and kissed her. Her lips parted as she kissed him back, over and over, until passion swallowed up everything but the two of them and the animal-like need roaring inside him.

But then Eve pulled away, and he felt bereft.

"We should get back to the ranch," she murmured.

"Right." He could make it that long, but how would he ever make it through the night without pillaging those sweet lips again?

He'd never wanted a woman more. And that frightened him.

SEAN SLOWED, AND A WAVE OF adrenaline shot through him as he spotted the strange car in the driveway in front of the ranch house. Troy was standing on the front porch next to an attractive woman who looked to be about his age, only much better preserved.

"Looks like Troy has company," Eve said. "I never considered that when I asked him and Collette to watch Joey. I guess I should have."

Sean didn't bother hiding his anger. "He knows how important it is that no one knows you're here."

"Maybe he didn't know she was coming."

Sean's irritation wasn't appeased, though he realized the sick rolling inside him wasn't just about Troy's lack of consideration for Eve.

This was his mother's house. The porch where Troy had sat with her on warm summer nights. Sean's mother, that Eve had claimed Troy worshipped.

He'd been out of prison mere months. It sure hadn't taken him long to find a replacement.

The woman was vaguely familiar, but Sean couldn't place her. She met him at the steps, all smiles as if she couldn't wait to see him.

"Sean Ledger. It's about time you came back to the ranch. I bet you don't even remember me."

"Can't say that I do."

"Ruthanne Foley. I was your mother's best friend."

And suddenly Sean remembered exactly who she was.

Chapter Eleven

Ruthanne had been in and out of their house all the time when Sean was a kid. Her husband had come over a lot, too. Sean hadn't liked him. He talked loud and was always telling Sean and his brothers they should go out-side and play, like it was his house instead of theirs.

He'd liked Ruthanne until the night he saw her with his dad out at the horse barn when neither of them knew Sean was watching. She'd tried to kiss his dad, but then his dad had seen Sean and pushed her away.

Sean had never told anyone what he saw that night, not even his brothers. But he'd hated it when Ruthanne came around after that.

For all Sean knew, it could have been as innocent on Troy's part as when Sasha Cahill had tried to jump his bones, but the old resentment rattled him all the same.

"Ruthanne heard I was sick and dropped by to bring a casserole dish," Troy said. "She's just leaving."

"News travels fast," Sean said.

"I ran into a nurse friend who works the E.R.," Ruth-anne said. "She told me the ambulance had bought Troy in with a heart attack the other night. I tried to call him, but he never answers the phone."

"Doctor's orders," Troy quipped. "I need my rest."

Troy was still holding the casserole dish, so, evidently, he'd met Ruthanne on the porch and not invited her inside. If they'd arrived a few minutes later, he and Eve could have avoided her altogether.

Ruthanne smoothed the front of her snugly fitted sweater and turned to Eve. "You must be a friend of Sean's."

"She is," Troy lied. "This is Ellen. She lives in Houston."

A nice recovery, Sean had to admit. Having anyone see Eve at the ranch was worrisome. He and Eve followed their hellos with a quick goodbye and left Troy and Ruthanne standing on the porch. They closed the door firmly behind them and Eve went off in search of Joey and Collette.

He followed to make sure she found them. When she joined them in the protected garden where Collette was on her knees helping Joey build a stone bridge for his cars, he returned to the kitchen. Troy was standing at the kitchen counter, closing the top on a bottle of pills. Troy swallowed a white tablet and chased it with a glass of water.

"I'm sorry Ruthanne ran into Eve like that, but I had nothing to do with her coming over. She just showed up. But no harm was done. She has no idea who Eve is."

"Did she see Joey?"

"No. Collette took him to the back of the house when we saw the car drive up."

Sean wanted to say more, but it was his own frustration pushing him. Troy couldn't have very well just run off Ruthanne with a rifle.

Sean went to the counter for a cup of coffee.

"I'm limited to a cup a day," Troy said, "but Collette made a fresh pot after lunch. It should still be drinkable."

Sean took a sip. "It's fine."

"How did the meeting with Bastion's sister go?"

"It netted her a gain of five thousand dollars."

Sean filled him in on the details and even mentioned the possibility that Orson might have had Brock Worthington killed.

Troy scratched his chin. "You're right. That sounds just like something he'd do. I can't believe I didn't think of that."

"We don't have proof," Sean said, "but the timing sure makes it appear suspicious." He carried his coffee to the table. The entire top was covered in computer printouts, yellowed newspaper and scribbled notes.

He found a spot just big enough for his cup. "What's this?"

Troy joined him at the table. "I've been collecting information on crimes committed in Mustang Run and neighboring towns within a year either way of the time your mother was murdered."

It was quite an impressive collection. "Did you gather all this by yourself?"

"Most of it, but Abel Drake's put me on some leads. He has a friend who was a Ranger back then, Trent

Fontaine. Trent came up with some information I would have never found."

"Like what?"

"An alleged rape in the northern part of the county one month before your mother was shot and killed. The woman claimed she came home and found a man inside her house rifling through her cabinets. He raped her, but left out the back door when her husband drove up. She called the authorities but was too embarrassed to press charges, so there was never any formal record of the crime."

"Were there others like that?"

"A rape and murder in a neighboring county that was never solved."

"What about forensic evidence?"

"Apparently there was nothing that could identify the killer. But back then CSI teams weren't what they are now, especially in rural areas. No one ever checked fibers or hairs or any of the other evidence they rely so heavily on now."

Sean scanned a couple of the newspaper articles. "You've done some pretty thorough digging. Who did you say hooked you up with the ranger?"

"Abel Drake. He's an old friend, used to live in these parts, but he has a ranch just east of Dallas now."

Sean spent the next hour going over the information spread across the table. The work represented a lot of time and effort. It was the kind of thing you'd expect from a man who was actually looking for his wife's killer.

OTHER THAN AT DINNER, Sean had seen little of Eve since they returned from San Antonio. She'd spent most of her time with Joey, who'd at least temporarily reverted to clinging and dogging her every step.

Sean understood Joey's deep-rooted anxiety better since he'd heard that the boy was there when his dad had died. He'd seen the blood up close and personal, the way Sean had when his mother had been murdered. Joey had been younger, likely understood less, but Joey's father had been alive and walking down the street with him one minute and dead the next.

There was too much violence in this country, too many kids who lived with nightmarish images forever seared into their minds.

Sean had buried much of his pain and fear deep inside him. Oddly, he became better at dealing with his own issues when he began to work with horses full-time. Horses responded to body language rather than words, to experiences instead of lectures. They made slow but steady progress, as long as the environment was conducive, trust was there and their basic needs were met.

Seems it was the same for people, even kids. It was pretty basic when you thought about it.

Except when you were dealing with men like Orson Bastion. Men without conscience or guilt, who killed without remorse whenever it suited them.

And Sean had no doubt that the kind of evil Orson possessed had started early in his life. Just because they had no record of it didn't mean it hadn't occurred.

Troy Ledger was not an evil man. So, if he had killed Sean's mother all those years ago, it would have taken some incredibly strong motivation or temporary insanity. But Troy hadn't claimed temporary insanity. He'd claimed innocence. And now he was, at the very least, going through the motions of looking for his wife's killer.

Sean's hodgepodge of thoughts collided with his equally jumbled emotions. The quietness of the house only added to the mix. His father had retired for the night. Eve was still back in her bedroom, though it was well past Joey's bedtime.

He was starting to think Eve was merely avoiding him. She'd thrown herself wholeheartedly into this afternoon's kiss. He was pretty sure it had left her reeling the way it had him. But she'd had time to think about it since then. She might just be smart enough to figure out that adding fiery passion to a deadly situation wasn't all that smart.

"Sean."

He turned at the sound of Eve's voice, though he'd been so lost in his thoughts he hadn't heard her approach. She was standing in the doorway, wearing the pale blue robe that always fired his imagination about the body beneath it. Desire rocked through him and his body hardened into a painful, throbbing need that devoured his control.

He walked over, took one end of the dangling belt between his fingers and tugged. The robe fell open revealing nothing but naked flesh.

Eve slipped her arms around his neck. "I got tired of waiting for you to come to bed."

Chapter Twelve

Sean's blood ran fire-hot through his veins as he picked up Eve and carried her to his room. Her arms and legs wrapped around him. Her fingers curled in his hair. But it was her kisses that drove him wild. Deep, wet, greedy, as if she couldn't get enough of him.

He let her slide down his body until her feet touched the floor. The pressure against his hard need triggered a thousand new emotions, all of them wild and tempestuous. He throbbed with a need so earthy and unfettered that he could barely turn the lock on the door.

Once he did, it was déjà vu, a repeat of night one. A sensual, frantic tangle of legs, arms and bodies. Only, this time Eve was the aggressor and there was no knife. No hesitation. No restraint.

She backed him against the wall, ripped open his shirt and smothered his bare chest with kisses. He tugged the robe from her shoulders and let it puddle at their feet. Kicking it out of the way, he fit his hands beneath her firm little buttocks, lifting and fitting her against him.

She pulled away just enough to slide her hands between them and unsnap his jeans. Lowering the zipper with one frantic jerk, she traced a searing trail down the length of his erection with her fingertips.

He should slow down, but he couldn't, especially not now, not with Eve's hands and mouth exploring him and finding every spot that drove him mad.

He slid his hands between her legs. She was already slick with desire. Blood rushed to his head. He'd never been this hot for a woman, never been this dizzy with desire. Never been so damned out of control.

He wrapped his hands around his need, trying desperately to hold back. "I have protection in my wallet."

"I haven't been with another man in years," she said. "After Brock, I got a clean bill of health. And there's no chance of pregnancy this week."

"It's been sixteen months for me. Two clean checkups since then."

Sean exhaled in relief and then was hit again by passion so intense he could barely stand. He lifted Eve and fit her over the throbbing length of his organ. She moaned as he thrust inside her.

And then there was no holding back. They exploded together in a frenzy of release that seemed to rock the whole room.

"I should have—"

Eve silenced him with a finger against his lips. "No shoulda-wouldas. That was exactly what I needed. The only question is how long before we can do it again."

If she kept curling around him as she was doing now, the wait would be incredibly short. This time, when he picked her up he carried her to his bed.

EVE CUDDLED IN SEAN'S ARMS, feeling as if she'd been painted inside and out with a sweet, golden brush of pleasure. The past week had been a nightmare. Tonight's sensual frenzy had provided the perfect release for the multitude of emotions that had run roughshod over her ever since she left Dallas for Willow Creek Ranch.

But it wasn't only about release for her. It was about Sean and the way he excited her by just brushing her shoulder when they passed in the hallway. About his blatant virility and the way he wore his jeans. About the way he handled Joey and looked after both of them.

She trailed her fingers down his abs. "Are you sleepy?"

"No, just regrouping."

"Tell me about you."

"There's nothing to tell. What you see is what you get."

"I know you've been in relationships. What happened that kept them from leading to marriage?"

"Nothing traumatic. I was engaged in college. We were planning to get married after we graduated and both got jobs."

"That seems smart."

"Real smart. It gave us time to figure out that we were heading in different directions. I couldn't see myself in a life that didn't involve horses. Once she got a job with a Madison Avenue advertising firm, she didn't see herself living anywhere but New York."

"So she called off the marriage?"

"It was a mutual parting of the ways."

"Were there others? I mean, others you were serious about? I'm not asking for stats."

"Good. I never kiss and tell—unless the kisses are as memorable as yours." He smiled at her. "Right now I'm thinking I should probably call everyone I know and shout about the thrill of you."

He kissed her again to make his point. Kissing made it really difficult to think coherently. But she did want to know why he was still single when he would have made such a marvelous husband and father.

"I'm being serious," she said.

"So was I." He stretched and put his hands behind his head, as if he needed to separate a bit from her before he could focus on the past. "I almost made it to the altar three years ago."

"What happened that time?"

"That time it was all my fault. Angie was great. We were the same age, both twenty-eight. And we both loved horses. She managed the dude ranch her father owned up in Colorado. I was working for a privately run horse-abuse facility at the time. I figured it was time I settled down, and this time all the external factors were in my favor."

"Only, you never married."

"Nope. A week before the wedding, I realized I couldn't go through with it. Something was missing. I had no idea what. I decided then that I was not meant for long-term relationships. So I paid all the nonrefundable wedding expenses, quit my job and moved on."

"What happened to Angie?"

"She was furious with me—until she met her real

Mr. Right. Then she called and thanked me. I went to their wedding. They have twin girls now."

At least Eve knew where she stood with Sean. He was not available for a long-term relationship. *So don't go building a dream around him,* she warned herself. She could get her head around that. It wasn't as if she was already planning to pick out furniture with him.

But as for not falling for him, it was way too late to convince her heart of that.

Sean turned and pulled her close again, nuzzling his face in her cleavage. "Time to make up for shortchanging you."

"You didn't. I asked—" She stopped talking as he slid his hand between her legs and sent vibrations of anticipation dancing through every inch of her. He clearly wasn't referring to their conversation.

"So show me the best you have to offer," she teased, easily falling back into the pleasure zone.

The lovemaking started all over again, this time slower, but no less exciting. Sean cupped her breasts, licking and sucking the nipples until they tingled, creating sensations in them she'd never imagined possible.

Impulsively she arched toward him.

"I love the way you open up to me, Eve. Sensually. Uninhibited. Like a woman who knows what she wants."

"What I want is you, Sean."

He kissed his way to her navel, teasing it with his tongue while his fingers explored her most intimate niches. She opened her legs wide, crazy for every touch, giddy from the surges of desire that sprung from deep in her core.

The sweet ache between her thighs intensified. He moved until his rock-hard erection throbbed against them.

"I want you inside me, Sean. Deep inside me."

"Once I'm there, I won't be able to hold off long."

"Then we'll explode together."

She was hot and slick and so ready for him that the first thrust almost sent her into orbit. Making love with Sean might not be this earth-shattering every time, but she couldn't imagine that she'd ever not want him inside her.

His breath came in hard, quick spurts. She closed her eyes and let the thrill take her, riding with him, to the crest and beyond.

Time stopped for an instant and then started again as Sean's spent body rolled off hers. He slid onto his back and pulled her into his arms.

"You're something else," he whispered.

"Is that good?"

"Nope. It's perfection."

The perfection was the two of them together. And even temporary perfection beat mediocrity hands down.

EVE SLEPT UNTIL SHE FELT A tug on her sheet.

"It's morning, Momma. I gotta go feed the horses."

Eve rubbed the dregs of sleep from her eyes, thankful she'd sneaked back to the room she shared with Joey and put on her pajamas in the wee hours of the morning. Eve glanced at the bedside clock and then back at her son.

It was indeed morning, ten before eight. Joey was already dressed in jeans, a blue pullover that was inside out and his boots.

She swung her legs over the side of the bed, biting back a groan at the unexpected ache in her thighs.

"Why don't you go visit with Troy while I get dressed," she suggested.

"I better go wake up Sean first. He's taking me horseback riding."

"What makes you think that?"

"He told me."

"When?"

"Yesterday, when me and him had a glass of chocolate milk on the back steps. You were in the bathroom."

That was the first she'd heard about it, but it made sense. Her leaving Joey with Collette yesterday had revived Joey's separation fears. The only time Joey had let her out of his sight after she returned from San Antonio was when she was in the shower. Leave it to Sean to give him something to look forward to.

"If Sean said he'd take you for a ride, I'm sure he will. But don't wake him. He'll come find you when he's ready."

"Okay." Joey picked up his hat and carried it with him. He wouldn't want to waste time coming back for it when Collette showed up to get him for the feeding chore.

Eve owed Gordon Epps a big thank-you for suggesting she and Joey hide out at Willow Creek Ranch. Had she stayed in Dallas… The possible outcomes were too distressing to consider.

She rinsed her face with cold water in the bathroom and then hurried to dress, choosing jeans and a long-sleeved, turquoise shirt that was one of her favorites. Using the mirror in her compact to check the results, she brushed on a hint of blush and smear of lip gloss.

Once she brushed and smoothed her hair, she looked closely in the mirror, amazed that last night's lovemaking didn't make her face light up like neon. But if there was any visible sign at all, it was in her eyes.

Now all she needed was word that Orson Bastion had been captured. Her hand was on the doorknob, when the now-familiar cold draft of air swirled around her, as if the ghost of Helene Ledger was trying to warn her of something.

The coolness vanished and the room became almost suffocating in contrast. Apprehension prickled the flesh on the back of Eve's neck. Rationality returned slowly. When it did, Eve dismissed all thoughts of ghosts and put in a call to Gordon Epps.

She was about to leave a message when he picked up the call. "Hello."

"Hi, Gordon. Hope I didn't disturb you."

"I was on the other line with Detective Conner."

She took a deep breath and dropped to the edge of the bed. "Bad news?"

"No news, except that he thinks you should return to Dallas. And it's obvious that he believes I'm in frequent contact with you. He pressured me again for a way to reach you."

"I hate that I'm forcing you to lie."

"I kind of got myself into that by calling you originally. But I think maybe you should listen to Conner, Eve."

"You think I should return to Dallas."

"Troy's a good guy and a tough old buzzard, but he's sick. It's unlikely either Dylan or Sean have experience with men like Orson. Besides, I think it might take a whole police department to stop Orson Bastion. Conner sounds as if he's ready to supply that now."

"If I agree to be bait."

"It's just my opinion, Eve. You do what you think is best, but don't ever start taking your safety for granted. You can't when you're dealing with Orson."

"I know that."

But she'd already given them bait. All they had to do was follow the money. She decided not to mention that to Gordon. She'd already involved him too deeply in her problems.

"I'll give it some thought," she said.

They finished the conversation, and this time when she started to the kitchen there were no cold drafts. Optimism filtered though the anxiety. With any luck, Orson would go to Alyssa for the money today and be back in prison before dark.

If not, she'd have to reconsider Gordon's advice. If it came down to her having to face Orson, then Conner and the Dallas Police Department really were her best option for getting out alive.

"NOW, WE'RE TALKING serious psychopath."

"None of this is etched in stone," Wyatt reminded

Sean. "It's not even allegations at this point, but just findings I thought you might find interesting."

Sean found them interesting, all right. Eve would find them bone-chilling. It was just one more thing he'd have to hit her with. But it shed even more light on the criminal mind of Orson Bastion.

"What's the likelihood any of this will be followed up on?" Sean asked.

"The first drowning falls under my jurisdiction."

"Does that mean you feel a cold case being opened?"

"At least a preliminary investigation. We'll decide whether or not to move forward after that. A reopening of Brock Worthington's murder trial would fall into the hands of the Dallas Police Department, unless there's an excuse to bring the FBI in on it."

Sean's suspicions about Bastion being involved in Brock's murder had led to Sean calling Wyatt this morning. The new information Wyatt had gathered had been lagniappe. If possible, the influx of data raised the danger bar even more.

He looked out the window and saw Eve and Joey returning from the horse barn. Joey was skipping along beside her, his boots kicking up dust. Sunlight shimmered in Eve's hair. She was smiling.

He didn't have the heart to chill her bones just yet.

"Gotta go," Sean said.

"Yeah, me too," Wyatt answered. "It's hectic on the homicide front this morning."

"Thanks for keeping me posted and for letting me bounce ideas off of you."

"No problem. Just watch your step and keep a cool head on your shoulders. Duking it out with a psycho is never a fair fight."

Eve and Joey stepped through the back door, lighting up the room as he broke the connection. A new plan was rapidly forming in Sean's mind.

Joey raced over to Sean. "Can we go horseback riding now?"

"I don't see why not, as long as your mother okays it."

"Can't my momma go, too?"

"Wouldn't be the same without her."

"Will you go, Momma?" Joey pleaded.

"Sure. Someone has to look after you hombres."

Troy joined them in the kitchen, no doubt lured by Joey's excited voice. "Did I hear someone say horseback riding?"

"Yes," Joey said. "Do you wanna go with us? You can ride your own horse."

"I'd love to, but I'm afraid it would go against doctor's orders. But I've been thinking. Do you know what this house needs?"

"I bet I know," Joey said. "It needs a dog."

Eve put a hand on Joey's shoulders. "Why do you think we need a dog?"

"When I wanted one for my birthday, you said our yard was too small and that we didn't have a fence. But his yard is bigger than a bunch of parks, and it has lots of fences."

"Good point," Troy said. "We do need a dog around

here, but I was thinking we need a Christmas tree. After all, it is December."

Joey's eyes grew wide. "Can we go buy a tree?"

"No need to do that," Troy said. "Cedars grow like weeds around here. I noticed a patch of them on that knoll west of Dylan's house. Several that looked to be a perfect size for a tree. I thought maybe you guys could pick one while you're out riding. If you find one you like, you can go back later, chop it down and bring it home in the back of the truck. That way you won't mess up the branches, dragging it behind your mount."

"Not a bad idea," Sean said. In fact, getting a tree for Joey was an excellent idea. It just surprised Sean that it had come from Troy. Seventeen years in prison, but he still understood what a Christmas tree meant to a kid.

"If you call, I can drive out and meet you with an ax and the truck," Troy said. "As long as you call before two. Dylan's driving me to the doctor shortly after that."

"Are you okay?" Eve asked.

"I'm fine. This is just a routine checkup, so don't go making a fuss. You just find us a tree," Troy said. "Helene always liked one that was just an inch or so shy of the ceiling."

His voice caught on Sean's mother's name. And a ridiculous knot formed in Sean's throat. "We'll find a tree. Now let's get out of here," he said, before he got tangled up in the facts, suspicions and bittersweet memories that would drag him back into his own nightmarish past.

There was already too much talk of Christmas, old

memories and new horrors about a killer who wanted Eve dead. And the day was only beginning.

EVE FELT AS IF SHE WERE living in an alternate universe as she watched Joey dash around the deep green cedars, choosing first one and then another as the perfect Christmas tree. He'd made more emotional strides in the last week than he'd made in the past two years. And this at a time when he'd been ripped from his home and plugged into a group of strangers.

The wide-open spaces seemed to work like a safety valve, giving Joey room to let off steam without constantly being inundated by different people coming and going, as he was at the crowded park near their Dallas home.

He was mesmerized by the horses, so much so that he'd bonded with Collette in order to help her feed them. That, and the fact that she offered no threat. She didn't bug him about being a baby when he wanted his mother around. She was loving and gentle and fun to be with.

Dylan and Troy were a different story. Joey was slightly wary around them, but if Troy kept coming up with ideas like Christmas trees, he'd move up the friendship ladder fast.

But Sean was the hero, the one to emulate. He had a way of making Joey feel independent without pushing.

Joey had stopped running around the trees now, and he and Sean were on their knees, studiously examining something in the grass. Eve left her comfortable spot on the grassy knoll and went over to join them.

"What have you two found so fascinating?" she asked.

"I saw a spider," Joey said, "but it got away before I could show it to Sean."

"Good," Eve said. "I like spiders that run away."

"Aw, I wanted to catch him and see if he was poisonous."

"I have a better idea," she said. "Let's pretend he is and leave him alone."

Sean gave Joey a very light but manly punch on the arm. "Women. They just don't get bugs."

"Have you decided on a tree?" Eve asked.

"We're stuck between two choices," Sean said. "Shall we let your mother have the deciding vote, Joey?"

"I betcha she picks the skinny one."

Joey pointed out the trees. The choice was a no-brainer. "The fat one will take up half the family room," she said.

"I told you she'd pick the skinny one."

"The skinny one it is," Sean said. "Dylan and I will come for it later today."

Eve eyed the tree again. "I hope it's not too tall." But it wouldn't be her and Joey's Christmas tree. Surely Orson would be captured by Christmas and they'd be back in Dallas. Away from the horses and wide-open spaces of the ranch.

Away from Sean. He was not a forever kind of guy.

Joey pointed to an aging oak tree about thirty yards away. It had apparently been hit by lightning at some time in the past, and one huge limb fell almost to the ground before stretching skyward again. "Can I go climb in that tree?"

"You might fall and—sure," she said, reconsidering. "Have fun, but be careful."

"A giant step for mothering," Sean said when Joey was out of earshot.

"I'm trying," she said. "It's hard to admit I got in the habit of being overly protective, especially with my being a psychiatrist."

Sean took her hand in his and pulled her down to the grass beside him. "I can see how protection can get to be a habit."

He toyed with a lock of her hair and for a second she thought he was going to kiss her. Instead, he let go of her hand and stared into space.

"Is something wrong?"

"I talked to Wyatt this morning while you and Joey were helping Collette feed the horses."

"Not more bad news. If it is, I don't want to hear it. All I want to know about Orson is that he's been arrested."

"I don't have any news that changes the current situation for the better or worse," Sean assured her.

"Then what is it?"

"There have been two other unexplained deaths that could be connected to Bastion."

"You mean besides Brock's?"

"Right. The first death happened when Orson was just twelve years old and swimming with a friend in a backyard pool."

"Did the pool belong to Orson's family?"

"No, it belonged to a family that was out of town. They managed to break the lock on the gate to get in. Details are sketchy, since the drowning was quickly concluded to be an accident, but the other boy was said to be a good swimmer. Orson claimed he got his foot caught in the drain somehow and got trapped underwater. He said he tried to save his friend, but that he died before he could get him loose."

"That could have happened."

"It could have. What makes it suspect is that Orson didn't admit to being with him when he drowned until another neighbor said he'd seen Orson break the lock on the gate. When confronted by the police, Orson admitted to being there, but said he got scared and ran home when the kid died in the water. The victim's body was found on top of the water with bruises around his legs."

Eve shivered at the thought of Orson's being capable of such cruelty when he was only six years older than Joey was right now. And if Orson had killed that boy, some family had needlessly suffered through the heartbreak of losing their child.

She looked to make certain Joey was still okay. He waved and grinned. She placed her hand on Sean's knee. "And the second instance?"

"It happened much later, during Orson's sophomore year in college. He and a girlfriend went to Cancún on spring break. She was found dead in the room, overdosed on booze and drugs."

"That one doesn't sound particularly suspicious."

"Except that the young woman's friends all said that she'd had a bad trip on acid the year before and that she hadn't touched illegal drugs since. It was also reported that Orson had flown into a jealous rage the day before and had accused her of getting it on with another reveler."

"But the death was still ruled an accident?"

"Yes. If Orson was involved in either of those deaths, he managed to present convincing arguments in his favor and was never considered a serious murder suspect."

"One of the characteristics of a true psychopath," Eve said. "Along with signs of cruelty showing up early in life. That's what was confusing in Orson's profile. Now even that part makes sense."

Sean put an arm around her shoulders. "Both events could be circumstance. I didn't tell you this to upset you, but I didn't want to keep things from you, either."

"I need to know the truth. It helps me to know exactly what I'm facing."

"You're facing a lunatic."

"That's not a psychological term."

"I'm not a psychological kind of guy. I'm more into the commonsense, big picture approach."

"Which means?"

"Sitting around waiting for Orson to either get captured or make his next murderous move is hell on your nerves, and it's not that great on mine."

"I can leave."

"Yeah, wondering if you're about to be killed at any second would make me feel great."

She threw up her hands. "What do you want, Sean? I'm definitely open to suggestions."

"Let's get out of here. The three of us. We'll fly to

Europe, take a winter vacation until Bastion is captured. It's not like I've got a job to hurry back to. And I've always wanted to visit Venice."

"It could take weeks or months before Orson is captured."

"It could take years, but we don't have to make a lifetime of decisions right now."

"You don't ever have to make a lifetime of decisions, Sean. You said as much last night."

"I knew that would come back to haunt me."

"I'm sorry," Eve said. "That just slipped out before I thought. I know you're trying to help, and I appreciate it."

"We can get a flight out tomorrow afternoon at three. They have first-class seats available and I have plenty of points to get them."

"How would a horse whisperer ever acquire that many points?"

"I'm good at what I do. A billionaire from Spain flew me over once a month for two years to work with his favorite mount."

"So you just checked the airline schedules without even asking me?"

Sean tucked a thumb under her chin and tilted it, forcing her to meet his gaze. "Say yes, Eve. I'll take care of everything else."

This was all happening so fast. On the surface, she loved the idea of running away to Italy with Sean. But if they stayed too long, she'd only fall harder for him. Joey would get used to having him in his life, only to lose him when this was over.

"I have to have time to think about it."

"I don't see what there is to think about. If nothing else, we'd have a great vacation."

He made it sound so easy. Maybe it was. "I'll give you an answer in the morning."

"And within twenty-four hours the three of us can be strolling along the Grand Canal."

ORSON KICKED THE BACK of the chair, sending the cheap piece of spindly wood banging against the wall of the deserted camp house where he'd been hanging out.

He hadn't broken out of prison to live like this. Mexico and señoritas by the dozens were waiting on him. He'd made three major mistakes in his life. The first was letting himself get arrested for the death of his worthless stepbrother.

The second was trusting his former cellmate Bodie Greene to follow Orson's exact plans for the murder of Brock Worthington. If Bodie hadn't screwed up, Eve would have gotten life in prison for the deed and Orson wouldn't have had to go to all this trouble to kill her now.

The third mistake was in not killing Eve when he'd had his hands around her bony neck. One more squeeze and she'd have died gasping for breath. He couldn't even blame Troy Ledger for that. The guy was just doing what your average halfway moral jerk did—saving a damsel in distress.

Orson wasn't average. He was Mensa-smart and brazen enough to do what other bastards in the world were too dumb to do. This wasn't how he'd planned to spend his last night in Texas, but it would be good enough to send him off with a bang.

He laughed at his own clever turn of thought.

Tomorrow he'd get the money from Alyssa and then he'd pay a visit to the basketball court in the park near his nephew's school. It would be much easier to kidnap him from there. Nick would love Mexico once he got used to it. And Alyssa would send money for years, in hopes Orson would keep her son safe.

It was a win-win situation.

Not quite as perfect as he'd planned. But close enough. All he'd miss was seeing Eve Worthington's face when her world went up in smoke.

Chapter Thirteen

Sean watched as Eve slipped quietly from his room. He'd tried to coax her into staying longer, but she insisted she needed sleep if she was going to make a make a major decision in the morning. And if she stayed, they both knew that one restless turn and touch in the night and they'd be in the throes of passion again.

The lovemaking tonight had been every bit as hot, as consuming, as it had been the first time. In some ways, it was even better, though he wasn't sure that was possible. He was learning where to touch her and how much pressure to use to make her moan in pleasure. Eve seemed to instinctively know how to drive him mad with wanting her.

But when the lovemaking was over, he'd felt the tension developing between them like sharp edges on a sparkling diamond. He'd probably been too honest with her last night when he said he'd never been able to make a relationship work long-term. But they sure wouldn't have a chance of making this work if he started out lying to her.

Yet, here he was, lying to himself, pretending that he

actually had a chance with her. She needed him now, but what was the chance she'd want him in her life when the crisis was over?

Too restless to think about sleep, Sean got out of bed and pulled on his jeans and the denim jacket he'd left thrown over the back of a chair. He'd never owned a robe in his life. Didn't plan to start now.

He wandered down the hallway to the extension that created one wall of the courtyard garden. He hadn't been in it since he returned. His mother had loved that spot, and Sean hadn't been ready to buck up against those memories.

He wasn't sure he was ready now, but he found his way there anyway. The garden was secluded, entered on one side through a guest room and on the other side via the master suite. Needless to say, Sean did not go though the room where his father slept in the big iron bed he'd once shared with Sean's mother.

Sean took a deep breath of the bracing air. And then he saw the figure standing in the shadows near the back wall. Startled, he started to dash back through the door and go for his gun.

"I guess you couldn't sleep either?"

His dad. "What are you doing out here?"

Troy stepped away from the wall. "Reliving the good times."

"Didn't the doctor tell you that you needed to get your rest?"

"Sometimes I rest better out here than anywhere else. Lots of nights when I couldn't sleep, I'd come out here to keep from waking your mother. She'd wake up, anyway, the first time she rolled over and I wasn't lying there beside her. Sometimes we'd dance in the moonlight. Mostly, she danced and I just held her until whatever problems that were keeping me awake seemed not to matter anymore."

"I don't need to hear this."

"I think maybe you do, Sean. You listened to your mother's family for years. You've heard exaggerated versions of all my shortcomings. You've heard how I was never good enough for Helene. You've heard how she planned to take you and your brothers and leave me. Now maybe it's time you heard my side of the story."

Sean dropped to the metal bench and propped his bare feet on a cold, hard stone. "Fair enough."

"Your mother was too good for me, Sean. She may have been too good for any mere mortal, but she was definitely too good for me."

Troy began to pace the narrow, meandering walkway. "She was upper crust. I made just enough money wrangling to pay the entry fee of every rodeo I could get to. But from the moment I met her, I knew that all I wanted was to love her and do my best to make her happy."

"So what went wrong?"

"Between us? Not a damn thing, except that it was a constant struggle to keep our heads about the poverty line. Your mother never complained, and she could stretch a dollar so far you'd swear it was made of rubber. She loved you boys and she loved me, and that was all she needed to make her happy. I know you were young, but you have to remember how happy we were back then."

The memories rained down on Sean with hurricane force. Laughing at Dakota's ridiculous knock-knock jokes. Taking turns jumping off Troy's shoulders at the swimming hole. Family nights when they watched movies together and had popcorn fights.

Happy was all he remembered until the happiness died.

"Why was Mother leaving you?"

"She was never leaving me. She was going to visit her parents, but she was never leaving me."

"But at the trial…"

"I know what some of the neighbors testified about your mother being afraid of me, or keeping secrets about me from her parents, Sean. All I can tell you is that if they were accurate, they were taking things out of context."

"Why would they?"

"Human nature, I guess. People got caught up in the heinous nature of the crime. The sheriff kept saying I was guilty and they started believing it. Not everyone, but enough that things just started snowballing against me.

"But it's my fault, too, Sean. I didn't fight for myself. I didn't care what happened to me. I couldn't stand it that I woke up in the mornings. I couldn't bear the thought of keeping on breathing and going through the motions of life when Helene would not be there with me. I just drowned in my own selfish grief."

The anguish in Troy's voice tore at Sean's soul. It

was difficult not to believe he was telling the truth. The man's soul was tortured. But Sean had needed to hear this years ago. He'd needed a father. He'd needed something to hold on to when he was only thirteen and his world was disintegrating in his hands.

"I wanted to die back then, too," Sean admitted for the first time in his life. "I tried to kill myself. I just didn't have the guts to pull the trigger."

Troy walked over and stopped beside Sean, so close that their shadows mingled into one. "I let you down, son. I let all of you boys down. Helene may never forgive me for that. I'll never forgive myself, but for what it's worth, I'm sorrier than you can ever know."

"I'm sorry, too. I'm glad we had this talk. I just wish it had come seventeen years ago, when I so desperately needed my father."

"I can't change the past. But I'm here now. The rest is up to you."

Sean felt a clammy emptiness invade his soul as he walked away. He wished that a few words from his father could change things the way they'd done when he was a boy. He wished he could reach out to his father and say that all was forgiven and that they'd just start over and things would be fine between them.

But words couldn't reach his soul. He didn't even turn when he heard Troy walk back into the house and close the door behind him.

EVE WOKE UP AT SIX, a full hour before the alarm clock would go off. She slid out of bed, a little nervous, but still eager to start the day. She'd lain awake for hours last night before she'd finally made a decision.

Going to Dallas and putting herself in Detective Conner's hands was risky at best. Staying at the ranch, hoping Orson Bastion wouldn't track her down, was like waiting on a lit fuse to blow. Given enough time, he'd find her. When that happened, she knew that Sean would do everything in his power to protect her and Joey.

That might not be enough. And even if it was, Joey would still be exposed to the violence.

Sean had the only viable solution. Change continents. Bastion would never travel to Europe to chase her down. Even if he had the money and the will, he wouldn't risk flying on a fake passport. More than likely, he wouldn't even risk airport security to fly inside the states.

As far as falling for Sean, that was a moot point. She already loved him. Joey's attachment was the more difficult issue, but somehow they'd work it out.

Eve spent the next hour packing. She wouldn't take much—one suitcase for her and one for Joey, plus a small carry-on. If she forgot something they had to have, they could buy it in Italy.

By the time she finished, Joey was twisting and turning. He'd wake soon, so she'd have to hurry if she wanted to be dressed before he got up. Rushing to the guest bath just down the hall, she brushed her teeth, washed her face and dressed.

"Momma. Where are you?"

Eve added the usual touch of blush and lip gloss and went back to the bedroom to check on her son. She'd tell Sean her decision right after breakfast. She'd wait until the last minute to tell Joey, leaving him just enough time to tell the horses goodbye, and not enough time to get anxious before they were off on their adventure.

Italy with Sean, instead of Texas with Orson Bastion. She pinched herself hard to convince herself she wasn't dreaming. The only thing that proved she wasn't was that tiny shred of apprehension that wouldn't quite disappear.

"EVE, THIS IS COLLETTE. Have you seen the morning news?"

"No, we're just having breakfast. Sean made pancakes. You should come join us."

"Don't let anyone turn the TV on until I can get there to pick up Joey."

The urgency in Collette's voice sent rivers of fear coursing through Eve. She pushed her chair back from the table and walked to the family room so that she was out of hearing range of the others. "What's happened, Collette?"

"It's bad, Eve. Really bad. But wait until I get Joey out of there before you deal with it."

"Just tell me," Eve insisted. "I can handle it."

"There was an explosion last night."

"Where?"

"In Dallas."

"Does this have anything to do with Orson Bastion?"

"Please, Eve. Don't make me talk about it. I'll start crying, and it's best if Joey doesn't see me that upset."

Eve's stomach churned. "Has there been another terrorist attack?"

"No, nothing like that."

"Then get over here on the double."

"I'm on my way."

Eve picked up the remote, fighting the urge to flick on a local cable news channel and find out what kind of explosion had Collette this upset. Whatever it was, she refused to let it sabotage her plans. Nothing short of Orson's arrest could make her want to deal with the kind of frenzied terror she'd heard in Collette's voice.

Sean came to the door of the family room. "Was that Gordon on the phone?"

"No, it was Collette. She's on her way over to pick up Joey."

"Is that all? You look upset."

"Collette sounded near hysteria."

"About what?"

"She refused to say, except that it's about something she doesn't want me to see on the news channel until Joey is out of the house."

Sean's muscles clenched and the veins in his neck bulged into corded lines. "It's that son of a bitch Orson again. I'd love to get my hands on that bastard and show him what it feels like to be on the receiving end of misery."

And Eve prayed he'd never get close enough to Orson to get that chance. She wanted him to stay far away from Orson's sick brand of evil.

"I'll see if Troy feels up to taking Joey for a walk to the horse barn. If Collette's that upset, she'll only frighten Joey."

Eve nodded and tightened her grip on the remote.

It seemed an eternity before she heard the back door slam shut.

"All clear," Sean said, as he joined her in the den. "Troy's got things under control."

Eve turned on the TV and read the rolling caption beneath the picture. An explosion in Dallas. Two police officers killed. And then she saw the image and she knew that Italy was officially off the table.

Chapter Fourteen

"A house explosion last night in a quiet Dallas neighbor-hood left two local police officers dead and the house in ruins. Neighbors as far as five blocks away reported being wakened by the blast. The owner of the house, Eve Worthington, was not at home when the explosion occurred. She has not been reached for comment, but we hope to have a statement from her soon."

The news went on and on. The words were like gar-bled static scratching across Eve's mind. She struggled to make sense of the continuous barrage of meaningless interviews with neighbors she barely knew and a police spokesperson who talked in circles, never zeroing in on the sordid truth.

A different reporter appeared on the screen. This one talked of Eve's connection to the prison system and mentioned that she'd worked not only with recently es-caped prisoner Orson Bastion, but with Troy Ledger. Apparently, they'd done their homework.

The reporter further mentioned that Eve had recom-mended against Orson's parole and that she'd gone on record as saying that she would trust convicted wife-killer Troy Ledger with her life.

The screen divided into two sections. The reporter on the right reminded the viewing audience that it was Eve's husband who was killed in a drive-by shooting in that same neighborhood almost two years ago. She questioned if the two events could be related.

The screen switched back to a view of Eve's house—or rather its charred remains. This time the view was much clearer. The chimney stood like a lone general whose soldiers had died in the flames. Part of a huge beam lay over the untouched brick mailbox at the street.

Joey's room was gone completely. All his favorite possessions had turned to ashes. All the things he should have gone home to when this nightmare was over were destroyed. Even the bed he would have been sleeping in if she'd stayed in Dallas had apparently become incendiary fuel for the blaze that had claimed their home.

Her stomach rolled.

She jumped up and ran to the bathroom, making it there just in time to throw up what felt like the lining of her stomach. Sean wet a cloth with cold water and held it to her head. She hated he was seeing her this way.

"There's no need to hear more," he said.

Tears burned in her eyes. "I've lost everything. Joey's baby book. My pictures. Letters from my mother before she died of cancer. My father's dog tags and the flag from the top of his coffin. It's all gone."

"Maybe not. You know how news reporters are. They

always show things from the worst possible angle. Some of the treasures may be salvageable."

"The house is gone, Sean. There is no good angle. I should have known Orson would win."

"He didn't win. You're alive, Eve, and so is Joey."

"But how many other people will have to die before he stops seeking his demonic revenge?"

Sean tried to pull her into his arms, but the emotional trauma wouldn't let her accept comfort. She beat her fists into his chest. "How many others? And how long before he finds a way to get to me?"

"He'll never get to you. I won't let him."

"You can't stop him. Can't you see that? No one can."

"I can stop him," Sean said. "And I will."

But he couldn't; and if he tried he'd end up dead. They might all end up dead. The next explosion could be here in this house, with them inside it.

Tears poured down her cheeks and shudders shook her body. This time, when Sean took her in his arms, she held on tight and kept holding on until she ran out of tears.

There was only one sane thing left for her to do, and it did not involve a trip to Italy.

THE FIRE HAD BEEN A SIGHT to behold. Eve's house had become a glorious inferno that lit the sky in brilliant shades of reds, oranges and yellows. Orson had been close enough to feel the heat and to hear the crackle and pop as the support beams fell and the wood splintered.

It had been quite a night, one that he hadn't spent in the mold-infested, mildewed cabin on Lake Livingston. This grimy motel room wasn't much better, but it was only for a night.

All that was left was for him to pick up the money from Alyssa and kidnap Nick.

Then look out, Mexico. Escaped convict Orson Bastion was headed to a bar near you.

Orson loaded his toothbrush with a minty paste and turned on the TV so that he could bask in his success while he brushed his full three minutes. He surfed three stations till he hit pay dirt. Ah, yes. They were even giving him credit for his handiwork. He walked back to the bathroom to spit.

When he returned, the reporter was talking about Troy Ledger and contrasting what Eve had said about him at the time of his release on a technicality, to what she'd testified at Orson's parole hearing.

She'd trust Troy Ledger with her life. Like the man could—

Orson choked on the toothpaste when the truth practically pounced from the TV and into his mind.

Eve had run to Troy Ledger when she'd heard that Orson had escaped prison. He'd saved her life once, so she assumed he could do it again.

Now they were talking about Troy's ranch in Mustang Run. This was priceless. There would be a slight delay in reaching Mexico while Orson devised a new strategy.

He could make good on his threat and avenge his mother's death. He owed that to Lydia and to himself.

"OH, NO. NOT AGAIN. This is exactly how it was the day Troy returned from prison."

Eve rushed to the front window and peeked over Collette's shoulder to see what she was talking about.

"It's the media sharks," Collette said. "They go on a feeding frenzy anytime they smell a story that involves the infamous Troy Ledger."

Eve stared, horrified at the crowds gathering not ten yards from the front door. "This is private property. They can't just drive onto this land."

"They can unless someone stops them."

"The sheriff should."

"My dad's the sheriff," Collette said. "He'd come and bring his deputies if Troy called him, but Troy won't. There's a bit of bad blood between them. It goes way back and is much too complicated to get into today."

Sean and Dylan strode into the room together. "Don't gawk at them," Sean said. "It will only encourage them to start popping flashbulbs."

When two more vans drove up, Eve said, "You should call the sheriff and have those people arrested for trespassing."

"I'm way ahead of you. Dylan and I have already hired an Austin security firm to disperse this crowd as peacefully as possible, and to stand guard at the gate to keep others from getting in."

"There will be some who'll just bust through the fence and tear up the pastures to try and get the scoop," Dylan said. "But we'll have guards around the house twenty-four seven."

"Then you expected this?" Eve asked.

"From the second you turned on the TV this morning." Sean put a hand on Eve's shoulder. "And don't start blaming yourself. You're the victim, not the aggressor."

But she was the one who'd brought this on the Ledgers—and while Troy was still recovering from a coronary attack.

"Has anyone seen Joey?" Eve asked, fighting panic when she didn't hear his miniature cars rolling up and down the hallway.

"He's watching Dad shave," Dylan said. "Dad's trying to convince him that it doesn't hurt when the hairs come off."

"He's not used to having a man in the house," Eve said.

"Okay, here's the new and approved house rules," Sean announced. "No female leaves this house without a male accompanying her. And by male, I mean an adult male, not Joey."

"Isn't that going a bit overboard?" Collette questioned. "The media mongrels may hound and aggravate us, but they're not actually dangerous."

"It's not the press they're concerned about," Eve said. "It's Orson Bastion. With this many reporters checking out everything in sight, it's only a matter of time until one of them reports that I'm here."

"I hadn't thought of that." Collette went back to the window, pushed back the curtain and looked out. "Your car's gone, Eve."

"I moved it into the large shed behind the house," Sean said. "It's no longer in the open, but someone will snoop around and get the license plate number. I moved the packages and the rest of your luggage that was in the trunk into the garden bedroom, Eve, in case you need them."

"Thanks." What she had with her now was all she had.

Joey came running down the hallway. "Guess what?"

"The circus is coming to town," Sean muttered under his breath.

Beside him, Eve whispered, "I'm pretty sure it's already here."

Joey asked his question again.

"Tell us." Sean moved to the window and closed the shutter, blocking out the sunshine along with the crowd.

Joey obliged, eager to share his news. "Mr. Ledger said we can decorate the tree today, and not with that old stuff you buy at the store. We're making our own decorations, and guess what else?"

Sean put his fingers to his temple as if her were concentrating. "We're going to string popcorn for the tree, and we can eat all we want."

Joey kicked the air. "How did you know?"

"I have super, bionic brain cells."

"And he did the same thing when he was a kid," Troy said.

Eve knew they were keeping this light for Joey's sake. She loved them for it, but it didn't change what she had to do. But first she'd decorate that tree and let Joey add his own special Christmas favorites. Then hopefully, she'd find a private moment to kiss Sean one last time before she took matters in her own hands. Well, hers and Detective Conner's.

ALYSSA'S HEART FLOPPED AROUND in her chest like a dying goldfish when the TV talked about Eve Worthington and her son. The boy was not even six years old yet, and he'd already seen his father shot down in cold blood. Now his house had burned to the ground.

They kept talking about Orson knowing the woman and how she was the shrink who said that if he got paroled, he'd kill someone else. Eve Worthington didn't know the half of it. Now that their mother had died, no one knew the truth about Orson and what he was capable of except Alyssa.

She had no doubts but that he'd blown up that shrink's house. He'd known how to make bombs since high school. He'd downloaded directions from the internet. Orson always said he could learn everything he needed to know from the internet. Everyone could, if they knew how to look for it.

But Orson wouldn't be satisfied with just blowing up that woman's house, not after what she did to him. Alyssa knew Orson was hanging around Texas for a reason. And it wasn't just the cash he'd had her get. If it had been, he'd have picked up the money yesterday.

He was going to kill that woman, and then her son would have nobody.

Alyssa had covered for Orson all his life. First it had been because her mother had made her. Now it was because she was afraid of him.

But killing a kid's mother just wasn't right.

Alyssa stuck her hand in her pocket and pulled out the card Detective Reagan Conner had given her. She had the money and the time and the godforsaken place to meet Orson so that she could turn over his escape funds.

She punched in the number and waited.

"Conner speaking."

"Detective, this is Alyssa Coleman."

"I was hoping we'd hear from you. Do you have information that will help us locate you brother?"

"Yes sir, I do."

BY FOUR IN THE AFTERNOON, all was quiet on the Ledger lawn. But even more disturbing for Eve than the hordes of noisy reporters were the armed guards who were being paid to keep the media and Orson Bastion away.

Joey in his innocence had said it best. "Momma, make those men go home."

She was about to do just that.

Eve ran her fingers along the back of the ornate wooden garden bench and listened to the soothing sounds of water trickling into the fountain just in front of her. The garden was just one of the things she'd miss about the ranch. Mostly, she'd miss Sean.

With luck she'd be back in a few days to pick up Joey, but she knew in her heart that things between her and Sean would never be the same once she left the ranch.

Dropping to the bench, she opened her notebook and began to write.

Dear Sean,

I know I'm a coward for not saying this in person, but it would only start an argument that I'm not willing to lose. I came here looking for a place to hide. I found that and so much more. You were great with Joey and you taught this stubborn psychiatrist who thought she knew it all a lot about boys—and about cowboys. All good, I might add.

So now I need to ask you a huge favor. Please watch over Joey for me until I can return for him. Hopefully, that will be in a few days, but it won't be until Orson Bastion is either dead or back behind bars. I've brought too much chaos and danger to the Willow Creek Ranch already. And I don't want Orson Bastion anywhere near my son.

FYI. When this is over, I'll be available for dinner on the Grand Canal. Or in a dimly lit bistro in Paris, Texas. Your call.

Ciao,

Eve

That should do it. Not too heavy. Not too light. And hopefully, the part about dinner wasn't too pathetic.

She sealed the envelope and dropped it in her pocket.

Taking out her phone, she punched in the number for Detective Conner.

"Conner here.

"This is Eve Worthington."

"I'm guessing your call means that you caught the morning news."

"The news that the two officers you would have used to protect me blew up with my house? Yeah, I heard."

"I would have had more than two on the scene if you'd been in the house."

"So you've said."

"I promised to protect you if you returned to Dallas. That promise still holds."

"So, do you have any other suggestions on how to use me as bait?"

"Look, Miss Worthington. It's been a rough night. I'm sorry about your house. Real sorry. I'm even sorrier that two young police officers lost their lives. And I'm plenty pissed off that we let Orson Bastion get away. So do me a favor and cut the sarcasm."

"I wasn't trying to be sarcastic, just realistic. I was also wondering why you didn't follow up on the money exchange between Orson and his sister."

"I can't discuss details concerning an ongoing case."

"Then can you discuss meeting me somewhere to figure out how I can help you flush out Orson?"

"I can arrange that. Why are you suddenly interested?"

"When Orson blew up my house, he also blew my cover. Soon, anyone who's interested will know that I'm staying at Troy Ledger's ranch in Mustang Run."

"Mustang Run is out of my jurisdiction. I can't promise any kind of protection unless you return to Dallas."

"Then let's make a deal."

"You sound as if you have terms."

"I do. Find a way to get me on every radio and TV station in the area. I want everyone to see that I'm back in Dallas. Leak where I'll be staying to the media, and then have enough men there to make sure you capture Orson Bastion while I'm still alive to celebrate."

"I can do that. I can also have a Texas Ranger pick you up at the Ledger ranch."

"That won't work. How about having him pick me up in Mustang Run? There's a big Baptist church on the highway, just after you pass the city limits sign. I'll be waiting in the parking lot in a black Honda."

"License plate number?"

She supplied it.

"I can have a ranger there in thirty minutes."

"I'll be waiting."

She went back inside just long enough to push the note under Sean's bedroom door. Then she went back to the garden and pushed the bench up against the stone wall that served as the back enclosure for the garden.

In seconds, she'd lifted herself to the top of the wall and jumped off on the other side. Her right ankle made an awkward landing. It smarted like crazy when she made a dash for her car.

Going though guards at the gate could present a problem, so she took Dylan's complaints about determined reporters at face value. She sped across the pasture, tearing down a couple of fences as she went, and doing major damage to her car's paint job.

When she reached the highway, she turned right.

That's when the doubts dragged her back into the confusing mire. What if she was making a major mistake? What if the detective couldn't protect her? What if she never saw Sean again?

What if Orson killed her as he had the others, and she missed out on the rest of Joey's life?

She tightened her grip on the wheel. What if this was the best option she had? Her gut feeling told her that it was. And at least, this way she could keep the danger far away from Joey.

Chapter Fifteen

"There's been a change in plans."

"What kind of change?"

The best kind, where Orson got to take care of things the right way. And since it was Saturday, Orson hadn't even had to work around Nick's school schedule. As he'd suspected, the kid was at the park most of the day.

"As you know, I didn't get a chance to pick up the money yesterday."

"Because you were too busy blowing up houses."

"You're getting a mouth on you, Alyssa. Mom wouldn't like it."

"Eve Worthington has a five-year-old son, Orson."

"I didn't tell her to have him."

"But she did, and he needs her. You've done enough damage to her, Orson. You don't need to kill her."

"Are you forgetting what she did to Mother?"

"Mother took her own life. That was not Eve Worthington's doing."

"Mother died because that snooty, pseudo-psychiatrist caused me to be denied early parole. Now she has to pay."

"Please don't kill her, Orson. Just this once, have a little sympathy for someone besides yourself."

"You sound so sweet and caring. Too bad that doesn't work on me. I'll kill her and leave her for Troy Ledger to find at his favorite little fishing hole. He can fish her right out of the river."

"Then I'm through helping and covering for you, Orson. Don't come to me for anything ever again."

"Don't be foolish. Drop the money off exactly as I explained to you. Mistakes will not be tolerated."

"I won't do it, Orson, not if you kill that woman."

"I think you will." He reached over and yanked the gag out of Nick's mouth. "Say hello to your mother, Nick. She's having a very bad day at work."

THE GUARDS AT THE GATE were a nice touch. Perhaps Orson had underestimated Troy Ledger. But he wasn't particularly disturbed by the unexpected militia. He appreciated modifications that challenged his intellect.

He'd acquired and studied an online survey of the ranch that Ledger's in-laws had ordered several years back. As a result, Orson knew exactly where Dowman River dissected Ledger's spread and created the fishing hole Ledger had gone on about with the other fishermen types in prison.

And if Orson remembered correctly, if he turned onto Willow Creek Ranch just south of the Dowman-Lagoste Bridge, he could drive all the way to the ranch house without having to cross Willow Creek.

He made the turn and slowed, getting his bearings. A black Honda came up behind him and rode his tail.

Not that it could legally pass him on this curving road. Orson checked out the driver in the rearview mirror.

A female, and on a practically deserted country road. She looked familiar. When she put on her blinker to pass, Orson pressed the accelerator. Once they hit the next curve, he slowed again.

She was familiar all right. That was Eve Worthington. He smiled and slapped the back of the seat. "Too bad you can't see what we're about to do, Nick. This is going to be fun."

EVE HONKED AT THE IDIOT in front of her and raised an angry fist. He knew she wanted to pass him, but every time she got the chance, he'd speed up.

Finally, they hit a straight section of blacktop and he let her go around him. She pushed the speed limit, trying to make up for time she'd lost fooling around with that imbecile.

He sped up as well. He was riding her tail, too close for comfort. She slowed for him to pass her. Being late to the Baptist church in Mustang Run was better than getting killed in the car.

The driver came up even with her and then bumped her from the side. Her car shimmied but stayed on the pavement. Irritation turned to apprehension. This guy was playing dangerous.

He sideswiped her again, this time so hard the car skidded onto the shoulder. She guided the vehicle back onto the road, then slowed to a near stop, praying he'd just drive off and cease his deadly intimidation.

There was a bridge just ahead, and if he ran her off

the road there, she'd be battered by the iron side rail. Both cars might plunge into Dowman River. One or both of them could get killed.

But the driver didn't wait for the bridge. He hammered his car into her back fender, knocking her sideways. She struggled to keep control of the car, but it skidded across the narrow road and went flying down an embankment.

When it finally came to rest, her car was practically lying on its right side. Her head seem to be spinning in dizzying circles. When she could finally focus, she got her first good look at the man who'd run her off the road.

Orson Bastion was only steps away.

Somehow Eve managed to unbuckle the seat belt and get the driver's side door open. She took off running for the woods, but before she made it out of the clearing, Orson's strong hands grabbed her from behind and threw her to the ground.

He planted his foot on her neck and pointed a pistol at her head.

"Take it easy and I won't kill you. Not here, anyway, and certainly not with the pleasant, quick death a bullet to the brain would provide.

"I have something much more torturous in mind for you. And then I will leave your body for Troy to find. Now, won't that be an exciting conclusion to the drama in our minds?"

SEAN HAD WANDERED all through the house twice, looking for Eve. He'd found Collette and Joey playing checkers in one of the spare bedrooms. Neither had seen Eve.

Sean stopped when he got to his own bedroom and stuck his head inside. No sign of Eve, but there was an unopened envelope on the floor, addressed to him. He picked it up and turned it over in his hand a few times, as if he could figure out who it was from by feel.

Finally, he slipped his thumb beneath the seal and tore the envelope open. He checked out the name at the bottom first.

Eve.

Apprehension sent him on yet another adrenaline high. There was no way a note from Eve could be good, especially when she was nowhere to be found.

Sean dropped to the side of the bed and read every word—twice—trying to make sense of why Eve would try a fool stunt like this.

Why go to Conner for protection when Sean was doing everything he knew to do to keep her safe? He had security guards at the gate, security outside the house, plus the three Ledger men.

Feeling positively betrayed, he took the note to Troy. "You know her," he said, once Troy had skimmed the note. "What do you make of this?"

"It's pretty clear that what she's asking is for you to take care of Joey while she goes to Dallas."

"I offer protection and she chooses the police. If you were me, what would you do in my situation?"

"I'd ask Dylan and me to stay here and protect Joey and Collette, while I went to Dallas and made sure Orson did not get his hands on my woman."

Sean was thinking the exact thing, not that Eve was acting much like she was his woman.

Not that he'd ever asked her to be.

Troy's cell phone jangled.

"Maybe that's Eve calling to say she's come to her senses," Sean said.

Troy took the call and shifted it to speakerphone.

"Hello."

"This is Detective Reagan Conner. Eve Worthington was supposed to meet a Texas Ranger at the Baptist Church in Mustang Run about ten minutes ago. She never showed up. I was wondering if you knew anything about that."

"Maybe she's changed her mind and is heading back here," Sean said, responding for Troy.

"That could be, but we received a phone call from an anonymous tipster a few minutes ago. She said that Orson was either at or heading to the Willow Creek Ranch right now. She said he plans to kill Eve and leave her body at Troy Ledger's favorite fishing hole."

Sean uttered a stream of curses.

"We're on it," Troy said. "How about sending that ranger down to the Dowman-Lagoste Bridge. And tell him to be on the lookout for Orson Bastion."

Troy killed the connection.

"The only fishing hole of mine that Bastion could possibly know about is the one just south of the bridge," Troy said.

"I know right where that is. Call Dylan. Tell him I may need backup. You and the guards stay here with Joey and Collette, in case Bastion doubles back here."

Sean raced out the back door without waiting for agreement. He could cover the distance a lot faster by horseback than by winding roads. And there was no time to waste.

EVE WATCHED ORSON'S MOVEMENTS, though she could do nothing to alter them. She was tied to a downed tree trunk with only her feet and hands free. He was busily tying lengths of rope around her ankles.

"Have you ever watched someone drown, Eve? It's a mesmerizing sight. They gasp for breath and fling their arms as if they've just jumped off a building and are trying to fly. Then everything just goes limp. They exhale bubbles like bizarre-shaped fish."

"You drowned that boy when you were twelve, didn't you, Orson? You killed him just to watch him die."

"My, you do surprise me. I'm sure you didn't discover that when you were digging around in my head. You were never good at that, you know."

"I learned enough about you to recognize that you're a psychopath." She had to keep him talking. The longer he talked the longer she'd stay alive, and the better her chances to be rescued, though Sean would never come looking for her after reading that note.

Still, she needed to keep Orson talking.

"You overdosed your girlfriend, too, didn't you? How did that go? Did you persuade her to take the drugs on her own, or did you just crush the pills and shoot them directly into her veins?"

Orson removed some three-holed bricks from a canvas bag and laid them at his feet. Then he picked up one and began to weave the rope that bound her right foot through the holes.

"I administered them through the veins. She was hardly worth persuasion. She'd slept with half my friends and then swore to me that she hadn't."

He picked up the next brick and began the rope weaving again. "That boy you asked about deserved to drown, too. He called my mother a whore."

"Was she?"

"Don't talk about my mother. You killed her. Isn't that enough?"

"Your mother committed suicide."

"Because you lied to keep me in jail forever. You had no idea what I was capable of. You're the reason Brock had to die, too."

"But now you're going to kill my son's mother. Isn't that just as wrong?"

"You should have thought about that before you ruined my life."

He held up one of her feet. The three bricks he'd weaved into the rope made the foot feel as if it was carved from granite.

"Time to go sleep with the fishes. And then your buddy Troy Ledger can come and catch you one day." He chuckled as he bound her wrists tightly and then untied her from the log. Circling a burly arm beneath her shoulders, he dragged her toward the water.

"Don't do this, Orson. Let me go free and I'll tell the parole board that I was wrong. I'll tell them anything you want."

"It's rather late for that. I no longer care what the

parole board does, and I never will again. If I went back to prison now, they'd make sure that I died there. But it doesn't matter. I won't be going back."

He shoved her into the water and the icy depth swirled around her waist and then up to her shoulders.

"Not quite deep enough yet," he taunted, "but don't worry. The end will come soon enough."

Weighed down by the heavy bricks, her feet began to sink into the mud. A few more inches and she wouldn't be able to keep her mouth and nose above water.

She would die here, just the way Orson had described the other drowning—flinging her arms the way she was now, wild but unsuccessful, with her wrists bound tightly. She'd struggle to keep her head above water, but none of that would save her.

The surface of the water reached her neck and sprayed over her chin. She thought of Sean and the way he smiled and tipped his hat. He was all man all the time. Yet he'd been so good with Joey. She'd worried that Sean wasn't a forever kind of guy. Now it turned out her forever might be measured in minutes.

She screamed for help at the top of her lungs.

She didn't want to die. She wanted to raise her son. She was all he had. She loved him so very, very much.

Water splashed into her mouth. Her movements became frantic as she fought to keep her head above water.

She screamed again.

She did not want to die.

But the mud was well over her ankles now and the thick, gooey mass just kept sucking her in.

Chapter Sixteen

The stallion's hooves flew across the uneven ground and through the carpet of brown leaves and high grass. Sean urged him faster still. He'd never get over it if something terrible happened to Eve.

He shouldn't have let her out of his sight. He knew how fearful she was of Orson, yet how protective she was of Joey.

A piecing scream reverberated through the trees. It was Eve. Orson must have her and be doing sickening, terrifying things to her.

Sean would kill him if he hurt Eve. He would. He'd kill him and be as heartless about it as Orson was with his crimes.

He urged his mount on. "Come through for me, Gunner. Come through for me this time and I promise you'll never become glue."

The scream sounded again. It was closer this time. Sean knew he had to be getting close to the bridge, and the old fishing hole was only another hundred yards or so downstream from there.

The evening was too quiet now. Sean longed for

another scream, any sound to let him know that Eve was still alive.

Something rustled in the woods to Sean's left. He readied his rifle but kept galloping. The next sound he recognized instantly. It was the gentle lap of water against the riverbank. And just off to the north he spotted the bridge.

He turned south, traveling along the river's edge until he spotted a car next to the treeline. He scanned the area, his finger poised on the trigger of his firearm.

No one was in sight. He slid from the horse's back and led the animal toward the car, alert for anyone hiding in the trees or jumping from inside or behind the vehicle.

Something splashed in the water, capturing all his attention. A head was bobbing frantically, barely staying above the surface. Sean dropped the reins and took off at a dead run.

It was Eve. Fighting for her life. His heart beat wildly, slamming against his chest as he dropped his rifle and jumped into the water, boots and all.

"Don't waste the effort."

Neck deep and dripping, Sean turned to see Orson Bastion standing on the bank with a pistol pointed at Sean's head.

"Kill me, but not Eve," Sean pleaded. "Let her go home and raise her son." He was feet from her, and her frantic gasps filled him with determination. He'd die to save her. He had no choice.

But his plea had no effect on Bastion. "Sorry. It's goodbye cruel world for both of you."

Before Sean could even make a last desperate grab for Eve, the sound of gunfire thundered across the water. He steeled himself for searing pain, or worse, the sight of Eve's beautiful face covered in blood. But it never came.

He grabbed for Eve, slipping his arm under her chin so that he could keep her from sliding beneath the water. "I've got you," he told her. Then he looked back toward the shore for Orson. He hadn't been prepared for the scene in front of him.

Orson was lying on the ground and Troy was standing over him, gun in hand.

"Need any help?" Troy called, not taking his eyes off the monster.

For Sean, relief had never felt so good. He finally remembered to breathe again. "A ride home in a warm car would be nice."

Struggling with the weight of the bricks, he dragged Eve to the shore. She took in huge gulps of air and tried to speak, but fear and the frigid water kept her chattering. "Th-thank y-you. Sean, I—I—"

He silenced her and carried her to the riverbank. She'd have plenty of time to thank him later. Plenty of time for him to tell her how his life had almost ended with hers.

Troy took off his jacket and threw it over her shoulders, and then he slit the ropes that bound her wrists and ankles.

Though she was safe now, Sean could not bring himself to let her out of his arms for even a second, but he leaned over for a glimpse at Orson. "Is he dead?"

"Probably," Troy replied, "but I'll call an ambulance just in case he isn't. And the ranger should be showing up here any second. Now you two best get in my car and start the heater. It's parked just on the other side of that hill."

"What happed to Dylan?" Sean asked, as he made sure Eve could walk to the car. "I thought you were sending him as backup."

"He's at home protecting the woman and Joey. I figured it's a father's privilege to come to the aid of his son."

He stopped and turned to look at Troy. "If you hadn't arrived when you did, we'd both be dead."

"'Bout time I did something right."

"You're always right in my book," Eve murmured through chattering teeth. "But thanks again."

"Yeah." Sean put one arm around Troy's shoulder. "Thanks, *Dad.*"

The emotion was genuine, and surprisingly, saying "Dad" out loud didn't feel half bad.

Epilogue

The presents had all been opened. Joey was on the floor with the golden retriever puppy Troy had given him for Christmas, after making sure it was all right with Eve. Eve had never seen her son so happy.

Collette wound the bright blue scarf around her neck. "I love this color, Eve. You give the neatest gifts. I should start taking you with me every time I go shopping for clothes."

"Sales start next week. And Troy, thanks for the gift certificate," Eve said. "I'm going to go out and replace some of what I lost in the fire."

The celebration continued, but Eve slipped away and walked out to Helene's garden. The pots of poinsettias Collette had scattered throughout the beds gave the whole space a festive look. It was lost on Eve.

She hadn't told anyone yet that this was her and Joey's last day on the ranch. It was time to move on. Orson had survived, but he was back behind bars where he'd no doubt stay. His nephew Nick was safe and back with his mother. Eve would get her insurance settlement from the house fire soon. And she'd found a house to rent, one with a fenced yard that was big enough for Joey's dog.

And while Sean still seemed absolutely crazy about her, he hadn't mentioned the possibility of a future together. She shouldn't be surprised. He was a fabulous lover, a brave protector, a genuine horseman and cowboy. But he was not a forever kind of guy.

Tears burned in the back of Eve's eyes as she dropped to the bench. She loved Sean, and she doubted she'd ever stop missing him. But she couldn't change who he was, and it wouldn't be fair to try.

"Eve."

She turned and saw Sean step out into the courtyard.

"You left before you opened all your gifts and before I told you my news."

Eve blinked repeatedly, determined to hold back the tears. "What is your news?"

"I put a down payment on some acreage near Bandera. I've decided to breed and train quarter horses."

So he had made his plans without discussing them with her. That pretty much said it all.

"If that's what you want, I'm happy for you."

"That's not quite all of it. I want to run a program where I bring out troubled kids on the weekends and let them ride and help with the horses. I know I won't reach all of them, but I think I can make a difference with some."

"You'll be great at that," she said honestly.

"Now, about the gift that you didn't open."

A tear escaped and she turned away from him. "I need to check on Joey. I'll open the gift later." She started past him, but he grabbed her arm and turned her around.

"Joey's fine. The gift can't wait."

He slid his hand down her arm and took her hand in his. Then he dropped to one knee. "I love you, Eve. I love Joey, too. Marry me so that we can be a real family. I need the horses, but we can have a place in town, too, if you want."

"The ranch is not a problem. I'd love living on a ranch. So would Joey."

"Then say you'll marry me."

She ached to say yes, but there was one question that needed answering. "Are you going to leave me standing at the altar?"

"Not a chance."

"How can you be so sure?"

"Because I was wrong about not being a forever kind of guy. I just hadn't met the right woman to share forever with."

"Are you sure?"

"Very sure. And if you don't say yes fast, I'm going to go crazy."

Her heart felt so full that it might burst from her chest. "In that case, I love you with all my heart, Sean Ledger, and yes, I'll marry you. I will so marry you."

He rose to his feet and touched his lips to hers with a kiss that promised a million golden tomorrows.

"I can't wait to start our new life together," Sean said. "Now let's go tell Dad that he's not losing a puppy, he's gaining a grandson."

* * * * *

Special Offers

Every month we put together collections and longer reads written by your favourite authors.

Here are some of next month's highlights— and don't miss our fabulous discount online!

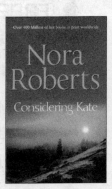

On sale 16th March   On sale 16th March   On sale 6th April

Mills & Boon® Online

Discover more romance at
www.millsandboon.co.uk

- **FREE** online reads
- **Books** up to one
  month before shops
- **Browse our books**
  before you buy

...and much more!

For exclusive competitions and instant updates:

Like us on **facebook.com/romancehq**

Follow us on **twitter.com/millsandboonuk**

Join us on **community.millsandboon.co.uk**

 Visit us Online

Sign up for our FREE eNewsletter at
www.millsandboon.co.uk

WEB/M&B/RTL4

The World of Mills & Boon®

There's a Mills & Boon® series that's perfect for you. We publish ten series and with new titles every month, you never have to wait long for your favourite to come along.

Blaze®
Scorching hot, sexy reads

By Request
Relive the romance with the best of the best

Cherish™
Romance to melt the heart every time

Desire™
Passionate and dramatic love stories

Have Your Say

You've just finished your book.
So what did you think?

We'd love to hear your thoughts on our
'Have your say' online panel
www.millsandboon.co.uk/haveyoursay

- 🌹 Easy to use
- 🌹 Short questionnaire
- 🌹 Chance to win Mills & Boon®
  goodies